Healing Montana Sky

BOOK FIVE OF THE MONTANA SKY SERIES

Healing Montana Sky

BOOK FIVE OF THE MONTANA SKY SERIES

DEBRA HOLLAND

Montlake
Romance

The idea for *Healing Montana Sky* came about when Mindy went into labor with her (now four-year-old) son, Adam. The baby became stuck and ended up being suctioned out while a team of nurses pushed on Mindy's belly. Only the miracle of modern medicine saved Mindy from the fate of Daisy Muth. One hundred and twenty years ago, Adam probably wouldn't have survived, either.

Nowadays, we take for granted that women rarely die in childbirth and we forget how, for much of human history, childbirth (and the complications from giving birth) was a primary cause of death for women of childbearing age.

Notes from the Author

Healing Montana Sky takes place in the spring and summer of 1895, overlapping in time with *Glorious Montana Sky* and *Painted Montana Sky*.

Antonia Valleau, the heroine in *Healing Montana Sky*, is illiterate, and her dialogue and italicized interior thoughts reflect her lack of education. But using the same simplistic and ungrammatical patterns when she's thinking would be burdensome to the reader. So I've chosen to have her thoughts read more smoothly.

Keep in mind that in previous generations, due to the intense labor required for sheer survival on the frontier, children were often left alone and expected to entertain themselves and do chores from a very early age. Children were also supposed to "be seen and not heard," and parenting wasn't as childcentric as it is today.

CHAPTER ONE

In the Mountains Above Sweetwater Springs
Spring 1895

Antonia Valleau cast the first shovelful of dirt onto her husband's fur-shrouded body, lying in the grave she'd dug in their garden plot, the only place where the soil wasn't still rock hard. *I won't be breakin' down. For the sake of my children, I must be strong.* Pain squeezed her chest like a steel trap. She had to force herself to take a deep breath, inhaling the scent of loam and pine. *I must be doing this.*

She drove the shovel into the soil heaped next to the grave, hefted the laden blade, and dumped the earth over Jean-Claude, trying to block out the thumping sound the soil made as it covered him. Even as Antonia scooped and tossed, her muscles aching from the effort, her heart stayed numb, and her mind kept playing out the last sight of her husband. The memory haunting her, she paused to catch her breath and wipe the sweat off her brow, her face hot from exertion in spite of the cool spring air.

Antonia touched the tips of her dirty fingers to her lips. She could still feel the pressure of Jean-Claude's mouth on hers as he'd kissed her before striding out the door for a day of hunting. She'd held up baby Jacques, and Jean-Claude had tapped his son's nose. Jacques had let out a belly laugh that made his father respond in kind. Her heart had filled with so much love and pride in her family that she'd chuckled, too.

Stepping outside, she'd watched Jean-Claude ruffle the dark hair of their six-year-old, Henri. Then he strode off, whistling, with his rifle over his shoulder. She'd thought it would be a good day—a normal day. She assumed her husband would return to their mountain home in the afternoon before dusk as he always did, unless he had a longer hunt planned.

As Antonia filled the grave, she denied she was burying her husband. *Jean-Claude be gone a checkin' the trap line,* she told herself, flipping the dirt onto his shroud.

She moved through the nightmare with leaden limbs, a knotted stomach, burning dry eyes, and a throat that felt as though a log had lodged there. While Antonia shoveled, she kept glancing at her little house, where, inside, Henri watched over the sleeping baby. From the garden, she couldn't see the doorway.

She worried about her son—what the glimpse of his father's bloody body had done to the boy. *Mon Dieu,* she couldn't stop to comfort him. *Not yet.* Henri had promised to stay inside with the baby, but she didn't know how long she had before Jacques woke up.

Once she finished burying Jean-Claude, Antonia would have to put her sons on a mule and trek to where she'd found her husband's body clutched in the great arms of the dead grizzly. She wasn't about to let his last kill lie there for the animals and the elements to claim. Her family needed that meat and the fur.

She heard a sleepy wail that meant Jacques had awakened. *Just a few more shovelfuls.* Antonia forced herself to hurry, despite how her arms, shoulders, and back screamed in pain.

When she finished the last shovelful of earth, exhausted, Antonia sank to her knees, facing the cabin, her back to the grave, placing herself between her sons and where their father lay. She should go to them, but she was too depleted to move.

Jacques appeared on his hands and knees, peering around the corner of the cabin. His dark eyes lit with pleasure when he saw her. The baby flashed Antonia his wide grin and scooted toward her. Only in the last two days had he gone from pushing himself across the floor to a hands-and-knees crawl.

Henri trailed so close behind Jacques that he had to walk wide-legged so he didn't step on his brother.

The baby reached her, placed his hands on her legs, and pressed himself up, grabbing at the front of her tunic. "Maa."

Antonia hugged Jacques. He'd soiled his rabbit skin diaper and smelled, but she held him close, needing to feel the baby in her arms.

He wiggled in protest.

She dropped a kiss on his forehead and reached up to her shoulder to unlace the leather ties of her tunic, pulling the flap down to free her breast. He began to suckle greedily.

Henri dropped to her other side and leaned against her.

Antonia put her arm around him. Just holding her sons brought her comfort but also increased her despair. *What do I be doin' now?*

Should I be takin' the boys and leave? Head for Sweetwater Springs?

Antonia shook her head. *No! I won't be leavin' Jean-Claude. Cain't leave my home.*

But without her husband to provide for them, she didn't know how long she'd be able to manage on her own.

Somehow, I'll be findin' a way, Antonia vowed.

❋ ❋ ❋

Three days later, Antonia took a final look around the log cabin. Just one snug room, made with Jean-Claude's and her own hands, it had sheltered her family for the last two years. Only the table and log chairs remained in front of the river-rock fireplace. She'd been dreading spending another long winter cooped up with a young boy and a toddler in the small space. Now, though, she'd give anything to stay, to experience the love and warmth once contained within these walls. But the house remained empty—not just of their possessions, which she'd packed on the two mules—but of the love, now lost to her forever, that had made the cabin a home.

The tears she'd held back since her discovery of Jean-Claude's body threatened to fall, and she abruptly turned and walked outside for one final look. The spring sun shone through the pines and dappled the needle-strewn ground. Her garden, now a graveyard, lay on one side of the cabin, surrounded by a high split-rail fence to keep out the deer. Before long, the forest would reclaim the plot she'd worked so hard to cultivate. She approached the grave, her heart as heavy as her steps.

Antonia reached the spot marked with a crude wooden cross, lashed together with leather strips, and sank to her knees. She wanted to throw herself over the mound and sob. But that act would frighten the children. She placed a palm on the dirt, feeling the loose soil shift under her hand. "Good-bye, my love."

The rest of the words clogged her throat. *How do I be tellin' a dead man that I'm a leavin' him?* Not that her husband was really here.

Antonia crossed herself. She believed Jean-Claude was in heaven, having sweet-talked his way right out of purgatory. He was probably laughing and telling stories to the angels, charming them as he had her. *I be the one livin' alone without him.*

Be I doin' the right thing...leavin'? For two days, uncertainty had weighed in her stomach like a rock, while her mind twisted between thoughts of Jean-Claude and debating plans for the future. *Can we be survivin' here?* The question had eaten at her. She desperately wanted to find a way to stay in her home. Although a good shot herself, Antonia couldn't take the children hunting. Nor could she leave them alone when she went.

She glanced over her shoulder at her older son.

Henri held the reins of the two mules, an unhappy expression on his face. The baby stood on tottery legs and clutched his brother around his hips.

Her heart twisted. How could she help her sons? They adored their father. Henri had cried himself to sleep last night. And her usually placid Jacques had fussed, waking up off and on. She'd barely had a wink of sleep.

Antonia motioned them to her.

Henri tied the reins to a branch and gently pushed Jacques to the ground. Her oldest son walked over, his feet dragging. The baby crawled after.

She patted the ground next to her. "Say good-bye to *Père, mon fils.*"

The boy looked from the mound to her, his face drawn and a sorrowful look in his eyes. "You say *Père* be in heaven, *Maman.*"

Jacques climbed on the grave and played with some loose dirt.

"He be, *mon petit cher.*" Aching with love for him, Antonia smoothed back the hair from Henri's face, wanting to find words to comfort him, to help her son understand. "His body lies here, though, and we are leaving." Her voice thickened. "So we're saying good-bye, although we'll never forget him."

Henri's face scrunched, and tears came to his eyes. He dropped to his knees and leaned into her. "Why he be a dyin', *Maman?*"

What be an answer to that? "I cain't tell you, Henri."

"I want *Père* back."

She put her arm around the boy and squeezed him close. "I be wantin' that, too."

Jacques crawled to them.

Antonia gathered the baby close, inhaling his scent. She gave him a squeeze, kissed his plump cheek, and stood. She tried to send Henri an encouraging smile, but her mouth wouldn't stretch, and it probably came out as a grimace. "Be you ready for an adventure, Henri?"

"Yes, *Maman,*" he said in a subdued tone.

Antonia missed her son's usual high spirits and gamine grin. *How long before they'll return?* She tried to suppress the secret fear that Henri would never again be the same, his happy personality buried with Jean-Claude in his grave.

"Up on the mule then," Antonia said briskly. "You be a big boy now and can ride by your lone self. I'm dependin' on you to be holding tight to your brother. Can you be doin' that?"

His expression brightened, which gave her a glimmer of hope, and he nodded.

Antonia helped him climb into the saddle and then lifted Jacques in front of him. Behind the saddle, she'd lashed their clothing and sleeping furs. "Hold him tight, now," she repeated.

"*Oui, Maman.*"

"In three days, Henri, we be arrivin' in Sweetwater Springs." She tried to instill some enthusiasm into her voice, but her tone sounded so heavy Antonia knew she'd failed. "You be havin' your first sight of a town."

The other mule was laden with Jean-Claude's rifle, his furs and hides, along with more of their meager possessions. A cast-iron Dutch oven and a metal bucket rode on top of the heap. Antonia shrugged into her own pack, hefted her rifle, and took the reins of both mules. Throat tight, she glanced behind for one final glimpse of her home and then resolutely faced forward, leading them down the trail.

CHAPTER TWO
On the Prairie Outside Sweetwater Springs

In the tree-shaded edge of pasture outside the barn, Erik Muth watched two newborn calves nurse, one on each side of their dam, and his chest swelled with satisfaction. Two heifers! *A double blessing and a good addition to my milk herd.* He'd been plowing a field when his favorite cow, Annabelle Lee, had disappeared from the herd, a sure sign she'd gone off to hide and birth her calf.

The cow wasn't hard to find. Trees grew only along the tiny stream trickling from the springhouse well and cutting through the pasture. Although he knew Annabelle Lee was an old hand at birthing her babies, he stayed with her to help with the delivery.

Erik stepped out of the shade and blinked in the bright sunlight. He hadn't realized half the morning had gone by already. He paused for a moment to survey his property, feeling a sense of pride at all he'd accomplished in the last six years. He took a deep breath of the fresh prairie air, inhaling the scent of turned earth and new growth.

Across the barnyard was his house, made with squared-off logs—a long, low building, nestled into the hillside. Two windows were set in the front and one on each side. A porch jutted in front. The sod roof kept the dwelling cool in the summer and warm in the winter. He already had a plan to expand his home—when the baby grew enough to need a sleeping room.

Erik squinted against the glare of the sun, trying to see his wife, Daisy, on the porch. He blinked, wondering why she wasn't there now. Usually after finishing the morning chores, weather permitting, she spent all her time out front, doing handwork or other tasks such as shelling peas or scrubbing clothes before she needed to start cooking his supper.

Maybe she's lying down. She'd become more and more tired as the months of her pregnancy crept by.

I'd better go check on her. He glanced down and saw his blood-and muck-stained hands and shirt. Knowing his sensitive wife would shrink from the sight, Erik figured he'd better wash up before he entered the house. As much as possible, he tried to shield Daisy—not something that was easy to do on a farm.

Erik strode to the barrel-well next to the springhouse and pumped water until it spilled into a small metal trough. He plunged in his hands, wetting his arms to his elbows to get off the blood from the birth. He rubbed his wet hands over his shirt but only succeeded in turning the red stain to pink. Then he picked up the trough and tossed the dirty water into the rosebush Daisy had planted near the left of the well. Some of the water splashed dirt on a tight bud that hung heavy on a branch, almost to the ground. Daisy had watched the bush for days, eager to see the first flower burst into bloom.

He picked up the bucket stored by the well, hung the handle on the top of the pump, and filled the pail. At her advanced state of pregnancy, his petite wife had difficulty carrying the water bucket without spilling, so he almost always brought in fresh water when entering the house.

He headed toward the porch, anticipating Daisy's reaction to his good news. She loved baby animals and would be doubly glad for heifers because they wouldn't grow up to be slaughtered. His wife shared his dreams of creating a prosperous farm, not just from the wheat he planted on the prairie, but from the dairy herd he planned to expand from the seven, no *nine*, cows he had now—including the five calves. He dreamed of fostering his family's legacy, making cheese, and selling his wares in town—maybe even shipping them off to some of Montana's cities.

As Erik walked, he could hardly keep the bounce from his step. And why should he? *Two calves when I expected one! And both heifers. A double bonus. Wouldn't that be wonderful if Daisy delivered two babies, too?* Then he sobered. His wife was too small to carry twins. But soon, they'd have the first of what he hoped would be a long line of children. *Only another month to go.*

He took a long step up to the porch, bypassing the two stairs, poured the water into the big pitcher set on a bench next to a basin, and set down the pail. He thought of washing up again, this time with soap, before dismissing the idea. Anxious to check on his wife, he tiptoed inside. Daisy was a light sleeper who complained if he woke her.

A quick scan of the room, half kitchen and half parlor, showed no wife. But a moan sounded from the next room, kicking his heart into fast thump-thumps.

He raced to the bedroom and saw Daisy on her back on the bed. She'd changed into her night shift, or maybe had never changed out of it. He didn't know.

Her face was pale and perspiring, her breaths harsh enough to hear. One hand was raised over her head, clutching a bar of the iron bedstead; the other rested over her mounded stomach.

"Daisy, sweetheart? Is it the baby?"

She slowly turned her head. Her blue eyes were sunken in her oval face. "Where were you? I called and called." Her voice sounded weak.

The accusation in her tone made guilt stab into him. He'd been so engrossed in delivering the calves that he hadn't checked on his wife as he normally did.

He sat on the edge of the bed and brushed aside the sweaty wisps of blonde hair that had escaped her braid. "Tell me what's wrong."

"The baby's coming."

"What! It's too early! We have to get you to the doctor." Erik bent, slid his arms under her back, and scooped up his wife. Seemed like a calf weighed more than she did, even with the baby inside her.

At the movement, she screamed and arched her back, kicking her feet. "No, no, no!"

Startled, Erik almost dropped her. He lowered her to the bed and gripped her hands, sitting down next to her.

Her face flushed red and crunched with effort. She squeezed his hand so hard pain radiated through his fingers. Grunting moans that didn't sound human came from her throat.

He remembered the panting the cow had done. "Breathe, sweetheart. That will help."

The contraction eased, and Daisy collapsed on the bed, panting. She started to cry. "I can't do this. I can't!"

Erik's mind raced. *What should I do?* He couldn't leave his wife and ride for the doctor. He'd be gone from her too long. Nor could he take her with him to town, lying in the wagon bed, bouncing over the ruts with those contractions. Might end up delivering the baby at the side of the road.

He released her hands and stood. *I need to ride for Henrietta O'Donnell.* But as Erik started to leave the room, he remembered his nearest neighbor telling him at the ice cream social that she was going home with her daughter Sally, who lived on the Thompson ranch with her new husband—on the far side of Sweetwater Springs. Henrietta had planned to visit for a few days and wouldn't be back yet.

He doubted there'd be time to ride for their closest neighbor on the other side, either. Not that he knew what childless, elderly Mrs. Knapp could do anyway. But she was a woman, so surely she'd know something about childbirth. *But what if she doesn't?* He couldn't afford a wasted trip.

Erik moved back to the bed and took his wife's hand. "Everything is going to be all right, dearest." He tried not to betray his feeling of panic. "I'm leaving you for a bit to go to the O'Donnells. I'll send Rory or Charlie for Dr. Cameron."

"No!" Wide-eyed, she clutched his arm. "Don't leave me!"

"Dearest, we need the doctor."

Another contraction came, and Daisy screamed the whole time, her fingernails digging into his skin.

Helpless, all he could do was hold her hand and make soothing noises, realizing there wasn't time to ride for help. With a sinking heart, he acknowledged delivering this baby was up to him.

"You did this," his gentle wife growled. "You put this baby inside me."

He tried to tease her. "I think we both made the baby, my sweet."

"I hate you!"

Shocked, Erik released her hand and stood. Daisy had never taken to his humor, and, of course, she wouldn't react well now to any attempt to tease her out of the seriousness of this situation. *I'm such an oaf,* he berated himself. *Just stand and take the blame. She's right that I was more eager for the act of making a baby than she was.*

"You'll never touch me that way again!"

Each word was a knife in his heart. They'd conceived this child in love. *She's in pain. I need to make allowances for her harsh words.*

To give himself a few minutes to recover, Erik strode over to a blue shirt hanging on a peg on his side of the bed. He removed the filthy one he wore and changed into the fresh garment before hurrying to the porch to leave the dirty shirt in the laundry basket.

When Erik returned to the bedroom, he saw that Daisy kept her face averted. Nevertheless, he took a seat and picked up her hand, bringing it to his lips.

Still, she refused to meet his eyes. "You need to put the waxed cloth under me so we don't ruin the mattress." She pointed a trembling finger at the bureau.

Erik took the cloth from her drawer, moved to the bed, and lifted Daisy so he could slide the material under her. Afterward, he prepared a warm, damp cloth and gently wiped the perspiration from her brow.

"My back aches."

"Turn over, and I'll rub you."

With a groan, she shifted to her side, presenting her back to him.

As Erik had so often in the past months, he massaged her tight muscles, pressing his thumbs into the knots.

She suffered his ministrations, seeming to relax. When Daisy finally turned over, she even offered a small smile. "Thank you. That helped."

He sat in the ladder-back chair next to the bed and rubbed her hand. "Soon, we'll be parents, dearest."

Her smile was strained. "I can't bear this, Erik."

He didn't know how she could, either. "Just keep thinking of holding our child in your arms."

She squeezed his hand. Her eyes drifted closed.

Some time passed in silence. Daisy even dropped into a doze. Then another contraction hit, and she began to scream and thrash on the bed. As he tried to hold her down, Erik couldn't help the clutch of fear in his stomach. *I'm not sure we can get through this!*

＊ ＊ ＊

Long hours passed. Darkness had fallen, and Daisy labored throughout the night. As each hour dragged by without the baby's appearance, his fear grew.

Through the window, Erik could see dawn smudge purple shadows around the house. His body felt heavy with fatigue, yet each contraction charged him with energy, only to leave him shaken when it passed.

Good thing all the calves were born, so I don't have to go do the milking. The animals could wait on their feeding until the child came. "If the child comes," he said out loud. Erik finally put into words the dread he'd struggled with for the last hours.

Toward dawn, Daisy had stopped moving. Even when a contraction hit, all she could do was moan. But something in those muffled sounds of pain frightened him more than her shrieks had. His wife had always been delicate, and the strength to battle childbirth had drained away.

Helpless, all he could do was hold her hand and wipe her sweating face. His coaxing, pleading, even ordering didn't make any difference. "Please, dear Lord," he prayed in a soft voice. "Let them make it through this ordeal."

The pains started to come quickly, rippling across her distended stomach. He pushed up her nightgown and moved her legs aside. To his relief, Erik saw the top of the baby's head. He gently touched the damp down. "Come on, baby," he urged. "Come to Pa."

Daisy lay still, her eyes slitted, half-open.

"Push, Daisy. You must push!" he demanded.

His wife didn't respond.

"Come on, sweetheart. You can do this."

Her eyes opened in response to his words. "Can't," she mouthed.

"You must." He moved to the middle of the bed and placed his hands above the mound of her stomach. "I'll help. You push. I'll press on the baby. Together we can do it." He kept talking, even as he saw her gather her strength to do as he asked.

She lifted her head, rounded her shoulders, and pushed. *"ARRRRRGGGGHHH!"*

He pressed, imagining himself pushing against the baby's feet.

All too soon, Daisy collapsed.

Erik rushed to peer between her legs. More of the baby's head had appeared, but not enough. "Again, Daisy," he directed. With one arm, he lifted his wife's shoulders, the other pressing against the baby.

His wife gave a halfhearted response before collapsing in his arms. This time, she wouldn't move, no matter how much he exhorted her.

Desperate, he lifted her, then climbed on the bed so he could stand and pick her up, hoping the position would aid the baby in coming out.

Erik struggled to hold his wife's deadweight in one arm while pushing on the baby with the other. Under his hand, he felt the baby move a bit. He shoved again and then another time.

The nightgown obscured his view, so he stepped off the bed, laid her back down, shoved up the material, and saw that enough of the head had come through. He pushed on her stomach with one hand and pulled the baby with another. The tiny body finally slipped free, followed by a gush of blood.

With awe, Erik held the slippery mite in his hands, noting that he had a daughter. "A girl!"

Thank you, dear Lord. Tears of joy pricked his eyes, and, unashamed, he blinked them away. He met Daisy's gaze, seeing the joy on her pale face.

He used the damp cloth to wipe the baby's face and nose, and then gave her a gentle smack on the tiny behind. She let out a feeble wail, and he laughed in relief. "That's it, love, my Camilla." Erik held the baby up so his wife could see, careful of the dangling umbilical cord.

Daisy watched the baby with dreamy eyes. Her lips moved in a slight smile. "Beautiful," she whispered.

Erik turned back to the task of pinching the umbilical cord, severing it, and tying it off.

He wiped his daughter's head, face, and body with a damp cloth, his movements careful. *She's so tiny and feels so fragile.*

He started to lay the baby on Daisy's chest, but something about his wife's still body sent a jolt of fear through him. Cradling the babe with one arm, he saw the pool of blood between his wife's legs. Fear shafted through him. *Too much blood!*

Erik set the baby on top of the blanket in the cradle in the corner next to the bed.

Camilla flailed her arms and legs.

Erik tucked the blanket over the baby's body. Moving to the bureau, he grabbed two flannel diapers from the stack that Daisy had put on top and used one to sop up the moisture between her legs. Red soaked the cloth. *If the bleeding doesn't stop, she'll die.*

Time passed in a blur. Erik massaged Daisy's stomach and kept changing the cloths as one became too sodden.

Daisy remained still, her lips bloodless, her skin as pale as marble. Slowly, the life light faded from her blue eyes.

Erik touched his hand to the side of Daisy's neck and didn't feel a pulse. Dropping to his knees by the bed, he placed an ear to his wife's chest. He heard only silence, instead of the familiar thump-thump.

"Daisy!" Erik jumped to his feet and grabbed the hand mirror from the bureau, holding it to her mouth, hoping against hope to see fog from her breath.

Nothing.

"No!" Erik dropped the mirror, barely hearing it shatter as it hit the floor. He collapsed on the bed next to her, pulling her body to him. He gently closed her eyelids and kissed her forehead. "Come back, love. Please don't leave me. Don't leave our baby. She needs you. *We* need you."

He hugged Daisy tighter, holding her for a long, sad moment. He lowered her to the pillow. "Thank you for our child, my love. I promise I will raise her to be a credit to you."

A whimper made him leap to his feet, bend over the cradle, and scoop up the baby, blanket and all.

I need to get to town, to the doctor, or our daughter will follow her mother to the grave.

❋ ❋ ❋

Antonia had been to Sweetwater Springs a total of three times. Once when they'd first moved to the vicinity of the town, and twice before Henri was born, when Jean-Claude had taken his furs to sell, and they had a chance to buy supplies. On those trips, she'd met no one, although she'd exchanged smiles with other women walking on the street or in the store. She vaguely recalled the shopkeeper, remembering the older woman as an unpleasant person.

Now, walking into town, leading the two mules, she was conscious of her grubby state and her Indian garb. She'd washed up at the last stream, but she still smelled like campfire smoke. The only dress she owned was from her girlhood and was threadbare and far too small, even with letting out all the seams. The other two she used to own had eventually worn out. Since they tended to spend summers with the Indians, it had been easier and more practical to adopt the clothing of the squaws—a long tunic that today she wore with leggings. Yet in this town full of white folks, she'd already drawn some astonished or condemning stares.

Feeling vulnerable, Antonia turned her face away from a man who leered at her, only to see a building under construction on the opposite side. The sounds of hammering slowed, and she didn't dare look to see if the workers also watched her.

Where should we go? On the three-day walk to the town, Antonia had plenty of time to think about what she could do to support her children. If Jean-Claude were alive, they could get by for almost a year on the sale of the furs. But with paying for shelter, food she hadn't grown or hunted, town clothing…. *Cain't last more than a season.*

As far as she knew, jobs for women were scarce. She could cross off the list teacher or anything else that required an education. She couldn't read or write. Washerwoman? Perhaps, although she had little practical experience with anything but using lye soap in a stream on the scant garb they wore that wasn't leather. Seamstress? She glanced down at her tunic. She didn't think there'd be much call for leatherwork in town. Saloon girl? Jean-Claude would turn over in his grave if she went anywhere near a saloon. *What will I do?*

Exhaustion weighed on her as heavy as her grief. Jacques had fussed much of the night, keeping her up trying to soothe him.

After the freedom of the mountains, walking through town felt uncomfortable, and Antonia had difficulty breathing. Even though the dirt street was wide, the buildings, both brick and the false-fronted wooden ones, seemed to press in on her.

"*Maman,*" said Henri, clutching his brother astride the mule.

Her son sounded worried. Antonia paused and reached up to touch his knee. "All will be well, *mon fils.*" She wished she could believe her words.

Antonia stopped in the middle of the dirt street. Although she should head toward the brick mercantile building to sell the furs, something about the white frame church drew her. Her childhood of following the army with her soldier father had made for a mixture of religious experiences, but in marrying Jean-Claude, she had become Catholic. Perhaps she could slip into the church and say a prayer, asking for guidance for herself and offering words for Jean-Claude. *Maybe my prayers can make up for burying him without a priest.*

She glanced up at the boys, sitting on the mule. Jacques slept in Henri's arms, and her older son watched her with solemn golden eyes. He had a smudge of dirt on one cheekbone, and a sprinkling of freckles across his nose had popped out from the last few days in the sun, away from the tree-shaded mountains. They'd be fine by themselves for a few minutes while she went inside to pray.

Antonia led the mules toward the church, conscious of tiredness weighing her down and the numbness in her heart. She stopped at a hitching rail at the side of the building. Before she could loop the reins over it, an elderly man in a black frock coat and clerical cravat strode up to her.

Antonia studied his austere, white-bearded face. With a sinking feeling in her stomach, she knew she wouldn't be allowed to pray in the church.

He stopped in front of her and gave a slight incline of his head.

Antonia braced herself. She'd be lucky if they weren't run out of town for being heathens. She made to turn around, but the man held up a hand, and she stopped, unable to meet his gaze.

He lifted his hat in greeting. "I'm Reverend Norton. Were you looking for me?" He studied her with piercing blue eyes.

"I be hopin' to go inside and pray." She glanced up at the boys. "My husband…he died a few days ago. Killed by a grizzly, he be."

His expression softened.

Antonia wondered if she'd misjudged him.

The man gestured to a small house behind and to the right of the church. "You've had a hard time of it, then. Why don't you come to my home? My wife can provide a meal, and I can offer an ear, some prayers, and, if needed, some advice."

At his kindness, sudden tears sprang to her eyes. She ducked her head to blink them away. "Mighty kind, preacher." Her voice sounded husky. "I be Antonia Valleau. My older son be Henri, and the baby be Jacques."

He smiled and tipped his head toward the little house, white-framed like the church. "Leave the mules and bring the children."

Antonia lifted Jacques down from the mule. The baby stirred but didn't awaken. He'd always been a good sleeper, something she was deeply grateful for.

The minister slipped his hands around Henri's waist. "Down you go." He lifted the boy to the ground.

Henri looked up at her for assurance.

"Follow the preacher," she told him.

They traipsed up the stairs and into a small main room. A slight woman wearing a blue dress appeared, drying her hands on a spotless apron. She had a sweet wrinkled face and white hair drawn back into a tight bun. She gave Antonia a welcoming smile.

Embarrassed by her Indian garb, Antonia shyly bobbed her head.

Reverend Norton gestured to the woman. "My wife, Mrs. Norton. Mrs. Valleau has just lost her husband."

Mrs. Norton frowned, concern in her blue eyes. She reached out and touched Antonia's arm. "You poor dear. I'm so sorry to hear that. Do you want me to take the children while you talk with Reverend Norton?"

Henri pressed against Antonia's side.

"They be not used to strangers."

Mrs. Norton gave an understanding nod. "Of course. Hopefully, they'll warm up to us. In the meantime, I'm sure you all are hungry. Let me dish up some food."

"Thank you kindly."

Reverend Norton opened the door to the right, ushering her into a small, cluttered room.

Henri, clutching the hem of Antonia's tunic, followed.

She took a chair across from the paper-and-book-covered desk, settled the baby against her, and patted the chair next to her for Henri to sit.

Her son climbed up gingerly, unused to chairs. In their cabin, they'd sat on crude stools padded with pelts and slept on furs on the floor. She hadn't sat in a regular chair since she was fifteen, about ten or so years ago, and had married Jean-Claude and set off for a life as a trapper's wife.

The minister sat on the desk chair. He glanced at her, white eyebrows raised, waiting for Antonia to begin.

The kind expression on his face encouraged her to talk. The words came out haltingly, but then sped up. Soon, she'd told him the whole sad story, pausing when she had to grope for a word. She'd grown so used to mostly speaking French with Jean-Claude, although she tried to use English with the boys so they'd know both languages.

He nodded and stroked his beard. "Your entire life has changed in the last days."

"I be so angry with him!" The emotion burst from her. "Jean-Claude killed them bears all the while we been in the mountains. Be he careless?"

At her outburst, she saw Henri's face go chalky. She warned herself to hush, but the feelings pulsed so inside her.

"I've observed that anger is a common reaction to a death caused by an accident," said the reverend. "Or in this case, a wild animal. I bet you wish you could give him a good scold."

Antonia stared at the minister. "How be you knowing?" She blushed, realizing whom she was talking to. "I be sure you've been doin' this often."

His expression grew somber. "Far more than I would like."

"Be…be it always this raw? Like knives stabbing into my heart?"

"No. But for a while, the pain will be overwhelming. At some point, which is different for everyone, some of the edges of your grief will cease to be so sharp."

Antonia shifted back in her chair.

Jacques stirred in her arms, made a little noise, and subsided.

Henri leaned his head against her shoulder.

She dredged up memories of preachers from her childhood. "You be not tellin' me he's an angel up in heaven? Me be thinkin' you're supposed to."

Reverend Norton gave her a wry smile. "Many ministers do say those kinds of things. Not that they say—" he hastily added "—Jean-Claude's an angel, for the angelic host isn't human—but they'll tell you his soul is at peace in heaven. A true statement...."

She wasn't sure what the preacher meant but didn't want to ask.

"However, I've found that the only time that statement helps is when the deceased has suffered before he or she died. Then the thought of the loved one no longer suffering does bring comfort. But your husband was a healthy man—one whom you expected to have many happy years with...to raise your sons together. You don't want him in heaven yet. You want him with you here on Earth."

Antonia swallowed the lump in her throat, feeling less weighed down by anger and guilt. "Yes," she whispered. "I thought I be selfish."

"No, my dear Mrs. Valleau. Just human. And the Lord who created us certainly understands our humanness."

Comforted by his words, she rubbed her hand over Jacques's silky hair.

The sleeping baby didn't stir.

"Thank you. The pain be still there, still be as strong, but mayhap I be a bit more able to bear it and all."

"Talking is very helpful. You've lived a very isolated life. And women, as I've observed and my dear helpmate has explained, need the companionship of other women. They need to talk about their feelings." A look of humorous bewilderment crossed his face. "So much so that it often makes my head spin."

She shrugged. "I never be around other women much. My ma, she died young, and I be raised in a fort. There be some officers' wives and daughters. But they be lookin' down on the likes of me—Pa being an enlisted man and all. After my marriage, Jean-Claude and me lived a bit with the Indians. Jean-Claude, he be French-Canadian but spoke Indian real good. Took me a while to learn, though. Still ain't all that good, though my Henri, here—" she touched his leg "—he be jabberin' away."

"Well, I hope you make your home in Sweetwater Springs. You will find some congenial feminine companionship here."

Congenial? What be that meanin'?

"I'll suggest starting with Mrs. Norton. Normally, I'd have a bed for you all, but my son and grandson have just returned from Africa. But if you don't mind sleeping on a pallet on the floor, you can stay here for a few days while you get your bearings. We can talk more later about where to go from there."

"We be used to sleepin' on the floor. Thank you kindly for your offer."

In her relief, Antonia squeezed Jacques, waking up the baby. He jerked to a sitting position, smiled at her with sleepy black eyes, and looked around the room. She knew the minute the baby realized he was in a strange place without his father, because his expression crumpled, and he laid his head back on her breast.

Her heart ached for him, and—she glanced at her older son—for Henri. *My two fatherless boys.* Somehow, she'd have to find a way to be both mother and father to her young sons.

CHAPTER THREE

Erik pulled the wagon to a halt in front of Dr. Cameron's house and set the brake, looped the reins. He'd never been to the doctor's before, but Daisy had, and she'd described the two-story white home with roses climbing over the picket fence.

He scooped up the baby from the straw-padded crate next to him and jumped off the wagon.

The doctor's office was around back, and he strode in that direction, carrying his blanket-wrapped daughter. There were moments on the hour-long ride that he wondered if they would make it here in time. Camilla looked so still and waxen. Then she'd move her hand or open her eyes, and he knew she still lived; thus there was a chance.

Erik pounded on one of the double doors.

Redheaded Mrs. Cameron opened the door. She was heavily pregnant, even more enormous than Daisy had been. "Why, Mr. Muth."

Just seeing her expansive belly made Erik shudder. He held up the baby. "My wife just gave birth to her and died."

"Oh, dearie me. You puir man. Come right in," she said in a Scottish accent. "The doctor doesn't have any other patients now, and he'll be able to see to the wee one."

Erik stepped inside a plain, double-doored entry, and then through a second set of doors into a hallway with a long cushioned bench along one wall.

She turned to the right and gestured him inside.

Two raised wooden beds with thin pads and clean linen stood in the middle of the room. Several straight-backed chairs lined the wall on one side of the bed. Shelves of jars holding liquids and herbs crowded the front of the room, and on a table between the beds metal instruments lay on a white cloth.

The red-haired doctor sat behind a desk in the back corner, reading a thick book. When he saw them, he stood. He was in his shirtsleeves; a long Prince Albert coat hung on a hook next to the desk. He moved to take down the coat, but hesitated.

Erik took quick steps to him and deposited the baby in his arms. "My wife died giving birth to her. She's come early."

Doctor Cameron laid the babe on the bed and unwrapped the blanket. He gently ran his hands over her body and then straightened. "She's tiny, which is to be expected with coming early. And your wife, I recall, was a small woman."

My dainty Daisy. Erik wanted to weep for all he'd lost, what he still might lose, but the tears wouldn't come.

"She's healthy, all things considered." Dr. Cameron picked up the baby, cradling her head with his hand, and handed her to his wife. "We'll need to find a wet nurse right away." His Scottish accent thickened. "The wee lassie does na have much time."

Dear Lord, please save her. Erik had never prayed so fervently before Daisy had gone into early labor, setting off this whole chain of events.

Using a damp cloth, Mrs. Cameron cleaned off his daughter with deft strokes. Although the baby was awake, she didn't even whimper. "What's the lassie's name?" Mrs. Cameron asked.

"Camilla."

"Lovely name, for a lovely lassie. Do you have baby clothes?"

Erik thought of the little brassbound trunk, filled with the tiny results of his wife's loving handwork, and wanted to smack a hand to his head. "I left everything behind."

"We'll find something for her."

"The closest woman is Mrs. Marshall," the doctor said. "Her daughter's almost ready to be weaned ana way."

Erik's stomach relaxed.

Mrs. Cameron shook her head, making her curls bounce. "She went to St. Louis to visit her mother."

Erik tensed, and his stomach tightened again.

The doctor's brow furrowed. "Mrs. Mueller?"

"Weaned the lassie two weeks ago. Her milk will have dried up by now."

"Patty, the saloon girl?" An anxious note crept into the doctor's voice.

"Eloped with a cowboy."

As the list went on, Erik's spirits dropped. Was there no nursing woman who could save his daughter?

"Mrs. Smith."

"I heard this morning and dinna have a chance to tell you. The wee babe died three weeks ago."

"They didn't call me?"

She swayed with the baby. "They woke up, and he was dead."

Dr. Cameron brushed his hand across his face. "We usually have a glut of babies. How can there not be a nursing mother in this town? Elizabeth Sanders, then. It's a two-hour ride to the ranch, though. Don't know if the wee lassie has the time."

Mrs. Cameron hurried toward the door. "I'll go have Mack hitch up the buggy and then fetch Reverend Norton. Not everyone can afford to have a doctor deliver their babies. He might know of someone we don't. Plus—" she gave Erik a sorrowing glance "—you'll want her christened."

Erik held in a groan of pain. *They don't expect my daughter to live.*

✻ ✻ ✻

A knock sounded on the door to the minister's office, startling Antonia.

"Enter," Reverend Norton called.

Mrs. Norton stuck her head into the room. "Pardon me for interrupting. Mrs. Cameron has an urgent message." She stepped back to allow a very pregnant woman with curly red hair piled loosely into a bun to precede her.

The new arrival wore an apron over her blue dress, as if in her haste she hadn't stopped to remove the covering. Mrs. Cameron's anxious green gaze landed on Jacques. Without even waiting for a greeting, she rushed into speech. "Are you still nursing the wee one, then?" she asked Antonia.

Puzzled by the question, Antonia nodded.

The woman threw up her hands. "Praise to Mary, mother of Jesus, and to all the saints." Then her eyes widened as if realizing what she'd said. Mrs. Cameron placed both hands on her chest and sent an apologetic glance at the minister. "I was praying to the Virgin in this case, Reverend," Mrs. Cameron rushed to explain. "She understands the needs of mothers and babes."

Reverend Norton frowned, but there was no disapproval behind the look. "Come in, Mrs. Cameron, and meet Mrs. Valleau."

Mrs. Cameron took a step into the room, but there was no space for her to go farther. She turned to Antonia. "We have a newborn whose mother has died. Will you come and nurse the wee one? For if she doesn't have sustenance soon, she's not long for this world."

Antonia's eyes widened at the extraordinary request. She glanced down at Jacques. *Have I enough milk to spare? We are barely surviving ourselves.* But she couldn't allow a baby to die. She nodded. "I be glad to help."

Reverend Norton waved in Alice's direction. "Mrs. Cameron, the wife of our doctor. Mrs. Cameron, this is a newcomer to our town, who has recently lost her husband."

A chagrinned expression crossed the woman's face. "I'm sorry for appearing so discourteous. Condolences on your loss. And that of your bairns."

"Thank you." Antonia stood. She set Jacques on her hip and held out her other hand to Henri. "Where be this babe?"

"Thank the good Lord!" Mrs. Cameron raised her eyes heavenward. "Now may we please be in time to save Camilla!"

❋ ❋ ❋

Erik cradled his tiny daughter with one arm. Camilla felt so light. He'd carried suckling pigs who weighed more than the little mite in his arms.

Now that his frantic dash to reach the doctor had ended with him holding his dying daughter and waiting, he finally had time to examine her. In the oval shape of her face and delicate features, he saw his wife again, and his heart ached.

He stroked a finger over the soft blonde hair on her head, barely more than fuzz.

A tiny hand flailed, as small as a coin.

He caught her wrist to study the slender fingers, the miniature nails.

Her fingers curled around his pinky, causing a wave of love to wash over him, the emotion so strong it made him dizzy. *This is what it means to be a father.* He hadn't known he could feel this way. Hadn't realized such a love was possible. He'd wanted his firstborn to be a son to help around the farm. Now, he wouldn't trade his precious Camilla for a schoolhouse full of boys.

He had a horrific vision of laying their daughter in her mother's arms and burying them both in a single grave, and his guts twisted.

Please, dear Lord. Let me keep her. I swear to be a good father.

The sound of the opening door made him look up. Erik's first glimpse of the woman wearing a leather tunic and leggings, russet hair caught in a long braid down her back, made him think Mrs. Cameron had found a squaw to nurse his baby. Not that he cared. Any breast full of milk would do. But then the woman stared at him with sad golden eyes, and he revised his estimation. Not an Indian, but Camilla's savior, nevertheless.

The woman held a baby in her arms. A boy. Plump, with big dark eyes and a gummy smile. *Please God, may my daughter soon look as healthy as he does.*

A young boy of five or six who had his mother's golden eyes followed on her heels and then leaned against her leg when she stopped a few feet away.

One hand on the mound of her stomach, Mrs. Cameron made breathless introductions that he barely caught.

Although the fact she was a recent widow and had left her home in the mountains penetrated his foggy brain.

Reverend Norton stepped into the room. "I've heard the tragic news. I'm so sorry to learn of Daisy's death. Mrs. Norton and I are here if you need us. If...the baby needs to be baptized right away. We'll be in the kitchen."

Erik wanted to shout, "NO!" But instead, he took a deep breath and gave the minister a nod of thanks before the man left the room. Truth was, he was grateful. *If my little mite isn't going to stay with me, then she'll need to be safe with her mother in heaven.* But he desperately wanted Camilla to live.

Mrs. Valleau handed her baby to Mrs. Cameron, and then reached out her arms for his daughter.

Erik hesitated. An unfamiliar paternal protective feeling made him reluctant to part with his child, but he forced himself to hand the baby to the woman.

"So tiny," she murmured softly, holding Camilla in one arm, while with the other hand, she unbuttoned a flap near her chest.

He caught a glimpse of a full breast with a dark nipple, so different from Daisy's small pink-tipped ones.

The woman fastened the baby to her nipple.

Erik turned away, embarrassed, waited a minute and thought it might be safe to peek from the corner of his eye. At first, Camilla didn't attach, and he began to worry all over again.

The woman gave him a reassuring smile. "It be takin' a bit of gittin' used to for one just birthed." The words held a slight French accent. "This little one be catchin' on, just you watch." She persisted in coaxing the child to nurse.

The baby's mouth closed over the nipple. She began to suckle, making tiny smacking noises.

Relief made Erik's knees weak, and he stepped back, collapsing onto a chair against the wall and dropping his head in his hands to hide his emotion. *Thank you, Lord. Thank you. Thank you!*

A hand dropped on his shoulder and squeezed. "You've had a hard time of it, Erik Muth," said Dr. Cameron. "It's early days, and I canna make promises. But the lassie is feedin' well, and that's a good sign. Mrs. Valleau seems to be an experienced mother, and her boys look healthy."

Erik wiped his arm across his face and lifted his head. "Thank you, Doctor." He looked over at the woman who was giving his daughter sustenance from her body. "Thank you, Mrs. Valleau. I don't have words to tell you how much this means to me."

She smiled. For a moment, the shadows in her eyes lightened. "Sounds like you just be doin' so."

CHAPTER FOUR

Since Jean-Claude's death, Antonia had been unable to feel anything but the heaviness of her grief, as if all her other feelings had frozen. Yet, looking at the child in her arms, so much smaller than her boys had been at their births, she felt a wave of love, of possession, as strong as the feelings she'd had when Jean-Claude had first placed each of her sons at her breast after their birth. "*Ma chérie,*" she murmured so softly only she and the babe could hear.

Don't be gittin' attached, Antonia told herself, glancing across the room at Erik, still sitting in the chair against the wall. She had no doubt the man loved his daughter. *Camilla be not yours to keep,* she reminded herself. *You be givin' her back.*

Henri came to lean against her, as was his habit. "*Maman,* I'm hungry."

Mrs. Cameron jiggled Jacques on one hip and extended a hand to Henri. "Of course, you are. Why don't you come with me? I'm sure you'd like a nice piece of bread with jam. We can give your brother a crust to gnaw on. Then I'll prepare a meal for everyone, and you can help me."

Henri looked to Antonia for permission.

She nodded. "Bread and jam be a treat. My young 'uns be not gittin' such as that."

Henri straightened looking more animated than she'd seen him since his father had died, and took Mrs. Cameron's hand.

Antonia detached the infant from her breast and placed her on her shoulder, patting the baby's back. "Camilla be a right purty name," she said to Mr. Muth.

The man stared at them, a strained look on his face. "My wife thought so, too."

"Sure be. No shortage of beauty in this'un, neither," Antonia said, although her even tone belied a pang at how close *Camilla* sounded to *Carmelina*, which is what she and Jean-Claude planned to call the daughter they'd hoped to have. *A child who'll never be born.* She strove to suppress the thought. She had more than she could bear with *real* losses. No sense mourning the ones that were only dreams. "What was your wife's name?"

He looked away. "Margaret. Although she hated that name. Everyone called her Daisy. She was adamant about not passing it on to a daughter. But now that she's not here, perhaps I should...in her memory..."

The baby let out a burp.

"Call her Camilla Marguerite," Antonia suggested. "She be named after her ma...but ain't quite the one your Daisy disliked."

"Camilla Marguerite," Mr. Muth repeated to himself and then gave Antonia a small smile. "I like that."

"I be sorry for your loss." The words came out sounding stiffer than Antonia intended.

He looked down. "I just left Daisy's body on the bed. I was frantic to get to the doctor. To save the baby."

"I think she'd understand. She'd want you to take care of her new babe."

His gaze looked haunted. Lines of exhaustion radiated from his blue eyes.

Antonia thought of the grave she'd left behind and put conviction into her voice. "She'd be a wantin' you to do anything to save her babe. *Anything!*"

Erik Muth straightened his back.

For the first time, Antonia really looked at him. She saw a big man who towered over her, which was unusual given her height, with shoulder-length blond hair bleached white by the sun, pale eyebrows, tired blue eyes, and a wide nose and mouth. He wore a bloodstained blue shirt. Above his close-cut tawny beard, his skin was ruddy, and he had a sprinkling of freckles across his nose, which gave him a friendly, open expression. Not a bad looking man, but very different from Jean-Claude, with his slender build, tanned skin, sharp cheekbones, exotic green eyes, and long, dark hair.

"I keep thanking you." His words came out in a slow rumble. "You're a stranger, and today, you've done more for me than anyone I've ever met. And I've been blessed with a lot of kindness in my life." He stared out the window, his eyes unseeing of the distant mountains. "I guess you can say I've been charmed. Got everything I wanted. My life plan was falling into place, step by step. Until today." He gave a slow shake of his head. "It's all been for naught."

Antonia glanced down at the baby, who'd fallen asleep. "Not be for naught. You can be takin' her now." With one hand, she pulled up the front of her tunic.

Erik rose and walked toward her. His hands fumbled as he took the babe and held her to him, looking helpless.

"Support her head," Antonia cautioned, as she tied up her tunic. "She be wobbly for a while."

Camilla stirred and opened her eyes.

"Hi, precious one," her father whispered, rocking her. An infatuated look spread over his face. He brought her closer and kissed her forehead.

Watching father and daughter made some warmth seep into Antonia's frozen heart.

"She's so tiny," he murmured, not taking his gaze off the baby. "How can she possibly survive?"

Dr. Cameron entered the room, came over to Erik, and peered down at the baby. "She nursed well?" he asked Antonia.

"Once Camilla caught on, she did fine."

"Camilla, eh. Lovely name for a lovely wee lassie." He stepped back and gave them both a serious look. "Now. We must speak of keeping her alive." He clapped a hand on Erik's shoulder. "What I propose will be hard to wrap your mind around, lad. But hear me out, will ya, then?"

Erik nodded.

The doctor lowered his hand to his side. "Camilla needs a wet nurse. There's no hope for her, else." He hesitated. "And someone to care for the wee lassie when you are working."

Erik ran a hand over his face, as if everything was too much for him to take in.

Dr. Cameron glanced at Antonia. "Mrs. Cameron tells me that Mrs. Valleau is a widow."

Widow. How she hated that word. *But now I be one.* She dipped her chin in acknowledgment.

He looked askance at Antonia. "Would you be willing to continue on as Camilla's nurse?"

"Oh, no," Antonia said before she thought. "I cain't." *I cain't be livin' with another man!* And how could she raise his baby, become attached to her, but have to leave when Camilla was grown enough to not need her care? Nor could she let her sons become attached to the man and child. The pain of having to leave again would be hard on them.

"Lass," the doctor said gently. "Mrs. Valleau. Without you to nurse her, the baby won't survive. As it is, her life will be touch and go. She'll need more care than a busy farmer, no matter how devoted a father, can give her."

As the meaning of the doctor's words hit, Erik first looked stunned. His face reddened as if he was going to cry. He took a shuddering breath. "The house isn't that big, but I could build a room for you and your children. Most of my money is invested in the farm, but I could pay you a little."

Her heart pounding, Antonia wanted to grab her boys and run back to the mountains to Jean-Claude's waiting arms. But Jean-Claude was buried in a cold grave. She had nothing and no one to run to. This would provide her and the boys some security. But still she wavered. Then she looked up at Erik Muth's face and saw the pain in his eyes, his imploring expression. She glanced at the little Camilla, already so dear to her. Did she really have a choice? She had nowhere else to go and couldn't let the child die. "I'll do it."

Mr. Muth's shoulders sagged in relief. He closed his eyes, took a breath, and opened them again. "Thank you. I promise to do everything I can to make life comfortable for your family."

Dr. Cameron smiled. "That's settled, then. I have a good feelin' about your wee lassie. I think with regular nourishment and the tender care she'll receive from Mrs. Valleau here, Mr. Muth, you just might be able to walk her down the aisle someday."

Will I be there to see Camilla wed? Antonia wondered.

"Mrs. Cameron has prepared us some food." The doctor waved toward the door. "I hope you like *haggis*." At their blank looks, he laughed. "I was just joking." His brogue deepened. "*Haggis* is liver, onion, oatmeal, and spices cooked in a sheep's stomach—an acquired taste. I left my wife fryin' up some bacon, and it smelled *vera* enticing. Come. Join us for a meal."

Antonia hadn't tasted bacon in ages. Yet, even the thought of a former favorite food did nothing for her nonexistent appetite.

The doctor nudged Mr. Muth's shoulder and urged him toward the door, the new pa glancing down at the sleeping child he held.

Antonia waited a moment before following the men. She needed to catch her breath, to brace herself for the new future.

✳ ✳ ✳

As Erik walked toward the kitchen, carrying his daughter, he doubted he'd be able to eat a bite. His stomach felt like a varmint had wrestled with his innards, a stone stuck in his throat, and grief weighed down his limbs. He just wanted to go find a cave, crawl inside, and hibernate away from the world for a while, but—he looked down at his daughter—doing so would mean giving up on his responsibilities. He had a child, a farm, and—he glanced over at Mrs. Valleau—now more people depending on him.

He stepped into the kitchen, crowded with adults and children. The smell of frying bacon made his stomach change its mind. His belly gave out a huge growl, which both embarrassed him and made him realize that he hadn't eaten since yesterday.

Mrs. Cameron stood at the stove cooking, while Mrs. Norton set the table with flowered china dishes of the type Daisy had coveted. He'd planned to get them for her as a

Christmas present. Pain stabbed him. *Why did I wait? Why didn't I make an effort to buy her more of the pretty things she wanted, instead of putting all my money back into the farm? Why did we argue about something so trivial? I was so selfish!*

Guilt settled in his stomach, the lump stealing away his appetite.

Mrs. Valleau had been standing silently to one side of the room, her body stiff. She seemed to be taking everything in.

Reverend Norton, seated at the foot of the table, waved for Erik and Mrs. Valleau to sit down. "Come, you two. You must eat." The minister gave him a glance of sympathy. "Even though you might think you aren't hungry, you must keep up your strength. Now more than ever."

He's right. But I don't think I could choke down a bite.

From her place at the stove, Mrs. Cameron glanced at him. "I figured a belated breakfast would be the easiest to fix. How does bacon, scrambled eggs, and toast with jam sound to you, Mr. Muth?"

Before he could answer, the boy, sitting at one end of the long kitchen table, holding his brother on his lap, spoke up. "Jam be good," he said, popping a crust in his mouth.

His English had a French accent, like his mother's. Both children had purple smears on their faces. The little one gave his mother an open-mouthed smile. He chortled and banged a fist on the table, still holding a jam-smeared crust. The older one swallowed his remaining bread in one bite.

Mrs. Cameron chuckled. "Plenty more where that came from. We've had several people pay the doctor's bill with saskatoon jam. We have a year's supply stocked up. That's on top of the jam left over from the previous year."

Mrs. Norton's face crinkled with good humor. "So do we. Such a blessing."

Mrs. Cameron glanced up at Erik. "You'll have to take several jars with you. And some of pickles and a few of applesauce."

Conscious he had his own doctor's bill to pay, Erik shook his head. "Thank you for the offer, Mrs. Cameron. But I can't deprive you of your jam."

She tsked. "Like I said, we have plenty. And more's bound to come in. You'll help me out by giving me some space in the pantry. Besides—" with her chin, she indicated the boy "—jam will help smooth the way with the laddie."

"Mrs. Valleau," said the minister. "Won't you sit with us?"

"I ain't got manners for company," she said, clearly embarrassed.

Erik, still holding Camilla, pulled out the chair next to the boy, whose name he didn't recall, and gestured for Mrs. Valleau to take a seat across from him. She did so, with a grace that he couldn't help noticing.

She surreptitiously touched the rose on the patterned plate already set in front of her, fingered the decorative handle of the silver knife, and then lowered her hand into her lap.

Erik took a seat across from her. He was grateful the meal was eggs and not beefsteak. *How would I cut my food while holding the baby?*

The doctor entered the room and headed toward the other end of the table. "If I'm lucky, I'll make it through the meal without being called out. I've missed a lot of meals this week." He patted his stomach. "Keeps me from growing out of my clothes."

Mrs. Cameron dished out generous helpings on all their plates. "Make sure you eat," she ordered Mrs. Valleau. "I can tell you've been doing without. Probably don't have much of an appetite given your sorrow. However, you're a nursing mother. Now you'll have two babies to care for. You'll have to keep up your strength for the wee bairns' sake."

Mrs. Valleau glanced at her boys, and then at Camilla. A resolute expression crossed her face, and she picked up the fork, scooped up some eggs, and took a bite.

"Try the jam, *Maman*," her boy said, picking up a strip of bacon and biting into it. His eyes widened. "*Très bon!*"

His enthusiasm required no translation.

Mrs. Cameron laughed.

Even Mrs. Valleau had a slight smile. "Henri be not used to pork, either, although he be likin' it. Bear, venison, duck, goose…but not pig."

"Well, I guess he'll have to get used to pork and chicken," Erik said, thinking about the livestock on his farm.

At the reference to their upcoming changes, Mrs. Valleau's small smile vanished, and she looked down at her plate.

Erik felt like a bumbling idiot. Yes, he'd just lost his wife, but he still had his farm. She'd not only lost her husband but her home, too. And her way of life. He wondered how she'd be able to adjust. His shoulders ached with tension. *Another burden.*

Mrs. Cameron bustled over. "Let me hold the wee lassie while you eat." She reached for the baby.

"What about your food?"

"I'll be fine. I had a head start on the bacon."

Carefully, Erik handed Camilla over to the woman.

The baby didn't stir.

Mrs. Cameron sat on the other side of him.

"I'll say grace," Reverend Norton said. He waited for them to bow their heads.

Before Erik closed his eyes, he noticed that Mrs. Valleau was half a beat behind everyone else, and he wondered if she usually prayed before meals.

The boy, Henri, didn't bend his head, instead stared at everyone with wide gold eyes.

I wonder if they're Catholic? Not that it mattered. Between the farmwork and the weather, he often didn't make it to church on Sundays. Although sometimes, Daisy had put her foot down and forced the issue of their lack of attendance.

Even as he thought the words, Erik realized he and Daisy would never have Sundays together again. Guilt swept over him. Daisy had enjoyed going to town, worshiping in church, and spending time with other women. Why, then, had he not seen to it she had more chances to do so?

How long will it take before I believe she's gone?

✳ ✳ ✳

Antonia wished she could do justice to the eggs and bacon, bread and jam like Henri was. The bacon, especially, smelled so good. But the food all tasted like wood to her. *Might as well chew bark.*

Yet, she realized the truth of Mrs. Cameron's statement about needing to keep up her strength. She not only had her boys depending on her but Camilla, too. She glanced over at Mr. Muth, who had stopped eating and seemed lost in unhappy thoughts. Perhaps the meat tasted like wood to him as well.

Mrs. Cameron cast a pointed look toward Mr. Muth's plate.

Obediently, he picked up his fork and began to eat.

She was glad to see that Henri, who'd only picked at his food since Jean-Claude's death, ate another helping.

Mrs. Norton started a conversation with Mrs. Cameron about some of the people in town. Their husbands joined in.

Too lost in her own thoughts, Antonia allowed their words to flow over her.

Dr. Cameron set down his glass. "Cleeves had a pig disappear, and an Indian was seen in the area."

Oh, no. Her gut clenching, Antonia sat up.

"After service on Sunday, Harrison Dunn told me a few of their cattle disappeared, and from the trail, he suspected rustlers. He reported the loss to Sheriff Granger."

Mr. Muth frowned. "Last week, the O'Donnells mentioned they'd lost four hens, with no sight of blood or feathers to indicate what had taken them. Quite upset, Mrs. O'Donnell was. The family relies heavily on their chickens. I hadn't realized more incidents had occurred."

Mrs. Norton placed a hand on her chest. "Do you think it's the work of Indians?" she asked in a timid voice.

A forbidding expression drew the minister's face into severe lines. "Let's hope that isn't the case. The last thing we need is folk becoming enflamed against the Indians."

"If they be, 'tis because they be starvin'!" Antonia said, her tone sharp. "The white men done killed off the buffalo, their main food. I be not sayin' that thievin' be right, or even that the Blackfoot be doin' such. But I do know their babes and elders be dyin'. Others be weak, vulnerable."

"I've seen some sad cases of grippe and malnutrition," the doctor commented.

"Sometimes the Indians come to our door," the reverend said. "And we never turn them away with empty hands. I don't know what more we can do." He glanced at his wife and his severe expression eased. "First of all, we must not let these rumors get out of hand. Sheriff Granger needs to know, of course. But she's a levelheaded woman, and I trust her not to act out of hand."

She? Antonia wasn't sure she'd heard right.

Reverend Norton must have seen her puzzlement, for he smiled and nodded. "Yes, our sheriff is, indeed, a woman.

Quite competent." He glanced around the table. "We may have no problem and these incidents all have natural explanations. Or they may be thefts and thus connected, in which case they may or may not be caused by the Indians."

Doctor Cameron glanced at the minister. "Between the two of us, we probably cover more ground around here and talk to more people than anyone else. We'll have to start asking questions…in an indirect way, of course. No sense putting any ideas in people's heads."

Reverend Norton rubbed his chin. "I'll talk to John Carter about the Blackfoot. Perhaps if we both write the Office of Indian Affairs, asking for more supplies to be distributed, that action could solve one or both problems."

"Be a start." Feeling somewhat heartened that, by coming to Sweetwater Springs, she might be helping the Blackfoot, Antonia took another bite of her eggs.

As everyone else returned to eating, silence fell.

After they'd tucked in a goodly amount, Reverend Norton cleared his throat. "What have you two decided to do?" He glanced from Antonia to Mr. Muth.

Mr. Muth flicked a look at her before turning to the minister. "Mrs. Valleau has agreed to come live at the farm with her boys and take care of the baby."

"Good. Of course, before you leave today, I'd like to baptize Camilla."

Mr. Muth set down his fork, an expression of concern on his face.

Reverend Norton held up a hand. "Not because I think she won't make it. I'm sure with Mrs. Valleau's tender care, Camilla will be in good hands. But I would suggest baptism for any infant who's in my vicinity when I know her folks live too far to attend church regularly."

"Of course." Mr. Muth's expression relaxed.

The minister indicated his approval with a stately nod. He looked at Antonia's boys, then at her. "I assume you're Catholic."

She nodded.

"I don't know if you've had a chance to avail yourself of a priest to baptize the boys. If not, I'll be glad to do it. Or, you can wait. A traveling priest visits Sweetwater Springs about once a month. Father Fredrick was just here, though. So it will be several weeks before the ceremony can take place."

Antonia had a panicked moment of wishing Jean-Claude was here to help her make the decision. They'd been married by a priest but had never lived near a church. And, if they had, she doubted they would have gone. Neither of them had been religious, although Jean-Claude had said a few times that he was more partial to the Indian beliefs than the Catholic ones.

Be it matterin'? She bit her lip, thinking rapidly. Reverend Norton had been kind. He'd counseled her, which had brought her some comfort. She could tell he was a good man and thought she'd like going to his church and hearing what he had to say. Furthermore, she doubted Jean-Claude would have cared, so she didn't have to worry about going against his wishes.

Antonia nodded. "I be likin' that plenty, Reverend Norton. Thank you."

His smile was warm, although his eyes still held concern. "No need to thank me, my dear Mrs. Valleau. I'm just doing my job. Now, the next question...a delicate, but necessary, question, I'm afraid. Do I perform a marriage ceremony for the two of you at the same time as the baptisms?"

CHAPTER FIVE

At the minister's words, Erik jerked up in his chair, anger flaring through him. He choked on the food in his mouth and had to cough, chew, and swallow before he could talk. Which was probably a good thing because the struggle kept him from cursing at the minister.

Mrs. Valleau came to his rescue. "I done buried my husband not five days past," she said, her voice thick with pain. "Mr. Muth, his wife, she be dyin' this day. We cain't marry. It be not right."

Seeing she was in agreement with him took the edge off Erik's emotions. But his agitation didn't die down.

The minister raised a hand as if to calm them both. "I understand the sentiment, Mrs. Valleau. If I were in your situation… where I'd lost my dear helpmate…." He gave a loving glance to his wife. "I don't know how I would be able to go on. I certainly could not remarry, especially on the day of her death."

Erik settled back in his seat.

"But you two will be living together…isolated…in a small home. Temptation will exist. Perhaps not for a while, but it will come."

Mrs. Norton carefully folded her napkin and set it next to her plate. "And, unfortunately, people will condemn and gossip."

Reverend Norton glanced at the baby, sleeping in Mrs. Cameron's arms, then looked at Henri before his gaze returned to Mrs. Valleau. "Such judgments may affect your reputation and that of your children."

Erik flexed his fingers. *I'll beat the tar out of anyone who dares say a word against my daughter!*

Mrs. Valleau waved her hands in a stopping gesture. "No. I be not marryin' again," she said, her voice shaking in distress. "Too cruel as to be a judgin' us."

Mrs. Cameron and Mrs. Norton exchanged concerned glances.

Reverend Norton sighed. "I certainly hope that is true, my dear Mrs. Valleau. However, if you change your mind...."

Erik set down his fork. "We will not change our minds." He put conviction into his voice.

The minister's suggestion banished the remains of Erik's appetite, and his meal sat uneasy in his stomach. He noticed Mrs. Valleau had stopped eating, too.

Her baby pounded his fist on the table. "Baa!"

Mrs. Valleau rose and picked him up. "Come, *mon enfant.* We be needin' to make you cleanlike."

"Use the towel by the sink," Mrs. Cameron said. She eased her way to her feet, the bulk of her pregnancy making her ungainly. Careful not to jar the baby, she handed Camilla to Erik and began clearing the dishes from the table.

Camilla stared up at him as if fascinated by his features.

As Erik looked at her little flowerlike face, he thanked God for her survival, yet worry persisted, and he wondered when he'd relax and trust that she was healthy. When she was eighteen? Fifty? He couldn't imagine this little mite a woman grown.

The doctor excused himself and left the room, only to return a few minutes later with a cradle, which he set next to Erik's chair.

The doctor's wife rested her hand on the mound of her stomach. "This is an extra one we have. We need it sometimes if a babe is ill," she said quietly.

Ah. He cast an anxious glance over his daughter's face. Her skin had lost the waxen tinge she'd had earlier, but that barely reassured him.

Mrs. Cameron turned back the blanket in the cradle. "You just set her in there, and I'll watch over her for you."

Mrs. Valleau's baby fussed a bit. She jiggled him on her hip. "Let me be a nursin' him. He might be fallin' asleep again. He be up most of the night."

Erik realized he'd have to transport the woman and her children to the farm. "Do you have possessions somewhere?"

"On the mules. I done left 'em tied up by the church. Didn't even water 'em, poor things. But we did be stoppin' at a stream just before town."

Erik nodded. "We'll take care of them before we set out for my farm."

"I be havin' furs that my husband done trapped and cured. I'd like to be tradin' 'em at the store. I be needin' things, and I don't want to go to your house empty handed."

Erik was going to retort that he didn't need anything, but the level of her chin made him stay silent. She had her pride, and far be it from him to step on it.

While he was in town, Erik knew he needed to pick up some things, too. Nails. A new hammer. He had compiled a list over the last weeks for the next trip to town, which of course he'd left at the house. At this moment, he had a hard time gathering his thoughts about what was written on the paper. Maybe if he looked around the store he'd remember.

Mrs. Norton touched his elbow. "When you're ready to go home, Reverend Norton and I will go with you. I'll help Mrs. Valleau prepare your wife's body. I imagine you'll want to bury her on your land, rather than the cemetery in town. Reverend Norton will be able to perform the service for you." The images caused by her words made him nauseated. "I need to go buy a coffin." Even as he made the statement, his mind screamed *nooooo*. The word echoed around his brain.

✱ ✱ ✱

After nursing her son and leaving the boys with Mrs. Cameron, Antonia led the mule, laden with pelts, toward the mercantile, while Erik drove his wagon to the cabinetmaker. As she walked, she replayed Jean Claude's stories of how he'd bargained with the shopkeepers. She might not know her letters, but her husband had taught her numbers and how to figure prices and money. She was determined to do as well as he had.

The spring sunshine shone warm on her face, and Antonia was able to muster up some gratitude that they didn't have to deal with rain, or even snow. *I don't need miserable weather to match my miserable circumstances.*

Keeping her gaze on the redbrick building across the street and close to the train station, Antonia tried to take determined steps to counteract her growing nervousness, which made the little amount of food she'd eaten weigh in her stomach as heavy as iron.

Based on Jean-Claude's past fur sales, Antonia had calculated the amount she thought this batch would bring and had figured out what goods they needed to start a new life. Now she could cross off many of the items on her mental list. At least by going to live on a farm, she wouldn't have to stock up as if they were starting from scratch.

Although she wanted to study the building—bigger than any she'd ever seen—that was under construction between the store and the train station, Antonia kept her gaze straight ahead. She didn't want to see any leers from the workers. Maybe later, when she was properly dressed, she could look.

Antonia tied up the mule in front of the redbrick building with black letters printed across the big window in the front. She reached up to take the top layers off the mule—the mink, beaver, ermine, otter, and a beautiful silver fox. She left the heavier elk, deer, and bear furs, including the uncured one from the monster who'd killed Jean-Claude, on the mule to unload on her second trip.

Usually, her husband would travel to Sweetwater Springs in the spring or early summer to trade the furs taken from the previous autumn and winter. But last spring he hadn't wanted to leave her alone with a tiny baby. Now that Jacques was older, Jean Claude had planned for them to take a trip to town in a few weeks. How painfully ironic that she was now the one doing the trading.

Her arms full, Antonia had to fumble with the door handle. By the time she entered the store, she was flushed and hot. The sight of so much merchandise—the colors, the smells—overwhelmed her senses. She paused to get her bearings, glancing over at a crock of what smelled like pickles. *When did I last eat a pickle?*

A tall man straightened from behind the counter. A narrow fringe of hair circled his bald head, and he had a squashed red nose. The shopkeeper eyed her clothing, and a sour expression crossed his face.

Perhaps he's eaten too many of his own pickles, Antonia thought, disliking the shopkeeper on sight. Once again she wanted to flee but felt trapped because there was nowhere to go. Her family needed this trade.

Antonia walked forward, as stately as she could, given the bundle in her arms. She set the pile on the counter and spread them out, so they lay in a neat display. "I be Mrs. Valleau. I be tradin' these. I be havin' more on the mule outside."

The man eyed her Indian tunic, and then ran a hand over the silver fox. His sour expression didn't change. "Well, get the rest then, woman."

Antonia bristled but held back a retort. She couldn't risk losing this sale. She turned and stalked out, leaving the door open so she didn't have to struggle with it again. Behind her, the man yelled about letting in the flies, but she pretended she hadn't heard him.

Antonia hefted the rest of the furs down, all but the uncured pelt of the grizzly that had killed Jean-Claude. She left that rolled on the mule, and then staggered back inside, dropping the bundle on the counter.

Mr. Cobb pointedly ignored her, instead striding around the counter, down the aisle and to the door, where he shut it with a snap before stalking back. He barely glanced at the pile on the counter. "I'll give you five dollars for the whole shebang, and that's it."

What?

Behind her, Antonia heard the door open, but she didn't turn, focusing her attention on the shopkeeper. *"Non!"* Fear and anger made the word come out as sharp as a knife. "These here be worth far more than five dollars."

"Not to me they aren't. Take the money and get out."

Antonia's thoughts raced. She couldn't accept that low offer. Yet, she also couldn't walk out of here without clothing for her and the boys, and with no money. Helplessness combined with anger, and tears welled up in her eyes. *Oh no, you don't be doin' that,* she scolded herself. *You be not weepin' for Jean-Claude, and you cain't let this miscreant be a makin' you cry.* With all her strength, she held on to her emotions.

The sound of firm footsteps came closer, but Antonia ignored them, wanting to get control over herself before she exposed any weakness to strangers.

Mr. Cobb's expression changed from contemptuous to obsequious. "Mr. Carter, welcome."

He sounds like he'd like to be wipin' this Mr. Carter's boots.

"Good day, Mr. Cobb," said a pleasant male voice.

Antonia turned to see a man in a blue suit and hat, far fancier than any she'd seen in years.

"No Mrs. Carter today?" Mr. Cobb asked.

"She stopped by the Mueller's place to pick up some of those big pretzels for the children." The man walked up the aisle. He smiled at Antonia and touched a finger to his hat.

She nodded, too upset to return his smile.

The man had a narrow face, thinning sandy hair, and kind blue eyes. His gaze lingered on her face. "I don't believe we've met. I'm John Carter, and I have a ranch out that-away." He waved his arm opposite from the direction she'd traveled to reach the town.

"I be Mrs. Valleau."

"Valleau sounds French." The comment sounded curious, not condemning.

"Yes, sir. My husband be...*was*—" Her voice wobbled, and Antonia took a breath to strengthen it. "French-Canadian." She touched the edge of a fur. "A trapper."

"I'm pleased to make your acquaintance, Mrs. Valleau. My wife, Pamela, will be along shortly, and I'm sure she'll be happy to meet you."

Although she detected nothing in Mr. Carter's expression to indicate his awareness of her strange dress, Antonia was sure Mrs. Carter wouldn't be so tolerant.

"What have we here?" Mr. Carter leaned over to examine the furs spread on the counter. "Your husband was a fine hunter, and he did an excellent job of tanning these."

A lump rose in Antonia's throat.

Mr. Carter ran a hand over the grizzly fur. "This one has more silver than the one I have at home." He rifled through the stack until he came to the pelt of a silver fox. "Ah. Mrs. Carter would like this to trim the white rabbit cape she has." He fingered the ermine. "This would make a beautiful muff. I believe these will make Mrs. Carter the perfect birthday gift." He looked from Antonia to Mr. Cobb and back. "Have you two finished negotiations?"

"We've barely begun," Antonia said in a bitter tone. "Five dollars ain't enough fer the whole lot."

The man narrowed his eyes at Mr. Cobb. "Surely that amount was a mistake?" The pointed stare he gave the shopkeeper made it clear his question was a statement. "The fox fur and ermine alone are worth more than that. Each."

Mr. Cobb shifted, and his glance darted away from Mr. Carter. "I'm full up. No call for furs."

"We're in Montana, man. There will be a call soon enough. Why else have that storeroom tacked onto the back of your shop if not to have a place for extra goods?" He let his words hang in the air.

When Cobb didn't answer, Mr. Carter turned to Antonia with a smile. "Course, I could always take the whole bundle. I'll make you a generous offer."

Mr. Cobb settled his hand on the top of the pile. "No! No cause to do that!"

Mr. Carter winked at Antonia before turning back to the shopkeeper. "Pay her fair, Cobb," he warned. "Then I'll buy the silver fox and the ermine from you. Otherwise, I'll finagle the whole lot right out from under you. And that deal will be exactly what you deserve." He didn't say, *for trying to cheat the woman*, but his silence spoke the words.

"All right," Cobb muttered in a grudging tone.

"I'll just wait right here for you to finish your transaction."

"No need to keep you waiting, Mr. Carter. Let me get you what you need."

"The lady was before me," the gentleman said firmly. "See to her needs first."

"Thank you kindly." Antonia conveyed through her expression how grateful she was for his intercession.

Cobb named a price that sounded similar to what she knew Jean-Claude had received in the past. She glanced at Mr. Carter, and he gave her a nod that approved the amount. Too distressed to bargain further, she nodded in agreement.

Mr. Carter smiled in obvious approval. "Keep the fox and ermine for me until I come to town without my wife," he told the shopkeeper. "Have to keep this a surprise."

Mr. Cobb jerked a nod. He scooped up the armful of furs. "Let me put these in the storeroom."

Seeing him hurry across the shop, Antonia realized she was watching the last of Jean-Claude's work disappear, and she almost cried out to stop the merchant. *Don't be ridiculous,* she scolded. *Jean-Claude would have sold them, too. And you still have the bear fur, and the sleeping furs, and…the boys.* She inhaled a steadying breath.

Through my sons, I'll always have Jean-Claude with me. I can get through this…for them.

CHAPTER SIX

As Erik drove the wagon down Second Street toward the cabinetmaker's shop, he cast an eye upward at the sky, judging the position of the sun. He couldn't believe after everything that had happened the time was only midday. *I never thought I'd be buying a coffin for my wife.* He remembered how Daisy had looked, lying on the bed in death, and could not even feel grief; his guilt was so strong it bound him like chains. *I just left her there....*

When Erik neared the shop, he realized he didn't have money with him and almost reined in the horses. *I need that coffin today!* Just the thought of his wife's body lying in the house another day...he couldn't allow that.

I'll have to give O'Reilly my pledge to pay.

Shame stuck in his craw at having to use credit again. Made him feel beholden—although he knew that wasn't the case. He had money squirreled away. Of course, most of their savings had been aimed to pay back the banker for the loan of money Erik had used to build the barn and purchase the three new milk cows.

Maybe Daisy was right. I was reckless, buying on credit. They'd fought about the decision, and, determined, he'd gone his own way. Afterward, she didn't speak to him for three days. Remembering made the heavy chains around his heart clank.

Erik flicked the reins, and the horses ambled on. He drew up before a wooden building with a false front. "Phineas O' Reilly, Coffin Maker, Carpenter, and Cabinetmaker" was painted in crooked letters above the dusty window.

In the past when Erik had seen the sign, he'd wondered why the man had chosen to put Coffin Maker first. Now he knew the answer. *Probably O'Reilly's most lucrative business,* he thought bitterly. Erik parked the wagon, climbed down, and went inside.

Phineas O'Reilly stood behind a wooden counter talking to Banker Livingston. Phineas was a burly man with a scruffy beard, and rusty red hair pulled back in a bushy tail. He wore a carpenter's smock over a dirty shirt and pants, quite the contrast from the handsome immaculate banker standing in front of him, wearing a fancy suit.

The carpenter gave Erik a quick nod but didn't break his attention from the banker.

Erik moved over to the front corner to inspect a side table with curved legs. He ran his hand over the smooth finish of the surface. *Daisy would love this.* Once again, pain stabbed him. *She's gone,* he told himself. *You need to accept the fact.* He moved over to examine a painted cabinet, flowers decorating the top and sides. *The man does good work.*

"I need wine racks," Livingston said. "I'm expecting a shipment from France, and the racks I have won't be big enough to hold them all." The banker waved his arms and described what he wanted.

Erik felt a flash of envy, wishing he, too, was ordering fancy wine racks, rather than a cheap coffin to bury his wife in. He'd never been inside the Livingston mansion, but judging from the outside, the house was a far cry from his humble abode. He made himself turn away from the comparisons by thinking about the room he needed to add on for the Valleau family.

Something else to eat away at my savings. For a moment, a crushing sense of burden weighed down on him. He stared out the window, not seeing the sunlit day but only empty darkness.

The two men finished up their business, and Erik listened to the conversation again.

"Mighty perty squaw came through town this morning," O'Reilly said with a wide smile, which showed missing teeth.

The carpenter offered the tidbits of gossip to the banker like he was handling him gold on a platter. Erik didn't know why O'Reilly didn't mind his own business. The man was worse than a woman with his loose tongue. At least Livingston didn't have that avid expression on his patrician face that overcame gossipers at the very hint of something new to ferret out about their neighbors' bad luck.

Daisy's death would provide the carpenter with fresh news. But short of stuffing a permanent sock in O'Reilly's mouth, there wasn't any way to prevent talk. By sundown, everyone in town would know of his wife's passing.

"I was just leaving the Cobbs' and saw the squaw," O'Reilly continued. "Two mules, one carrying good-looking pelts. Two little ones. No man in sight. Shore was a tempting piece. Stopped by the church, she did."

Livingston looked like he'd sucked sour milk. "Surely, you don't find an Indian woman attractive?"

Erik clenched his fists, wanting to punch the banker. *Not a good thing to do to the man who holds my note.*

O'Reilly laughed and slapped his leg. Sawdust flew into the air. "Shore do. Any woman's attractive when you don't have one of your own."

Erik couldn't stop the wave of anger that propelled him forward. "I've met the *lady.*"

The men turned to him, surprise on both their faces.

He strove to relax his hands, keep his tone even. "Mrs. Cameron introduced Mrs. Valleau to me a few hours ago. Seems like a fine lady. Well mannered. Soft spoken. *White.*" He clipped the last word.

Livingston's lord-of-the-manor gaze swept over Erik like he was a peasant.

For the first time today, Erik was aware of his uncouth appearance—the blood- and sweat-stained shirt and work pants, the heavy boots. *Livingston must think I have no idea about real ladies and good manners.* But he stood tall, a couple of inches taller even, than the elegant banker. Looking him eye-to-eye, Erik refused to let the man shame him.

Seemingly unaware of the undercurrents, O'Reilly made a disappointed sound. "Guess she's got a husband around someplace."

Erik almost revealed more information about Mrs. Valleau. But a protective instinct clapped a figurative hand over his mouth. Learning the woman was a widow, no matter how recent, could make her fair game for the unwed O'Reilly, which could cost Erik his wet nurse.

The banker excused himself without, thank goodness, reminding Erik that the payment on the loan was due next month.

As soon as the man left, Erik paused, reluctant to mention his wife's passing. Buying Daisy's coffin would make her death a fact. But an uncomfortable silence lingered between him and O'Reilly, forcing Erik to launch into an explanation of why he was here. "My wife died in childbirth today."

O'Reilly put on a professional solemn face. "Sorry I am to be hearing your bad news, Muth. You'll be needin' a coffin then? Did the child live?"

"Yes, and yes. A daughter."

O'Reilly tugged on his beard. "I'm glad the baby survived."

"She's not out of danger yet. Came early." In spite of his reluctance to talk, his anxiousness about his daughter tumbled out.

"Sorry to hear that." The carpenter crossed himself. "Say a prayer for her, I will."

Erik found himself softening toward the man. "Obliged."

O'Reilly cleared his throat and got back to business. "I don't recall your wife all that well. Height, width?"

Erik's hands spanned the air to indicate Daisy's slight stature. *She's tiny enough to lay her head right on my heart.* Just the thought that he'd never hold her again made his chest ache and his arms feel empty.

A gleam lit O'Reilly's blue eyes. "I have one like that. Mahogany, polished inside and out. Silk for her to lie on. A right fittin' resting place."

Guilt almost made Erik say yes. Daisy deserved a beautiful casket to cradle her as she lay in the dark grave. But he knew that if he gave in, the cost would wipe out the money they had saved toward paying back the loan. She liked beautiful things, his Daisy did. But she also had a practical streak. If he spent the money they'd saved on her casket, she'd probably come back from heaven and haunt him. *Well,* he amended, knowing Daisy wasn't the haunting type...*she'd give me a piece of her mind.*

Strange to think he'd welcome one of his wife's dreaded scolds. *If she came back to me, and I made her angry, I'd just grab her up in my arms and squeeze the ire out of her. She'd screech away, and I'd hug her all the more.*

With his thumb, O'Reilly gestured behind him. "Come on back and take a look at what I have. Once we're done, I think I'll mosey off to Main Street. See if I can get an eyeful of that woman again. Maybe there's no husband after all. You said she was at Doc's?"

"Lady," Erik corrected through gritted teeth, resisting the urge to pick up the man by the front of his shirt and slam him against the wall. "Mrs. Valleau is a lady."

A feeling of urgency made him hasten to conclude the wretched business. The new widow had suckled his newborn daughter. Saved Camilla's life. *She deserves my protection.*

❊ ❊ ❊

Antonia saw Erik Muth come through the door of the shop and relaxed her shoulders in relief. Although the man had been a complete stranger only a few hours ago, now his familiar presence reassured her.

He glanced at her and Mr. Carter, his eyebrows pulling together in a frown. "Have you finished your transaction, Mrs. Valleau?"

"Almost. Mr. Carter lent a kind hand to help me."

His eyebrows relaxed.

Mr. Carter gave them a curious glance, obviously wondering how they knew each other. Antonia didn't want to offer an explanation in front of Mr. Cobb.

Erik walked over to a barrel of nails, reached in and picked one up, rolling it between his thumb and forefinger.

Mr. Cobb came into the room, followed by a stout woman in a blue dress.

The woman gave Antonia a sharp glance from her close-set brown eyes. She pursed her lips. "I'm Mrs. Cobb. Mr. Cobb has filled me in on the situation."

Surely it will be easier dealing with a woman. "I'll need a new dress."

"You certainly do." The woman frowned, her face settling into a disapproving expression. "Can't have you traipsing around looking like a heathen. And from the sight of you, you'll need everything from the inside out."

Antonia's hackles rose. She held onto her temper by imagining Mrs. Cobb captured by the Indian braves and forced to live in their camp. The thought of the disagreeable woman wearing the garb of a squaw almost made her grin. She might just hunt down some of Jean-Claude's Blackfoot friends and see if they'd oblige.

"You're in luck." Mrs. Cobb eyed Antonia up and down. "I think we have something that would fit you. On sale even, because the color doesn't suit most women. Nor does the size. I was out visiting when Mr. Cobb made the order." She shook her head in disapproval. "Can't trust a man to do anything right when it comes to women's fashions."

Mr. Cobb made a garbled sound of protest.

His wife ignored him, bustling around the store, gathering articles of apparel, picking up some, muttering and putting them down before finding another. She held up a pair of knickers trimmed with crocheted lace.

The knickers were far finer than any Antonia had worn before as a young woman. Later, she'd followed the Indian custom of going without. Her cheeks heated, and she had to resist running over and snatching the drawers away from the shopkeeper and hiding them behind her back.

An uncomfortable look crossed Mr. Muth's face. He dropped the nail back into the barrel and pointed to the other side of the store. "I'll go look at the tools." He hurried over to the wall where several hammers hung and lifted one off.

Mrs. Cobb waved to an inner door. "Follow me, Mrs. Valleau. I allow ladies to change in our private quarters." The shopkeeper, her arms full, disappeared through a door.

Antonia cast a helpless look at Mr. Muth, who'd been watching her, instead of looking at the hammer he held.

Manlike, he made a face and shrugged, before turning to set the tool on a rack.

Antonia followed Mrs. Cobb into a short hallway and through another door. She stepped into the room and stopped short in surprise at the elaborately decorated parlor.

Even the few times she'd been in the quarters of the officers' wives, she hadn't seen so many pieces of fancy furniture. Each seemed to be buried under other objects. Chairs and a settee overflowed with cushions, and every surface—whether tables, bookcases, or shelves on the walls—brandished vases, figurines, boxes, and other decorative objects. The scent of dried rose petals in a glass bowl wafted to her. The constricted space made her feel big and clumsy.

"Come along, Mrs. Valleau," Mrs. Cobb said in a sharp tone of voice. "I need to get back to the store. It's a busy day for us, and I don't want Mr. Cobb to handle everything alone. That man can upset my careful record-keeping in a matter of minutes."

Antonia edged around a table that held several framed photographs and a carved box.

Mrs. Cobb led her to a bedroom housing an elaborately carved four-poster bed and pointed to a flower-painted screen in the corner. "Go behind there. Put on the drawers and chemise, then I'll help you with a corset." She glanced at Antonia's waist with a pinched expression of disapproval.

Antonia found herself hustled behind the screen, and her fingers shook as she unfastened the Indian garb and slipped out of it. *Good thing Mrs. Cobb doesn't know I'm not wearing anything underneath my tunic.* Pulling on the drawers and chemise, she realized how fine and light the material felt against her skin compared to the leather she'd worn for so long.

"Are you finished, Mrs. Valleau?"

"Yes."

Mrs. Cobb pulled aside the screen. "Raise your arms." She whisked the corset around Antonia's waist.

The garment was one she'd never worn before, and her initial curiosity lasted until Mrs. Cobb pulled the strings so tight Antonia couldn't breathe. Then the woman gave a yank that made Antonia's eyes bulge out.

"There." Mrs. Cobb's voice oozed satisfaction. "You do have a nice waist, after all, and no need of padding for your hips."

Antonia had no breath to protest as the woman hurried her into a petticoat, followed by a shirtwaist and skirt made of golden calico with little rose buds. She wished she could examine the material, far prettier than anything she'd ever worn.

Mrs. Cobb pinched the cloth at Antonia's waist and pursed her lips. "Too loose. This will have to be taken in."

Antonia drew breath to argue, only to find her ribs constricted by the corset, so just a tiny gulp of air made it into her lungs. "I'm dizzy. I need to sit down." She took a few steps and tried to collapse on a wooden chair in the corner, but with her body imprisoned, she found that all she could do was lower herself to the edge of the seat.

Mrs. Cobb didn't seem to notice Antonia's distress. The woman walked back and forth, her gaze narrowed on the dress's shape.

"We don't have a tailor or dressmaker in town. More's the pity. All the women do their own sewing and mending. So you'll have to take in the dress yourself."

I'm not about to take in this dress. Antonia rose, careful to not fall over. If she collapsed wearing the contraption, she'd never be able to get off the floor. Without a word, she glided toward the screen.

"Mrs. Valleau. What are you doing?" Mrs. Cobb tried to wave her back. "I didn't bring another dress for you to try on. I have a green one, though, that might suit you. Wait right here, and I'll bring it in."

Antonia stepped behind the screen and pulled it closed. Moving as best she could with her waist locked up, she shed the dress, and then fumbled at the strings of the corset. Once they'd loosened, she took a deep inhale, grateful to breathe, and worked off the offending garment, letting it drop to the rug.

Then she put the dress back on. This time, the waist was still loose, but not so much. She'd lost weight in the last few days. Hopefully, when her stomach wasn't so knotted, and she could eat again, she'd regain her figure. The dress would fit just perfect then. She smoothed down the creases and stepped out from behind the screen.

An oval mirror stood in the corner of the room, and Antonia moved toward it. She'd seen her face in a smaller one before when she lived at the fort with her father. Since then, pools of clear water had sufficed, providing a blurry reflection. So the woman staring back was almost a stranger.

The gold in the dress made her eyes stand out and burnished her complexion. The sight moved Antonia in some strange way she had experienced only once as a child, when an officer's wife had given her a hand-me-down dress. Usually, she'd run around in cut-down boy's clothing.

As a girl, Antonia had dreamed of wearing a gown like this. Regardless of the compliments her husband had lavished on her, she'd never considered herself pretty, for her features were too strong.

With a surge of feminine pleasure, Antonia thought of the stunned look on Jean-Claude's face when he caught sight of her in the dress. As soon as the boys slept, he'd release her from the gown, and they'd make energetic love. Another reason not to wear that corset.

Realization hit her as hard as a blow to the stomach, and she almost collapsed. Jean-Claude would never see her in the gold dress. Her lip quivered, and she bit down to avoid screaming. Her future stretched out, devoid of husbandly warmth and caresses.

How can I possibly bear it?

Only the thought that the shopkeeper would return in a moment kept Antonia upright. But she turned away from the mirror, unable to bear the sight of herself.

❀ ❀ ❀

Erik had only the slightest acquaintance with John Carter, the foremost rancher in the area, and his wife. They'd exchanged greetings at the ice cream social—had that really been only a few days ago? But the man had a stellar reputation for fairness and integrity, and his wife was known to be equally as kind.

Carter strolled through the store, looking calm and confident. The man was well groomed in a dark-blue suit. Instead of using one of the baskets stacked near the door, he picked out items and carried them: a trowel, a jar of peaches, a can of mineral spirits.

Erik glanced down at his bloodstained shirt. *Ruined, suitable only for the barn.* Best buy a new one, although he begrudged spending more money. But with all that was going on, it wasn't fitting to wear the shirt in town. He wandered over to shelving that went from floor to ceiling, filled with clothing. He fingered a tan one, then picked up the shirt and held it against him. Looked too small. He tried for another in the same color. Also too small.

Engrossed in searching for a shirt, Erik didn't pay any attention to someone entering the store, nor the secretive female voices gossiping at the counter. But when he saw John Carter stiffen and turn, Erik caught a mention of Mrs. Valleau's name. The critical tone of the voices left no doubt what they were implying.

Rage, deep and dark, exploded. He'd born too much this day to have the woman who'd saved his daughter treated thus. Erik tossed the shirt to the floor, turned on his heel, and stormed over to the front.

Mrs. Cobb leaned over the counter, her head near another woman's—the Widow Murphy.

Erik had stayed at the widow's boarding house for a few days when he first came out here. *Nasty old witch.*

Before he could say the cutting words that wanted to boil out of his mouth, Antonia entered the shop from the other room. She stood in the doorway, clad in a yellow dress that made her golden eyes striking, transforming the plain widow he'd seen earlier into a stately and attractive woman. Yet the vulnerable look on her face made him aware of how difficult this all must be for her, used as she was to living in the wilderness.

He took a decisive step forward. "Mrs. Valleau."

"Mrs. Valleau!" Mrs. Cobb cut in, a scandalized expression on her face. "You're not wearing a corset." She cleared her throat. "Ladies *must* wear them."

Mrs. Murphy wagged her head, making the wattle of skin under her throat shake. "Saw her ride in, I did. Dressed like a squaw. Wouldn't expect her to know how to dress decent."

Antonia paled and half turned, headed toward the other room.

Erik took a few steps to stop her from fleeing. "Do not speak to my wife-to-be in that manner," he ordered.

Antonia gasped and whirled around.

Play along, Erik told her with his eyes.

"What are you saying, Mr. Muth?" Mrs. Cobb said sharply. "You have a wife. Bigamy is illegal in this state, you know."

"I'm well aware of that fact, Mrs. Cobb." Erik did his best to sound pompous and authoritative. "Actually, I am premature in my announcement by a few minutes. My wife, Daisy, has died in childbirth, although my daughter lives. Our baby would have joined her mother if Mrs. Valleau hadn't stepped in to nurse her."

Mrs. Cobb stepped back in apparent shock. "I'm sorry to hear of your wife's passing," she said as if by rote. "Yet, she is released from this vale of tears."

Anger flushed his body. *No, I will not strangle the woman.* Erik took a deep breath, striving to keep his tone even. "Mrs. Valleau's husband passed away recently, leaving her with two little boys. She and I have agreed our mutual need will supersede our grief for our spouses and the conventions of mourning. After we conclude our business here, Reverend Norton will join us in Holy Matrimony." He hoped Mrs. Valleau would turn his lie into the truth.

He glanced at Mrs. Valleau, who stared at him with wide eyes. Was there a hint of humor in their depths? The thought she might find this discussion with Mrs. Cobb as absurd as he did lifted his spirits just a bit. He liked that he might have alleviated her pain for a few short minutes. A shared sense of humor eased many of the stresses of life, and the two of them would certainly need that advantage if they chose to marry in grief instead of love.

Mr. Carter stood on the outskirts of the circle of people. From the rigid stance of his body, Erik could see the rancher was disturbed and would step in if need be. Yet he had a sense the man was allowing Erik to handle the situation.

"Well," Mrs. Cobb huffed. "If Mrs. Valleau is recently widowed, she can't go around wearing gold. She needs black."

Widow Murphy sniffed. "And you getting married on the same day your wife has died? Scandalous."

"Do you have a black dress that will fit Mrs. Valleau?" Erik asked the shopkeeper, trying to keep his tone even.

Mrs. Cobb glanced over toward the dress section. "No."

"Then gold will have to do, which is fine with me. Black would be too painful for us both."

Even Mrs. Cobb had enough sensitivity to keep her mouth shut.

The door opened, and Pamela Carter whirled in. She saw her husband first, and a happy smile lit up her plain, plump face. She held up a parcel wrapped in string. "Success! Mrs. Mueller had just taken out a batch. I had to wait for the pretzels to cool a bit." Seeming to become aware of the tension in the air, she lowered her arm, her expression becoming wary.

John Carter took a long step toward his wife and held out his hand. "You're just in time, my dear. There's someone I want you to meet."

Mrs. Carter put her gloved hand in her husband's, and he drew her forward.

Erik realized the Carters were heading toward Mrs. Valleau, and he stepped out of their path, hoping Mrs. Carter wouldn't be offended by Antonia's lack of a corset like Mrs. Cobb and Mrs. Murphy were.

As the couple passed, Mrs. Carter gave Erik a friendly smile and a nod of acknowledgment.

John Carter bowed slightly to Mrs. Valleau. "How fine you look in that dress. The color suits you."

Mrs. Carter cast her husband a curious glance, but her friendly smile stayed in place, and she didn't seem put out by his admiration of another woman.

I should have been the one to compliment Mrs. Valleau. Seems Erik could do nothing right this day.

Mr. Carter gestured to Mrs. Valleau, introduced the two women, and quickly explained the circumstances.

Mrs. Carter's expression softened. "Oh, you poor dear. I can't even imagine what you must be going through." She leaned forward to embrace the new widow.

As Mrs. Carter hugged her, Mrs. Valleau stood wide-eyed and stiff, as if not knowing how to respond.

Mrs. Carter didn't seem to mind. She glanced at Erik then placed a sympathetic hand on his arm. "What you *both* must be going through. How can we help?"

Erik snuck a glance at Mrs. Cobb and Mrs. Murphy. Both had identical grimaces on their faces, as though they'd just drunk sour milk.

John Carter gazed at his wife with approval. He leaned forward to say something and hesitated, his ears reddening. "Please reassure Mrs. Valleau that she can refrain from wearing a corset and still be a lady."

Not by expression or posture did Mrs. Carter betray any astonishment at the improper conversation. She scrutinized the yellow dress. "You're so slender, Mrs. Valleau, that you don't even need a corset." She touched her waist. "Not like us, eh, Mrs. Cobb, Mrs. Murphy?"

Mrs. Cobb's face reddened, and Mrs. Murphy ruffled up like a chicken. But neither said anything, apparently not wanting to offend the foremost lady of Sweetwater Springs.

Mrs. Carter raised her chin. "The essence of a lady comes from within," she said in a gentle but firm tone. "A lady can wear rags, but as long as she holds her head up and carries herself proudly, people will see her, not her clothing."

Mrs. Murphy made an outraged choking sound.

Mrs. Carter sent a pointed look toward the two gossips. "A lady always seeks to educate herself and is kind to others."

Color came back into Antonia's cheeks, and she straightened her shoulders.

Erik wanted to cheer. Relief relaxed his anger. He didn't dare turn to look at the two biddies, who, by Mrs. Carter's descriptions, definitely were not ladies.

Mr. Carter swung around and pinned Erik with his gaze. "Duly noted there's to be a wedding soon, Muth. May Mrs. Carter and I invite ourselves to attend?"

Why the man's offer would make tears spring to his eyes, Erik didn't know—perhaps because such a busy, important rancher extended kindness to a prairie farmer—basically a stranger. Manfully, though, he choked them back. "I—" he glanced at Mrs. Valleau "—we'd be obliged."

Mrs. Valleau tried to smile, but the sadness on her face wasn't chased away by the turning up of her lips.

John Carter shot Erik's shirt a pointed look. With a wave of his hand, he urged Erik toward the shelves. "I imagine you'll want to get back to shopping. Mrs. Carter will help Mrs. Valleau with whatever else women need at times like this. Then—" he lowered his voice "—you can get cleaned up and warn Reverend Norton he'll be performing a ceremony, since I have the impression he doesn't know."

Erik shot Mr. Carter an ironic glance. "The reverend had the idea in the first place. Neither Mrs. Valleau nor I could stomach it, though."

Mr. Carter glanced toward his wife. "I can understand not wanting to jump into another marriage after the loss of one so beloved. In fact, Muth, I can't imagine ever marrying again."

"Then you know our sentiments exactly. But Reverend Norton was right. We must."

"But, when I think of my children as babies, vulnerable—my youngest daughter isn't strong and still gives us anxious times—I'd do anything to save them. *Anything.*"

Somehow, having the prominent man echo Erik's dilemma made him feel more resigned to his choice.

Mr. Carter fell silent for a moment, staring at the wall of folded clothing. "I have a feeling...in time this hasty marriage won't be bad at all. Mrs. Valleau seems a good woman. I think you'll be able to make a comfortable life together."

Erik's doubts must have shown on his face.

"I'm not saying you won't have a sorrowful time to get through first."

First? Erik didn't think he'd ever get through this wretched, sorrowful time.

CHAPTER SEVEN

Erik hesitated outside the church door, wondering if he could, indeed, go forward with the wedding ceremony. *I must.* Stiffening his spine, he pushed open the door and walked into the small vestibule, where he took off his coat and hung the garment on a peg next to some others.

His brief consultation with Reverend Norton had resulted in a flurry of wedding preparations on the part of Mrs. Cameron and Mrs. Norton, and he'd had a chance to wash up and change.

He straightened the new navy-blue shirt he wore, and then ran his hands over his hair, which he'd slicked back with water, using a borrowed comb. In his haste to get Camilla to town, he hadn't thought to don his hat. With no other reasons to delay, Erik gathered his courage and moved into the church.

The Nortons and Camerons waited near the front.

Reverend Norton stood near his wife, who sat on the piano bench. The Camerons were in the first pew with Henri. Dr. Cameron held the Valleau baby in one arm, while keeping a supportive hand on the young boy's shoulder.

Henri looked at Erik with a blank expression in his golden eyes, then he glanced away.

A vase of pink Lenten roses stood on the altar. A well-used Bible and a prayer book lay in front of the flowers.

Mrs. Cameron cradled Camilla in one arm. In her other hand, she held a bouquet of more Lenten roses.

Just the sight of his daughter gave Erik some strength to see this farce of a wedding through. *No, not a farce.* He strove to find a better way of describing the marriage he was about to enter.

It's like a hiring-out for work, Erik tried to tell himself. *No, better still, going into business together. That's it! We'll both bring needed skills to the job of raising a family and working a farm. Mrs. Valleau will be my partner.* Erik suspected he could be a good business partner to her, even if he couldn't be a loving husband.

Putting his forthcoming marriage in that context eased Erik's mind somewhat. Even though he'd only known Mrs. Valleau for less than a day, he hoped she'd have a similar practical approach to their union.

Erik walked over to Mrs. Cameron. She'd changed into a nicer dress—green, which made her eyes brighter. She angled the baby toward him so he could see her.

For the first time, he could admire his daughter without feeling a clutch of fear in his belly. Mrs. Cameron had dressed Camilla in some sort of white garment, and she looked like a little angel. *She's so tiny. So delicate. So precious.*

He bent down and kissed Camilla's forehead. *I'm doing this for you, my love.*

Reverend Norton glanced out the window. "They're coming."

Mrs. Cameron held up the bouquet. "Let me give Mrs. Valleau the flowers." Carefully, so as not to jostle the baby, she glided down the aisle.

In Dr. Cameron's arms, Jacques stirred and opened his eyes.

He gave Erik a sleepy smile.

Reverend Norton walked over to the front of the altar and waved for Erik to join him. "Come stand here."

Feeling his heart pinch, Erik followed Reverend Norton's orders, taking a position in front of the minister. *I'm really going to do this.* His stomach churned, and for a brief moment, he wondered if he would lose his last meal.

The minister gazed at him, compassion softening his austere face. "I will say prayers for your family daily," he murmured so only Erik could hear.

The comforting words settled his stomach a bit. "Thank you, Reverend. We'll surely need them."

From the back of the church came the sound of people entering.

Reverend Norton picked up his prayer book from the altar and angled to face him. The man who'd married Erik and Daisy now prepared to say the words of the marriage service over Erik and another woman. *A stranger.*

Mrs. Norton began to play *Blest Be the Tie That Binds.*

But, when Erik turned and saw his bride walking toward him on the arm of John Carter, and witnessed the sadness in her eyes and the pallor that lay under her tanned skin, compassion rose in him.

Antonia passed through a beam of sunlight that made the golden dress blaze.

For a moment, Erik's heart stuttered.

She moved like a queen, shoulders erect, chin lifted, floating toward him with that grace he admired. Then she stepped beyond the light and became the woman, vulnerable and frightened.

Erik held out his hand and took hers.

Her fingers trembled.

He gave them a reassuring squeeze and drew her to stand beside him before the minister.

❋ ❋ ❋

Clutching a bouquet given to her by Mrs. Cameron, Antonia moved up the aisle in a daze, barely hearing the sound of music. She leaned on John Carter's arm more than she normally would have, given he was a stranger, and she wasn't the leaning type. But her knees trembled, and she felt grateful the gold dress hid her weakness from the small crowd of people waiting at the front of the church. *Somehow, I be gittin' through this.*

Mr. Muth and Reverend Norton stood at the front of the aisle before the altar. Her groom had washed up and donned the new shirt, which made his eyes look sky blue. He was big and handsome, with wide shoulders, although she preferred slender, green-eyed, brown-haired Frenchmen to ruddy, blond Germans.

He didn't watch her approach with the look of a bridegroom, his eyes full of pride and eagerness. Instead, his expression looked sad, his eyes shadowed. She supposed her face looked the same.

Be two people ever more unwilling to wed than we? The few couples whose ceremony she'd witnessed had taken the steps to marriage with joy, and, if not joy, at least practical anticipation. Not with pain and a sense of betraying a beloved spouse.

She couldn't help contrasting her first wedding—how she'd almost flown to Jean-Claude's side, so eager was she to join herself to him that she seemed to have wings on her feet. How he'd laughed, not out loud in front of the priest and their friends, but with his eyes. She'd been so happy that day....

In the front pew, Dr. Cameron held Jacques, who bounced when he saw his mother. Henri stood next to the doctor. Her older son wore a confused expression on his too-thin face.

For his sake, Antonia tried to compose herself enough to send him a reassuring smile, which she wished was real.

Across the aisle, Mrs. Cameron and Mrs. Carter stood together. Mrs. Cameron held the sleeping baby in her arms. Both women smiled at Antonia, as if trying to give her strength and encouragement.

Mr. Carter escorted her to the front of the church.

Mr. Muth gave her a slight turn of his lips and held out his hand to her.

Mr. Carter uncurled her arm from his and stepped back.

With trepidation, Antonia reached out to Mr. Muth. His hand felt large and callused, his fingers thicker than Jean-Claude's. His hand tightened around hers, and she wondered if he needed support as much as she. The thought made her more sympathetic to him.

Reverend Norton gave her an understanding smile.

Tears welled up in her eyes. Through an effort of will, she didn't let them fall.

"Dearly beloved," the minister said, his voice gentle.

Antonia stared blindly at him, letting the words of the service wash over her, repeating the vows she was prompted to say.

In minutes, Reverend Norton joined her in Holy Matrimony to a man she'd known for a few hours…changed her from Antonia Valleau to Antonia Muth. *But nothing be changed inside me.* In her heart, she remained Antonia Valleau. She knew she would *always* be Antonia Valleau.

After the marriage ceremony, the minister baptized the children. Camilla never woke up, looking like a sleeping angel.

Jacques squealed with laughter when the water touched his head, making everyone, even Erik, chuckle.

Henri's solemn expression never changed.

Then, with Mr. Muth holding his baby, and Antonia carrying Jacques on her hip and holding Henri's hand, they walked back down the aisle—a makeshift family.

✳ ✳ ✳

On the hard seat of the jouncing wagon, Antonia bounced beside her new husband, holding Camilla, wrapped in a blanket, who'd fallen asleep again after nursing. Her wedding bouquet, stems wrapped in a damp towel, was wedged between her side and the end of the seat.

They rode in silence, obvious discomfort radiating from both. She supposed the man's thoughts were as dark and heavy as hers.

Early on, the uniqueness of the transportation had worn off, and she shifted on the wooden bench, careful not to wake the sleeping baby in her arms, and wished she'd thought to pad the board with one of the sleeping furs before they'd set out. She pulled her new brown shawl closer around her shoulders.

Antonia checked on her boys, who rode in the back of the wagon, next to the pine coffin. They seemed fine with this new form of travel. Jacques grasped the side of the wagon, bending his knees and straightening them in a bouncing motion, while Henri held him in place. Her baby son would be tired soon and need to sleep. The two mules were tied to the back of the wagon.

Next to Henri was a round woven basket with a flat top—a wedding gift from the Camerons. Inside were enough jars of jam and pickles to last them quite a while, as well as two fresh-baked loaves of bread wrapped in a towel, dropped off by Mrs. Mueller, who'd already heard the gossip. The baker had wished them well with a thick German accent. The Carters had provided a wedding cake bought from the bakery, as well as a glass stand and cover.

Antonia was touched by the generosity of the townsfolk, who only hours before had been strangers. She just wished she had gotten to know them under better circumstances.

Behind the Muths' wagon, the Nortons drove in a shabby surrey, and the Carters trailed the group in a big black vehicle that reminded Antonia of a stagecoach. Both couples intended to help her settle in…and to bury Daisy.

The farther they moved from the mountains, the flatter the land became. She looked up at the beautiful blue sky, loving the broad arc of color. In the mountains, she usually only saw parts of the sky through the dense trees. But now, the vastness of the grassland was inspiring—and perhaps overwhelming. "Look, Mr. Muth," she said, pointing with her chin to the hawk floating overhead.

"What?" He gazed upward but didn't focus on the bird.

"The hawk. See how he be just floating there. I wish I could fly like that."

"Just hope it stays away from Daisy's chick—" he stuttered out the end of the word "—ens." There was a brief silence before Mr. Muth stiffened his shoulders. He gave her a quick glance. "I'm sorry, I shouldn't have said that."

For a moment, she experienced a sharp poignant longing for Jean-Claude, who would have loved to soar with the hawk and usually understood her flights of fancy. But the pain in Mr. Muth's eyes made her try to reach out. "It be like that for me, too. Like he be not gone, really. I keep thinking of things I be tellin' Jean-Claude. Or I start to be sayin' something to the boys about their father and have to…" She made a chopping motion. "I don't mind if you be speakin' of Daisy. How can we not be sharin' 'bout the two people we loved so much?"

He nodded, and his stiff shoulders relaxed. "Maybe you should start by calling me Erik."

"Erik," she repeated. "I be Antonia."

"Pretty name. How did you come by it?"

"My father…he be a poor soldier. He be givin' me a rich, educated-sounding name." Antonia omitted telling him she didn't have the education to match the name.

"Well, he succeeded."

Silence drew out between them, long and uncomfortable.

Erik flicked the reins. "I don't know what to think…what to do. I've never been through this before."

"Me, neither. I be only five days ahead of you, eh? So I be not much help."

He gave her a bitter smile. "I haven't yet buried my wife, and now I have a new wife."

"I done buried my husband six days past, and now I have a new husband," she echoed, trying to match his words. Antonia remained silent for a moment, thinking. "Do you think be easier—" she mused out loud "—to come to a new marriage…a hasty one with a stranger…and *both* be filled with pain over the loss of a beloved mate…than when just one person be sufferin'?"

Erik heaved a heavy sigh. "Is it better or worse that way? I don't know." He looked at her with sad blue eyes. "Is it better or worse that we've both lost spouses we love, rather than beginning with someone who is available to love us, and we have a free heart to give them?"

"Or to be startin' out fresh? Strangers still, but with no connection…but also no pain?"

He shrugged. "Don't think either is easy. But maybe we'll both be more…tolerant of each other because we know the other's hurting, and we understand."

Tolerance. She supposed it was a good word when applied to people in general. *But to a marriage?*

Antonia's throat clogged. *Yes, I 'spose tolerance be important there, too.* Yet, she couldn't bear the thought of spending the rest of her life being tolerated instead of loved.

CHAPTER EIGHT

The faint wagon track through the grass led between two hills. Erik lifted his chin. "On the other side, you'll see my...uh, *our* farm."

Antonia straightened, relieved to be near the end of the journey. She was hot and sticky, and she needed to use the privy, wash her face and hands, and stretch her legs. She shifted on the hard seat.

Camilla, who'd woken a few minutes earlier, protested the movement.

Antonia rocked the baby until she calmed, and then stared ahead, anxious to see the first sight of her new home.

The barn came into view first—a big building gleaming with whitewash.

Astonished, Antonia turned to Erik. "Your barn be bigger than the church!" She looked from the building back to him. "You must be havin' a lot of livestock."

"Eight cows and nine calves. Delivered twins—" he paused to think "—yesterday. Right before Daisy went into labor."

Judging it best not to pursue the subject, Antonia let it drop, instead staring avidly around her. Several small buildings were near the barn. A chicken coop, she guessed from Erik's earlier mention, although she couldn't say what the rest were.

The house came into view, a long, low building about three times the size of her cabin, with a broad porch and windows with real *glass*. She and Jean-Claude had never lived in a house with glass windows. Her brief burst of excitement over the barn was banished by a feeling of guilt for her disloyalty. *Our cabin be suitin' our needs just fine*, she reassured herself, or maybe she reassured Jean-Claude's spirit.

Erik's home was built into a hill. Grass waved from the sod roof. Antonia wondered whether, if she stood on the far side of the hill, she'd even be able to tell there was a house. She discretely wiped the perspiration from her brow with her sleeve. Hopefully, the sod roof ensured the house would stay comfortable in the summer heat and winter cold.

Antonia hoped Erik wouldn't expect her to share his bed tonight. *Or ever*. She swallowed down her fear. He seemed a reasonable man. Surely, he'd give her time. She glanced at her husband, sitting next to her, his jaw clenched. *Maybe he'll need time, too.*

* * *

Although he heard Carter's offer to see to the care of Antonia's mules, Erik shook off the offer, telling himself he couldn't have one of the wealthiest men around tending to his livestock. But really, Erik knew he wanted to avoid entering the house and seeing the body of his wife. He still couldn't wrap his mind around the fact that he'd slipped another woman into Daisy's place before she was even cold, much less buried.

Carter seemed to understand. He allowed Erik to take the lead, but refused to be banished to sit in the rocker on the porch like Reverend Norton, who retired there after helping unload the mules. Instead, Carter took the reins of one of Antonia's mules and fell in step with Erik as if they'd worked together for years. But the rancher did pause when they entered the big barn, gazing around and obviously taking everything in.

Truth was, Erik had raised the barn to match his dreams, not to match his pocketbook, which is why he owed the banker for the loan. The barn cost more than the house—a sum Daisy hadn't appreciated spending. Some of their arguments involved the amount of money he'd invested. She'd wanted to go about building a smaller barn and increasing their herd more slowly with capital they'd acquired, not borrowed.

He'd built sturdy and large, with space for the wagon, stalls for the team and two other horses, and twelve stalls for the milk cows. On the other side, dug into the hill for coolness, lay the dairy room. Overhead, a hayloft took up a third of the space.

"Mighty fine barn you have here, Muth," Carter said.

If he'd heard the rancher's comment yesterday, Erik's pride would have soared as high as the clouds. But today, buried under the weight of his grief and guilt, only the faintest feeling of satisfaction stirred.

Out in the pasture, a cow mooed.

Carter shook his head. "Why don't you let me see to the horses, and you do the mules?" He raised a quick hand to Erik's shoulder and squeezed. "As much as you'd like to, you can't be delaying." The rancher's blue eyes showed sympathy and understanding. "The moon is bright enough. Won't bother me to drive home in the dark. But I don't know about the reverend."

Guilt prodded Erik. "You've been right neighborly to come out here with me." He strove for some levity. "And we aren't even neighbors."

"This is Sweetwater Springs. We're all neighbors here. You should have seen the passel of people who showed up unannounced to spruce up my ramshackle house when I first brought Mrs. Carter here from Boston. Doubt there was a body left in town." His mouth turned up at the memory. "You'll have plenty of opportunities to help others out when they hit hard times."

"Suppose I will." *I'd much rather be on the giving end.*

Carter's expression sobered. "You given any thought to where you want the grave?"

No! Erik wanted to howl out the word. He clamped down his teeth to keep the noise in and shook his head.

They began to unharness the horses and mules, wipe them down, grain and water them.

"It's a hard decision, where to bury," Carter said as he curried. "Not one I've had to make, but my parents sure did. My six-year-old sister was the first person they laid to rest there." His voice hitched. "Then came my grandparents. Now my parents sleep beside their daughter. There was a time when I thought my little Lizzy would join them. Her illness was the most frightening time of my life. More painful even than my sister's death…than when each of my parents died."

Somehow, the man's words comforted Erik. He thought about them as he pumped water outside and brought buckets to the mules' stalls. Carter hadn't lost a beloved wife. But the rancher knew about the death of loved ones, knew grief. And the feeling that he wasn't alone in suffering was enough to give Erik strength for what came next. "'Bout a quarter of a mile from here is a place only as wide as this barn. Circled by gentle hills. Protected…."

"Sounds fine. But if it's a quarter mile, we'll need to get your team hitched again. That's too far to carry a casket, at least for just the two of us."

"You're right. Guess I should choose someplace closer."

Shaking his head, Carter held up his hand. "Go with your instincts. Our graveyard is about half a mile from the house. Close enough to know they're there and to visit when need be, but not so close as to make you remember and hurt whenever you see it."

Erik let out a big breath. "I need to dig the grave so we can have the service and get you all headed home."

"We'll dig the grave together."

❊ ❊ ❊

Leaving Jacques to play in the wagon with Henri, Antonia paused at the porch of the house, waiting for Mrs. Carter and Mrs. Norton to catch up with her.

Mrs. Norton carried Camilla, tucked in the crook of her arm, and Mrs. Carter held the glass cake stand containing their dessert.

"Thank you," Antonia told them. "For helping us through this."

"It is our Christian duty to help," Mrs. Norton said with a gentle smile. She shifted Camilla.

Mrs. Carter raised the cake to her. "And it's what friends do. We've made new friends today."

"Yes," Mrs. Norton added. "The Lord's blessing in the midst of a dreadful day of pain."

Antonia remembered her manners, although she'd never entertained other ladies. But she recalled as a girl watching the major's wife interacting with other soldiers' wives. "Won't you come in," she said, inviting them into another woman's home as if it were her own, which, now, she supposed it was.

She snuck a quick glance at two rocking chairs on the long porch, imagining sitting in comfort while she worked, watching the boys play in the yard. *Much more comfortable than the split log stoop I be usin'.*

Feeling disloyal, Antonia stepped into the room, then moved to the side so the other women could follow her. Her first impression was of roominess and fine furniture. On second inspection, she realized the house wasn't as big as the Cameron's, nor was the furniture as ornate. Comfortable, she reckoned, and found herself relaxing a bit, while she studied the space.

A warm breeze rushed through the open door, freshening the stale, fetid air. She shuddered at the reason but saw no body and felt momentary relief.

The room combined a kitchen, dining area, and sitting room. Antonia eyed the big black stove that dominated the kitchen area and wondered what it would be like to cook on it, instead of using the fireplace or Dutch oven. A table, a counter, open shelves stocked with dishes and pantry items contained more possessions than she'd ever owned. A window above the dry sink provided a view out the side of the house toward the road. The windows on both sides of the front door let in plenty of light, and Antonia couldn't resist peeking out of one to see Erik and Mr. Carter leading her mules toward the barn and Reverend Norton unloading the wagon. She lifted the sash to let in more air.

"Good idea," said Pamela Carter, opening the window on the other side of the door. "Where is Daisy—" She bit off the words.

All three women glanced around. They spotted an open door, probably leading to the bedroom.

"In there," Mrs. Norton said. "God rest her soul." She took off her threadbare wool shawl and faded black bonnet and hung them on a hat tree near the door.

Antonia stepped out on the porch. "Henri," she called.

Reverend Norton walked out of the barn. "I'll get them." His voice carried across the yard. He helped Henri climb off the wagon.

The boy ran to her.

Reverend Norton lifted Jacques and carried him to the porch.

Jacques stretched his arms toward her.

"Thank you," Antonia said, taking her son. After holding Camilla for so long, Jacques felt heavy. She shifted him to her hip. "Henri." She pointed to one of two leather chairs in the living area. "I want you to sit there and hold Camilla like you do with Jacques. And keep an eye on your brother. I'll get Mrs. Cameron's basket. Then you and Jacques can have a piece of cold chicken."

"And jam after?"

She nodded, liking the eagerness in her son's voice.

A slight smile broke over Henri's face. He moved to the chair and sat. With a startled expression, he ran a hand over the leather cushion and bounced a bit, as if enjoying the padding.

Once Henri was settled, Mrs. Carter handed him Camilla.

He propped an elbow on the arm of the chair to brace the baby, his hands protectively around her small body.

Pamela removed a patterned shawl and her hat—an elegant burgundy straw with dyed feathers of the same color circling the brim—and hung them next to Mrs. Norton's. She placed her hands on her hips and surveyed the kitchen. "Why don't I start supper so it will be ready after the…"

All three women glanced toward the open bedroom door.

Mrs. Norton took Antonia's hand. "Leave the washing and dressing of the body to me. I've done it many times, and I think you have had enough to cope with today."

Antonia nodded, grateful to be spared that difficult task.

"If you could bring me some clean rags and a pail of water...." Mrs. Norton disappeared into the other room, closing the door behind her.

Mrs. Carter started poking around the kitchen. "There must be clean rags around here somewhere." She opened a drawer under the counter. "Ah, here they are. I'll give them to Mrs. Norton."

Antonia stared at the bedroom door, wondering if it was cowardly to leave the unpleasant task to Mrs. Norton. Her thoughts jumped back to the sight of Jean-Claude and the grizzly, and her stomach churned. Resolutely, she turned away, relieved to be spared. "I'm gittin' the food basket from the wagon and a pail of water." Grateful for a moment alone, Antonia slipped out of the house.

One of the men had left the basket on the porch. A pail stood near a washbasin. Hastily, she washed her hands and face, choosing the soap scented of lavender instead of one that smelled of bay leaves, which must be Erik's. *Will he be mindin' that I smell like Daisy?* She picked up the pail and hurried to the well—the pump was an unexpected luxury.

The late afternoon sun had begun to cool. A budding rosebush grew nearby, and Antonia made a mental note to pick some when they bloomed to place on Daisy's grave. She made a stop at the privy, pumped some water in the trough by the well to rinse her hands, and filled the bucket.

She moved to the house, trying not to look at the coffin in the wagon. When she walked through the open door, she saw the two other ladies had made themselves at home. Antonia smiled at her sons.

Someone must have brought the basket inside, for it sat on the table, contents scattered across the surface.

Mrs. Carter had tied on an apron with blue embroidered flowers across the top and hem over her dress. "Daisy Muth left a well-stocked larder," she said in approval. "That will make cooking meals easier for you." From a shelf, she picked up a tin box decorated with red flowers painted across the top and held it up. "I found Daisy's recipes. That will help you make Mr. Muth his accustomed meals."

Shame rose in Antonia. She couldn't read the recipes, but didn't want the women—or Erik for that matter—to know of her ignorance. She gave a quick nod of agreement, mentioned bringing the water to Mrs. Norton, and escaped from the conversation. Walking to the bedroom, her chest tightened and her breath came in gasps. *What am I going to do?*

CHAPTER NINE

John Carter had insisted on finishing up the grave and sent Erik back to bid his farewell to Daisy. At first, Erik argued, and then the man firmly said that digging the grave was good for him. He was counting his blessings with each shovel full.

Erik wanted to curse at Carter for that statement...for having a beloved wife, children, prosperous ranch, when he had.... But he'd sucked up the feeling, remembering he was beholden to the man.

He detoured to the barn to grab some of Antonia's possessions, taking up a big parcel wrapped in hide. As he approached the porch, he could see Reverend Norton sitting on the rocker, a Bible open on his knee. Erik climbed the steps and set down his fur-wrapped bundle.

"The womenfolk chased me out," Reverend Norton said, looking up from his reading. "They want to prepare the body. You wait here until they're ready."

Erik felt a surge of gratitude for the reprieve from having to see his wife in the rigors of death. He remembered how Daisy's body had looked when he left, and he'd dreaded seeing her again that way.

The minister rocked his chair. "I decided the best help I could be was to sit here and pray for you and your new family."

"I appreciate that, Reverend. We're certainly in need of prayers."

The minister patted his Bible. "The Lord promises He won't give us more than we can bear, but He certainly comes mighty close at times."

Like right now.

"He brings us comfort as well."

Erik thought of his beautiful baby, of the support from people he'd barely known before today. "But there's so little compared to all the pain."

"We receive small doses to sustain us. Sometimes from different places. Not much, perhaps, if you look at them individually. But they all add up to enough to keep us going, until someday, we find the pain is lessened."

Antonia poked her head out of the doorway, and, when she saw Erik, she stepped outside. "Mrs. Norton wants to know which dress you want Daisy buried in?"

How in the heck do I know? Suppressing his irritation, he rubbed a hand over his head, as if the gesture would give his brain some energy to think. "Her best dress, I guess." But then he paused and held up his hand, signaling her to wait. Daisy was awfully proud of her navy-blue dress with the puffed sleeves and the lace around the collar and neck—the one her parents had sent her at Christmas. But he'd loved his wife in her second-best dress, a light blue shirtwaist and skirt that made her eyes match the sky. *That's the one.* He described it to Antonia.

Giving a nod, she vanished into the house.

Erik walked over to the pitcher and ewer, set on a bench at the end of the porch, and washed his face and hands. With a sigh, he settled down to wait. For the first time, fatigue hit him, and he realized it had been a long time since he'd slept. He thought about getting up and poking around the kitchen for something to feed his guests, but he didn't have the strength. Thank goodness, Mrs. Cameron had sent along a basket of food. *That will have to do.*

Mrs. Norton came out onto the porch. She looked at him, compassion in her eyes, and nodded.

It is time. With a heavy sigh, he stepped over the threshold and into his comfortable main room.

On the braided rug, Mrs. Carter knelt in front of Jacques, holding his hands and letting him bounce up and down. "Ma, Ma, Ma," he chanted, grinning.

Antonia sat in the rocking chair, nursing Camilla. She looked up when he entered, her eyes shadowed. She didn't say anything.

But Erik could feel her gaze on him as he crossed the room to enter the bedroom. He paused at the door, then with a deep breath forced himself to enter.

His wife lay on the big bed, a cover pulled up to her shoulders. She looked almost relaxed, her eyes half-lidded, her mouth slightly open.

If he squinted, he could believe she slept. But when Erik touched her hand, he failed to feel any warmth, any life, and he knew Daisy was really gone.

Erik let out a slow exhale, maybe the first deep breath he'd taken since this whole tragedy started. He dragged the ladder-back chair to the side of the bed and settled onto it. He rubbed his hand down Daisy's unresponsive arm, desperately wishing she'd open her eyes and come back to him. Yet at the same time, he knew she wouldn't.

Baby Jacques crawled through the open door. He reached Erik's leg and pulled himself up. The baby solemnly glanced up at Erik and patted his knee, as though comforting him.

Erik gave Jacques a small smile.

The baby reached out one chubby hand toward the bed, trying to touch Daisy.

At first, Erik was tempted to push away Jacques's hand. But something in the little one's face stayed him—curiosity, but also tenderness beyond his years. It seemed to him as if briefly an old soul peeked through those dark eyes, lending an elder's wisdom and compassion to the baby's countenance.

With one finger, Jacques touched Daisy's hand in a tender gesture that brought tears to Erik's eyes. He rubbed a hand over the boy's black curls, feeling a connection to the child, akin to the love he had for Camilla.

The wise look on the boy's face faded, and then Jacques was only a baby, whose legs gave out. He plumped down on his bottom, then turned, and crawled out the door.

Erik stared after the baby, feeling awe and the first stirrings of peace since Daisy had gone into labor. Then he pushed the strange incident to the back of his mind and turned his attention to his wife. "Daisy, we have a beautiful daughter. Thank you for giving her to me. I swear I will do everything in my power to keep her alive and happy."

He paused, not wanting to say the next words. "For Camilla's sake, Daisy, my love, I've taken another wife. I think you would like her. She's saved our baby, Daisy. And for that alone, she'll have my undying gratitude."

A fanciful thought struck him, and he stopped to think it over, feeling that maybe it wasn't so fanciful after all. "Perhaps, my dearest, you already know this. Maybe the first thing you did after crossing through those pearly gates was arrange for someone who would save our daughter...and thus save me. Maybe we'll all save each other."

Erik brushed back the hair from her forehead. "And sweetheart...if you haven't already met him. Go seek out a man named Jean-Claude Valleau. Tell him I promise to take good care of his family. I'll provide for them as if they were my own."

Swallowing hard, he leaned over and pressed a last kiss onto her forehead. "Good-bye, my love."

* * *

In the other room, Antonia picked up her baby son when he crawled to her and hugged him. The other two women had stepped outside to give Erik privacy, taking Henri and Camilla with them. But Antonia felt she should stay near Erik if he needed her—not that she knew what, if anything, she'd be able to do for him.

Jacques laid his head on her breast, and she took a seat in the leather chair. She couldn't help overhearing Erik talking to his wife, and she didn't want to disturb him by closing the door. But as the conversation continued, Antonia was grateful she hadn't, for his words deeply touched her.

A powerful emotion flowed through her body, comprised of pain and gratitude, and the beginnings of affection for the man she would now call husband. This time, she couldn't stop the tears that rolled down her face. But they weren't just for her loss or that of her boys', but also for Erik and Camilla. *And Daisy, too.* She leaned her head against Jacques's and let them flow, 'til the wetness dripped on his curls.

As she cried, Antonia echoed Erik's prayer that Jean-Claude and Daisy meet up and together watch over the two families, who, from necessity, had now become one.

* * *

The burial party formed a semicircle around the open grave with the coffin resting inside. Reverend Norton stood at the head, near a cross Erik had quickly lashed together, a prayer book in his hands.

Gentle hills ringed the area, shutting out the sight of the house and the barn. A breeze swept through the group, bringing the scent of grass and dust, and ruffling the women's skirts.

Antonia held Jacques, while Henri clutched her skirt. At the house, she had broken apart her wedding bouquet and passed out flowers to the mourners. Although, at Mrs. Norton's suggestion, she'd held back one bloom to save as a keepsake.

Erik stood next to her, nearest the minister. On Antonia's other side, Mrs. Norton held Camilla, who watched the proceedings with her unfocused blue eyes. Then came the Carters who stood close enough for their arms to touch.

Everyone, even Jacques, carried one of her roses, denuded of thorns, although his had lost most of the petals. There'd been just enough flowers to provide one for each person.

Reverend Norton bowed in prayer. When he lifted his head, he looked at Antonia. "Before we begin," the minister said, "I'd like to take a moment to say a few words for Jean-Claude Valleau, who didn't have the benefit of a formal funeral."

Antonia suppressed a gasp of shock.

"I didn't personally know Jean-Claude Valleau, but through his wife and sons, I have come to know him—as a man who loved his family and did his best to provide for them, even when the task was dangerous for him to do so. Therefore, I also see him as a brave man. We ask that God have mercy on his soul and give comfort to his widow and children. And when we hear the words of the service for Margaret Marie Muth, we remember Jean-Claude Valleau as well."

Tears pricked Antonia's eyes.

Erik glanced at her; then seeing her emotion, he tucked his hand under her elbow.

The gesture brought her unexpected comfort.

The rest of the service passed in a blur of words and grief. Antonia let her mind drift, for if she focused on the grave, the sight brought to mind another shallow one filled with the body of her husband, and once again, she shoveled dirt onto her beloved—the sensations as vivid as when they happened six days ago.

"The Lord giveth, and the Lord taketh away." Reverend Norton's words brought her to the present. "Blessed be the name of the Lord."

They echoed his words.

"Into His hands, we commit the spirits of Margaret Marie Muth and Jean-Claude Valleau. May we rise in glory to see them again. Amen."

"Amen," everyone murmured.

Reverend Norton looked at Erik and made a small throwing motion.

Erik tossed his rose into the grave. In a flutter of pink petals, it landed on top of the coffin.

The rest of them threw their flowers into the opening.

Jacques held onto his, and his brother reached up and pried the flower from his clutched hand. "Ba!" Jacques protested.

Antonia jiggled him, while Henri dropped the rose into the grave.

There was a pause, and Reverend Norton led the women and children toward the wagon and buggies, while the two men made quick work of filling the grave.

Antonia glanced back, saw the mound over Daisy, and bit her lip, wishing for some way she could comfort Erik. *But how can I do that when I can't even comfort myself?*

Still, when he climbed on the wagon and settled himself in the seat next to her, she reached over and placed her hand on his leg for just a moment. With the small gesture, she tried to convey her support and understanding.

He gave her a quick sideways glance and a slight nod.

Small gestures will have to be enough.

CHAPTER TEN

After the Nortons and Carters left, silence settled over the house. The new family sat around the table. Antonia held Jacques, who was almost asleep. On her right, Henri nodded over his tin plate. The baby slept in a cradle near Antonia's feet.

Outside the windows, the velvety purple dusk softened the landscape and darkened the interior of the house. A glass lamp burned on the table, another luxury Antonia wasn't used to. At night, the fire had been their only illumination, and in the warmth of summer, they often let it go out after she'd cooked supper. The breeze through the open window brought the faint smell of kerosene her way.

Erik sat across from her. The lamplight cast shadows over his weary face. He rubbed a hand over his eyes.

He's probably desperately tired but doesn't want to go sleep in the bed where Daisy died. Antonia didn't blame him. She wouldn't want to, either. "You probably didn't sleep last night."

Erik shook his head. "Daisy was in labor the whole time."

The words had to be said, and Antonia braced herself for the conversation. "Why don't you go on off to bed?"

He shifted. "Don't know how I can…"

Antonia hastened to talk over his words. "The boys and I be used to sleeping on bearskins on the floor." She pointed to the corner of the main room where Erik had piled their possessions. "We be spreadin' them there and be just fine. Don't you be worryin' 'bout us at all."

His brows drew together. "You sleep on the floor?"

"Yes." She tried for a brave smile. "All of us be together like a litter of puppies."

"Sounds cozy in the winter."

"It be so. Iffen one of the boys leaks through his..." She shook her head.

Erik let out a brief bark of laughter. "Bet that would be mighty uncomfortable." His expression sobered. "I could take the floor, and you all could have the bed."

She shook her head. "No, I'd rather keep the ways the boys be used to. Later, after they be familiar..."

"I'll build you all a bedroom."

Antonia let out the breath she hadn't known she was holding. *Thank goodness, he doesn't expect us to sleep together as man and wife.* "I'd be much obliged...."

He made a cutting-off motion. "We're yoked now, you and I and the children. No obligation about it. But...tonight's not the time to ponder the wherefores." He glanced at the table and looked helplessly at the cluttered kitchen. "Daisy's ghost will probably haunt me for saying this. She was awfully particular about a tidy kitchen...but let's leave the dishes be. They'll still be here in the morning."

Antonia nodded.

He gestured toward the rifles resting on top of a bookcase. "I'll make a rack for your rifle next to mine."

She followed his gaze to the gun over the door.

Erik lifted his chin to the pile of their belongings. "Tomorrow, you can unpack and put away everything."

Antonia thought of the awkwardness of placing her possessions among Erik and Daisy's.

He seemed to understand for he ran a hand over his head. "Anywhere you choose will be fine. I'm sure I can get used to the changes."

Unspoken between them was the knowledge of how much bigger change they'd suffered. Clutching Jacques, Antonia started to rise.

Erik waved for her to remain seated. "I'll spread out the furs, then you can lay the little shaver down. I'll watch over the babies while you and Henri use the privy. Then I'll take my turn. I'll bring in water from the well for washing up. You don't mind cold?"

"We'll make do for tonight."

"We have a basin in the bedroom, but mostly, we wash up on the porch unless it's too cold." He glanced down at his new shirt. "Except when I'm too grubby, then I just stand on the dirt near the well and toss the water over me."

"Sounds like that be a fine plan."

Erik pushed the two chairs together. He knelt by her furs and unrolled the bundle. Then he spread them out to form a comfortable nest. He raised an eyebrow in askance at Antonia.

"That looks fine." She rose and laid Jacques down. Then, placing her hands on Henri's shoulders, she urged him to his feet. He made some sleepy protests, but she guided him out the door and to the privy.

As they walked through the deepening shadows, Antonia uttered a prayer of gratitude, thanking God for bringing her here. If she had to lose Jean-Claude, the Lord seemed to have provided a satisfactory situation to their dilemma, with a man who seemed hardworking and considerate. That didn't make the pain of Jean-Claude's death go away, but the tight band of fear she'd worn about her body had loosened like that awful corset, and Antonia could take a breath of relief that she and her children had landed in a safe place. She prayed it was so.

Once inside the house, Erik turned toward the bedroom then lingered, his body conveying tenseness. "Do you have a nightgown to sleep in?"

In the summer, she and Jean-Claude slept nude. But she couldn't scandalize her new husband by telling him that, so she shook her head.

"Daisy's will be short on you, but I guess that doesn't matter. Let me get it."

He took longer than she expected to return. She knelt to tuck Henri into bed and kiss his forehead before rising to her feet again.

Erik emerged from the bedroom carrying a folded white bundle. He thrust it at her, his expression almost angry.

Feeling uncomfortable, Antonia took the soft garment and held it, waiting for him to leave.

Erik waved toward the cradle, which earlier he'd brought from the bedroom. His daughter was snuggly tucked inside. "You'll be all right with the two babies?"

"Jacques usually be sleepin' through the night. Camilla be wakin' for feedings several times, but don't you be worryin' 'bout that." She hesitated. "I be findin' that sleep don't be comin' easylike since Jean-Claude died."

"I don't suppose it would."

She shrugged. "Although I be sure some was due to me a worryin'. Maybe it be different for you. But this be a hard, hard time. Take what sleep you can be gittin'." Antonia leaned over to blow out the light from the glass lamp.

"Wait," Erik said. He walked over to the lamp. "Turn down the wick before you blow it out. The wick will stay cleaner and burn brighter that way."

Antonia hoped he wouldn't see the red flaring in her cheeks. She didn't want Erik to know how long it had been since she'd used an oil lamp. *I have a lot to learn.*

"Good night." He moved through the darkness with the ease of knowing his home and shut the door of the bedroom behind him.

Quickly, Antonia took off her new dress and slipped out of the undergarments. She spread them over the chair so they wouldn't wrinkle, and then pulled on Daisy's nightgown, which smelled like lavender and cedar. The sleeves stopped mid-arm and the shoulders were snug. She ran a finger around the cuff, feeling the thread pattern of lace.

Her hand went to her throat, to the lace that edged her collar. She'd never owned anything with lace on it before. She remembered, as a girl, longing for beautiful clothing with pretty fabric, embroidery, ribbons, and lace. *I've gotten my wish.* The irony of the situation almost made her weep.

The gown came to her knees, and, in feeling around the front of the garment, Antonia couldn't discover any panels for breast-feeding. She frowned, realizing she'd have to push the material up to her shoulder when nursing one of the babies.

Antonia dropped onto the bedding between her sleeping sons and pulled up a fur to cover herself. Through the open window, she heard an owl hoot. A cloud must have moved across the moon for the grayness she saw through the window faded to black.

Lying in complete darkness, unable to sleep even though she felt exhausted, Antonia couldn't stop her mind from thinking. Too much had happened today—this week—for her thoughts to calm. Everything should feel comfortable— the furs beneath her, the familiar sounds the boys made in their sleep, but she was already on edge from listening for

Camilla—a reaction she remembered from when her boys were newborns.

The baby in her cradle made a little sucking noise in her sleep—a reassuring sound. But still, Antonia knew she'd be waking often to check on frail Camilla.

Even in the blackness, Antonia could feel the difference in the space around her. She didn't feel snug, cocooned by familiar log walls. The sounds and smells differed. She missed the wind whispering through the trees, carrying the smell of pine and lulling her to sleep. Here, the breeze brought the smell of dried grass, dirt, and cow droppings.

Antonia started to relax, her eyelids growing heavy, when a creak from the kitchen area brought her wide-awake. With her heart thudding, she listened intently. Then she realized the sound was only the house settling, and she subsided. She'd moved enough through the years to know it took time to become used to new creaks and groans that a house made. But with familiarity she'd stop hearing them—probably far quicker than any other adjustment she'd make to her new life.

❃ ❃ ❃

Erik couldn't ever remember dreading going to sleep. But tonight, his feet dragged as he approached the bed. Mrs. Norton had made the bed with Daisy's company sheets, and he felt some relief that he didn't have to sleep on the soiled bedding.

He sat in the ladder-back chair and pulled off his boots and socks, then stood and divested himself of his clothes. He fished under his pillow, grateful to discover that Mrs. Norton had replaced his nightshirt where it belonged, and yanked the garment over his head.

Once he slid into bed and pulled the sheet and blanket over him, he tried to relax. The sheets and pillowcase smelled of the lavender Daisy had tucked between the folds. A familiar smell, but not as comforting as the scent and feel of his wife lying next to him.

Erik stared unseeing into the darkness, reliving the events of the day. He replayed Daisy's death over and over, wondering if there was anything, aside from finding her early enough to get her to the doctor's, he could have done differently. But he didn't see any other path but the one they'd taken.

His thoughts turned to Antonia and his mixed feelings about the woman. He shouldn't resent her presence, but he did. He pondered the emotion—an odd feeling, really, because of his gratitude toward her and the fact that he liked her, which was a blessing given that he could have ended up with a wife he disliked.

Wife. He was the one who'd jumped to suggesting matrimony, something he didn't want. But to see Antonia attacked by those women after all she'd endured was just too much for a man to bear.

Marry in haste, repent at leisure. The old adage taunted him. He'd almost repented when he'd taken Daisy's good nightgown from the hope chest at the foot of their bed. Resentment had stabbed him that he had to give the garment to a stranger.

For a moment, Erik had buried his face in the soft cotton material and drank in the scent of cedar and lavender, remembering his excitement when he'd first seen Daisy wearing the nightgown on their wedding night—how his fingers fumbled with the small buttons, his rough hands snagging on the fine fabric. He'd felt like a clumsy oaf, all the more so because Daisy had been fearful, while he'd been crazy with excitement and love. He'd believed that night would be the beginning of a long life together—the days and nights stretching into the horizon. Never had he dreamed they'd be cut short.

He'd emerged from the memory when a practical inner voice reminded him Antonia needed the nightgown and urged him out of the room. He'd given her the garment, hoping he appeared civil, but he suspected perhaps not.

Finally, exhaustion pulled him under, and he slept.

❋ ❋ ❋

Erik awoke. From the gray light, he could tell it was time to rise and see to the stock. He reached a hand for his wife, only to realize he was alone in the bed. Daisy must be up already. He listened for the sound of her cooking breakfast and sniffed the air, hoping to smell bacon frying, but then realized the door was closed.

That's odd. He turned his head, saw the pristine pillow next to him, and like a blow, the memory returned.

Erik groaned as everything that happened yesterday came crashing back. He knew if he stayed in bed for a minute longer, he'd start bawling like a calf who'd lost his mother. Forcing himself to sit up, he pulled off his nightshirt, rose, and moved to the washbasin on top of the dresser.

His muscles ached like he'd plowed a thousand acres, and he walked stiffly like an old man. When he picked up the pitcher of water, intending to pour it in the ewer, he realized that Daisy's bloodstained nightgown was soaking inside.

The sight of the rust-colored water nauseated him, and Erik turned away, deciding to wash up outside. Then he remembered his daughter, and a sudden fear that she might have died during the night made him don his clothes, grab his boots, and rush out of the room in stocking feet.

Antonia slept curled up around Camilla on the pile of furs. Henri sprawled on his back on her other side, and next to Camilla, Jacques sucked his fingers.

Looking at the peaceful tableau settled Erik's stomach. He crouched at the side of the makeshift bed so he could see Camilla's chest rise and fall. *She made it through the night!* He closed his eyes in relief and said a silent prayer of thanksgiving.

Opening his eyes, unable to resist, he carefully maneuvered Camilla away from Antonia, who didn't stir. He wondered how much sleep she'd gotten last night. *Probably not enough.*

Erik held his daughter for a few minutes, searching her features for signs of Daisy, and marveling at her eyelashes, the softness of her skin when he ran his finger gently across her cheek, half hoping she'd wake up.

Antonia sighed and shifted. The bearskin slipped aside.

He looked at her more closely. The nightgown was pushed up to her hip, exposing long, shapely legs. Her calves and feet were tan, fading into creamy white skin, where her dress had protected her limbs from the sun.

His reaction to the woman shamed him. *Daisy is barely cold in her grave*, he chastised himself. Turning abruptly, he laid Camilla in the cradle, which he moved to give Antonia a view of the baby that she'd see as soon as she woke up. He gently pulled the bearskin back over his new wife's body, hiding temptation. Quietly, so as not to wake them, he went out the door.

CHAPTER ELEVEN

*A*ntonia *stepped from the shelter of the forest into a green meadow cupped under a brilliant blue sky and scattered with colorful flowers.*

Jean-Claude waited for her in the middle of the clearing, his stance uncharacteristically still. But when he saw her, he cocked a grin and held out his arms.

Joy filled her, and she ran to him, buoyant with happiness, her feet barely skimming the grass. The distance wasn't far, yet for all her lightness, Antonia seemed to take forever to reach him. Just as she touched his outstretched hands, something pulled him away and out of her sight. "Wait," she cried out. "Jean-Claude!"

Antonia awoke saying his name. For a moment, she stared at the unfamiliar wooden ceiling of the house, disoriented. Then memories flooded back, bringing with them a wave of pain, and she longed to return to the dream—to somehow reach him. For the space of several breaths, she allowed the desolate feeling to engulf her.

The feel of small hands pushing on her breast brought her to the awareness of Jacques at her side, and she shoved down her emotions. As tempting as it was to wallow in her grief, she had three children depending on her.

She glanced at Jacques, his eyes still sleepy, then over at the cradle. After the last nursing, she'd fallen asleep with

Camilla in her arms. Erik must have taken his daughter at some time in the last few hours and put her back in the cradle. She heard no sound, so the baby must be sleeping.

Antonia turned to Henri, sprawled on the other side of her.

His long eyelashes feathered his cheeks. His features were relaxed, not tight with the strain he'd been carrying since his father's death.

She listened, but heard no noise from the bedroom and figured Erik might have left to go milk the cows.

Jacques pushed against her breast again. "Maa."

"Patience, my son," Antonia murmured, dropping a kiss on his forehead.

She decided to let Jacques nurse a bit, more for comfort than substance, for she needed most of her milk for Camilla. Perhaps just a little in the morning and at night, for both mother and son still needed this special time together more than ever. She bunched up the nightgown for him to find her breast.

While Jacques suckled, Antonia closed her eyes, trying to pretend that she was back in her cabin, with Jean-Claude outside, perhaps going for water. But while the bearskins of her bed were familiar, the smell of the room differed—lacking the scent of pine from the forest outside her window. Even through her closed eyelids, Antonia sensed the greater space around her and the differences in the angle of the light.

After she'd nursed Jacques, she snuggled with him for a few minutes, wishing she could postpone the time when she needed to rise. She was tired from the broken sleep due to caring for Camilla. Unlike when her boys were newborns, last night she'd a hard time falling back asleep, her grief for Jean-Claude keeping her awake. Now lethargy—exhaustion and a heaviness of spirits—weighed her down. She suspected without the children to prod her into an awareness of her responsibilities, she might lay here for hours, maybe even all day.

Jacques stirred from her arms and crawled off to explore his strange new surroundings.

Antonia forced herself off the furs. She stared at the new dress she'd carefully laid over the chair, wondering if she should don the garment and take the chance of ruining the only white woman's clothes she possessed, or if she should once again put on her old tunic. *Will Erik mind?*

She could use Daisy's aprons to protect the dress but decided she would rather be comfortable. She shed the nightgown and donned her regular garb.

She scooped up Jacques and took him with her to the privy, changing the moss in his rabbit fur diaper and wondering what she'd do when she ran out. Camilla's woven soakers, knitted by Daisy, were too small for Jacques. She shrugged off the worry for a later time.

When she'd returned to the house, she saw Henri was just stirring.

He gave her a sleepy smile, just like she'd seen almost every morning until Jean-Claude's death. How she wished she could prolong the moment for him. But even as Antonia had the thought, she saw awareness of their new circumstances wake him all the way. She set Jacques on the floor.

Henri's eyes widened, and he glanced around, and then his expression crumpled as if he was going to cry.

She swooped in on Henri, dropping to her knees to hug him. "I know, *mon fils*. We be sad. We miss *Père* and our home. But we must make the best of things. *Oui?*"

He pulled away and stared at the floor. *"Oui, Maman,"* he said quietly.

"We have bread and jam. Would you like some?"

At his vigorous nod, she smiled and rubbed his head. The treat would be a temporary distraction. She doubted the novelty of jam would work for long. Either they'd run out, or Henri would become so used to the sweet that the food wouldn't distract him.

"*Bon.* Rise and use the privy. I be readyin' your victuals."

She stood. "When you come back, watch your brother, eh? I'm going to look around and find where everything be."

He went out, and Antonia rummaged through the kitchen. She avoided glancing at the stove that seemed to dominate the area—big and menacing. She'd never used one in her life, only cooking over an open fire or in the fireplace. But this house didn't have a fireplace. *I can build a campfire outside and use my Dutch oven.*

She dismissed the ridiculous idea as soon as it came to her. Erik would think he'd married a crazy woman. But when even getting out of bed took effort, the task of learning to cook on the stove seemed overwhelming.

I can figure out the stove. I've certainly done far harder tasks this week.

In the cupboard, Antonia noted earthenware and tin plates, knives and forks, and more pots and pans than she'd ever seen in her life. *Far more than I know what to do with.*

In the backside of the kitchen, she saw a door set into the wall and opened it to find a large dirt-walled pantry dug deep into the hill the house was built against. On the left, she found shelves burrowed into the walls holding colorful glass jars filled with canned fruits and vegetables, long-necked brown bottles with neat handwriting flowing across pasted-on labels, and various crocks that must also contain preserved food.

The relief she felt at seeing such bounty nearly made her sink to her knees. *My boys will not go hungry on this farm.*

On the shelf near the bottom, empty jars taunted her. Canning was another skill she'd never learned. When the garden started producing or she foraged for berries, she'd need to find someone to teach her. She thought of kind Mrs. Norton, perhaps easier to approach than Mrs. Cameron or Mrs. Carter, and wondered if she could ask for her help in exchange for a portion of their labors.

On the right side of the room, a short string of onions and one of garlic dangled from the ceiling above a line of earthenware crocks. She lifted the lid of a crock to see beans inside. A second crock held oats and a third cornmeal. When she opened the fourth, the smell of lard and something meaty came her way. She peered inside and saw a few sausages on the very bottom of the crock. She hadn't eaten one in years.

Another held ashes, but when, puzzled, she poked a finger into the middle, she saw a big ham nestled inside. Her stomach grumbled.

Baskets holding eggs, potatoes, carrots, and apples were set deeper into the pantry. Although the egg basket was full to the brim, the others were low, but still a marvel. If this much food remained after the long winter, Antonia imagined in the fall, the pantry must have overflowed—far more than the two of them could eat.

The more she explored Daisy's kitchen, the more inadequate Antonia felt. She'd always thought she'd done a good job of keeping her family well fed. But she'd relied heavily on the game Jean-Claude hunted and trapped, as well as the fish he caught. In her garden, she had grown pumpkins, squash, sunflower seeds, sweet potatoes, corn, and beans. And she'd often taken the boys and foraged for the berries, leaves, and roots of wild plants.

In her pack, she had leather bags of dried food—meat strips, berries, squash and cantaloupe, as well as parched corn and nuts. From the Blackfoot, she'd learned to make pemmican—dried meat pounded to small pieces, mixed with berries or chokecherries, and marrow grease. The light-weight circular patties stored well and were easy to travel with. She'd depended on them during their journey to Sweetwater Springs and only had a few left.

Standing in the pantry, Antonia had never felt more alone. She was used to spending long hours in solitude while Jean-Claude was out hunting, but then she'd never felt lonely. Now, with three children a few feet away and a man some-where about the place, she became aware of the isolation in her heart—something her children, no matter how beloved, or an unfamiliar new husband—could assuage.

The feeling took Antonia back to her childhood. Even when surrounded by people at a fort, as a motherless girl and with her father a soldier, she was often left to fend for herself. Then she'd grown older and met Jean-Claude, tumbling into love with the handsome trapper and adoring him with all of her starving heart. And in the most blessed of miracles, he'd returned her feelings, and eventually had given her Henri and then Jacques to love and nurture.

My sons. The children are my purpose. Since her husband's death, taking care of them had been her driving force. Without her boys, she might have cast herself on Jean-Claude's grave, wallowing in her grief until she followed him to heaven.

And now I have a daughter—the fulfillment of a dream—in the middle of a nightmare. Tears pricked her eyes.

"*Maman?*" Henri called. "Jacques is hungry."

Antonia sniffed back the tears and rubbed her arm across her eyes, scrubbing away any betraying moisture. "I'm sure he be not the only hungry boy around." She put false lightness into her tone.

Backing out of the pantry, Antonia found a knife and took the bread from the breadbox and cut a slice, spreading a thin layer of red jam over the surface before handing a piece to Henri and one to Jacques. Looking around the kitchen, she wondered what to make Erik for breakfast. *Does he eat the kind of food we had yesterday at the Camerons?*

Antonia frowned at the stove. Even with her lack of experience, she could probably manage to boil eggs and fry some ham. Glancing out the window, she saw a trio of rabbits and made up her mind. "Stay here, Henri. Watch your brother," Antonia ordered. She started to race for her sling, but figured she had it packed too deeply and veered toward her rifle. *The rabbits will make the perfect breakfast.*

✳ ✳ ✳

After milking the cows in the field and taking the milk to the springhouse, Erik entered the barn to feed the horses. For the first few minutes, he inhaled the familiar smell of animals, manure, and hay, and could almost pretend nothing in his life had changed. *Daisy is in the kitchen preparing breakfast while I go about the morning chores. All is well,* he tried to tell himself as his thoughts skittered away from the dark knowledge that the opposite was true.

One of Antonia's mules looked over the stall door. A jolt of reality charged through him. *Even my barn is no longer the same.* The pain almost blinded him. By rote, his body performed the routine tasks of caring for the livestock.

Erik couldn't help contrasting the feeling of jubilation he'd experienced at the birth of the two heifers—*was it really two days ago?* He couldn't be sure. Years seemed to have passed.

Will I ever feel so happy, so...satisfied again? Such feelings seemed as far from his current grief as the mountains were from the prairie. *If I am ever happy again, it probably won't be for years—maybe when I'm seventy.*

Outside the open barn door, the crack of a rifle made him almost jump out of his boots. *What in tarnation?*

Two more shots rang out. His heart leaped into his throat, and Erik lunged out of the stall, shutting the door behind him. He grabbed the pitchfork that leaned nearby and raced through the open barn door, cursing that he didn't have his rifle nearby.

In the yard, he glanced frantically around. Everything looked peaceful. There was no sign of an intruder. He wanted to yell for Antonia, but didn't know if calling her would put her or the children in danger.

Carrying the pitchfork like a spear, he sprinted toward the house, only to skid to a stop when he caught movement to the left.

Antonia—clad in her Indian garb—walked around the corner of the house, an expression of satisfaction on her face. She carried a rifle in one hand and three limp rabbits in the other. She cast him a startled look and took a step back.

With his hair probably standing on end like a spitting cat's, brandishing the pitchfork, Erik knew he must appear as if he were the very devil himself. He stopped and clutched his chest, where his heart pounded so hard it made his ribs hurt.

Antonia hastened to his side. "Erik, what be wrong?"

"Everything's wrong!" he snapped. "Starting with the fact that you frightened the bejeezus out of me. Dear Lord, Antonia, when I heard the gunshots, I thought—" His voice hitched. Erik forced himself to steady it. "I thought the worst."

She looked from the rabbits to him. "I be gittin' us some breakfast meat."

"That's breakfast?" The words came out sharp enough to cut.

She flushed but met his angry gaze. "You don't be likin' rabbit stew?"

"Rabbit stew for breakfast? What happened to ham and eggs, pancakes, biscuits and gravy, toast with jam, bacon, sausage, porridge, stewed fruit?" He ran out of all the breakfast items he could think of.

She looked at the ground. "I be not knowin'."

Her quiet words deflated him. "Forgive me. I'm acting like a jackass." The apology came out sounding stiff. "You frightened me. I reacted poorly. This is your home now. Everything in it belongs to you as well as me. Why don't I show you around after breakfast, so you'll know where everything is?"

She nodded.

Just like that his anger dissipated, and he remembered to feel grateful for her. "When I saw Camilla breathing this morning.... She was the most beautiful sight!"

Antonia's small smile showed her understanding. "With each of my sons when they been new, but especially Henri, I'd check to see him breathe. The relief at each one..." She let out an audible breath. "Even more so with Camilla. I be lookin' keenlike on her four times last night. She took the teat but twice."

"Thank you for your care of her." Erik reached out to take the rabbits.

She swung them out of his reach. "No need. "I be doin' it. You must have plenty of work already."

Puzzled, Erik studied her. "I do," he said slowly. "But are you sure?"

"Did I tell you Jean-Claude be a trapper?" She gave him a faint smile and shrugged. "Yesterday be a blur, and I cain't remember half of what I done said to no one."

"Me, neither. A few minutes ago, I couldn't remember what day it was." Erik pointed to the house. "The meat storage is on the north side. Plenty of hooks for hanging game. Shed attached to it is where you can dress them. You'll find everything you need." He glanced at the barn. "I really should be getting back to my chores."

With the hand that held the rifle, she gestured toward the barn as if urging him in that direction.

Erik walked away from her, his thoughts churning. While he was glad about the lack of danger, he couldn't get over Antonia's matter-of-fact attitude about shooting and skinning the rabbits. His sensitive Daisy couldn't even bear to wring the neck of her chickens.

This new marriage will take a lot of getting used to.

❋ ❋ ❋

Erik took a seat at the table and looked around. Antonia sat opposite him, Jacques on her lap.

The toddler had smeared jam on his face, obviously having begun on breakfast earlier.

Henri sat to his mother's left.

They all watched Erik with solemn eyes, their bodies stiff. Discomfort lay heavy in the air.

Erik glanced at the bowl in the center of the table, stacked with hard-boiled eggs, and winced. He liked his eggs fried and flipped over, the yokes poked and spread over the surface, and turned again. He surveyed the rest of the food. Antonia had set out half a loaf of bread, but she hadn't already sliced it. An open jar of jam was next to the bread, a knife stuck into the middle. He didn't see any butter. A plate held slices of ham. At least those looked just the way he preferred his ham, lightly browned in spots.

Daisy hadn't permitted jars or crocks on the table, and she always scooped jam into a small saucer. She'd also insisted on dishing out the food onto their plates before placing them on the table. "I don't run a boarding house," she'd stated in the beginning of their marriage. She'd liked things fancy, had his wife.

He glanced over at Antonia, who was watching him with an anxious expression, and flinched, wondering if he'd have to start thinking of Daisy as his *first* wife. *No! Even if it's the truth, I can't bear the thought.*

Lest Antonia see the resentment in his eyes, he lowered his gaze to his empty plate, trying to talk himself out of his ill humor. *This situation isn't her fault. She's as unhappy as I am.*

He glanced down at the cradle where Camilla lay. The baby was awake and her blue eyes—Daisy's eyes—gazed at the ceiling. He wondered what she saw up there, what she was thinking. *Do newborn babies think?*

Erik gathered his wits enough to speak. "Shall we say grace?"

Antonia gave him a blank look, glanced at the table in puzzlement, and then around the room as if searching for something. Her wary gaze returned to him.

Erik didn't know what to say to her obvious bewilderment. They'd prayed before the meal at the Cameron's house yesterday, and she'd seemed ill at ease then, but he supposed she'd been as numb to what was happening around her as he'd been.

Deciding to go ahead, he clasped his hands together and bowed his head. "Lord, we are grateful for your blessings." He said the words by rote, but resentment churned in his belly.

He didn't feel blessed, or grateful. *Perhaps I should find a different prayer?* He let out a sigh. *Another change.*

I'll figure out a prayer at the next meal.

He reached for the bowl of eggs. Antonia hadn't used Daisy's prized rose-patterned serving platter—the one she'd inherited from her grandmother. *Who would have thought a simple meal could be so fraught with changes—with pain?*

With a spoon, he took three of the eggs and deposited them on his plate, and then passed the food to Antonia. She took one for Henri, and one for herself.

Discretely, Erik glanced over at the stove, trying to see if Antonia had boiled coffee. But he couldn't see any on the stove. Nor, when he sniffed the air, did he smell the rich scent. *I'll have to show her where everything is.*

Was there ever a more awkward meal? He reached for the loaf and cut off a slice, wishing Antonia had made toast. "Would you like some?" He extended the piece to her.

She nodded.

He deposited the bread on her plate.

Erik looked at his stepson. "Henri?"

The boy bobbed his head, his gaze sliding away.

After Erik set the bread on Henri's plate, he pushed back his chair and strode to the larder. He returned with a crock of butter, which—disregarding Daisy's rule—he put on the table, not wanting to take the time to scoop some spoonfuls into a serving dish. "I'm making an egg sandwich," he announced, taking a seat. After buttering his bread, he passed the crock to Antonia.

With a wide-eyed expression, she stared at it. "Butter be a rare treat."

Curious, he cocked his head.

"Ain't many cows at an army fort," she said, accepting the crock. "If there be any, the milk and cream goes to the officers' table. And Jean-Claude and I never be havin' a cow."

A small feeling of pleasure rushed through his discomfort. *At least, I can give this family dairy products.* "Well, from now on, you'll have plenty of milk and sour milk, cream and butter."

"We'll enjoy that." Her small smile didn't reach her eyes.

Not knowing what else to say, Erik focused on eating, for his body needed the sustenance. He usually had a hearty appetite and devoured a lot of food at each meal. But today, the knot in his belly kept him from feeling hunger, which was a good thing given the scanty nature of the breakfast.

From the slow way the others ate, they seemed to feel the same. Only Jacques seemed comfortable, gnawing on a crust of bread and stuffing small bites of egg from his mother's plate into his mouth.

He peeled the hardboiled eggs, and then sliced them, piling them on the bread he'd already buttered. As Erik chewed, he wondered if he should say something to Antonia about how he liked his eggs cooked, or if that would hurt her feelings. He'd already gotten angry about her shooting the rabbits, which was enough chastisement for a new wife for one day.

Erik pondered the dilemma, wondering which would be worse—making her feel bad about her cooking, or eating hard-boiled eggs for the rest of his life? And what if she found out the truth? Would she feel bad because he hadn't told her? He couldn't help thinking such trivial questions were ridiculous given the nature of the changes they were going through.

But Daisy had always been firm with him about the importance of honesty. One of their early arguments had been when she discovered he didn't like salt in his stew. She'd blown up at him for not telling her right away, when he'd thought he was sparing her feelings. *Are all women like that, or just Daisy?*

Erik let the others finish before talking again. "I know this is all new to you—not knowing where everything is…figuring out a routine and all." He waited for her to say something.

But Antonia watched him, her golden gaze impassive.

He wished he knew what she was thinking. "I don't know what you like or want. What will please or displease you. Nor do you know those things about me. Normally, we'd discover those things when we were courting…."

"Perhaps not." She gave a wry twist of her lips. "I know Jean-Claude and I learned much about each other after we were married. But, then again, we didn't wait long to wed after we met."

"Daisy and I grew up together…went to school together. We knew from the time we were young that we'd marry someday." He paused, remembering…. "We were apart for several years after I moved to Sweetwater Springs to establish the farm. We wrote back and forth. Then she insisted on waiting no longer. I agreed. Against her parents' wishes, she joined me here, and we were wed."

"You be lucky, knowin' her for so long," Antonia said in a wistful tone. "Although from Jean-Claude's storytellin', he be wild when he be young. Perhaps 'tis best I be not knowin' him."

Jacques bounced, as if to get down.

Antonia set the boy on his feet.

The baby promptly plopped on his bottom and crawled away from them, heading toward the door.

Antonia glanced at her oldest son. "Henri, take Jacques outside and watch him good. Be stayin' close and no goin' into the barn unless Mr. Muth be with you."

"*Oui, Maman.*" The boy slid off his chair and hastened after his brother, opening the door and coaxing the baby to crawl out. He followed Jacques, shutting the door behind him.

Erik frowned, wondering how to begin the discussion. "Perhaps it's best if we set everything out on the table."

Her eyebrows pulled together in puzzlement. Her gaze flicked between his plate and the dishes, obviously wondering if he wanted more.

"I mean, strive for honesty between us."

Her brow relaxed. "Yes."

He gestured toward the eggs. "For example...I'd like to tell you how I like my eggs done, but I don't want to be critical."

She bit her lip. "We didn't eat chicken eggs. Other types, sometimes."

"Antonia," he said in a gentle voice. "Even if you had chickens and cooked eggs every day, you wouldn't know how *I* like them."

"You be right. This be plumb different for me."

"That's why we need to talk."

She gave him a direct look. "How be you likin' your eggs, then?"

He thought of the topics that were far more important than eggs, even though that's what he'd started with. "How 'bout I show you tomorrow?"

She let out a sigh, as if in relief. "That be good soundin'."

He glanced at the cradle.

Camilla waved her hand in the air. She kicked off her blanket. "Perhaps we should decide how the children address us. Your boys are now my stepsons. They can hardly call me Mr. Muth. And Camilla will only know you as her mother."

Antonia reached down and pulled the blanket over the baby. "Jean-Claude was French Canadian. Henri called him *père.*"

"And I've heard Henri use *maman* with you."

"That's right."

"The boys could call me Pa. That's different enough from père."

She gave a decisive nod. "Yes. Then when I say *père*, they know I mean Jean-Claude. And Pa will mean you."

"And the same for you—*Maman*. And Ma for Daisy." For the first time, he saw warmth in her golden eyes.

"Thank you."

"For what?"

"Keeping Jean-Claude—" Her voice broke. "Honorin' his memory."

"Not trying to take over from their father." He gave a bitter twist of his lips. "My daughter will never know her mother, except through what I tell her."

"Jacques won't remember his *père*. I hope Henri will, though."

Camilla started to fuss.

Antonia leaned forward and plucked the baby from the cradle. Holding her in the crook of one arm, she raised her hand to let down the flap of her tunic and hesitated. Her cheeks reddened. She seemed more modest today than yesterday.

Corresponding heat flushed Erik's face and burned the tips of his ears. "I'm your husband," he reminded her, his voice thick. "Would you prefer me to turn away when you nurse my daughter?"

She looked down and jiggled the baby.

Erik imagined what Daisy would feel if she were the one to survive and take on a marriage of convenience. His modest wife would probably hide away in the bedroom each time she fed Camilla, rather than expose herself to a strange man— new husband or not.

Now that he thought of it, he figured Daisy probably would have nursed in private with him as well, although he hoped she soon would have become comfortable to do so in his presence. "I can leave the room," he offered, but hoping to stay.

Antonia rubbed a gentle hand over Camilla's fuzzy head. "No." Her voice was soft. "I be uncomfortable. But that be...*must be* changing." She untied the strings, and the flap dropped, exposing a full breast, the brown nipple enlarged for nursing.

Erik had a sudden image of cupping her fullness. Her breast would fill his hand. His groin tightened, and he imagined her naked in his bed, as he explored her body, so different from his petite wife. He and Daisy hadn't been intimate for months, not since she'd had morning sickness.

I've gone without too long, Erik told himself, trying to stifle his sudden desire, feeling guilty about lusting after another woman with his wife newly dead. Although, perhaps, his reaction boded well for future intimacy.

What if Antonia doesn't feel the same about me? The specter of never again having marital relations made his physical reaction die away.

Erik forced himself to give his attention to the next topic he wanted to discuss, but the fear about his future intimacy with Antonia, or lack thereof, burrowed into the back of his mind. "Speaking of Henri...he needs to go to school."

She gave a sharp indrawn breath and met his gaze.

"You don't want that?"

Antonia made a negating gesture. "*Non.* I mean no. I do. It be my dream for him. But it be so far to town."

"Yes. But many children walk from even farther away. I certainly did."

"Gittin' an education's important, an' all. It be just…" She glanced down at the baby.

"Too many changes all at once," he guessed.

"Yes. He never be parted from me for more than a few hours when Jean-Claude took him along to check the trap lines."

"Well, it's going to be another change for him, that's for sure. Has he had any teaching at home?"

She shook her head.

"We can wait a couple of days before Henri starts. First give him time to adjust to living here." He wrinkled his brow, thinking. "The way I've lost the days I'd better make sure we don't start him on a Sunday."

"I don't have no notion what day it be. We never kept track." She shrugged. "Didn't matter."

Erik stood, walked to the shelf, and took down the almanac. He had to think before he could remember the date. He flipped open the pages until he found Tuesday. Then he brought the book over to Antonia, setting it on the table in front of her. He tapped the date. "There you have it."

Her expression blanked. She looked where he pointed, but didn't say anything. Finally, she looked up at him but couldn't hold his gaze. "That be fine."

She's lying. Erik didn't challenge her. He nodded, as if accepting her words at face value, but all the while, knowing that neither of them believed anything about their lives would be fine.

CHAPTER TWELVE

Henri wandered after his brother, who crawled across the yard, stopping to examine every rock and weed. Sometimes, he had to stoop to keep Jacques from putting a clump of dirt in his mouth, but mostly, he took small steps after the baby.

He snuck an upward glance at the sky, and then looked back at the ground. The vast expanse made him dizzy, pressing down on his head and making his middle cramp. Although the bread and jam had tasted good when he'd eaten it, now the food didn't sit too well in his stomach, feeling more like one of the rocks he'd just pried out of his brother's little hand.

Henri looked toward the barn and wondered if Kenny and Rocky missed him. He always visited them first thing in the morning, helping *Père* feed and water the mules, groom their coats, and muck out the stalls. Surely they felt as lost in that big ole barn as he did here by the house. *Or maybe they like it better?*

Back on the mountain, their shed had been small and dark. But *Père* said it was sturdy and kept out the bears and mountain cats. *Be there bears on the prairie?* He gave a fearful glance around, but he didn't see any sign of wildlife but a red-tailed hawk floating in the sky.

The bird swooped to the ground and then flew up with a mouse in its claws.

He glanced toward the barn again, the pull to go to the mules so strong he took a few steps in that direction before he stopped, remembering *Maman* had told him not to go there unless Mr. Muth was with him.

Jacques crawled toward the house. He stopped at the stairs to the porch, using the first step to lever himself to a standing position. "Ba, ba." He smacked the wood, obviously pleased with himself. He swiveled until he saw Henri. "Baa."

"Baa," Henri mimicked.

The drone of *Maman* and Mr. Muth speaking came through the open screen door. He didn't pay them any mind until he heard the man say his name.

"Henri needs to go to school."

School? Maman had told him about school. He strained his ears to hear the rest of the conversation. *Maman*'s voice was softer, her words harder to make out, but the concern in her tone came through clear enough.

I don't wanna go to school. His stomach ached, and Henri wondered if he was going to be sick. *If only I could run away— back home, back to* Père. Not that he wanted to leave *Maman* and Jacques...

With a sigh, he sat on the step next to his brother, remembering how they'd played on the stoop the morning *Père* died. How both of them had laughed and laughed.

Now everything had changed, and he didn't like it one bit. Although Mr. Muth seemed nice enough, Henri didn't want another *père*. He wanted his own *père* back. *I want to go home!* He thought again, feeling helpless.

Jacques scooted over and patted Henri's knee. "Baa?"

Henri tried to smile. "Baa." But his heart wasn't in the game.

Jacques's face fell, as if he'd sensed his brother's feelings.

Not wanting the baby to let out a wail that would disturb the adults, Henri grabbed Jacques's hand. "Come on. Let's walk."

His suggestion worked.

Jacques gave him an open-mouthed grin—the one that usually made Henri laugh back. *Grenouille, Père* teased when Jacques smiled like that. *Maman* would scold, although her mouth turned up, so she wasn't really angry, and tell *Père* not to call the baby a frog.

Père *will come for us. He won't leave us here without him.*

※ ※ ※

Carrying Camilla, Antonia followed Erik from the house, squinting at the brightness of the sun. She'd grown too used to the tree-shaded mountain and wondered if she'd ever adjust to the openness of the prairie.

Henri held Jacques's hands, allowing the boy to walk in front of him.

Her oldest son still looked sad—haunted eyes, mouth pulled down, and shoulders slumped. But Antonia was relieved to see Jacques had a smile. He always loved playing with his big brother.

Henri saw them and slowly steered the baby their way.

Jacques smiled at her, obviously proud of his accomplishment. "Maa." He pulled away from Henri, sank to his knees, and crawled over to her.

Antonia handed Camilla to Erik and picked up her son.

Jacques patted her cheeks with his dirty hands. "Maa," he repeated.

She kissed his cheek, shifted him to one arm, and held out her hand for Henri. "Mr. Muth is showing us his farm."

"*Our* farm," Erik corrected.

Although Antonia sent him a polite smile for his inclusion of them, she doubted this place would ever feel like *our* farm. "Henri, Mr. Muth and I spoke some on our new family. We always be rememberin' *Père*." Her throat tightened, and she had to pause before she could continue with the words she hated saying. "We be always lovin' Père. He be a good father to you, and we be never forgetin' him." Her lips trembled, and she pressed them tight.

With a sideways glance at her, Erik seemed to note her distress, for he came to her rescue. "Yesterday, when your mother married me, we became husband and wife. She will now be a mother to my baby, Camilla...her *maman*."

Antonia reached out to touch the baby's foot. "And Mr. Muth be a new father for you boys." She took a breath and rushed out the words. "You be callin' him Pa."

Henri backed away, shaking his head.

"I be sorry, *mon petit fils*. But this be the way 'tis." She tried to keep the sorrow from her voice.

"Baa," Jacques added, seemingly unconcerned by the strained emotions flowing around him.

Carefully holding Camilla to his shoulder, Erik squatted so he was eye-level to Henri. "I know this is hard, boy. Hard for all of us. I can't be your *p*ère. But I promise to be the best pa to you and Jacques that I can be."

Henri twisted away from Erik, pressing close to Antonia's side. "No, *Maman*. *Père* be comin' for us and take us home."

Henri's words twisted like a knife in her stomach. *If only that be true!* Antonia had a brief flash of longing before firmly suppressing the feeling. *No sense wishin' for something that be never happenin'.*

Erik rose to his feet.

She glanced at her new husband, afraid of what she might see. *Be he angry?*

Erik rubbed Camilla's back, his gaze on Henri, compassion in his blue eyes.

Relieved, she turned back to her son. "*Père* be *dead*, Henri." She made her tone gentle but firm. "The grizzly bear done killed him. He not be coming for us, no matter how much we be wishin' on such a thing."

The boy scuffed the dirt with his foot and then shot her a quick glance as if to verify her words.

"Our life is here, now, with Mr. Muth, your new pa." Releasing his hand, she gave him a one-armed hug. "In time, this will not seem so bad, *oui?*"

"*Oui, Maman.*" Henri didn't sound convinced.

Erik waved to a whitewashed house, not much smaller than the log home she'd left behind. "That's our henhouse. Henri, let me take you to meet the chickens. I think you're big enough to help your mother take care of them."

I be takin' care of them? Antonia didn't know anything about chickens. Once again, she realized how ignorant she was of the basic knowledge other white women took for granted. At least, Erik didn't seem to notice her reaction.

"Daisy was mighty proud of her chickens. Good layers all, although Penny's falling off. I briefly fed and watered them last night. But Daisy usually lavished a lot of attention on them." A guilty expression crossed his face, and he took a ragged breath.

Antonia didn't know what *lavished* meant, but she could guess. She glanced over at the henhouse. She'd never been around the *les poulets.* At the various forts she'd lived at, the camp cooks jealously guarded the flocks, and no one was allowed near. She hoped these ones were friendly.

"Come," Erik said. "Watch what I do; then tomorrow you can take over their care." He glanced down at the baby in his arms. "Ah…"

"Let me take her." She set Jacques on the ground near a pile of rocks she knew would interest him. Then she reached for Camilla and gathered the baby to her. After holding Jacques, the infant seemed so tiny, so frail. Antonia cuddled her close and pressed a kiss to the baby's forehead.

She followed Erik to the henhouse. Up close, she marveled at the windows with glass panes. *Why, my cabin be not even havin' glass! And here I be proud of the screen tacked over the windows to keep out the flies.* She'd carefully taken down the screens, rolled them up, and brought them with her.

Erik unlatched the door and stepped back to allow the chickens to surge outside. "We need to lock them up at night to protect them from predators. We have fifteen in all. Daisy liked to keep an eye on them. She'd sit on the porch and do handwork. We used to have a dog to protect the flock, but he died a few months ago. We were going to wait until after the baby came to get a new one."

The white, black, and brown chickens rushed out of the doorway, clucking and spreading their wings. They chattered in obvious excitement, seeming happy to stretch their legs. Some stopped to peck for bugs, but the rest must have been hoping for feed, for they scurried toward Erik.

"Sorry, birds." He stepped back. "No food for you yet." Erik glanced down at Henri. "Can you go get the feed for me?" He pointed toward the barn. "Just inside the door on a shelf." He made a turning motion to the right with his hand so Henri would know where to look. "There's a metal pan and a gunnysack with some feed. The bag's almost empty, so I think it's light enough for you to carry. Do you think you can do that?"

Henri glanced up at Antonia, seeking her approval.

Antonia nudged him with her arm. "Show Mr. Muth...
uh, *Pa*, what a helpful boy you be." She tilted her chin. "Go
on now."

Henri moved from her side in obvious reluctance. Then,
as if eager to get the errand over with, he broke into a run,
vanishing through the doorway.

Antonia watched him, her stomach churning, hoping he
wouldn't need her assistance. Henri had always taken pride in
helping her and Jean-Claude, and she hoped aiding his new
father would support the development of their relationship.

Henri emerged from the barn, carrying the pan with the
sack on top.

"Well done, *mon fils.*"

"I knew you could do it." Erik gave Henri a smile and nod,
taking the pan from him. He upended the sack then held
out the pan to Antonia so she could see the contents. "Some
cracked corn and grain. 'Bout that much each time."

Antonia noted the level of the feed.

He picked up a handful and scattered the grain.

Chickens attacked the feast.

"Daisy named them all." Erik tossed another handful.
"She could tell them apart. I only know about half. Let's see if
I can remember which is which." He pointed at one. "Penny
stands out with her copper-colored feathers. The little lady's
coming to the end of her laying life and should end up in
the frying pan soon. And Sadie is...was—" he continued with
only the slightest stutter of words "—Daisy's favorite. Treated
that chicken like a pet, she did." His voice caught.

Antonia rushed to speak, hoping to distract him. "Iffen
you don't know what they be called, Henri can give 'em
names. He be plumb good at that."

Erik swallowed and nodded. "The rooster is Bert. The ole
boy likes to keep an eye on things. As does this one, eh, Miss

Mae." He stooped to run a hand over the neck and back of a white-feathered chicken.

Miss Mae wiggled and fluttered her wings in apparent enjoyment.

Erik kept rattling off names and pointing to the various birds. Then, he finished feeding them, upending the pan to shake out the remaining kernels.

Antonia gently swayed with Camilla and concentrated on following his directions and watching what he did. Feeding the chickens seemed easy enough. So did filling up the water pan from the well.

Erik took down a long-handled wire basket that hung from a big hook under the eaves. "This is how Daisy carried the eggs, although sometimes she just used her apron." His gaze slid away from Antonia's Indian garb.

Her cheeks heated. *Does he disapprove?* But since he didn't say anything more, she pretended nothing was wrong. "We be gatherin' them." She glanced at Henri. "Eh, son? You be careful?"

Henri nodded.

Before Antonia followed Erik into the chicken coop, she glanced at Jacques, sitting in a broad patch of dirt.

He'd become engrossed in a stone that he'd picked up and was carefully studying.

Since the rock was too big for Jacques to swallow when he inevitably tried to put it into his mouth, Antonia let him be, figuring he'd be safe for a few minutes. She walked into the henhouse, inhaling the smell of straw, wood shavings, and droppings that covered the floor.

The interior was surprisingly light with sunshine streaming from windows on both sides. A few feet off the floor, straw-filled wooden boxes lined the walls. Some held eggs in various shades of tan. A few stragglers, perched on wooden branches that reached from wall to wall, stretched their wings and made a trilling noise. She sensed their unease with a stranger.

Erik glanced up at the roof, which was a foot above him. "I built this high enough so I could stand upright inside without worrying about hitting my head."

Henri entered, and the three of them seemed to take up the available space.

Erik motioned to a nest holding three eggs. "Go ahead, Henri. Pick them up."

Gingerly, the child reached for the first one.

Erik held out the basket.

Henri set the egg inside and added the second. After the third, he moved to the next box without having to be prompted.

Small steps, Antonia told herself in relief. *He be making small steps into getting settled in this new life. Each a sign that he be all right. Or so I hope.*

Erik scooped some straw from an empty nest. "Clean out the droppings or any broken eggs, removing all wet or soiled straw, and replace the straw or shavings. The straw is in the barn, and the shavings are at the woodpile." He gave them a brief upward turn of his lips. "I'll show you where both are."

"Shouldn't be hard to figure out where."

He dipped his chin in a *you're right* motion and then gestured toward the floor. "When we rake out the henhouse, we save everything for the garden."

Antonia nodded in agreement. She'd used the manure from the mules for her garden in the same way.

By this time, Henri had collected all the eggs that were left unattended.

On a nest in the corner sat a black chicken, a baleful look in her eyes.

"Nanette is broody." Erik set down the basket. "That ole biddy doesn't like me and isn't about to let me or anyone else get her eggs. Watch what happens when I try." Slowly, he stuck his hand toward the hen, aiming for underneath her body.

Lightning fast, she struck at him with her beak.

Antonia gasped.

At the same time, Henri jumped back and pressed against her side.

Erik didn't jerk away his hand like she expected. Instead, he allowed the chicken to continue attacking him. "It just pinches. Doesn't hurt bad." He withdrew his hand and winked at Henri. "Scary critter, isn't she?"

Henri responded with a vigorous set of nods.

"When I was your age," Erik said in a reminiscing tone. "I hated gathering eggs from broody hens. In fact, once I got a switchin' from my ma for letting one mean ole bird keep her eggs for days. Then my pa took me aside and taught me this trick."

He edged around them toward the door and took down a small shovel hanging on the wall. "Now, you want to move slow and careful to not hurt her with this." He positioned the edge of the shovel in the straw in front of the chicken.

Nanette pecked the shovel, her beak making *ting, ting, ting* sounds.

Erik slid the shovel under the chicken's breast and lifted an inch. "She can't see me. And I'm protected by the metal." He stuck his hand under Nanette and brought out an egg, holding it up with three fingers. "*Ta-da!*"

Henri pulled away from Antonia's side. He took the egg from Erik and, stooping, he settled it on top of the pile in the basket.

Still holding the shovel in place, Erik glanced at Henri. "You want to try? I felt another two under there."

Antonia bit her lip to still an instinctive protest. *Henri can be doin' this. Jean-Claude already had the boy be helpin' with the traps—a far more dangerous task.*

Arm outstretched, Henri leaned forward and slid his hand under the hen, groping for an egg. He pulled it out and flourished his prize like Erik had, although he didn't say *ta-da.*

"Well done." With his chin, Erik indicated the hen. "One more."

Henri pulled out the egg and laid it safely in the basket.

Erik bent to pick up the basket. "You two will gather eggs again tonight. Are you comfortable doing it by yourself?"

Antonia exchanged glances with Henri. "We be."

"Good." Erik motioned them to the door and led them outside.

Jacques had found another stone. Banging the two together, he yelled, "Baa!" He made no move toward them, seemingly content to play with the rocks.

Erik scooped up the boy, rocks and all, and settled him against his side, appearing completely familiar with hauling around young uns.

Jacques didn't seem to mind, flashing her a wide grin. "Maa!" He waved one hand, narrowly avoiding clipping Erik in the head with a stone.

Antonia said a quick prayer of thanksgiving that her youngest had returned to his usual cheerful self. She settled Camilla in her arms and glanced at Henri, wishing the change would be as easy for him.

"The springhouse." With his free arm, Erik waved toward a small stone house on their left. The building was about the size of the chicken coop and had a white door. Instead of a window, a square of metal vents allowed air to flow in and out. A small stream of water trickled out of the side and through the cow pasture. "That spring is the reason I chose this land. I knew I needed cold storage for my dairy products and meat, as well as fresh water for the livestock."

They didn't stop to view the springhouse, instead the group headed directly toward the barn and through the open door. Once inside, Erik set down Jacques.

The boy plopped on his bottom and banged his rocks together. "Ba. Baa!"

With the soaring ceiling, the barn looked bigger than the church in Sweetwater Springs. The smell of hay from the hayloft filled the room. Aside from the mules, Antonia didn't know much about livestock, nor had she been in many barns. But this one seemed well kept, with several empty stalls big enough to hold six cows each.

Even the tools lining one wall hung in a straight line, and the aisle was swept clean of debris. The place was as different as could be from the small shed that had housed their mules.

Antonia wondered if the mules were as unsettled by their new home as she was or if they enjoyed their new quarters. She lifted Camilla to her shoulder, pressed a kiss to the baby's downy head, and rubbed her back.

A fat tabby sat on a straw bale, watching them with alert green eyes.

Erik walked over to the cat and rubbed her head. "Eh, Delilah. Catch anything for me today?"

The cat tilted her head.

He scratched under her chin. "I think we'll have kittens, although we have to wait a bit. You'll like that, eh, Henri?"

The boy shrugged.

"Henri's never seen a barn cat," Antonia explained. "He only knows the big mountain cats—dangerous they be. But I recall kittens. Sweet little 'uns."

"They are. And plenty of folks looking for one. The kittens will go fast." Erik took them around, pointing out everything in great detail. He showed obvious pride in his barn and livestock. While he talked, he seemed to forget his sadness. His shoulders straightened, he gestured with his hands as he spoke, and his expression grew more enlivened.

Antonia studied him, seeing Erik as a *man*, not as a grieving widower, new father, or unwanted second husband. She saw the strength in his large frame, the light in his blue eyes when he discussed his plans for a dairy herd, and remembered the gentle way his work-worn hands had earlier cradled his daughter.

How would I be feelin' about Erik if I met him before Jean-Claude? Would I be drawn to him? Antonia thought perhaps she might have and, for a moment, wondered what their life together would have been like if they'd met and married when they were young.

Feeling disloyal, she turned away from the sight of him. With all the agony she was now experiencing, Antonia wouldn't trade the years with Jean-Claude, even if the price for the joy of that time was living in pain for the rest of her days.

CHAPTER THIRTEEN

For a few minutes, Erik had forgotten. His barn—only a year old—and the livestock within were his pride and joy. Seldom did he have visitors to show around the place. Antonia and Henri made the perfect audience, looking about with curious golden eyes and taking in everything. Their obvious awe of the place gave him a warm feeling of satisfaction.

They stopped at the stalls where the mules poked their heads over the doors.

With a flash of animation, Henri hurried over to the nearest mule, rubbing the nose, and murmuring what sounded like French.

The boy looks like he knows what he's doing, Erik thought in approval. *He's certainly old enough to have chores.* At about half his age, Erik and his brothers had started helping their father. "I've fed and watered the horses and mules but haven't had a chance to muck out the stalls yet."

Guilt stabbed him. He'd never neglected his livestock before. "It's been several days for the horses, actually. Perhaps you can help me with that, Henri?" He made his voice sound hearty. "Truth be told, I could use another hand around here."

The boy gave him a sideways glance but didn't answer.

Antonia briefly touched her son's shoulder before returning to rubbing Camilla's back. "Of course. He be a good worker." Although Antonia said the words to Erik, her gaze rested on her son. "Eh, Henri?"

"*Oui, Maman.*"

"Then we'll begin after I finish showing you around." Erik pointed toward a smaller door on the backside of the barn. "The pigsty is out there. And I want you to meet the cows in the pasture. I have twin calves. Born...born—"

The memory of that morning hit him like a mule kick to his gut. Walking to the house, feeling elated about the birth of the calves, not knowing that his wife had gone into labor. *If I'd been there when her pains first started, I could have bundled her into the wagon and rushed her to the doctor. My pride, my selfish neglect, caused her death.* The image of her laboring to push out the baby came to him, of the unstoppable blood, the light fading from her eyes...

His chest tightened until he couldn't breathe. *I need to get some air.*

"Erik?" Antonia shifted Camilla into the crook of one arm, stepped forward, and touched his shoulder.

Unable to bear any comfort, he pushed away her hand, turned, and jogged down the aisle, bursting out of the open doors. The bright sunshine was a shock to his watering eyes, and he had to blink back moisture to see. A wrenching ache clutched his gut, and all he could do was run from the pain.

Unthinking of where he was going, Erik hurried past the springhouse. He picked up speed, blindly racing along the pasture fence. He gulped for breath, trying to force air into his constricted lungs. But something else took up the space in his chest—something dark and heavy.

Without conscious volition, he moved toward Daisy's grave. In the distance, he saw the cross like a beacon and headed toward it.

At the edge of the mound, Erik's knees crumpled, and he threw himself down. A heavy sob broke through the constriction of his body and burst from his mouth. Sprawled across the grave, he dropped his head into the crook of his arm. Inhaling the smell of the newly dug earth, he wept.

* * *

Her hand still outstretched, Antonia watched Erik flee.

The cat leaped off the straw bale and followed him outside.

Camilla made a noise, as if sensing her father's obvious distress.

Her stomach tight, she lowered her arm to cradle the baby and rocked her, trying to recover from Erik's rebuff. His rejection of her attempt to comfort him stung, making Antonia wish she'd never reached out in the first place. *I already have enough pain, without feeling hurt by him, too.*

At the same time, Antonia was distressed by her strong reaction—so unlike her, especially when she knew all too well how grief grabbed one at the oddest moments. *And married or not, I'm a stranger to him.*

"Where be he going?" Henri asked.

Antonia stared after Erik. "I don't be knowin'." She thought through what had happened. Although she didn't know why the mention of the twin calves had caused him to become upset, she'd become familiar with how waves of sorrow crashed down without warning.

I probably be doin' the same thing, if he be tryin' to comfort me. But the matter-of-fact words didn't make her feel better.

"*Maman?*"

How to be explainin'? "Mr. Muth…ah, your new pa be sad. Camilla's mama—his wife, Daisy—died like *Père* did."

"We done bury her like you done with *Père* in the garden."

"Yes. Just as we be sad about *Père,* he be sad about Daisy."

"Will he cry?"

"Maybe. Or maybe he be trying not to cry."

"I be tryin' not to cry."

Antonia shifted Camilla, so she could rub Henri's head. "So do I. But maybe sometimes we be needin' to."

Henri glanced around the barn. "We could be muckin' up."

He's so thoughtful. Tears pricked Antonia's eyes. "You be a good boy, *mon fils.* You be doing *Père* credit." She stooped to kiss his forehead.

From his expression, Henri seemed pleased, but he squirmed away.

Straightening, she stood and looked around. Although in some ways the barn was an even greater contrast to the shed she'd left behind, Antonia felt more at home here than she did in Daisy's kitchen. Mucking up after animals was pretty much the same, no matter how fancy the surroundings.

Erik had stacked the small pile of possessions they hadn't brought into the house in the corner by the door. She'd left their homemade rake behind but brought Jean-Claude's store-bought shovel. She pointed to their things. "Find our shovel, and then be startin' with our mules. I be doin' the horses."

He retrieved the shovel.

"I be fetchin' the cradle for Camilla and bringin' Jacques and his rocks near. Then we start mucking up for your new pa." Just the thought of tackling the chores—something she could do for Erik—released the tightness in her chest.

* * *

Henri opened the stall door and propped the shovel in the corner. The mule nudged him. Although he felt a little guilty about having favorites, he loved Kenny better than Rocky and knew the mule loved him back. *Père* always said Rocky was as stubborn as a rock.

Feeling sad at the thought of *Père*, Henri hugged Kenny's neck as high as he could reach, inhaling the comforting smell of the mule's hide.

Kenny snuffled Henri's shoulder.

Feeling a little better, he led the mule out of the stall and tied him up in the aisle.

A shovel and rake hung on the wall, and *Maman* took them down, walked over to the nearest horse stall, and set the tools against the door. She checked on Camilla in her cradle, and then glanced through the door to where Jacques played with his rocks.

I be explorin' later and bringin' Jacques some more.

Henri glanced at the back door, remembering the muck-heap he'd seen outside. At home, they'd just shoveled and raked everything out of the shed and around the corner to pile near the garden. He looked at the clean concrete floor of the center aisle. Seemed like a long way.

He looked up at *Maman* and waved from the door to the floor of the stall. "How we be gittin' this out?"

Maman pursed her lips in the way that mean she was thinking. She walked down the aisle, her head turning back and forth, obviously looking for something.

Curious, he followed her.

"There." She pointed to a single-wheeled wooden cart, shaped like an arrowhead, tilted into the corner at the back of the barn. "A wheelbarrow."

Henri had never seen anything like it. At home, they'd heaped the droppings onto pine boughs and dragged them to the dung heap.

Maman walked over and stepped between wooden poles attached to the back, grasping them and lifting. She turned the wheelbarrow in his direction and pushed it toward him.

Fascinated, he watched the wheelbarrow come toward him, feeling some excitement break through the heaviness that had weighed in his chest since *Père* died.

The cart wobbled at first until *Maman* figured out how to balance properly. She set the back end down in front of Henri. "*This* we be usin'."

"Can I be tryin'?"

She nodded and moved to let him pass, and then tapped the poles. "Grab both these shafts and be liftin' 'em at the same time. Then be holdin' steady."

Henri stepped between the shafts and hefted the handles. The wheelbarrow was heavier than *Maman* made it look, and he could barely lift the back legs. He staggered several steps and the wheelbarrow wobbled.

With a clutch of fear, he wondered if it would tip to the side. He tried to compensate and the other side dipped. His arms grew tired, but, determined to make the wheelbarrow move where he wanted it to go, he didn't want to stop.

"Take's a mite of practice, it do," *Maman* said.

His muscles aching, breathing heavy, Henri pushed the wheelbarrow down the aisle, dropping it to a stop in the doorway of the barn. Triumph filled him. He glanced up at *Maman* and saw pride shining in her eyes.

"Well done."

Her expression and quiet words made him feel good, like he'd accomplished something for both of them.

Jacques, apparently entranced by the sight of the wheelbarrow, abandoned his rocks and crawled toward it.

In one of her gestures of affection, *Maman* rubbed the back of her hand against Henri's cheek. "The wheelbarrow be too heavy when it be full. So I be wheelin' out, and then you be drivin' back, *oui?*"

Jacques reached up for the edge of the wheelbarrow.

Maman made a grab for the handles so the baby could pull himself up without toppling the thing over on him.

Once Jacques reached his feet, he flashed them his *grenouille* grin and banged on the side of the wheelbarrow.

"Jacques be wantin' a ride."

"We start, he won't want to be stoppin'," *Maman* warned. "We be finishin' the work first. Then we can be puttin' some straw inside and givin' him a ride."

Henri hurried back to the stall, anxious to get finished so he and his brother could play.

❋ ❋ ❋

Erik trudged back to the barn, fighting the compulsion to turn and head in the other direction. He'd treated Antonia rudely—run out on her, allowed his emotions to rule him and make him weak.

A mourning dove perched on the barbed wire fence, the soft *ooo-ahhh croo-ooo-oo* sound so familiar he rarely paid attention. But today he glanced at the gray bird, fancying the mournful coo was a tribute to his grief for Daisy—even though he knew the bird was probably just calling to its mate.

He stopped and eyed the prairie—not his fenced-in pasture or the planted acreage, but the other direction—at the vast emptiness of the undulating grasslands, green with spring. He usually liked to think in terms of conquering this land—building a homestead that would last for generations.

Someday, he hoped his great-grandson would walk in his footsteps and feel a similar connection with this patch of earth.

But today, the wind rippling through the grass made him think of the ocean—the endless body of water that he would never see. *Cast adrift.* The nautical term came to his mind. He couldn't remember from where he knew it. *Moby-Dick,* perhaps? Or maybe *Twenty Thousand Leagues Under the Sea?* The library in his hometown had been quite extensive. Having plenty of books was one of the things he missed about living alone on the prairie. Not that Sweetwater Springs had a library, anyway.

The two words suited his mood, and he repeated them. *Cast adrift.*

Erik turned and looked toward his barn and his house—once his stalwart anchor—or so he'd assumed. Prior to Daisy's death, he'd always approached his home with a sense of wellbeing. He'd taken pride in his accomplishments—of carving a farm out of the raw prairie with his own back and hands.

But now, the dreams he'd woven about the place had turned to ashes. For he suspected, his wife, not his farm, had been his anchor.

Weeping at Daisy's gravesite had relaxed the tight band of sorrow around his chest. He took a deep breath, needing air in his lungs before he could once again begin to journey the rest of the way home.

As Erik walked, his legs felt wooden. Guilt alone spurred him on. He'd run out on Antonia and Henri, leaving them to think who-knows-what about him. He'd left the work undone….

The press of his responsibilities weighed on him. For the first time in his life, Erik wanted to turn and run away—just head out toward the horizon and never look back.

Just thinking such thoughts made him feel more guilt. He was a father, a husband, a farmer. His new family and his livestock depended on him. The usual routine of farm life, as backbreaking as the work could be, had always brought him a sense of stolid comfort. *I've certainly been a man who liked his routine.*

I wonder if I'll ever feel that way again.

Stopping by the springhouse, he crouched to splash water over his face and rinse his hands at the tiny stream rather than bothering with the pump at the well. He took the dipper from the hook on the wall and scooped up a long drink. Standing, he drank. Then he flung the rest of the water on the rosebush and rehung the dipper on the hook.

With a heavy breath, Erik headed to the barn. *I still have a lot of mucking out to do.* The thought made him tired. Seemed as if he'd been up for days, not only a few hours.

Just outside the door, the sound of clapping and a peal of laughter stopped him in his tracks. *What in tarnation?* He plunged into the gloom of the interior, and his eyes took a minute to adjust.

With a bent-kneed walk, Antonia headed down the aisle, pushing his wheelbarrow.

Jacques sat in the front on a pile of straw, holding on to each side, a wide smile on his face. He chortled, and then let out another gleeful shriek.

His mother kept the handles of wheelbarrow low, so the baby wouldn't tip, even though that angle must be punishing on her muscles.

Henri, too, looked almost happy. He bobbed up and down and clapped his hands.

Erik couldn't help feeling a flicker of their pleasure. Immediately, he chastised himself. *How could I possibly have any good feelings when Daisy lies cold in her grave?*

Antonia headed the wheelbarrow toward Erik.

For the first time, he saw her with a wide smile and a light in her golden eyes and was struck by the realization that another woman existed within her—different from the grief-stricken one he'd briefly gotten to know. *This* Antonia, although not classically beautiful, had a vibrancy and strength that was almost more appealing than beauty.

Feeling guilty, Erik suppressed the thought. *Guilt, guilt, guilt. Everywhere I turn, I feel guilty!*

When Antonia caught sight of him, she gasped and halted, setting down the wheelbarrow. She straightened, her shoulders stiffening, as if expecting a reprimand.

Instead, the reprimand came from her youngest son. "Maa!" Jacques protested. "Maa!" He banged on the side of the wheelbarrow.

Watching the light drain from their faces made Erik feel like an ogre. *Do they see me as a somber authority figure?* He didn't like the idea. Of course, he thought of himself as a serious-minded man. But he liked a laugh as much as anyone. He tried to remember the last time he'd laughed but failed. *But I smile a lot. Surely, I must.*

Antonia gestured to an open stall. "Camilla's in there in her cradle."

Erik made himself smile. "I'll bet my daughter wishes she were old enough to ride with Jacques," he said, striving for a joking tone.

Her shoulders relaxed. "You don't be mindin'?"

He rubbed a hand through his hair, vaguely wondering where his hat was. *Did I even put it on today?* "They are only boys. They need to have fun. Especially now."

"Thank you." The words sounded heartfelt.

"Felt good to see you all happier, even if just for a moment."

She let out a sigh. "Hard for them, this be. Yet, to laugh when their father be dead feels wrong." Her voice dropped. "Jean-Claude be always laughin'. Tellin' stories and makin' us laugh."

Envy stabbed him. His reaction took him by surprise. *Am I jealous of a dead man? Of a man who made his family happy?*

Erik didn't like the idea. A childhood memory came to him—his pa pushing him around the barnyard in the wheelbarrow when he was just a tyke. How he loved the feeling of flying. Even better, how good—special, even—he'd felt because his busy father had taken a few minutes to play with him. The memory made him smile at Henri. "How 'bout when I finish mucking out the stalls, I put you in the wheelbarrow and push you around? We'll go fast."

Henri's eyes widened with obvious pleasure, but his gazed darted back and forth between the two adults.

Antonia nodded at her son, her smile warm. A moment later, she turned that smile on him.

Something eased inside Erik. After all he'd done wrong in the last two days—mistakes that would haunt him all his life—he'd finally done something right. Maybe it wasn't much when stacked against his mistakes, but the feeling brought him a little comfort.

Antonia exchanged a conspiratorial look with Henri. "Perhaps, the chores be done, eh? Or the muckin' out at least be done."

He moved to peer into Shandy's stall. Sure enough, Erik saw clean straw on the floor. "Well, I'll be." He stepped back and gazed at Antonia in astonishment. "You did that?"

She motioned between her and Henri. "We done it."

His throat tightened, although this time not from grief. Mucking out was man's work. Or so Erik had always assumed. His ma and sister never labored in the barn. Course there was plenty of boys around for that—he, his three brothers, and his pa. And Ma and Kirsten had their hands full just keeping the family fed, much less all the other chores womenfolk were responsible for. Daisy had only fed and watered the livestock and milked the cows during the couple of times he'd been sick. But she'd never mucked out. He doubted the idea to do so would have even occurred to her.

"Thank you." Once Erik forced out the words, talking didn't seem so difficult. "That's a lot of hard work."

"I be not afeared of hard work, and the wheelbarrow be makin' the chores a real treat."

He couldn't imagine mucking out was any kind of treat. "Why don't we take the wheelbarrow into the yard where there's more space?" Without waiting for an answer, he leaned over and picked up Jacques. Before the boy could squawk about being taken from his ride, Erik lifted him high in the air.

Jacques squealed with laughter.

The boy's open-mouth grin went right to Erik's heart, planting the seeds of a father-son bond.

Antonia glanced into the stall at Camilla. "She be sleepin'."

"Then we'll leave her be for a few minutes." He hefted Jacques and cocked an eyebrow at Antonia. "Boy or wheelbarrow?"

"Well, you have my boy. I be takin' the wheelbarrow."

He tilted his head, motioning for her and Henri to precede him.

Antonia pushed the wheelbarrow out the door.

Henri followed, glancing over his shoulder at Erik and Jacques.

Once outside, out of habit, he looked at the sky. In the distance, pewter-gray clouds had built up. They'd have rain soon, hopefully light enough that he could still plow. He handed Jacques to his mother and stepped between the shafts. He grasped them firmly. "Climb aboard," he told the older boy.

Gingerly, Henri lifted his leg over the side of the wheelbarrow and scooted up and over the edge. Once he settled in the middle, he stuck his legs forward and grasped the sides.

"Here we go." Erik started at a walk, taking care to avoid running over any rocks. "You doing all right in there, Henri?"

The boy nodded.

Erik wished he could see the child's face. *Is he smiling?* "Want to go faster?"

"*Oui!*"

Erik picked up the pace.

"Faster!"

At his small stepson's command, Erik obliged, breaking into a run. He charged past the house and up the road a ways before slowing to catch his breath. *I've become an old man. I used to run for miles.* He thought with nostalgia about the boy he'd once been. *When did I become so staid?*

Henri twisted to look back at him. "Again!"

"Let me catch my breath, Mr. Impatient. Then you watch out."

Eyes bright, Henri gave an eager nod.

It did Erik's heart good to see the lively expression on the boy's face—to know he'd been the one to make the boy happy. He took a deep breath, preparing to break into a run. "Hold tight, now." He took off, racing as fast as he could, only slowing when he neared Antonia, who held Jacques in her arms.

She watched them with a sad smile on her face, her eyes bright with tears.

When they stopped, Erik tried to hide how out of breath he was.

"Did ya see me, *Maman*?"

"All the way." She sent Erik a grateful glance. "You made him smile. Such a gift for me to see."

"He made me smile, too," Erik admitted. "And, in these dark days, genuine smiles will probably be few and far between for us."

Jacques pointed at the wheelbarrow and squirmed to get down.

Antonia set him on his feet. But before the boy could drop to his knees, Erik scooped up Jacques and placed him in front of his brother. "Hold him tight now, Henri," he commanded. "We'll go slow."

Erik picked up the wheelbarrow and began to walk.

Jacques let out a squeal. "Baa!"

Erik winked at Antonia and angled the wheelbarrow toward the road, grateful for the temporary respite from mourning.

CHAPTER FOURTEEN

Two days later, the rain came in a gentle shower. Erik had borrowed Antonia's mules and chose to stay outside plowing the field. He wore a floppy-brimmed hat and a slicker to protect him from the worst of the wet, but she'd made him promise to stop if he became too chilled.

Inside the house, Antonia kept a fire burning in the stove, and the room, as big as it was, remained a comfortable temperature and didn't smell as smoky as she was used to. She'd forgotten how a stove was a more efficient way to heat a house than a fireplace.

She did a final rinse of Daisy's nightgown and the bedding that Mrs. Norton had soaked. Antonia had been too busy the previous day to tackle the chore. Once she'd wrung out the water, she laid them over the porch rail protected by the roof for later when the rain stopped and she could hang them on the clothesline.

The babies soon became tuckered out. She nursed Camilla until she was almost asleep and then placed her in the cradle.

Jacques was delighted to be allowed to nap on Erik's soft bed, and he quickly fell asleep.

Antonia placed pillows on both sides of his body so he wouldn't roll off, and then stood for a moment, watching him, love expanding her chest. She searched for Jean-Claude's features in his chubby face. But this sturdy son took after her side of the family. He had her father's build, as well as his bark-brown eyes, and the curl to his dark hair.

With a sigh, she returned to the other room and washed the breakfast dishes, while Henri dried, and then she unpacked her belongings and further explored the house. She stopped before the shelf of books and took one down. She'd never held a book before and reverently turned the pages, looking at the incomprehensible print and wishing she could understand the meaning of the words.

Henri drifted close to peer over her arm. "What's that?"

"A book. There be stories in here."

"*Père* told us stories."

"Aye, he did. And if we could write 'em, they'd be in a book like this. Other people could read 'em and learn his stories.

Henri's puzzled expression didn't clear.

"I cain't explain better. You need schoolin' to know what be here." She tapped the open page of the book. "I ain't never had none. But things gonna be different for you." *Now be a good time to tell him about school.* "You'll have chances I ain't had. You be goin' to school where you can learn to read and figure numbers. Tomorrow, you be startin'. Mr. Muth, um Pa, will drive you to town in the mornin' when he takes the milk and eggs to the store."

"Be you comin'?"

"No. Only children go to school."

He lifted his chin and crossed his arms. "Then I ain't goin'. I be stayin' with you and Jacques and Camilla."

"Oh, yes, you be goin'," Antonia said firmly to counteract her son's unusual display of stubbornness even though she longed to pull him into her arms for a reassuring hug.

Truth be told, she didn't know if she could bear to be parted from him, either. "You ain't growin' up like me, with no book learnin'. People put great store in education, and I ain't got none."

He hung his head.

Placing her hand under his chin, Antonia lifted his face until his gaze met hers. "Soon you be learnin' your letters, and then you be readin' this book to me." She put enthusiasm into her tone. "That be a fine treat, aye it be." She released his chin and ran the tip of her finger over some of the words in the book. "Just think, someday you be knowin' all these. I'll be right proud of you, Henri."

Before he could respond, a knock sounded at the door.

Startled, she replaced the book on the shelf and hurried to open the door. Just before Antonia reached for the handle, she glanced down at her Indian garb, and with a stab of embarrassment, wished she had time to change. Squaring her shoulders, she opened the door.

A woman with a dripping bonnet and damp coat stood there, clutching a big burlap package to her chest, the handle of a basket over her arm. Behind her, a mule was tied to the railing. The rain had let up to a sprinkle, so she must have ridden a ways to be so sodden.

"Land sakes!" Antonia exclaimed, astonished to have a female visitor. "Come in out of the wet." She stepped back and held open the door.

"Sure, and this is nothing. I grew up in Ireland, and we had our share of wet days," the woman said with a beautiful accent. "Although, when I was twelve, our family immigrated to Virginia—a much warmer climate."

"Go stand by the fire," Antonia ordered. She grabbed the hat rack by the door and moved it near the stove. "Hang your hat and coat to dry, and I'll find you a cloth to wipe yourself with."

She glanced at her son. "You be seein' to her mule, eh?"

Henri jerked a quick nod and scampered through the door.

Antonia walked over to close it behind him but stood a moment watching his actions to make sure he was comfortable with the mule.

Henri petted the mule's nose, before unwinding the reins and leading the animal toward the barn.

She closed the door. Feeling nervous about her very first *company*, Antonia hurried into the bedroom for a towel.

In his sleep, Jacques had moved from the middle of the bed to end up next to one of the pillows.

Antonia tugged him back into the center, checked on Camilla asleep in her cradle, and took Daisy's good towel from the trunk, grateful to have something nice to offer to the woman. She returned to the other room and handed it over.

"Thank you." The woman dabbed at her face. She had beautiful dark-red hair, with only a few threads of gray. Her brown woolen dress hung on her thin frame as if she'd recently lost weight. "You'll be thinking me foolish to venture out on such a day, and you'd be right. I'm Henrietta O'Donnell, and we are your nearest neighbors—thataway." She waved in the direction of Sweetwater Springs.

"Right pleased ta meet you."

"When the Nortons stopped by to tell Rory of Erik and Daisy...and you being a newcomer to these parts, why, I just had to come over and make you welcome." She picked up the basket from the table and handed it to Antonia. "Irish soda bread and oatmeal cookies. Fresh baked."

Flabbergasted, Antonia looked from the basket to Mrs. O'Donnell. "You came all this way in the rain for a visit?"

Henrietta laughed, giving animation to her face. "Oh, no. There wasn't a sign of rain when I left the house, else my dear Rory would have forbade the journey."

Since Jean-Claude had never forbidden her anything, she stiffened. The idea of Mr. O'Donnell telling his wife what-for didn't sit well with Antonia.

Her thoughts must have shown on her face for Mrs. O'Donnell patted Antonia's arm. "I've been quite ill, you see. Even though I'm on my feet and out and about—why, I'm just back yesterday from a visit to my daughter—my family worries about me. My husband's cossetting is driving me out of my mind."

"Be you dry enough, Mrs. O'Donnell? Your husband wouldn't be thankin' me if you come sick again."

"Call me Henrietta. Us being such close neighbors and all. My coat and hat bore the brunt of the wet, and with this nice heat from the stove, why, the rest of me will soon be as dry as toast."

Hoping her neighbor had judged rightly, Antonia glanced toward the pantry, thinking about its contents. "Can I be gittin' you something to eat? To drink?"

"A cup of tea would be lovely."

Tea? Antonia had a moment of panic. She'd brought some herbal teas with her. "I be havin' sassafras, chamomile, or mint. Is that what you mean?"

"No need to fret yourself." Henrietta pointed at the shelf near the stove. "China tea is in that blue tin canister. In fact, why don't you let me brew the tea for us? I imagine I'm more familiar with Daisy's kitchen than you are." Her voice caught.

Antonia saw the pain underlying the woman's friendliness. *Should I be pretendin' there be not a bear in the room, or shoot for the head?* But as much as she didn't want to talk about death and grief, she'd never been someone to shirk her duty or keep her tongue behind her teeth when plain speaking might be better. "Daisy's death be a powerful loss," she said in a quiet voice. "Suspect you'll miss her, eh?"

Henrietta's eyes filled with tears. "I couldn't believe the horrible news." She pulled a handkerchief from her sleeve and dabbed her eyes. "If only I'd been home. Maybe I could have helped."

Antonia recognized that kind of guilt. *How many times since the death of my man be I wishin' I'd a told him I'd a hankering for fish that day? He'd a headed a different direction and never come upon the grizzly.* "Daisy be awful tiny," Antonia offered, remembering when she paid a respectful visit to the body and from the size of her nightgown. "Don't know if even Doc Cameron could have saved her."

"I worried about her being so small-hipped. But I never said a word. I didn't want to put any fears in her head that she didn't already have. A woman has enough to worry over at such a time."

Antonia remembered birthing her boys and shivered. *A woman always fears dyin' when givin' birth.* "Would you like to see the babe?"

Henrietta gave her a tremulous smile. "I would, indeed." She pulled a handkerchief from her sleeve and dabbed her eyes before blowing her nose. "Dearie me. My daughter's with child, and I was so excited for the news and didn't allow myself to worry. But now...." She shook her head. "At least, living on the Thompson ranch, Sally's not isolated. Two other women live there, and plenty of men to fetch the doctor."

Antonia motioned for Henrietta to follow her into the other room and pointed at the cradle.

"Ah." The woman stooped to touch Camilla's hand. "So tiny. Sure and she's a perfect babe," Henrietta whispered. She placed a hand to her mouth, obviously overcome with grief.

Not knowing what to say, Antonia left the room to give the woman privacy. Sadness overwhelmed her, and she dropped into a chair, thinking about neighbors and friendships. Many people would carry the memory of Daisy. If he chose, Erik could speak with others who'd cared about her.

Only me and the boys be a mournin' Jean-Claude. Living isolated, moving every few years to follow the game...they didn't have friends, although Jean-Claude did try to visit the Indians at least once a summer, bringing gifts of game. She wondered what the tribe would think of his absence this year.

Antonia took a shuddering breath to control her feelings and stood, moving to take down the tea canister. When she pried open the lid, she peered inside to see small brown leaves that emitted an earthy scent and figured she could brew this the same way she did chamomile.

Footsteps sounded behind her, and she turned to see Henrietta enter the room.

The woman's eyes were red, but her face looked composed. "This will not be an easy time for you or Erik, Antonia... may I call you by your beautiful given name?"

She nodded.

"How may we help you two?" Henrietta walked over and took the canister from Antonia's hand, then moved to the stove. She briefly touched the side of the teakettle, gauging the warmth.

Watching her neighbor prepare tea, Antonia thought about the woman's question and couldn't come up with an answer. *Nothing can fix the pain this newly patched together family be sufferin'.*

Henrietta brought over cups on saucers and gave one to Antonia. She set the other on the table and took a seat. "Have a cookie. These are Rory's favorites. I had to leave half the batch at home, or I might never have gotten away from the house." She opened the cloth lining the basket to expose cookies ringed around the bread. She offered the basket to Antonia.

"These be a rare treat for me." Antonia took one and bit into it, savoring the sweet oat taste and remembering back. The last time she'd had cookies and pie was at her wedding to Jean-Claude. When she sipped the tea, the flavor lingered, delicate and fragrant.

In silence, the women drank their tea and finished a cookie.

Henrietta set down her teacup. "My dear Antonia, since we are to be neighbors, and, I hope, friends, I would like to be frank with you." She paused, obviously waiting for a response.

Not sure what to say, Antonia responded with a wary nod.

"Mrs. Norton gave Rory a quick recounting of your circumstances." Henrietta raised a hand to ward off a potential protest. "Not in a gossiping manner, you must believe. But because she knew that the more information we had, the more we could be of assistance."

Antonia took another sip of her tea.

Henrietta made an up-and-down gesture in Antonia's direction. "I know you had to buy a gown for your wedding. And I suspect you have no other dresses?" She made the comment a question. "And Mrs. Norton mentioned your son was dressed in Indian garb." She held up a hand. "Not in any critical way, mind you. If there's a woman who doesn't care about appearances it's Mary Norton. But she knew I might have a solution."

Ashamed, Antonia looked into her teacup, seeing the dregs of the leaves plastering the sides and bottom. "We have no other clothes."

"So I suspected. I'm sure you're used…as we are…to making do. Why, for Christmas, I made over an old silk dress from when I was young for my oldest daughter Sally. Served as her wedding dress as well."

Not sure where this conversation was headed, Antonia placed her teacup on the saucer.

Henrietta took a deep breath. "Well, I think there must be something we can do to alter Daisy's wardrobe to fit you." She wrinkled her nose. "Even if the colors that suited her won't show you in the best light."

Antonia didn't care about colors. Just having some work clothes so she wouldn't ruin her gold dress was enough for her.

"Now, I know for a fact Daisy had leftover material from one of her skirts, for she planned to make the baby—if it was a girl—some dresses from it. If we let out the side seams and attach that cloth to the hem—put some braid or tatting over the join…. You'll still have to buy a shirtwaist, though. Or the material to make one."

Henrietta made the idea of making over Daisy's skirt sound easy, and her neighbor might be right. Hemming and such, Antonia could do. But making a pattern and sewing a shirtwaist was beyond her experience.

"The two dresses she wore during her pregnancy will be plenty wide. Hopefully, there's enough at the shoulder seams to let them out. If we cut the sides, bringing in the waist, then we can piece those strips to the bottom. Course, they might still be a little short. But for house dresses, they should do the trick."

"Clever to think of such."

"Practical, dearie," Henrietta corrected. "With three daughters and little money for clothing, I've learned to make do. I've another idea. Daisy was not the only small woman in Sweetwater Springs. Maybe you can sell or trade her clothing to another woman in exchange for money or material. Or maybe even to Mrs. Cobb at the mercantile, although you won't get as good of a price from her."

Antonia sat back in her chair. "I never be thinkin' of such a solution."

Henrietta beamed. "You let me handle the matter. The next time I'm at church, I'll approach some of the women I think might be interested." She pursed her mouth for a tad of time. "Mrs. Gordon, the schoolteacher, comes to mind. But then again, she seems to prefer wearing gray or green."

"But would Erik mind?"

Henrietta shrugged. "I doubt he'll care if *you* use the dresses, although he might mind someone else doing so. If that's the case, then we won't do it." She glanced out the window. "There's still time for me to help you get started on altering one.

Antonia gazed at her. "Why, you be like a whirlwind."

Henrietta laughed and made a twirling motion with her forefinger. "This fills me with energy. I was sick for far too long, and I've missed my daughter so. Sally married at New Year's and moved to the Thompson ranch.... I must confess to moping, although I've tried to hide my low spirits from my family. So this project is perking me right up."

This is what it's like to have neighbors. A warm feeling settled in her stomach. The idea that she might be aiding Henrietta as much as the woman was helping her appealed to Antonia.

Her neighbor waved toward the bundle she'd left on the chair. "I brought my son Charlie's old clothes from when he was your boy's age. Charlie's thirteen now."

Such generosity. Antonia gaped at the woman before catching herself and offering her thanks.

Shaking her head, Henrietta waved away her appreciation. "Might as well put them to good use. They've sat useless in a box for too many years."

"Henri can be wearin' them to school and church."

"You probably wonder why I've held onto Charlie's clothes for so long, instead of doing something useful with them." Henrietta glanced away, swallowed and looked back. "We had another son, who I thought would grow into them, but Paddy didn't live past his fifth birthday, and then I'd hoped we might have another boy. But Paddy was the last…"

"I be sorry," Antonia said, knowing the pain of losing a child aches in a mother's heart for all her lifelong days.

Her neighbor sniffed and pulled out her handkerchief again, blowing her nose. "This is certainly a day for sorrow, isn't it?" She tucked her handkerchief back into her cuff. "Mourning is such an odd experience—crying one moment, laughing the next, and then crying again. Ah, lass, the changes life brings."

"My boy starts school tomorrow." Antonia heard the uncertainty in her voice as she spoke of the change to come in her life. "I want him to go, yet—"

"You don't know if you can let him out of your sight for so long." Henrietta finished Antonia's sentence for her. "Why, I had the hardest time sending Sally off to school on her first day." She smiled, as if remembering. "A milestone, it is, but I cried, nevertheless."

Antonia didn't know what a milestone was, but she wasn't about to interrupt and ask.

"Our young children stay with us all day, every day, unless they are with their father for a while. We are rarely parted from them. Then, all of a sudden, we send them off to town for most of the week. I certainly missed Sally. Worried about her. I had an easier time with Charlie, because I knew what to expect. Also I didn't have to fret because I knew Sally would take care of him. But I found letting go of my twins was hard, for I was all alone without my children at home. Then, saints be praised, I came to enjoy doing my work without them underfoot. Sure and I do like having a little time for myself."

"Did Sally walk to school and back by herself?"

"The first three days, I insisted her father take her behind him on the mule and go and pick her up, too. But after that, she walked. Course, town isn't as far for us as it is for you."

"It still be a far piece. And I fret about him being alone...."

"Why, he won't be alone, Antonia!" Henrietta exclaimed. "Or least not longer than from here to our place. Charlie and my twins will walk with him."

Gratitude rushed through her. In that moment, Antonia knew she'd been wrong to believe nothing the O'Donnells could offer would diminish her family's pain. She'd never known how grief shared, assistance offered, could bring comfort. *How could I be knowin'? I never had no neighbors afore. Visitin' the tribe wasn't the same as havin' someone be livin' close.*

With a sense of wonder, Antonia glimpsed a whole new future spreading out in front of her, the possibilities as vast as the blue sky over the prairie—living as part of a close-knit community. On the day of her arrival in Sweetwater Springs, she'd been too numb, too frightened, to fully appreciate what the Nortons, Camerons, and Carters had done for her—for all of them. Now she could see how much their help had aided her—probably Erik as well.

With sudden longing she wished Jean-Claude could be here with her. *We be experiencin' this together.*

But even as Antonia thought the words, she realized such a future could never have been. Her husband had thrived in the solitude of the wilderness—in exploring new territory and doing for himself. For the last couple of years, he'd chafed at living so long in one place, even as he'd recognized the need to do so. But he'd intended to uproot the family once the winter had passed.

With sadness, she remembered how a few weeks before his death they'd argued about leaving. She'd longed for roots and an education for her children, but Jean-Claude wanted new hunting grounds, planning to move even farther away from Sweetwater Springs. *And I would have gone along with him.*

If Jean-Claude had lived, I never be findin' this kind of settled life, never realized what I be missin' or the cost to my children.

Antonia felt a pang of betrayal to think of her husband with complaint…to wonder if she'd have become dissatisfied with their way of life or even worse, with her husband. She thought of the dream she'd woken from this morning, of Jean-Claude in the meadow. How she'd thrown herself into his arms. *Be it really only a few days ago?*

Now, if Jean-Claude appeared, alive and well, and held out a hand, would I go to him? The thought that she might reject her beloved husband made Antonia's heart ache.

❋ ❋ ❋

The next morning as dawn was breaking, Erik drove the wagon to town. He was tired from not sleeping well, but he was determined to start his stepson at school.

Henri huddled next to him, dressed in Charlie's clothes and too-big cap, which tipped low on his forehead. He held Erik's old slate in his gloved hands.

This early, the air was chilly, and one of Antonia's bear-skins was spread over them—far more efficient for keeping warm than a woolen blanket. In the back, Erik had piled straw to support the cans of milk—though they often clanked together—and a basket of eggs for the mercantile, and Henri's lunch pail, as well as to provide some cushioning for the O'Donnell children they'd be picking up this morning. He'd tucked a blanket back there for them as well.

The pale rays of sunrise lightened the purple dawn shadows. The dew lay heavily on the prairie, sending up the scent of green grass and shy wildflowers. A wren almost hidden in a thicket broke off its song as they passed.

So far neither man nor boy had uttered a word.

Henri slumped in his seat, his body speaking of his utter dejection at the prospect of attending school.

With each creak of the wagon wheels, Erik grew guiltier. He kept arguing with himself that he was doing the right thing in taking Henri to school today. The boy was already far behind others his age, and only a few months were left in the term before summer vacation. Plus, attending school would go a far ways to helping Henri adjust to his new life.

But still, like a flea-bitten dog chasing its tail, Erik's doubts skittered around his mind. After all, the boy had just lost his Pa and been uprooted from all he knew. *Should I have taken him away from his mother so soon?*

From time to time, Erik eyed Henri, feeling prompted to impart some sage advice. But, truth be told, he didn't know what he could say to make the first day of school easier for the child. *Once he makes friends, everything will be different.*

But will such a quiet boy be able to do so?

A man with three brothers should know tips for teaching a boy how to make friends. The best Erik could come up with was to pick a fight. He imagined telling Henri, *"You pummel each other and roll around in the dirt. You'll forget what caused the argument in the first place and become the best of friends."* After all, that's how he'd acquired his childhood sidekick, Tom.

No, that isn't the best advice.

When Erik was Henri's age, he had a gang of friends, which included his brothers. They didn't have much playtime—just before and after school and during recess—or sometimes when chores were done. He remembered sailing bark boats on the pond, games of tag, hide-and-seek, or cowboys and Indians. They teased and argued and played tricks on one another.

Happy memories. Thinking about his childhood made Erik's lips curve, yet sadness weighed heavy in his belly. He'd left his gang and his family behind when he'd come to Montana, determined to homestead his own land, to forge his success. Once Daisy had arrived, he hadn't given much thought to his family and friends. Farmwork kept him too busy and tired to mull over old memories and wonder what everyone was up to now.

Sometimes, letters from his mother mentioned the news of his friends. Except for Tom who'd joined the army, everyone else had settled nearby, some on their parents' farms.

When Erik had thought of his old friends, he nurtured a vision of a triumphant return home to brag—in a modest way—about his life. Daisy and their passel of children would travel with him—a goal his wife shared. She, too, looked forward to flaunting their success before their hometown. He'd just wanted to visit with the people he cared about.

Abruptly, Erik realized he had to write to his parents about Daisy's death and that they now had a new granddaughter *and* a new daughter-in-law. But even worse, he had to write to *Daisy's* parents.

Remorse filled him, thinking of their pain and grief when they learned of the loss of their treasured only daughter. They'd never forgiven Erik for leaving Indiana in the first place, because they hadn't wanted Daisy to follow him.

When she became pregnant, his wife had wanted to return home until after the baby was born. Her parents had money and a servant girl for the house. Daisy wouldn't have to do any chores and would be cossetted through her whole pregnancy.

Erik hadn't let her go, insisting he would take care of her and that he wanted to be there when his baby came into the world. Secretly, he feared she might not return after she'd become reacquainted with the relative luxury of her parent's home. He'd known she'd sometimes found the work of a farm wife more than she could—or wanted to—handle, and he'd taken on as many of her duties as he could manage.

Doubtless her family would blame him for her death—*not that they'd be wrong.*

With dawning horror, Erik realized that if he hadn't married Antonia, he would have been faced with Daisy's formidable mother arriving to take care of Camilla. Maybe she'd even force him to let her take the child back with her to Indiana. *When I write to them tonight, I need to stress that Antonia is nursing Camilla, and the baby is thriving in her care.*

In the distance, the O'Donnell farm grew bigger. Like his place, the house was set well back from the road, and he saw the three children trudging down the mule track to meet him. They'd probably reach the road before he arrived, but Erik had arranged with Henrietta for them to keep on walking toward town. He'd pick them up whenever he caught up with them.

The memory of his encounter with Henrietta O'Donnell yesterday banished any lingering panic about his in-laws. He'd walked in on Antonia and Henrietta engrossed in altering one of Daisy's dresses, which they'd spread out on the table.

After his initial surprise, Erik had accepted his neighbor's condolences and agreed with her idea of making over some of Daisy's clothes for his new wife. He'd put his foot down, though, on the idea of bartering clothing. He didn't need to unexpectedly come face-to-face with a woman wearing one of Daisy's dresses. *Perish the thought!*

After the women were through, he'd sent Henrietta home with some hens to replace the ones that had disappeared—hopefully, not stolen by Indians—and in appreciation for her help with his new wife's and stepson's wardrobes. He'd also filled her basket with some eggs and one of the Nortons' jam jars.

Truth be told, he was relieved Henrietta had accepted Antonia, and the two looked to be starting a firm friendship. His new wife needed the support and guidance of other women, and he was glad to see his neighbor looking in far better health than Henrietta had been since she took ill.

When the wagon reached the children, Erik pulled up, setting the brake.

The O'Donnell siblings were dressed warmly in shabby coats, scarves, hats, and gloves, and carried their books and slates.

"Good morning, Charlie, girls." Erik didn't say the twins' names because he could never tell the two apart. The identical ten-year-olds had their father's navy-blue eyes and dark hair, as did thirteen-year-old Charlie and Sally, their older sister who'd gotten married.

"Hello, Mr. Muth." Charlie grinned. "Thanks for the ride." He gave Henri a short salute. "Howdy, Henri."

The boy mumbled a hello.

"You probably know I'm Charlie." He tugged on the nearest girl's braid, lifting the end to show the blue ribbon. "This is Idelle. Her color is blue."

Idelle grimaced and elbowed him.

With a cheeky grin, Charlie released her and pointed at the other girl. "Isleen has the green ribbons. Don't worry. I won't let them switch colors on you. We all promised Ma we'd be friendlylike."

Knowing Charlie was a talker, Erik cut short the introductions. "Into the back you all go. And cover yourselves with the blanket."

"A ride under a blanket instead of a long, cold walk? Boy, are we lucky." Charlie flashed him a grin and set his schoolbooks over the side of the wagon. The girls did the same with theirs.

Once the children had clambered aboard, Erik released the brake. Then he hesitated. "Would you like to ride in the back?" he asked Henri.

The boy shook his head.

Maybe he will tomorrow. Erik flicked the reins, and the horses started up. They traveled the rest of the way to Sweetwater Springs listening to Charlie's constant chatter.

When they reached the town, they drove past children walking or riding to school. From the back of the wagon, Charlie called out greetings.

Henri shrank down under the fur as if he wanted to hide, although his gaze darted around, taking in the sights of the town.

The boy had probably been overwhelmed when he'd arrived here after his father's death and hadn't noticed much.

Even this early, men were hard at work on a nearby office building and farther down the street on the banker's new hotel going up near the railroad station. A breeze blew the smell of sawdust their way, and the sounds of sawing and hammering rang through the air.

Erik pulled up before the school, set the brake, and tied off the reins, taking the fur off of them.

Charlie launched himself over the side, grabbed his things, and called, "See you later, Henri," and tore up the steps of the school.

"Here you are, Henri." Erik tried to make his tone hearty but suspected he fell flat. After checking to make sure the O'Donnell twins were out of the back and headed toward the school steps, he walked around the wagon to escort Henri to meet the teacher. They'd arrived early enough that she hadn't yet appeared on the steps to ring the bell.

Henri's eyes widened, and he pointed behind Erik.

He turned to see the Thompson children riding their horses, while their mother, Samantha, drove a tiny buggy pulled by a pair of her midget horses from Argentina that had some fancy Spanish name. One was brown with a black mane, and the other gray.

Erik had seen the miniature horses once before and was just as taken by the little critters this time around. He glanced down to see his stepson's reaction and was equally taken by the wondering expression on Henri's face. He looked from the boy to the equipage and had an idea.

Taking a breath, he girded himself to go over and speak to the wife of one of the richest ranchers around—someone, like John and Pamela Carter, whom he'd barely said "good-day" to before. But if doing so would ease Henri's passage into school, he'd put himself forward.

He tilted his head in the direction of the Thompsons. "Come on. Let's go meet the little horses. Maybe Mrs. Thompson will allow you to pet them."

The eager expression on Henri's face spurred Erik forward, the boy walking at his side.

Mrs. Thompson, a beautiful redhead with sky-blue eyes, set the brake of the buggy and glanced from him to Henri.

On the verge of introducing his stepson, Erik hesitated. He doubted word of Daisy's death and his remarriage had traveled as far as the Thompson ranch. *How do I explain?* Dread filled him as he realized this probably wouldn't be the first awkward introduction he'd have to make.

Mrs. Thompson leaned forward, her gaze intent. "The children brought the tragic news home with them. I'm very sorry for your loss, Mr. Muth. So shocking. Why, I'd just spoken to your wife at the ice cream social."

"Thank you," he mumbled, not sure what to say.

Her gaze traveled to Henri, who'd drifted closer to the small horses. "My Falabellas have been known to work magic on children who are hurting," she said to Erik before shooting a quick glance toward the schoolhouse, then back to him. "I believe there's time." She shifted, grabbing the side of the buggy.

Erik extended a hand to help Mrs. Thompson out.

Her youngest son rode over to them. Daniel Rodriguez Thompson, who looked to be about eleven, had the golden skin and dark hair of his Argentine father, but his eyes were the same blue as his mother's. "Hiya, Idelle," he called to the twin remaining outside. He saw Henri and raised his slanted eyebrows. "Who are you?" he bluntly asked, his curiosity obvious. Without waiting for an answer, he dismounted. "I've never seen you before."

Appearing shy at the older boy's attention, Henri ducked his head and didn't answer.

Erik lowered a hand to his stepson's shoulder. "This is Henri Valleau. Henri Valleau *Muth*," he said, making a spontaneous decision to add his name to the boy's in the same way Wyatt Thompson had branded Samantha Rodriguez's sons as his own when he married her—including the three adopted ones. "This is his first day of school, and he doesn't know anyone."

Daniel bounced on his toes, the motion making him appear not much older than Henri. "Not anymore. Now he knows me, don't ya, Henri?"

"He's shy, too," Erik quickly added, not wanting Daniel to be discouraged by Henri's silence.

Daniel's mother extended the reins of the buggy to her son. "Why don't you take Henri for a quick ride so he can become acquainted with Chico and Mariposa? Just to the train station and back, mind you." She glanced at Erik. "If that's all right?"

"More than all right," he assured her, feeling an enormous sense of gratitude. He'd only hoped for Henri to be allowed to pet one of the little horses. Falabellas, he corrected himself. He held out a hand to his stepson. "I'll hold your lunch pail and slate."

"Come on, Henri!" Daniel handed the reins of his mount to his mother and climbed into the buggy, sliding over to make room for Henri.

With a quick smile at Daniel, Henri lost no time in crawling in next to the older boy.

Daniel flicked the reins, and the Falabellas took off at a trot.

Erik watched them for a ways before turning to Mrs. Thompson. "I'm mighty grateful for your kindness and that of your boy. In the last few days, I've rarely seen Henri smile much and decidedly not at *all* this morning. He's never been to school before."

Mrs. Thompson, too, stared after the buggy. "Poor boy. His life has been upended." She gave Erik a determined glance. "I'm certainly glad I drove in with Daniel today. I'd heard Mack Taylor has a litter of puppies at the livery stable, and I've come to pick out one for my children, especially

Christine. Our other dog is so old, and I don't think she's going to make it much longer."

Erik thought back to losing his dog—watching the animal grow old and struggle to move. The pain of the old boy's death, the shadow that walked at his heels for days…. "I know how that feels."

"It's not fair that our dogs don't have longer lives. When I get to heaven, I intend to scold God for that."

Erik couldn't help but smile at the picture her words made, even if she sounded somewhat sacrilegious. "St. Peter might not let you through the pearly gates."

Her eyes twinkled. "Guess I'll have to hide my intentions better from the Almighty beforehand." She glanced back at the boys and smiled. "Look, Henri is driving."

Erik squinted over the distance and almost didn't recognize his stepson, for Henri's eyes sparkled and a spirited expression transformed his previously wooden countenance.

As she watched them, Mrs. Thompson's expression saddened. "Daniel was about Henri's age when his father died. Such a dark, difficult time for us." She hesitated and touched Erik's arm. "What I'm about to say isn't to hurry you through your grief, as some—no *many*—will try to do. For I know all too well how mourning has its own seasons, and the winter of sorrow can feel interminable. But I want to give you hope…that happiness and love can await you on the other side—in the springtime, to continue the metaphor."

Erik wasn't sure his winter would ever end. But with both hands, he grasped the hope Mrs. Thompson offered, for he and Antonia, as well as their children, deserved the arrival of spring. "Thank you for…" His throat closed, and he couldn't finish the words.

Daniel pulled the buggy to a stop in front of them, a grin on his face, eyebrows riding high.

Henri leaned toward Erik. "Did you see me drive, P-Pa?" he asked in an excited tone.

This is the first time the boy has spoken directly to me. The first time he's called me Pa. Magical miniature horses, indeed.

Touched, Erik wished he had a wagonload of money, so he could afford to buy Henri a Falabella. But such an indulgence was beyond his means. He had a loan to repay and a family to raise. "I did see you. You did a fine job, son. A fine job, indeed."

From behind him, a clanging sound jolted Erik. He turned to see Mrs. Gordon on the steps, gray gown billowing in the breeze. Bell in hand, she summoned her students.

Erik held out his hand for the reins of Daniel's horse. "I'll take him to the livery for you. We can't have Daniel being late after he's befriended Henri."

With a quick smile, Mrs. Thompson placed the reins in his hand.

Erik tied them on the hitching rail.

Mrs. Thompson hurried to Daniel's side of the buggy and took the reins from him, while the boys climbed out. She waved good-bye before taking a seat.

Erik waved back, more of a salute really, wanting the gesture to acknowledge the woman's kindness. Lowering an arm to Henri's shoulder, he steered the boy toward the schoolhouse.

Daniel fell into step on Henri's other side. "You'll sit with Tony Barrett and Luke Salter. They're your age." He scrunched a face. "And the girls. Lizzy Carter and Krista Swensen."

When they reached the steps, Daniel dashed inside. "Talk to you at recess, Henri," he called over his shoulder. "I'll introduce you to everyone."

Erik paused at the foot of the stairs to make eye contact with the teacher.

Mrs. Gordon was a brown-haired woman about Daisy's height. The schoolmarm was married to a man even taller than Erik—a relative newcomer to Sweetwater Springs, who now owned the newspaper and the new office building going up.

Rather than climb the steps to tower over her, Erik stayed where he was. "Good morning, ma'am."

"Good morning, Mr. Muth. I see you've brought me a new pupil."

"This is my stepson, Henri Valleau Muth. He's never been to school before, so he's starting from scratch."

Mrs. Gordon had big gray eyes, which now brimmed with compassion. "I'd like to express my condolences on the loss of your wife." She looked down at the boy. "And to you, as well, Henri, on the death of your father."

The bad news certainly has traveled fast. "Thank you, ma'am. We are dealing as best we can."

"I'm sure you are, Mr. Muth." She gestured to Henri. "Come inside, and I'll make sure you're settled."

Erik stooped to look Henri in the eyes. "You mind your teacher, now."

Henri gazed at him, his wooden expression returning.

"School won't be so bad. You'll see," Erik said in an encouraging tone. "And you've already made new friends with Daniel, Charlie, and the twins. When you get home, you can tell *Maman* how you drove the little horses. Just think how she'll want to hear all about that, and everything else you do at school as well!"

Henri's lips quivered into a tiny smile.

"Good boy." Erik gave him a brief squeeze around his shoulders and walked toward Daniel's horse, surprised by a surge of emotion. *I feel as though I've become attached to that boy—like a father.*

Erik glanced at the mercantile, thinking through the list of what he had to buy. Impulsively, he decided to purchase some candy as a treat for Antonia and Henri. Then, after he dropped off the milk and eggs and did his shopping, he'd have the far less pleasurable task of driving to O'Reilly's carpenter shop to pay for Daisy's casket.

His gaze drifted toward the livery, his first stop to drop off Daniel's horse. Remembering Mrs. Thompson's errand to get a puppy, Erik made another spontaneous decision.

CHAPTER FIFTEEN

The inside of the schoolhouse, which seemed to Henri to be almost as big as the church and his new pa's barn, was packed with more people then he'd ever seen in his life. The sound of voices filled the room and buzzed in his ears.

Mrs. Gordon directed him to hang up his coat on a peg by the door.

Henri stuffed his mittens into the pocket, draped his scarf over the top, and then his cap. He set his lunch pail on a shelf with everyone else's and took his slate with him.

When he turned, Henri saw rows of tables and stopped moving, wishing he didn't have to go any farther into the room, that he could go home. Just then he didn't care where home was, Henri just wanted *Maman*.

He glanced at a shelf holding more books than Pa had. *I'll learn to read those books for* Maman. He curled his toes in Charlie's hard leather shoes lest his feet take him out the door.

Mrs. Gordon patted Henri on the shoulder. "The students are arranged by age. The youngest sit at the tables in the front and the oldest in the back."

The noise of the room stilled as the children turned to look at him.

Many of the students had lighter skin, as well as hair and eye colors he'd never seen in children before. He would have wanted to look his fill at them. Instead, feeling like a mouse eyed by a flock of hawks, Henri took a step back, only to be constrained by the teacher's hand on his shoulder.

"Don't worry," Mrs. Gordon said in a cheerful voice. "You aren't the only newcomer." She gestured to a boy sitting in the middle of the room who looked to be Daniel's age. "Micah Norton arrived here from Africa not too long ago."

Micah must have heard his name for he glanced over, the expression on his face sullen.

His vivid blue eyes made him seem familiar, but Henri knew he'd never seen the boy before. *Norton, like Reverend Norton? He must not want to be here any more than I do.* Somehow, the thought of a fellow sufferer made him feel better.

Mrs. Gordon patted his shoulder. "And my own niece, Natalia Stevens, is paying us a visit."

Henri wasn't sure what a *niece* was.

"Since Natalia plans to be a teacher, she is assisting me with my pupils." She waved to a young brown-haired woman who was tying a ribbon on a little girl's braid. "Come here, Natalia, and meet Henri Valleau Muth."

Natalia wove through the tables to them, smiling at each child she passed. She wore a dress almost the color of the flowers *Maman* held when she married Pa and that they threw into Daisy's grave. She had a friendly, freckled face and the same gray eyes as his teacher.

The smile Natalia gave him eased some of the tightness in his belly.

"Natalia, dear. Will you take Henri to the end of that table there? Once we finish the pledge and prayers, I'd like you to start teaching him the alphabet as far as he can go by lunchtime. Uppercase letters only. He can use his slate."

"Yes, ma'am." Natalia beckoned for Henri to follow her.

When Henri hefted his slate, the chalk and a piece of cloth tied to a string through a hole in the bottom swung free. He made a grab for them. Pa told Henri to loosen the chalk once he was at his desk and tie it back up again before going home so he wouldn't lose it.

Last night, Pa had showed him how to use the chalk to scratch marks on the slate. He would have liked to draw more, but Pa said he had to take a bath in the tub and go to bed.

Remembering that unpleasant experience—especially how the soap stung his eyes—made Henri wrinkle his nose. *I hope I never have to take a bath again.*

Natalia patted the end of the table. "I sit here when I study with a pupil. Take a seat while I obtain a primer."

What's a primer? Henry slid onto the bench. He laid his slate and the piece of chalk on the desk in front of him.

She walked over to the shelf of books, selected one, and returned to the table. She set the book on top and patted the cover in obvious affection. "Battered old thing. This primer's been used to teach a lot of children."

When Natalia sat next to him, Henri caught a whiff of something sweet. *She looks and smells like a flower.*

Mrs. Gordon walked to the front of the room. "Good morning, students."

"Good morning, Mrs. Gordon," everyone chorused.

The teacher waved in their direction. "I'd like to welcome another newcomer to Sweetwater Springs, Henri Valleau Muth." She smiled at Micah Norton. "Isn't it so exciting to make new friends?" Her gaze swept the room. "I know you all will extend a warm welcome to Henri."

Natalia whispered to Henri what he needed to do. Bow his head for prayers, and hold his hand over his heart for the Pledge of Allegiance.

The children all recited the prayer and pledge together, the words filling the room in a rolling beat that reminded him of the rhythm of Indian drums. The sound thrummed in his ears. Henri followed along as best he could, although most of what they said didn't make sense.

Afterward, Mrs. Gordon gave directions to the students.

"Never mind her," Natalia said in a low voice. "Just listen to me." She picked up his slate and the chalk. "First, we will learn an *A*. Watch me make it. Up one side and down the other." As Natalia talked, she drew two slanted lines, with another in the middle. "Now you try." She handed him the chalk.

Henri imitated what he'd seen her do, making an *A*, which looked similar to hers.

Natalia shot him a look of astonishment. "Very good, Henri. I thought you didn't know your alphabet."

For the first time, Henri had a good feeling about school. He pointed to the letter. "Shaped like a teepee, it be. Or an arrowhead."

"Why, Henri, I do believe you're right. I've never seen a teepee or an arrowhead, only had them described to me. Quite an interesting observation. I wonder if any of the other letters will evoke images for you."

Why does she have to use such big words?

Natalia motioned to the slate. "Go on, make some more until you fill up the whole slate."

Henri bent to his task. Engrossed in learning, he didn't notice the morning speeding by.

Mrs. Gordon clapped her hands. "Lunch time. Enjoy your recess."

The room, which had been silent except for the sound of the teacher's voice and a student answering her question, erupted into noise as the pupils surged from their seats.

"Just wait a minute for the herd to pass," Natalia said. "You did bring lunch?"

"Ha," Henri laughed. "They be not *cattle*."

Natalia laughed, too. "You're right. However, you're supposed to say, 'they *are* not cattle,' not 'they *be* not cattle.' Now repeat after me. 'They *are* not cattle.'"

"They are not cattle," Henri echoed, the sentence sounding strange to his ears. *They are not cattle,* he repeated to himself.

"Take your food outside. You'll have time to eat and play awhile. When you hear the bell, come back in. You've done well on your letters. I'm going to advise my aunt that we switch to numbers for the afternoon."

Right then, Henri became aware of hunger pinching his belly. Although reluctant to leave Natalia and join the herd, as she'd called them, he wanted to eat. His lunch pail was the second to last on the shelf. He grabbed the handle and trotted out the door and down the steps.

At the bottom, Henri came face-to-face with two smaller girls who were holding hands. One had braided hair the color of the sun and wore a dress that reminded him of sage leaves. She studied him with eyes as blue as a robin's egg.

Fascinated by her coloring, Henri stared back, wishing he could touch her cheek to see if the pale skin felt as soft as Camilla's. But he didn't know her and wasn't sure if he should do such a daring thing.

The sunny-haired girl was the first to speak. "I'm Krista Swensen, and this is Lizzy Carter."

Carter? He looked at the other girl.

Lizzy shrank closer to Krista. A ribbon the color of the sky at dusk was tied around her head, matching her eyes and dress and holding back her flowing brown hair. She peeked up at him through long eyelashes, gave a tiny smile, and then slid her gaze away.

Like Micah, Lizzy seemed familiar to him, although this time he knew why. Henri wondered if he should say something, but he didn't know what.

"Come on, Henri," Daniel yelled, running past him with a smack on the shoulder. "We're gunna play ringer. You can watch and learn how."

Bewildered, Henri stared after him.

Most of the girls sat at a long table under the thick branches of a huge oak. He saw the O'Donnell twins on the end.

The boys ate as they walked, heading to an open area on the other side of the tree.

Henri couldn't see the reason for their direction, for only some thin boards and long sticks lay on the ground, but he followed them anyway.

One of the older boys stopped and eyed him. "*Henri*. Frenchified name. Can't you go by a good ole American one?" His lip curled.

The boy was almost the size of *Père*. The look in the boy's brown eyes reminded Henri of a badger they'd once trapped that spit and snarled at them before *Père* killed it.

"Heard your ma dresses like a squaw."

Another boy, about the same size but with the dark skin and hair of an Indian yet wearing the same type of clothing as the other students, shot Henri a slight smile and nodded before shoving the first one on the shoulder. "Leave him be, Ben."

"Why should I do what you say, Injun?"

Seeing the Indian boy made Henri feel better. He hadn't forgotten his Blackfoot friends, even though he and *Père* and *Maman* hadn't visited the tribe since long before Jacques was born.

The Indian boy didn't say anything, merely raised an eyebrow and cocked a fist.

A third one about their age approached. "Knock it off, Ben and Hunter, or recess will be over by the time we get started." He spoke the words in a calm tone of command.

Seeing his blue eyes and hearing the way the third boy spoke made Henri realize he must be a Carter, for he sounded just like his father.

Without waiting for a response, the Carter boy picked up a narrow board, scraping the edge across the dirt until he made a clear, flat space. Then he tossed it down and chose a stick, drawing a large circle on the ground. When he finished, he made a line under the bottom of the circle and another one across the top. He threw the stick next to the piece of wood and pointed at a thin boy with hair the color of carrots. "Matthew, you won last time, so you lag first."

Matthew extended his hand to show a small green ball made of glass. "Better watch out. I've made a special wish on my marble here. You all might never have a chance to play."

Henri edged closer to see the marble.

Ben pulled out a red-and-white one from his pocket. "You should make a special wish, Matthew, seeing as you Salters only have three marbles between the four of you." He tossed his into the air, and then snatched it. "We're playing for keeps."

The Carter boy shot him a disgusted look. "Don't you get tired of saying that every time, Ben Grayson? We play for fair, and that's that!"

Ben caught Henri staring at him. "What you looking at Frenchie? Go over where you belong." He pointed to a spot beyond them where the younger boys were drawing circles in the dirt, apparently separating themselves by age.

Ben's badger look and mean tone gave Henri a belly ache. Carrying his lunch pail, he shuffled away from the group. He looked for Daniel, but he was in the midst of several other boys his size, talking and gesturing with his hands.

Henri turned and walked past a group of girls who'd finished eating. Two turned a long rope in circles, and another jumped through it. He paused for a minute, thinking the jumping looked fun and wondering if he could try. Then he realized that only girls were lining up. Shrugging, he drifted toward the school.

Three older girls sat on the steps, eating and talking, their heads together in what looked like a serious discussion.

He climbed past without them seeing him and slid through the partially opened door.

Mrs. Gordon and Natalie, their backs to him, wrote on the big slate in the front of the room.

With the quiet *Père* showed him when hunting, Henri took his pail of food and moved to the corner and sat with his back pressed against where the two walls joined. The students' tables hid him from the view of his teachers. He pulled his knees to his chest and wrapped his arms around his legs. Dropping his head on his arms, he pretended to be home— his real home, not the farm—moving silently through the leafy evergreens, needles thick under his moccasins, their spicy scent filling his nose. *Père* had taught him to know each bird and animal, and he listened to the sounds of the forest.

He found his favorite place, a hidden burrow made by the toppling of several massive pines, and crawled inside. In his den, Henri had often made believe he was an animal—a wolf, a bear, or a fox. He strained to remember the feel of the forest and, after a few minutes, almost forgot the voices of children playing, the hard feel of the wooden floor, and the smell of chalk and books.

After a while, Henri felt peaceful again, although he still ached with longing for his den and his life before. A rumble from his belly made him remember he hadn't eaten, and he rummaged in the pail for the food *Maman* had packed—cold baked potatoes, some nuts, and bread spread with butter and huckleberry jam. He bit into the bread, savoring the sweet taste.

The only good thing about the changes be this bread and jam! Then he thought of Pa, Camilla, and the horses, and Natalia…. They were all good, too. Henri wished he could have them *and Père.*

No sooner had he eaten when the clanging of Mrs. Gordon's bell brought an end to recess. He scrambled to his feet just as the children poured through the door, setting their pails on the shelf. Since they seemed to be going to their places, he did likewise, taking a seat.

With a smile, Natalia walked over to stand in front of him. She tilted her head in inquiry. "What is it, Henri? When I sent you outside, you had on a happy expression. Now you look the same as you did when I first saw you this morning. Has something upset you?"

Henri looked down, not knowing what to say. He glanced across the room at Ben, who slouched in his seat, an open book in front of him.

Natalie followed his gaze. "Ben Grayson." Her words were clipped. "He's such a troublemaker. What did he do to you?" She slid into the seat.

The kindness in her gaze coaxed the story out of him.

When he finished, she patted his arm. "I'd tell you to not pay him any mind, but that's hard to do with a bully like Ben Grayson."

Bully? Henri didn't know the word.

Natalia studied his face and said, "Someone who's mean and pushes people around." She pursed her lips. "Well…he is right about one thing. You do have a French name. The American version is *Henry*, with a *huh* sound. If you want, we could change it. What do you think about that?"

"A chicken be *Hen*ree," he muttered.

She laughed. "Oh, Henri, how funny."

Liking that he'd made her laugh, Henri sat a little straighter.

Natalia tilted her head so she was close to him. "My grand-father's name is Henry. A good solid name." She touched Henri's nose with the tip of her finger. "I think he'd be pleased to share it with you." She gave a decisive nod. "Henry. Sounds very dignified. Something I'm sure you'll be when you grow up."

Puzzled, he looked askance at her.

"Dignified...Reverend Norton is dignified. Although, from what I've seen of his son—Reverend Joshua Norton, who's also Micah's father—he's not so dignified, maybe because he spent so much time in heathen Africa and lived in a hut.

More words I don't know.

She ruffled his hair, seeming to understand. "I'd show you Africa on the globe, *Henry,* but first, I'd have to explain some geography to you. I think we'd best concentrate on learning your numbers and work up from there. After we work on your numbers, I'll teach you how to spell your new name."

Numbers. At last, something I know!

❉ ❉ ❉

Henri's absence left behind an emptiness that lingered in Antonia's awareness all morning. *He'll be home tonight,* she kept reassuring herself and managed to feel grateful for that fact. Jean-Claude's death had taught her not to take her loved ones for granted.

But even with Jacques's babbling, to her, the house seemed silent. She hadn't realized how much she and Henri spoke to each other during the day. This morning, she had only her thoughts for company.

Today, she wore Daisy's altered blue-flower print dress with an apron over it. The dress buttoned down the front, making it easy for her to nurse the babies. As she worked around the house, Antonia was aware of the material of the skirt swishing around her legs. Once she'd gotten tangled in the hem and almost tripped herself. *Why be women wearin' such no-sense dresses?*

With two babies in constant need of her attention, Antonia was slow to finish her chores. She'd always counted on her oldest son's help with Jacques, and now she had no one to guard or play with him.

What do women who have twins or several babies in a row be doin', especially if they have no older child to be helpin'? She answered her question. *Likely, they be goin' mad.*

A few hours later—for all that Antonia had been listening for his arrival, eager to hear news of her son—Erik caught her by surprise when he walked through the door as she sat in the big chair nursing Camilla.

Jacques, standing with one hand holding onto a kitchen chair while he pounded on the seat with the flat of his hand and chanted, "ba, ma, ba, ma," was probably the reason she hadn't heard the wagon.

When he saw Erik, her boy shouted, "Pa!"

Erik's eyes lit with surprise, and he grinned at Jacques before nodding hello to her. He unwound his scarf, took off his coat and hat, and hung them on the hat rack. With two big steps, he reached Jacques and scooped up the boy, tossing him into the air, obviously enjoying the child's chuckles.

Antonia suppressed a proud smile. All morning, she'd been trying to teach Jacques to say *Pa* but had no idea her clever boy would say the word at just the right time.

Still holding Jacques, Erik strode over and crouched down to eye Camilla. "How's my little girl doing?"

At the sound of his voice, the baby shifted her eyes toward her father but didn't stop suckling.

He rubbed his daughter's downy head. "I think that's my answer."

Antonia couldn't hold back her curiosity and concern. "Henri?"

Erik stood and again lifted Jacques into the air, smiling at the child's laughter. "Well, my dear Mrs. Muth. I can report with some certainty that both your sons are doing well." He lowered Jacques until they rubbed noses.

Her son chuckled.

Although hearing him call her *dear Mrs. Muth* cost her a pang, Antonia suspected Erik might have also suffered a similar emotion upon naming her thus. But he didn't show any sign of distress, acting as if they'd been married for years and had many such conversations about the children.

"As you can expect, Henri never said a word to me and barely one to the O'Donnell children. But once we got to town, he perked up when he saw Mrs. Thompson driving their little buggy down the street pulled by two midget horses. Yay high, they are." He held his hand palm down at his hip. "Falabellas are what they're called."

She raised her eyebrows in skepticism. "Those be mighty small for horses."

"You wait until you see the critters," he said in a teasing tone. "Then you'll believe me." Holding Jacques with one arm, he bent his knees up and down while they talked to keep the child content. "The Thompsons are kind people, or so I'd heard, for I didn't know them beyond a mere acquaintance. Their situation is not unlike ours, in that they'd both lost first spouses, although years prior. Samantha Rodriquez, as she was called, had a son, Daniel, and adopted three more, and Wyatt Thompson had a daughter. Sometime, I'll tell you the tale of those ruffian twins of hers."

"What did Henri do?"

"I introduced him to Mrs. Thompson and Daniel. He's about eleven. She'd heard about Daisy and you and offered kindly condolences. Then, low and behold, she had Daniel give Henri a ride in the little buggy. Even better, Daniel let Henri drive the Falabellas. I tell you, Antonia, no prince in a royal coach was happier than your son in that moment."

Antonia's deep sigh of relief seemed dredged from her toes.

Camilla loosened her mouth from Antonia's nipple.

She raised the baby to her shoulder, holding her against a clean rag, and patted her back. The baby omitted a loud burp.

Erik looked over at them with a smile and shook his head. "I can't believe the noise that comes out of such a sweet little mite. She sounds like the roughest teamster."

Antonia pretended to frown. "Just as well she be comfortable." She moved the baby to her other breast. "No sense havin' a fussy babe with air in her stomach. I promise the wailin' that be comin' then be makin' your own stomach ache."

Erik set Jacques down.

The child clung to his leg like a sucker vine.

Carefully, Erik shuffled sideways across the room, dragging the boy on his leg.

Eyes bright, Jacques held on tight and chortled at the new game.

"Daniel promised to introduce Henri to the children his age." Erik took up the story. "Then Henri met his teacher and got all shy again but not as bad as before. Mrs. Gordon also expressed sincere condolences, both to me and Henri."

Antonia liked the sound of this teacher.

"All and all, I couldn't have hoped for a better start to his first day of school."

"Thank ye for all you be doin' for my boy."

"He's my boy now, too," Erik said quietly, a firm set to his jaw. "But there's something else I did that might upset you."

Her stomach tightened with dread.

"I told you about the Thompsons. Well, Daniel goes by Daniel Rodriquez Thompson. So, liking that idea, I did the same thing with Henri. Introduced him as Henri Valleau Muth."

You be havin' no right! A surge of anger and protective-ness had Antonia biting her lip to hold in the hot words. Grappling with her feelings, Antonia bent her head, pretend-ing to look at Camilla, but really she was avoiding Erik's gaze. The child in her arms—already *her* babe and loved with the same fierceness she felt for her sons—cooled her wrath. Truth be, if Daisy stood before her, demanding back her daughter, Antonia would not give up the baby.

Erik has the right to be tackin' his name onto Henri's.

Despite her fear of Jean-Claude being lost as this man took over their lives, she'd received nothing but kindness from Erik Muth. And their family would be better off if he came to love her sons as his own…if they all shared the same name.

"Becoming a father to these little shavers of yours, Antonia…." Erik spoke into the lengthening silence.

She looked up and met his solemn gaze.

He ruffled Jacques's hair. "Let's just say the boys are good for me."

"You done right," Antonia admitted. "Be hard for me to swallow at first hearin'. But I be grateful for your care of 'em."

As if relieved, Erik rocked back on his heels. He glanced out the window. "I have one more field to plow, and I'd best be getting on with it." He turned back to her. "We missed washday yesterday. Best do that all today while the weather's good. Do you need me to get out the tub for you?"

Why be yesterday washday? Antonia almost opened her mouth to ask but just as quickly held in the question to avoid showing her ignorance. She hadn't needed to wash clothes for years since hers had long since worn out. Their leather garments didn't need the same kind of care. But in the early days of her marriage, she'd beaten the clothing on rocks in a stream.

She cast her memory back to her childhood, to the women of the fort working together on laundry day to wash clothes and linens. The youngsters—both boys and girls— had hauled pails of water and stirred the loads in the tubs with wooden paddles. As she grew older, she'd taken her turn at scrubbing clothing on the washboard.

Her stomach relaxed. *Although doin' laundry be heavy labor, based on what I recall, I can figure it out on my own.*

Erik's gaze lingered on Camilla at her breast. "The tub is in the barn—the same one you used for bathing," he said referring to the baths they'd taken the night before. "Opposite the door where the tools are hanging. You'll find the paddle and washboard there, as well as the can of soap shavings. The bar of soap, as you know, is in the kitchen. Do you want me to bring everything in and haul you some water? Daisy usually did the wash on the porch unless it was too cold. Saved her from having to mop up the floor."

Antonia looked down at Camilla. "Could you be bringin' everything while I finish feeding her? Then I'll be cookin' up something for you to eat."

Erik pried a protesting Jacques off his leg, deposited him next to her chair, and left the room. He returned a few minutes later with two pails of water that he poured into the empty stew pot and set on the stove. Making two trips, he filled the kettle and another pot as well, then stirred up the banked coals inside the stove and added some wood. He went outside again.

A few minutes later, she heard the clang of metal outside, and then the slosh of water.

Antonia finished nursing, burped Camilla again, and moved to lay the baby in her cradle. Lying on the fur she'd spread on the floor of the main room, she cuddled with Jacques, allowing him to nurse as the quickest way for him to fall asleep, although she doubted she had much milk left for him.

Once she saw Jacques slept, she rose. A glance at the cradle told her Camilla had fallen asleep as well. The baby seemed to need more rest than her boys had. Antonia hoped that was just because she'd come early and was so small. Or maybe because she was a girl? *I'll ask Henrietta when next I see her.*

While the water heated, she sorted through Erik's and Daisy's clothing. She set aside the whites—mostly Daisy's undergarments, which were edged with fancy lace—and added her own from yesterday, even though they were new and she'd barely worn them.

Once the water boiled, Antonia poured out all the containers into the tub on the porch, adding soap shavings, which she stirred with the big paddle until they dissolved. The soap smelled sweeter than the harsh lye soap she'd always used, and she wondered what Daisy had added to make the difference. After dropping in the whites to soak, she hauled water inside to heat for rinsing.

She began scrubbing the garments on the washboard and quickly realized Erik would need to make her a table to raise the tub higher, for if she had to bend over all day, her back might end up with a permanent curve. When Antonia finished cleaning the whites, she emptied out the soapy water over the front of the porch, first by scooping out several full buckets, then hefting the tub onto its side, using her arm to keep the laundry from falling out. She added fresh hot water, stirring with the paddle. When the water cooled enough for her to put her hands into, one by one, she wrung out the pieces of clothing and placed them on a towel she'd laid on the floor next to her.

Once the whole load was done, Antonia poured a measure of soap shavings into the tub and tossed in the colored clothing, mostly Erik's shirts. She gathered up the wet laundry and stepped off the porch, walking around the house to the clothesline.

Two lines ran from the side of the house to an upright pole with a cross piece on top. The sprouting garden lay on the other side. With her arms and back already aching, Antonia hauled the damp load to the clothesline, sopping the bodice of her dress.

Earlier this morning, she'd hung up the bedding and Daisy's nightgown, making several trips back and forth from the porch rail to the clothesline. Now, she realized that with her arms full, she had no available hands to drape the garments over the ropes and growled in frustration.

Once again, she searched her memory of those long-ago washing days and recalled the women using baskets to hold the laundry. Shaking her head over missing such an obvious solution, Antonia backtracked to the porch where a big wicker basket hung by a handle on the wall. Awkwardly, she managed to one-handedly take it down and then dumped the clothing inside.

She walked into the house to check on the babies. Reassured the two slept soundly, Antonia went out to the porch, lifted the basket, and hauled it to the clothesline. There she flung the garments over the rope and smoothed them out. She returned to the house to start all over again with the colored clothing. And she still had Erik's heavy work clothes to tackle last. They would require longer soaking and scrubbing.

Several hours later, Antonia stepped away from the clothesline, digging both fists into her sore back muscles, and stretched, surveying her handiwork with a feeling of satisfaction. On the two lines, clothing, diapers, and bedding waved in the breeze. *I be sure glad washday only comes once a week!*

Something tickled her memory, and she followed the thought back to the past and groaned, remembering. *Ironing day comes after washday!* At the fort, while laundry was a communal chore, shared by all the women, each family was responsible for ironing their own clothing and bedding. *Ironing be even more tedious than washin', for I cain't be lettin' my attention stray, else I scorch something.*

In frustration, Antonia wondered if she even needed to iron at all. Out here on the prairie, no one would even know. And maybe Erik wouldn't notice wrinkled sheets.

Antonia glanced at the sun, realized she'd better get supper started, and headed for the house. As she climbed the steps to the porch, she told herself she'd rest for a few minutes and watch for Henri's return. She angled the rocker so she could view the road, and, with a weary sigh, sank into the seat. She hoped to see the tiny figure of her son walking home from school, but he wasn't in sight.

Just as she began to rock, Antonia heard Camilla's cry and knew the baby had probably awakened Jacques as well.

Her boy could sleep through most things, but not that insistent wail.

Feeling exhausted to her bones, she tilted the chair back one more time. She was a strong woman, used to working hard and taking pride in her accomplishments. But dealing with grief and her changed life, sleeping poorly, fretting for her son, caring for two babies, and doing all the chores of a farm wife had taken their toll today. She wondered how long before her body adjusted to this new life.

Out in the pasture, she saw Erik driving the cows to the barn to be milked. She pushed to her feet, knowing she had two sleepyheads who'd want snuggling and need changing, probably at the same time, and she had supper to make. *God should have made mothers with more arms—a set for each child.*

Newborn Camilla needed her care, and, indeed, Antonia wanted to do everything she could so the baby would thrive. Yet, she felt guilty for neglecting Jacques, who was used to far more of her attention than he'd received lately. She hadn't even found time to sit and play with him. She fretted about her small son—his father dead, a new home, and his brother gone all day. Most of the time he seemed his usual happy self, but all these changes were bound to affect him.

To her relief, after she changed them, Antonia was able to bring both babies out to the porch and fit them on her lap. Camilla didn't take up much space, and Jacques was content to lay with his head on her shoulder while she rocked. Soon he'd wake up all the way, eager to play. *Hopefully, Henri be home by then, so I be free to cook supper.*

A gust of wind, stronger than the afternoon breezes, blew across the yard, setting the skirt of her dress fluttering. Erik must have finished the milking for she spotted the cows back in the pasture. *Tomorrow,* she remembered from one of Erik's casual mentions, *I'll be makin' butter.* Trepidation fluttered in her stomach. *Something else I never be doin' afore.*

In the distance, she saw Henri headed her way, one arm carrying books and his slate. Her heart gave a heavy thump of relief and anticipation. She wanted to run to her boy and throw her arms around him, but the two little ones anchored her to the rocking chair.

The wind picked up, causing Henri to hold onto his cap. He left the road, crossed the yard, and saw her. He waved, which, when a gust tugged the brim, almost cost him his cap. Smacking a hand on his head, he broke into a run.

"Look, Jacques," Antonia said, setting him on the floor. "Henri be home. Go to your brother."

"Ha." Jacques flapped a hand in Henri's direction.

Henri ran up the steps, stopping only to rub his brother's head before rushing to her.

Antonia rose to give him a one-armed hug. "It's good to see you, *mon fils.* Come inside, have a bite to eat while I cooks up some supper. I be waitin' to hear how your day be."

As she was about to guide the boy to the door, one of Daisy's chemises blew by, followed by a shirt of Erik's. "Oh, dear." Releasing Henri, Antonia hurried into the house and deposited Camilla in her cradle, returning to fetch Jacques. "Watch the babies," she commanded Henri, setting her youngest son on the floor. "I be grabbing those clothes."

Racing outside, she snatched up Daisy's still-damp chemise, now covered with dirt, and then hurried toward Erik's shirt, which was also filthy.

"Antonia!"

She glanced up to see Erik hurrying toward her. He didn't have the milk buckets, so he must have taken them into the springhouse.

"There's a storm coming up." He pointed in the direction opposite Sweetwater Springs.

She turned to look. A fat swirl of dark-blue clouds covered the horizon. Weary and too busy looking the other direction for Henri, she hadn't even noticed the storm's approach.

A jagged flash of lightning cut the sky. Another of Erik's shirts flew off the clothesline and headed in their direction, only to crumple to the ground.

Erik glanced from his shirt to the dirty clothes in her hands. "Next time use clothespins."

Clothespins?

The wind gusted harder and more clothing sailed from the lines. In dismay, she watched them land in the dirt. *All my hard work be for naught!*

Erik picked up his shirt and thrust it into her hands. "I need to get the cows into the barn before the storm hits. You'll have to take in the laundry by yourself." He turned and ran toward the pasture.

The power of the wind kicked up, sending dust swirling into the air.

Squinting to protect her eyes, Antonia moved against the gusts that billowed her skirts and slowed her progress. Gasping for breath, she reached the house, hastening across the porch to open the door. She threw in the clothes, uncaring where they landed, for she'd have to wash them again anyway.

She grabbed the laundry basket to hold the clean laundry still hanging on the lines. Once she stepped around the corner of the house, the full force of the wind slapped her, almost tearing the basket from her arms. With one eye on the approaching storm and the other on her task, she pulled off the clothes and linens, dropping them into the basket.

Finished, she lifted the basket, and the wind at her back pushed her toward the house. Once through the door, she deposited the basket in the corner.

Henri watched her with anxious eyes.

"A storm's coming, son. I need to be gittin' the rest of the laundry in, while Pa's roundin' up the cows. Keep watchin' the babes."

From his spot on the floor where he sat with Jacques, Henri nodded his understanding.

Antonia carried the basket outside, but left it on the porch where the rail would keep it from blowing away. She bundled up her skirts with one hand, cursing that she'd even worn the unwieldy dress today, and dashed into the yard, chasing down her laundry.

A blur of white cloth blew past her. Antonia made a grab and missed, watching as the pillowcase plastered against the fence to the pasture. She ran to peel the cloth off the barbed wire.

With a stick, Erik herded the cows across the pasture toward the barn.

Even without counting, Antonia could tell some animals were missing, and he'd have to go back for them. Turning away, she hurried to catch one of Daisy's petticoats.

The afternoon darkened. When she looked to the horizon, she spied a monstrous cloud with an eerie greenish tinge around the edges that had blackened the sky, moving toward them faster than she could believe. The hackles on her neck rose.

Thunder rumbled. Lightning forked, far too close for safety.

Antonia whirled to look for her husband and saw him running toward Annabelle Lee and her two calves. He'd told her how much that cow meant to him. "Erik!" she yelled to get his attention, hoping he'd hear her. Cupping her hands around her mouth, she tried again. "Erik!"

He glanced over.

She pointed toward the storm. "We got to be gittin' in the house *now!*" She prayed he'd choose common sense over his livestock.

He veered away from the cow and sprinted toward the gate.

Relieved, Antonia turned to run toward the house. There was a leaden pause to the air as the wind abruptly died. Without warning, rain pounded down so hard she couldn't see more than a few feet in front of her.

With an ear-piercing screech, the wind roared back to life, tangling her sodden skirt around her ankles. Imprisoned by the heavy material, she couldn't catch her balance. She tripped over a stone, falling to the ground hard enough to knock the wind out of her.

Thunder crashed overhead. Simultaneously, lightning struck the pole of the clotheslines, so close Antonia could feel the heat. A scream of terror wrenched from her throat. The vivid light seared her eyes, and a deafening noise made her ears ring. An acrid smell filled her nose, and she couldn't breathe. Or maybe that was the weight of fear pressing on her chest.

"Dear God, Antonia!" Erik grabbed her under her shoulders and yanked her to her feet. Once he had her upright, he circled her waist with his arm and held her against his side.

Bending into the wind, they headed for the house. The several dozen steps to get there seemed to take them forever. Finally, they reached the scanty shelter of the porch.

"Inside!" Erik ordered, pushing her toward the door and followed on her heels.

She stumbled into the house.

Erik slammed the door behind them.

"Maman!" Henri cried, throwing himself at her.

She tightened her arms around him. "It be all right, son." Her voice sounded husky, and her knees trembled.

Erik pulled the two of them into an embrace, burying his face in her hair. "The lightning blinded me. All I knew was it struck near you. When my vision cleared, and I saw you on the ground...." He groaned into her hair. "I thought...I thought...." He shuddered, obviously unable to say the words.

"My skirt tripped me." Held against his solid chest, Antonia could feel him shaking, or maybe that was her. She slid her free arm around his waist, needing to be even closer to him. "If I hadn't fallen, I be hit for sure." Tears welled. "I would have left my babies behind." She buried her face between his shoulder and neck so her tears wouldn't spill over, but despite her best attempts they did, running down his skin.

"Shhh, shhh. You're safe now. God sent an angel to tangle your skirt, that he did. To keep you here for your family who needs you."

Antonia inhaled a sharp breath and raised her head, looking at him. "You be right!" The thought of such divine intervention filled her with awe, chasing away the vulnerability she'd felt since the storm hit. *Thank you,* she sent the simple prayer heavenward. *Thank you, thank you!*

They huddled together for long moments, seeking comfort as the thunder roared overhead. The house filled with bursts of white flashes, and the walls shook from lightning thudding into the ground. The babies started to cry.

Erik straightened, but not before he pressed a kiss to Antonia's forehead and another on her cheek. He released her to lean over and give Henri a big hug. Then he picked up Jacques, holding the boy close and kissing the top of his head.

He handed the child to her, as if knowing she needed to feel her baby safe in her arms.

Finally, he lifted Camilla out of her cradle and rocked her, kissing his daughter's forehead and rubbing her back to soothe her.

Seeing Erik's obvious care for them—his need to reassure himself of each family member's well-being—touched something inside Antonia, melting the edges of the ice she'd carried in her chest since Jean-Claude's death. *We be formin' a connection—a blessin' blown in on the winds of a storm.*

CHAPTER SIXTEEN

Holding only Camilla wasn't enough. His daughter had stopped crying, and Erik shifted her into one arm so he could drop the other around Antonia's shoulders and pull her to his side. To his surprise, Henri moved to face them, circling their legs with his thin arms and pressing his face into his mother's stomach.

They stood together for another few minutes, listening to the sounds of the storm, until Erik had somewhat recovered. He squeezed Antonia's shoulder, released her, and tried to lighten the tense mood. "Losing two wives in one week would have been too much, don't you think?"

Antonia gave a shaky laugh, leaning into him and resting her head against his shoulder.

Her height made the position feel intimate. "Everyone in town will start thinking I'm Bluebeard."

She lifted her head to look at him. "Who be this Bluebeard?"

"He's from a fairytale by Hans Christian Anderson. How about I read you the story after supper?"

"Supper!" Antonia pulled away from him. "You must be plumb starvin'." She glanced down at herself. "We be wet. And now we got the babies damp. Best change first."

With sudden concern, Erik lowered Camilla and fingered her dress. "A bit damp. I think if we change her right away, I'll have done her no harm."

Antonia ran her palm over the soft chamois shirt Jacques wore. "He be fine." She set him down and reached for Camilla. "Her first." She took the baby from him and headed for the bedroom.

"Keep an eye on your brother," Erik told Henri. He waited until the next lightning strike passed and dashed outside to close the shutters on the windows, so he could block out the sight of the lightning, at least in the main room. He didn't dare move off the porch to shutter the bedroom window. No sense making himself a target.

He hadn't put on his coat, and the howling wind flapped his shirt and whipped his hair over his eyes. Once he covered the windows, he was left in pitch darkness and had to feel his way toward the door.

Erik had never forgotten how, when he was a child, lightning had killed one of their neighbors as he hurried home from the fields carrying a metal rake. The man died instantly, burned to a crisp, leaving behind a widow and three small children.

The thought of how close Antonia had come to the same fate struck fear inside him once again, making him dizzy. He thrust his hands into his pockets to still their shaking and gulped for air.

Erik had never been much of a praying man, but this week he'd made up for that, petitioning the Almighty, nay, battered with his fists on heaven's very gates, demanding the Lord save Daisy. Afterward, left broken by grief and guilt— ignored, he felt—Erik had gone as far as questioning the very existence of God.

Leaning his back against the wall for support, grateful he wasn't a widower again, he sent up a prayer of thanksgiving. Then he thanked the Lord for his new family, who were proving to be such an unexpected blessing. His feelings for them were tangled up with his grief for Daisy and perhaps would always be.

Comforted by the act of praying, Erik was able to move again. He carried the rocking chair into the house, figuring the little ones needed extra soothing.

Light glowed from a lamp on the table and another on the counter in the kitchen area where Antonia worked. A candle protected by a glass chimney burned on the small table next to the big chair.

Antonia must have felt the need for extra light tonight. Erik didn't blame her. He set the rocking chair in the available space in the living area and hurried into the bedroom to change. Wearing dry clothing, he emerged and walked toward Antonia and the children.

She had changed into her Indian garb and had unfastened her braid, brushing out her hair and leaving it loose in a dark fall to her waist. She held Camilla in one arm, while Jacques whined and pressed against her leg, chubby fists clenching her tunic.

Henri stood on his mother's other side—not holding on, but looking like he wished to.

With her free hand, Antonia tried to assemble the ingredients for their meal but was hampered by the children made fretful and clingy from the constant barrage of thunder and lightning.

Antonia turned and frowned in obvious frustration. She held out his daughter. "Fussing, she be, not likin' the ruckus outside."

"None of us likes the ruckus outside," Erik said in a wry tone, taking the baby from her.

She waved him toward the rocking chair. "Make yourself be useful, Pa. You can hold both Jacques and Camilla at the same time, so I can be about the business of cookin' supper."

Holding his daughter in one arm, he stooped to wrap his other arm around Jacques's middle and lifted the boy.

Jacques wailed at being taken away from his mother. He kicked and arched his back, holding out his hands toward her.

Erik clamped the boy tight to his side to keep him from slithering out from under his arm and hurried to the rocking chair. He maneuvered the two babies so they each sat on one of his legs, their heads resting on his arms. Once he started rocking, both Jacques and Camilla settled.

To keep Henri occupied and out of his mother's way, Erik called the boy over and had him bring the slate and sit on the floor next to him. He asked Henri to draw the letters and numbers he'd learned in school today.

With no available hands, Erik could only verbally instruct Henri when his stepson made a mistake. But, for the most part, the child did fine on his own. He seemed to have gotten *A* through *H* down, although his *B* faced the wrong way, and his *1* through *10* looked good.

Although his insides still hadn't settled, and he was in the midst of one of the worst thunderstorms he'd weathered in the last few years, Erik still enjoyed the homey domestic scene, perhaps more so because of what had gone before. He looked forward to reading *Bluebeard* to an audience unfamiliar with the story, although if Henri stayed awake, he might have to stop before some of the grim parts.

Antonia seemed to have recovered her customary equanimity. She hummed as she worked, stirring something in the frying pan, not even flinching when thunder boomed overhead.

He couldn't help marveling at her calm. Daisy had always hated storms, ducking at each flash of lightning as if she were about to be struck and complaining all the while—as if she held him accountable for the weather. More than once, Erik had lost his patience and informed her that he did *not* possess the power to calm the wind and rain.

He tried not to think of the elements pounding on Daisy's lonely grave. The image of her lying cold under the earth made his heart heavy. *She's not there,* he reminded himself. *She's safe and warm and happy in heaven.* But he couldn't quite shake his melancholy at the thought of his wife in a box under several feet of dirt, and he wondered if Antonia had similar thoughts about Jean-Claude's solitary resting place on the mountain. Somehow, that seemed even more tragic, for at least Daisy was laid to rest nearby.

He worried about the fate of Annabelle Lee and her two calves unprotected in the field. The thunder and lightning were enough to put off the cow's milk. He hoped the lightning wouldn't strike the barn. A fire, even if quickly drenched by the rain, would deal a devastating blow to his finances— one that could cause him to lose everything.

The rumbling thunder didn't cease, as if the storm had decided to settle over their farm and stay awhile. Sometimes, the wind pushed down the stovepipe, making the stove belch ashes and noxious fumes into the room.

Antonia seemed to take the hazards in stride. Once she turned and sent him a rueful smile. "Cookin' in a fireplace durin' a storm be far worse, eh? I usually give up and have jerky or pemmican or some such."

He admired her, this new wife of his—the matter of fact way she'd gone about making a new life for her family, her obvious love for his daughter, the small ways she'd begun to take care of him…. Yes, in a short time, Antonia had become very dear—as confused and guilty as such emotion made him feel.

* * *

Sometime during the night, the storm left as abruptly as it had come. In the early morning darkness, with just a hint of light to make gray shadows in the room, Antonia awoke in Erik's arms, feeling languid and warm. He laid on his back, with her body tucked against his side, her head on his shoulder. Inhaling the scent of his skin, already familiar, and feeling the softness of the bed underneath them, she felt cocooned and safe.

Jacques slept at her back, and Henri behind him, the four of them snug like peas in a pod. Since the thunder and lightning made everyone uneasy, they'd piled together on Erik's bed, the children quickly falling asleep. Later, when she'd nursed Camilla, she'd put the child back in her cradle.

In the hush of the morning, still only half-awake, Antonia tried to keep guilt at bay and allow herself the luxury of a few dreamy moments. *Be it wrong to pretend that I love this man, and he loves me? Be I betrayin' Jean-Claude, or be I takin' what comfort I can find?*

She hadn't slept in Jean-Claude's arms for a long time—not since Jacques was born, anyway. The baby had slept between them. Now she regretted their assumption that plenty of time lay before them to wake in each other's arms. They'd even joked about when Jacques was weaned that he'd share a pallet with his brother. For the first time since Henri's birth, they could sleep without children and, perhaps, Jean-Claude had laughed, quickly make another.

Erik stirred, tightening his arm around her.

Antonia let out a ragged breath, resolving to savor this time with Erik, not fret over a past she couldn't change. Gradually, she drifted back to sleep.

A short while later, she felt Erik move from her side. She opened her eyes and saw him already half-dressed, his back to her, as he shrugged himself into his shirt. She wished the room had more light to better view the muscles of his broad back.

When Erik finished, he turned toward the bed and caught her watching him. "Morning," he said softly, sitting on the bed to take her hand. He pressed a kiss to her palm.

The touch of his lips on her skin sent tingles rushing through her.

"Are you all right after last night's storm?"

"I be fine." Antonia shifted closer to him and had to suppress a wince, when her muscles throbbed. *Maybe not be so fine.* But she didn't want to complain. The plowing and planting Erik had recently done probably made him just as sore.

"Good." He leaned down and kissed her forehead. "I'll bring in some milk for breakfast."

Antonia sent her husband off to the milking with a smile and lingered in the warm bed for a few more minutes. Last night, she and Erik had resolved that Henri wouldn't attend school today. The road would be too muddy for the wagon, and the way was too far for him to ride alone. But still, all too soon, she'd have to be up and about her day—for one thing, she had most of the laundry to do all over again. She suppressed a groan at the thought.

The need to use the privy finally pushed her out of bed. Without bothering to dress, she shoved her feet into her moccasins, and, still wearing her nightgown, went outside. She picked her way through the mud and around puddles until she reached the outhouse. Afterward, she washed up, left her muddy moccasins on the porch, and dressed in her Indian garb. *I might never again wear a dress around here. Only when I go to town.* She hoped Erik would not care what she wore.

Aiming to cook breakfast, Antonia hefted the ham from the pantry, cutting off several slices to fry. When the slabs sizzled, a cloud of sweet scent rose into her face, and her stomach clenched with hunger. Once finished, she cut small pieces for Jacques and Henri and then gobbled up a few for herself like the chickens after grain.

Far sooner than she'd expected, Antonia heard Erik's footsteps on the porch, sounding heavy and slow, not at all like the firm stride she'd heard when he'd left the house.

He walked inside, his shoulders slumping and his features drawn, looking much the same he'd done on the day Daisy died. Without even bothering to take off his hat and coat, he strode to the big chair and dropped into it, lowering his face into his hands.

Her stomach clenched with dread. She moved the pan to the cooler part of the stovetop and rushed over to him. "Erik?" She placed a hand on his shoulder.

He didn't answer, only moved his head back and forth, his face still buried in his hands.

"Erik." Her tone sharpened with fear. "Tell me what be wrong!" She removed his hat, dropping it on the floor.

He let out a shuddering breath and raised his face to her. "Lightning struck and killed Annabelle Lee and one of her calves. I know I should butcher them right away so we can use the meat, but I couldn't face it, Antonia. Not yet. It's too much."

She sucked in a sharp breath of understanding. She knew that cow was his favorite. Another painful loss for him. Not the same as a wife, but perhaps felt all the more deeply because he was already vulnerable from grief.

"I be sorry." She squeezed his shoulder.

"When Annabelle Lee birthed twins, I felt on top of the world—my world, anyway. I had this vision, Antonia, of the prosperous life ahead of me. But instead, fate twisted my dreams. Will everything be taken from me now?" He let out a harsh breath.

Not everything, she wanted to protest but held her tongue, saddened to see such a strong man brought low by trouble. She understood how he felt. After Jean-Claude died, she'd struggled with similar fears.

Until now, Antonia hadn't realized she'd felt more secure since marrying Erik and moving to the farm. *Erik has given me that—a respite from those fears.*

Antonia wished she had an answer—one that would make everything right for him. But all she could do was haltingly explain her thoughts. "That be life, Erik. Like the harvest, eh? Some years the crops be good, and the cupboards full. Other years, they fail, and times be hard. You don't stop plowin' and plantin'."

He leaned back in his chair, staring blankly at the ceiling.

She wasn't sure he'd even heard her.

But then, Erik reached up and briefly covered her hand with his and squeezed before lowering his arm. He didn't move again.

Antonia waited for a few silent minutes, and then pressed a kiss to his forehead. "Eat your victuals, now, while they's warm. The little 'uns had some afore you came in."

With determination, she walked to the door. *I might not know how to read and sew shirtwaists and bake cake, but I know how to butcher a cow! Not that a milk cow be makin' good eatin'.*

I can't take away his pain, but I can ease his burdens.

CHAPTER SEVENTEEN

As if in repayment for the storm, the weather for the next month alternated between rain and sunshine, followed by several days of unseasonable heat. The spring vegetables Daisy and Erik had previously planted in the garden shot up. The garden was six times bigger than the small plot she'd left behind. Each day while Henri was in school, Antonia spent long hours hoeing the weeds while the babies stayed in a sheltered corner—Camilla kicking and mewing on a blanket and Jacques playing in the dirt with a spoon and some rocks.

From time to time, they had visitors. Henrietta dropped by to help Antonia with making over Daisy's wardrobe, and elderly Mr. and Mrs. Knapp, the neighbors on their other side, made a condolence call.

Once, Reverend and Mrs. Norton drove out to see how they were managing. The minister privately spent time with Antonia, and she welcomed the chance to talk freely about Jean-Claude and her grief for him—for speaking about a former husband to a current one wasn't easy. She knew the visit did her good, and she suspected Erik's own talk with Reverend Norton was also beneficial. But neither of them shared what they'd discussed with the minister.

Erik had taught her how to make butter, an area where Antonia's physical strength came to her aid, for pumping the churn up and down was a tedious and tiring chore. After a few awkward attempts, she soon made butter that her husband said was as good as Daisy's. He added her butter to the milk and eggs he took to the mercantile.

During the babies' naptime, Antonia often took the rifle and rode out on one of the horses to hunt game. She left the babies near Erik so he could watch over them while he planted the fields. He'd rigged up a straw-filled box for them to sleep in that sheltered them from critters.

Antonia brought back prairie chicken, pheasant, a wild turkey, plenty of rabbits, and once a deer. Because she wanted to share the chores, she continued to be the one who dressed out the game.

Erik had taken a while to adjust to her hunting ability, but one day, he gave her a quiet smile and expressed appreciation for how her efforts allowed him to concentrate on plowing and sowing the fields, while she augmented their larder. He even joked that he might never have to hunt again.

His praise warmed her heart.

In preparing the wild game for meals, Antonia was able to serve the kind of food—mostly stews—she was used to making. She hadn't had a chance to visit Henrietta to learn how to bake desserts, but so far, Erik hadn't complained about her cooking.

During their quiet evenings, instead of the stories Jean-Claude would spin about his day, often making her laugh, Erik would read a book or the weeks-old newspaper, while she mended clothes. Henri would do his homework at the table.

If he had any questions, she'd told her son he was to ask Erik. Thus, often her husband sat next to Henri, gently instructing and correcting his letters and sums, as well as teaching him proper grammar, although he didn't correct the boy at other times.

So far, Erik hadn't questioned why Antonia wasn't the one helping her son. She tried to absorb everything he was teaching Henri, hoping that she too would learn enough to read and speak properly. Sometimes, when her husband wasn't around, she'd ask Henri to draw letters for her on his slate. But it seemed a long way from learning the alphabet to actually reading.

Tonight, Antonia perched in what had become her chair and mended a tear in her husband's shirt. Henri had already nodded off over his slate, and she'd put him and Jacques to bed on the bearskin.

Across from her, Erik sat in silence, and she wondered why he wasn't reading like usual. She thought back through the day and realized he'd been unusually silent at dinner, too. Well, she amended, *unusually silent for Erik.*

Is he upset with me? With one of the boys? Missing Daisy? She couldn't think of anything that she or the boys might have done wrong, so she figured his withdrawal might be about grief. She was all too familiar with the longing for a lost love, the ache of missing him, of wanting his presence, right here, right now, often accompanied by an intense burst of anger that he was gone. She hated how the yearning for Jean-Claude could seize her in its grip and shadow her every footstep.

In spite of their growing closeness, Antonia didn't doubt Erik had times of looking over at her sitting in Daisy's chair, and wishing his wife was still there. Mayhap this was one of them.

Should I ask?

Antonia debated for a while. When she'd finished repairing the rip in the shirt—not with the tiny, almost invisible stitches Daisy used but with serviceable ones, nevertheless—

she folded the garment and set it aside. She picked up one of Daisy's aprons that she'd taken to wearing, intending to attach the corner of the pocket where the edge had pulled away. "You be silent tonight, Erik."

He stirred and gave her an absent-minded smile. "I guess I was out on the prairie, thinking things through."

Curious, she set down the apron and stared at him, waiting.

He let out a sigh. "I was as pleased as punch when my cows dropped their calves. But at the same time, one cow alone requires a lot of feed, especially if I want her to keep a good supply of milk. Now that I have more..."

"What be you thinkin' of doin'?"

"There's all that wild hay out there, just waiting to be cut. We've had a spell of hot days, and I want to take advantage of the weather, for it won't last. Now's a good time to gather in some of the new grass before it flowers. I usually harvest a batch at this time, using a scythe." He swung his arm in a demonstration. "At the end of the summer, the Knapps, the O'Donnells, and I will band together to rent a mowing machine."

"I never be hearin' of such a thing." Antonia thought of the laborious task of using a long knife on hay—holding a clump and chopping off the bottom—that she'd done to gather fodder for the mules while Jean-Claude was out hunting. "A marvel."

He gave her a brief smile. "If you let a lot of high grass grow around the fields, you make a good place for bugs and everything else to hang around. I try to get to those areas once or twice over the summer. In the past, working by myself in the grasslands, I could harvest enough to keep the animals through the winter." He leaned forward. "But with the new cows, the herd is bigger. I'm debating about hiring a man to help me and bring in more hay. I just don't know if I'll make the money back that I pay him in savings from not having to buy any."

"What be havin' an extra man do?"

"I scythe the hay, but I also have a sickle another fellow can use. Better yet, he can bring his own scythe. We rake the hay into rows—windrows—to dry, turn the windrows a few times to dry the batch underneath. Hopefully, the day after, we toss the dried hay into the wagon. Then I have to climb into the wagon and stomp on the hay to pack it down. Jump out, pitch more in, stomp it down, until the wagon is full. Then I start all over again with the cutting. With another man, I could work twice as fast."

"You don't be needin' to hire anyone. I can be helpin' you."

He shook his head. "It's hard work, Antonia. Especially backbreaking those last few hours of the day. And what would we do with the children? It's hot out on the prairie with no shade."

"If we be cuttin' the hay, we'll put 'em in the wagon." She made a spreading motion with her hands. "Be puttin' up the canvas top so they'll be shaded. Henri watches the babies."

"He'll have to miss school for a couple of days...." Erik rubbed his chin. "I don't like it, but missing school is a given in a farming community. The boy's been doing well with his studies. That little whippersnapper is smart."

She glowed at his praise of her son.

Erik jumped to his feet and began to pace the floor. After a few minutes, he said, "That just might work. At least, we can give it a try. I'll have to ride over early and tell the O'Donnells not to expect us while the weather holds." He stopped in front of her chair and grinned. "What do you say, wife? If it's sunny, shall we spend the day on the prairie tomorrow?"

An unexpected feeling of warmth washed through Antonia. He never called her "wife" before, and, for the first time, she felt hopeful, like maybe they were forming a team, able to pull together in harness. "I think that be a fine idea, husband. I be packin' us food."

"We'll need to bring water, lots of water, for the horses and for us." His face sobered. "I'm warning you, it will be hot, thirsty work, Antonia, and there's no water where we're going. You sure?"

"I be sure."

"Good then. We'd best get an early night." He leaned over and gave her an unexpected kiss on the cheek. "Thank you."

Antonia could feel a blush creep into her face, and she hoped he couldn't see it in the lantern light.

He turned, and, with another smile, went into the bedroom, and closed the door.

Needing time to recover from the intensity of emotions churned up by the storm and sharing a bed, Antonia had moved back to sleeping on the bearskins with the children. Since Erik didn't protest, she'd suspected he, too, needed to pull back some.

Antonia stared at Erik's closed door, the feel of his kiss lingering on her skin. She reached up and softly touched her cheek.

❋ ❋ ❋

In the shadow of a hill, Erik pulled the team to a halt. He studied the prairie before him. The golden grass undulated in the slight breeze, and the sharp blue sky almost hurt his eyes. For as far as he could see, no trees broke the horizon.

He'd timed their arrival perfectly. The sun had just risen enough, and the day hadn't yet become too warm. The dew was still on the grass. The first hour or two would be the easiest before they became hot and tired. *And sore.* He didn't want to think about how much his body would hurt tonight. *A necessary evil.*

He braked, tied off the reins, climbed down, and then went around to take Camilla from Antonia and helped his wife off the wagon. Wearing Jean-Claude's leather britches, with one of Erik's cotton shirts tucked into them, her sleeves rolled up past the elbows, Antonia navigated getting down far easier than if she'd worn a skirt. She'd shocked him when she first came out of the bedroom wearing men's clothing.

He'd almost protested her choice of apparel, ready to order her to change into proper clothing, or even her Indian garb. Luckily, common sense had taken over his thoughts before he opened his mouth and said anything that might cause trouble. Men's clothing was far more practical for what they were about to do, and no one was around to notice, anyway. All he'd done was insist on her taking along one of Daisy's sunbonnets to protect her face from becoming burned.

Surely, I'll get used to seeing Antonia in her new raiment and won't keep ogling the outline of her legs and having thoughts....

Erik wrenched his mind back to where it should be—on the job at hand. He handed Camilla back to Antonia and reached up for Jacques. He put his hands on the little boy's sides and lifted him high in the air, just to see his reaction.

Jacques squealed with laughter, making Erik chuckle in response. He set down the little one, patted his head, and reached up for Henri, and lifted him over. The solemn boy didn't crack a smile. *Someday,* he told himself. *Someday, that child will smile at me. Me, not some charming little horses.*

He left the little ones in Antonia's capable hands while he unloaded the tools from the wagon, as well as the cask of water for the horses. Then he spread the blanket over the straw underneath the canvas.

Antonia laid Camilla down.

He scooped up Jacques and placed him in the corner of the wagon bed, then helped Henri climb in.

The boy had brought his slate, intending to practice his letters—if Jacques allowed him to. Henri settled himself next to the babies, near a small Indian basket that held crude wooden toys.

When he had a few minutes of free time, Erik had started carving some animals. He wasn't proud of his efforts, but he needed to make the toys in haste. He'd do a better job when winter hit, and he was homebound.

Erik hefted the crock of water with the wooden cover, placed it in the other corner, and set the dipper on top next to two glass jars they'd use to drink from. Then he went to the front of the wagon to unhitch the horses, staking them on a grassy hillock and filling their bucket with water.

Antonia repeated instructions to Henri that she'd told her son earlier, and then with a nod to indicate she was ready, walked to Erik's side.

He gave her his extra pair of leather work gloves and pointed to the spot where he wanted to start, about thirty feet away from the wagon—still within eye and earshot of the children.

Erik took out the sickle and handed it to Antonia, keeping the scythe for himself. The wooden handles were smooth. He'd taken care to rub linseed oil on them when he put them away for the winter. He pulled work gloves out of his pocket and put them on.

He made a back-away motion with his hand and took his first swing. It was awkward, as first swings always are. Usually, he'd settle into a rhythm fairly quickly, but today, conscious that Antonia watched him, he fumbled, cutting the grass in a jagged swath. Embarrassment made him clumsier. *She won't know the difference,* he tried to assure himself, shooting a glance her way to see if she was watching.

Antonia wasn't looking at him but at the sickle in her hands. She looked a strange sight, wearing Daisy's pink sunbonnet and men's clothes. Amused, he relaxed—until she bent over to grab a handful of grass, her hand about ten inches from the ground, and swung the sickle to cut the stems.

The sight of her bottom outlined against her pants made Erik realize he needed to face away from her if he wanted to get any work done today. Not for the first time since Daisy's death, desire stirred. While the familiar rush made him uncomfortable because he wasn't directing those thoughts toward Daisy, he had an odd sense of gratefulness to feel alive in that way again.

He bent to his task and soon put his uncomfortable reaction to his new wife out of his head.

✳ ✳ ✳

At first, Antonia relished the work. She breathed in the smell of cut grass, heard the swish-swish sounds of Erik's scythe, enjoyed the exercise, and took satisfaction in seeing the swath of mowed grass she left in her wake.

After an area was cleared, Erik sharpened their blades. Then they moved to a fresh spot and started again. After an hour or so, Antonia's muscles began to ache. After several hours, her back hurt, and she took longer to bend and grab a handful of grass.

In spite of the mildly warm morning, she soon heated up, and sweat soaked the chemise she wore under Erik's shirt.

The dust from the hay built up in her mouth and nose, causing her to sneeze. Underneath the sunbonnet, her sweaty head itched, but if she ignored the feeling, it went away, only to return a few minutes later. She gritted her teeth and kept going.

After a while, Erik walked toward her, carrying two long hay rakes. He handed one to her. "Time to make windrows."

Nodding, she accepted one.

"Rake the hay together into long rows to dry." He demonstrated. "Keep them high and airy," he ordered. "The more air they get, the better."

The raking was a welcome change from cutting, giving her tired back and shoulder muscles a break. But, all too soon, they finished, leaving five neat long rows, and returned to cutting.

Several times, Antonia would halt and go check on the children, who seemed just fine without her hovering over them. While she was there, she poured herself a drink, and she'd take the glass jar of water to Erik, who'd give her a grateful smile. Once, when Camilla became fretful, she stopped to nurse the baby. Then she returned to her cutting or raking.

As the day went on, Antonia became hot, tired, and itchy. Finally, when the sun had moved overhead, and her stomach sent out rumbles of hunger, she saw her husband pause, take off his hat, wipe an arm over his forehead, and replace his hat.

Erik caught her glance and walked over. "Let's eat." He laid down his scythe.

Grateful, she set the sickle next to his scythe, then stripped off her work gloves and dropped them on top of the tools. Side-by-side, they walked toward the wagon. She pushed the sunbonnet off her head, letting it dangle down her back.

Erik opened the back of the wagon and motioned for Henri to get out.

Henri scrambled down.

Knowing he needed to move after such a long time sitting, Antonia pointed to the row of cut grass. "Run to that hill. By the time you be back, the food be out."

With a grin, Henri took off, holding his arms out as if he were flying.

Antonia set Jacques on the ground and let him crawl after Henri. She untied her sunbonnet strings and dropped the head-cover inside the wagon, then scooped up Camilla and sniffed. Making a face, she held the baby away from her and smiled. "Stinky poo. You be needin' a change."

By the time Erik was done with filling the horses' water bucket, Antonia had Camilla changed and the boys washed up and ready for lunch. She spread the blanket in the shade of the wagon and took out the basket of food and the crock of water.

With a groan, Erik dropped to the blanket. He pulled off his hat and wiped an arm over his sweaty forehead.

Glad he wasn't as unfeeling of the physical discomfort as he'd seemed, Antonia sank to her knees. She pulled out a clean cloth from the stack she'd brought, dipped it into the water, wiped her face and hands, and then handed it to him. "I'm plum clean starvin', and I bet you be, too." She opened up the basket holding food that could keep outside of the cellar—jerky, pemmican, pickles, some raw carrots, cold boiled potatoes, and bread and jam for dessert.

Erik wolfed down the food, and Antonia wasn't far behind, only slowing enough to make sure the boys ate. But since she'd given them snacks earlier, they weren't too hungry.

Once the sharp pangs of her hunger stopped gnawing into her gullet, Antonia slowed her consumption, enjoying the break, feeling her muscles relax, although they ached plenty.

When he finished his victuals, Erik picked up Camilla, who'd been staring at them with curious blue eyes.

The baby gave him a gummy smile.

Erik kissed his daughter's forehead. "You're so clever, learning to smile at your pa." He lay down and tucked the baby next to him. "Let's rest a few minutes longer. We've done good work so far."

Both Henri and Jacques had sleepy eyes, so Antonia motioned to Henri to lie down next to her and pulled Jacques by her side. The thick grass underneath the blanket cushioned her sore muscles. She let out a sigh and relaxed.

Jacques rummaged for her breast, yanking on her shirt.

She pulled up the material, curled on her side, and let him nurse for a minute until he fell asleep.

A small snore from Erik made her realize he napped with the children. Gently, she moved Jacques to the side to sleep by himself, then she buttoned her shirt and turned. She was going to elbow Erik awake, but relaxing felt so good. *Just a few more minutes,* she told herself.

Propping up on one elbow, she watched her husband, liking how sleep softened his face into boyishness. If he'd been Jean-Claude, she'd have pressed a kiss to his lips before snuggling close for a few more minutes of rest. But he was Erik, and she rolled onto her back, intending to give him just a little more time before waking him up. Instead, she drifted into slumber, too.

A tickle on her nose pulled her out of the comfortable dream-place. She made a noise of protest and brushed at it, not wanting to awake fully.

A laugh sounded near her ear.

She slowly opened heavy eyelids to find herself face-to-face with Erik, only a few inches between them.

His eyes smiling, he brushed her forehead with a blade of grass.

Dreamily, she watched him watch her. She liked the shape of his nose, broad and straight. *A strong nose for the strong face of a strong man.* Then awareness jerked her completely awake, and she gasped.

Erik's eyes lost their smile, and he pulled back.

Antonia sat up. "Goodness." She checked to see that the children still slept, and then reached for her sunbonnet. "I not be intendin' to fall asleep." She set it on her head and tied the strings.

"Me, neither." Amusement gleamed in his eyes. "But the sun is still overhead, and I don't think we've slept long. We'll be all the better for a short rest."

Careful to not wake his daughter, Erik crawled off the blanket and rose to his feet.

Antonia followed, and he reached down to help her up.

Her muscles had stiffened, and, grateful for the support, Antonia allowed him to pull her to her feet. She tottered a tad before her legs unkinked. With a wince, she stretched her upper body, limbering up her back.

From the corner of her eye, she saw Erik do likewise.

He picked up the rake from where it stood propped against the wagon. "You keep cutting. I'll rake the hay into windrows."

She reached for the sickle. Just curling her fingers around the wooden handle hurt. She didn't have blisters, her palms were too callused for that, yet her skin burned as if heat built up underneath the calluses. *I can do this*, Antonia told herself, and bent to her task.

CHAPTER EIGHTEEN

Once Jacques woke up and Camilla still slept, *Maman* let the boys out of the wagon, but only when she and Pa were raking. Once he was out of her sight, Henri slipped off his moccasins, wanting to feel the texture of the springy grass beneath his bare feet. He found a stick and swished it around, pretending to be cutting hay. Then he took off, running big circles around Jacques. "Catch me. Catch me, Jacques!"

His brother crawled to him, laughing.

Before Jacques could get close, Henri raced off, making the baby switch directions.

After a while, Jacques became impatient with never reaching his brother. He scooted toward a nearby boulder. When he reached it, he stretched his hands along the top and pulled himself up. Then he looked for Henri. "Haari!" He grinned. Letting go, he toddled a few steps, then ran out of steam, and toppled to the ground, crawling for a bit. He found a feather and picked it up, backing into a sitting position and studying his find.

Getting an idea, Henri gathered flowers and found two pheasant feathers that he brought to the boy, scattering them on the grass in front of him.

Jacques chortled. "Ba! Haari!"

Knowing Jacques would stay busy for a while, Henri ran straight through a patch of wildflowers, delighting in their bright colors. He stretched out his arms and twirled until he was dizzy and collapsed on the ground, inhaling the sweet smell of the flowers, while the crisp blue sky spun high above his head.

When the sky stilled, Henri scrambled to his feet and headed back to where his brother sat.

Since he could tell Jacques was still engrossed with his flowers and feathers, Henri trotted over to examine a spot where only a few strands of prairie grass grew in a rocky patch. Seeing a small flicker of movement near the ground in the center of the area, he quickly stilled.

He crouched and became a hunter. Bent over, sneaking upon his prey, he padded closer. Pebbles dug into his feet, and Henri wished he hadn't taken off his moccasins. He squinted to examine the ground. Several minutes passed before he saw a horny toad blending in with the gray-brown dirt.

The horny toad didn't move. Only the mouth opened and closed.

Henri watched, remembering *Père* catching them for him to play with. Once he'd taken one home for several days until *Maman* grew tired of helping him find beetles and grasshoppers to feed it. She made him let the horny toad go.

He narrowed his eyes at the critter. *I can catch one by myself. Jacques will want to play with it. Maybe I'll be taking it home with me. Won't be too hard to find bugs for its meals.*

Henri moved closer to the horny toad, noting the small spikes near the back of the head, the single row of light-colored scales along the sides. Even though the creature was motionless now, the horny toad could move right quick when it took off.

He inhaled a deep breath, like *Père* had taught him, almost hearing his father's voice in his ear. *"Concentrez-vous, mon fils."*

I be lookin' sharp, Père. With a frog hop, Henri pounced, both hands closing around the horny toad. The critter was a small one, and his fingers caged it. The creature remained still, its body soft, despite the spiky-looking hide.

A feeling of triumph filled him. *"Je l'ai fait, Père!"* he said, as if his father stood watching. Then more quietly, he repeated the words in English. "I did it."

Out of the corner of his eye, he could almost see *Père* laughing with pride at Henri's feat. With sudden hope, he glanced in that direction. But no one was there. His catch of the horny toad lost all meaning, and his elation drained away.

Slowly, Henri sank to his knees. Sadness blew into him like the wind. His chest hurt. Opening his hands, he released the horny toad and watched it skitter under a pile of rocks.

I wish.... But he already knew wishing with his whole heart wasn't enough to bring back *Père.*

Henri rose and turned to check on his brother and find his moccasins.

Jacques sat in the same place, waving two feathers.

Beyond him, *Maman* and Pa raked hay. *Maman* stopped and shaded her eyes, looking for them. She smiled and waved, gesturing for him to return with Jacques.

One more time, he glanced back to where the horny toad had disappeared, hoping to see....

A gust of wind fluttered the grass.

With heavy steps, Henri turned and moved toward his family.

✳ ✳ ✳

When Camilla wails reached him, Erik's conscience bit, and he called a halt for the day. He looked around the broad area they'd cut—the windrows rolled into small stacks to protect them from the dew that would come overnight—and had the satisfaction that they'd accomplished twice as much today than if he'd been on his own. He glanced over at Antonia.

She pushed back her sunbonnet and ran an arm across her forehead.

"You go take care of Camilla and the boys, and I'll hitch up the horses."

With a tired smile, she nodded.

Once he'd harnessed the team, he took the empty keg and bucket back to the wagon, smiling to see Henri writing on his slate.

Antonia stood in the shade. The baby suckled at her breast, and Jacques clung to her leg. Fatigue shadowed her eyes, and guilt stabbed him.

She worked beside me without complaint all day. He hadn't given a thought to her well-being, assuming that when she'd had enough, she'd start complaining. That's what Daisy would have done. He thought back through the day and realized he'd been the one to stop them for lunch. The oddest feeling of pride in her and disgust at himself tangled in his chest.

"Sit and rest," he ordered, pointing at the blanket. "I'll pack up."

She sank to her knees, clutching the baby.

He picked up a jar, filled it with water, and handed it to her. Then he scraped the bottom of the crock to get the last of the water with the dipper and took a draught.

After he'd drunk his fill, Erik quickly put the tools in the wagon. He lifted the boys into the back and then reached down a hand to help Antonia to her feet.

His wife leaned on him more than he figured she would have normally done, and his guilt deepened. He kept a steadying arm around her while escorting her to the wagon. Then he took Camilla while Antonia climbed up.

His daughter squirmed in his arms and let out a squawk, anxious to return to her feeding, which she did as soon as he lifted her to Antonia.

Once in the wagon, Erik would have liked to urge the team to a faster pace so they could return home sooner, but he couldn't be sure Jacques was secure.

Dusk was settling as they approached the house. Although the guilt continued to stab him, Erik had the livestock to attend to. The needs of his wife and family would have to come second.

As he unhitched the horses, groomed and fed them, then milked the cows, Erik pondered the realization that something had changed today with his relationship with Antonia. That *something* felt both good and bad. While his hands went about their familiar tasks, he puzzled out what was different.

He realized, for the first time today, Antonia had felt like his *wife*, his partner, and that was progress. Yet, if he became close with her, what did that mean for his memories of Daisy?

Erik had struggled with these feelings since the storm but with the press of planting, taking care of the livestock, making repairs around the place, and driving into town every day, he'd been able to push them aside. He had no doubt he'd loved Daisy, loved her still, would always love her. So, how could he also feel satisfaction and an odd sense of intimacy and partnership with Antonia?

Deciding such thoughts and emotions were too much for his tired male brain to figure out, Erik resolved to put them from his mind. He finished the milking and brought the pails into the springhouse, filled a pitcher with chilled milk, and carried it to the house.

Antonia had set out supper, and the boys had clean faces and hands. She looked like she'd washed up, too, although she hadn't changed clothes, and tiredness made her face look drawn.

He smiled at her and set the pitcher on the counter.

She took it and poured four glasses.

Erik went back on the porch to wash up. When he came inside, he saw the table was set, and everyone was waiting for him.

Camilla slept in the cradle near Antonia's feet.

He claimed a seat and gave thanks. Then they set to, as if they'd never eaten before. The meal was cold from the springhouse and pantry: pheasant, hard-boiled eggs, bottled green beans, potatoes, applesauce, and bread and butter. Even Henri, who never ate as much as Erik thought a boy should, piled into his food.

The milk went down as quickly as the food, until, at the end of the meal, the boys nodded over the scraps left on their plate.

Antonia gathered up the children and took them into the bedroom, tucking them into the bed. She placed the cradle next to them. Later, when it was time for Erik to go to bed, they'd transfer the boys to the pile of furs in the main room.

His wife returned, lighting an oil lamp before she sat again at the table. She placed it between them.

Erik used his last bite of bread to slop up the little bit of applesauce left on his plate, and then leaned back, too exhausted to move. He looked at Antonia.

The lamplight burnished the gold of her eyes. The shadows hid the tired lines of her face.

Once again, he felt that sense of connection that had gnawed at him earlier. "Thank you."

She gave him a puzzled look.

"For helping today."

With a shake of her head, she made a dismissing gesture.

He captured her hand in his, curled his fingers around hers, and lowered their joined hands to the surface of the table. "You were a big help to me today. Henri, too, what with him keeping an eye on the babies. I'm grateful. You worked as hard as a man." He broke eye contact to look down. "I'm ashamed to say, I treated you like a man, too. Didn't stop enough to rest. Assumed you'd tell me when you needed to stop. But you kept up with me the whole way through."

Her hand moved, and he thought she was going to pull away. But Antonia surprised him by turning up her palm and clasping his. "I didn't need to stop, or I would have."

"I can see how tired you are. How sore and stiff."

She gave him a wry smile. "Course I be tired and sore and stiff. You be, too."

He started to protest.

She held up her other hand to stop him. "I'm proud of what we done today, Erik. Please don't be snatchin' that away by criticizin' yourself."

He shook his head, feeling the pressure behind his eyes that seemed to hit him so often since Daisy's death. He waited awhile until he could speak without betraying any emotion. He was about to order her to bed…to tell her that he'd go haying alone tomorrow, to give her a day to rest. But he paused, realizing that wisdom dictated he ask Antonia's opinion. "I can do it alone tomorrow."

She gave their clasped hands a little thump on the table. "You'll do no such thing, Erik Muth. We'll all go together."

Smiling, he brought their joined hands to his mouth and placed a kiss on her wrist. "So be it."

CHAPTER NINETEEN

The next morning, Antonia woke from a deep sleep to see the house filled with morning light. *I've overslept.* The lack of sound from the bedroom told her Erik must be up and about, and her conscience prodded her to get out of her bed of furs.

Still drowsy and in no mood to jump up, she glanced over at the boys, surprised that they hadn't woken her. Antonia watched them for a moment, thinking how beautiful they looked to her and how very blessed she was to have them.

Thoughts of Jean-Claude didn't bring the usual pang of grief, just a feeling of gratitude and warmth. Curious, she probed at her emotions. Her circumstances had changed so completely since Jean-Claude's death—her day-to-day life, her focus—everything so different than before. In some ways, Antonia felt years had gone by since that day she'd buried him in the mountain garden. In that respect, perhaps she was luckier than Erik, for he still lived in the same surroundings and had to struggle with a stranger and her children stepping into Daisy's place.

Antonia wasn't foolish enough to believe her grief had passed. Nor did she want the feelings to wane, for a beloved husband and the life they'd shared deserved to be mourned. *No, this be just a respite.* She repeated the word, *respite.* From

Henri at his lessons and Erik in his everyday speaking, she was learning new words, new—proper—ways of saying her thoughts. And this, too, moved her further and further from Jean-Claude.

Judging from the way her grief ebbed and flowed, Antonia was fairly sure something soon would happen, perhaps in just a few hours, which would once again make her want to weep or kick the side of the house. *Although, if I be lucky, this be a good day.*

"Thank you, Jean-Claude. Thank you for giving me our children," Antonia said aloud, hoping he could hear her. It wasn't the first time she'd made the statement, and it wouldn't be the last. *I'll be eighty years old and thinking the same thing. Although, God willin', I be givin' thanks for children and grandchildren...and maybe great-grandchildren.*

Antonia sat up, but then wished she hadn't moved. Every muscle ached from the haying. She had to suppress groans of pain as she rose from the pile of furs and struggled to her feet. Leaning over, unable to stand upright without hurting, she hobbled to the table to take hold of the back of a chair, where she forced her stiff body to straighten.

As she creaked and inwardly groaned through dressing, the walk to the privy, and the washing-up afterward, she wondered what Erik had planned for the day. Antonia figured she'd go find him after she fed the chickens. But needing some willowbark tea to soothe her aches and, she suspected, her husband's aches as well, Antonia first stoked the stove.

When Antonia moved the teakettle, she found it full, even though she knew she'd used up the water the previous night and hadn't refilled it. She must have slept too deeply to hear Erik moving around, and she blessed his thoughtfulness.

Since the children were still sleeping, and the tea needed to steep, she headed out to feed the chickens and gather any eggs they'd already laid. Once she brought the pan of feed and opened the door of the henhouse, the birds flocked to her. The chickens hadn't taken long to transfer their loyalty from Daisy to her. *Whoever feeds them...*

By now, Antonia had learned to distinguish the twelve birds they had left after Erik gifted three to Henrietta. The black-and-white one was the fastest, beating the others to attack a bug. Little brown Sadie needed extra feed scattered at her feet, but not until the rest of the hens were busy pecking away at their food and wouldn't notice. Otherwise, some of the bigger birds pushed her out of the way. Penny, a copper-colored hen, was the most affectionate, seeming to enjoy being petted.

The birds joined Antonia when she worked in the garden, pecking at the weeds and worms she uncovered. She'd come to enjoy their company, although she had to watch Jacques, who loved to crawl after them. So far, they'd evaded him, but she could tell he'd be walking any day now. Already, he could take a step or two on his own before dropping back down to his knees. Once sturdy on his feet, those chickens would be in trouble.

After Antonia had fed and watered the chickens, she gathered the eggs—another task she'd become adept at. *Even with the broody ones*, she thought with pride.

Then the black one managed to nip the back of her hand.

Antonia winced and shook her head. *Spoke too soon. I be not moving fast enough today.*

Carrying the wire basket of eggs, she strolled to the barn to return the pan. Her muscles had loosened up, making it easier and slightly less painful to move. Before going into the barn, she glanced at the house and strained to hear any sound the children might have made. So far, no cries told her the babies were awake.

Looking down, she saw the copper-colored hen had followed her, wanting attention. Forgetting her stiffness, Antonia crouched, and then regretted the movement before she'd gone far, but it was too late to stop her downward momentum. Her leg muscles protested, and she made a sound of pain.

Setting down the egg basket, she scooped Penny into her arms and stood, running her fingers over the hen's back.

The bird shifted, fluttered her wings, and gurgled softly.

"Like a cat, you be, Penny. Likin' being rubbed." The two of them had developed this morning ritual. The hen's feathers were soft, and Antonia found petting the chicken soothing. A few times, when she felt in need of comfort, if Erik wasn't around and the babies napped, she sought out the chicken and took Penny to the porch, sitting in the rocking chair with the bird in her lap.

Erik walked out of the barn, carrying the hay rakes. He stopped when he saw Antonia holding a chicken. "What have we here?"

"Penny follows me. Not just for food."

"For affection." He smiled. "Sadie always trailed Daisy around for petting. Guess Penny's taken a liking to you."

Penny likes me better than Daisy. She'd assumed the chicken had acted the same with both women. The thought gave her a secret little thrill.

"There be willowbark tea a brewin' for your aches and pains."

His eyebrows raised in surprise. "That's thoughtful of you. Give me a few minutes." He continued on to the wagon and set the rakes in the back, propped against the side, then moved around the barn and out of sight.

Deep in thought, she stroked the chicken, wondering why Erik had seemed surprised by the offer of tea and why

Penny liked Antonia better than the woman the hen had always known. *Mayhap neither hen nor man be receivin' enough attention from Daisy. Could be she stopped doing as much when she became pregnant.*

To Antonia, Daisy seemed the perfect wife. In comparison to her, she'd felt gawky and ignorant—just as when she was a girl—and supposed everyone else viewed her the same way.

Only a chicken but still.... In gratitude, she gave the hen some extra attention before setting her down and picking up the egg basket. As she headed toward the house, Antonia wondered if Erik would take a liking to her as well. *Not more than Daisy, a course.* She accepted that Daisy would always have first place in his heart, like Jean-Claude did in hers. *But I'd be a liking to be a close second.*

She chided herself for indulging in fanciful thoughts. *Erik be caring about me, and I be caring for him. Best not think about more.*

❋ ❋ ❋

Today's haymaking was much a repeat of yesterday. After getting the children settled in the wagon and the horses picketed, Erik and Antonia spread out the mounds of hay to dry in long windrows. Then they moved on to cut a new section. Erik was intent on being more solicitous of Antonia, insisting she halt for some water or to spend time with the children.

Finally, she shot him a glance that told him to stop.

He chuckled. While he felt half-dismayed she didn't appreciate his attempt to be a better husband, he was also amused that he'd already learned to read her so well.

After lunch, the children napped beside them on the blanket in the shade of the wagon. Henri had exhausted himself "helping" gather the hay, and he slept mouth open, sprawled between the babies.

Erik propped his arms on his knees and looked over the horizon. Lines of thin clouds feathered across the sky. A warm breeze ruffled the windrows, carrying the scent of mown grass their way. He watched a hawk glide and dive, pouncing on its prey. With mighty wing flaps, it rose, a hapless mouse clutched in its talons.

Antonia sat straighter and smothered a yawn.

"Don't get me started." Even as Erik said the words, he, too, yawned. "I know better than to lay down today. Probably would fall asleep. But we can still take a few minutes to sit here. Not too often we have some quiet time without a child awake." Then, concerned lest Antonia think he was criticizing her boys, he shot her a contrite look. "That's not a complaint."

Antonia patted his leg. "Didn't take it to be." She'd taken off her sunbonnet as soon as they'd sat in the shade and tossed it next to his straw hat at the edge of the blanket. A spiky wisp of hay speared through the waist-length braid she wore over her shoulder.

Ever since the storm, they'd been more comfortable around each other, venturing small touches. He plucked the hay from her hair and held the piece in front of her face, so she could see what he'd taken. Playfully, he tickled her nose with one end.

"Oh, you." She wrinkled her nose and swatted his hand out of the way.

"Do you feel you're settling in all right?"

"As well as be expected." Antonia pursed her lips, obviously thinking. "Perhaps I be a tetch better than that. Ain't sayin' it be easy, mind you."

As she spoke, he dipped his head in slow nods. "I think I can say the same."

"I be thinkin' something this mornin'." She hesitated. "Livin' together must be harder on you. Us 'uns here takin' Daisy's place. Jean-Claude...he be left in peace on the mountain."

Erik dropped the grass. "No one to disturb his memory?"

"Aye."

"Sometimes it *is* hard. Pain comes like stabbing me in the chest with a pitchfork." He pantomimed running himself through. "Then other times, it's just plain uncomfortable—living with strangers who are now supposed to be family."

A quick duck of her head told him she agreed.

"Getting better, though. We are becoming a family in truth. There's been more good as well. Even a save-my-sanity, grateful-to-my-bones kind of good. I don't know how I would have gotten through this time without you." He reached over and touched Camilla's foot. "And she's still with us, which is the biggest gift of all. I hold on to that when Daisy's loss hurts the most."

"Bein' with her be healin' me, too."

He nodded. "I'd known Daisy most of my life, decided early on I'd marry her someday.... She's woven through my life history."

"I be fifteen when I met Jean-Claude, and we hitched up."

He raised his eyebrows. "That's really young."

"My pa, he be glad to have me off his hands. Never done paid me much mind."

"A fort's not a place for a young lady without a mother. How old are you now?"

She shrugged. "Ain't figured it out in a long while. We be wed four years afore Henri's birth." She counted silently on her fingers. "Twenty-five."

"When's your birthday?"

"Don't know that neither. Pa said I was born during the first snowfall. He was stationed at Fort Ellis."

"In Montana, could be August, September, or even October if we had a long Indian summer that year," he said in a joking tone. "But we should probably stick to September. Mine is March twenty-fourth. I'm twenty-seven. But you need a birthday so we can celebrate. Why don't you pick a date in September, and we'll use that?"

"Celebrate?"

She doesn't know about birthdays. A glimmer of an idea entered his mind, and he decided not to tell her. Better to surprise her when the time came. "What about the boys?"

"My Henri be a winter baby. Born smack in the middle of the darkest nights."

"Late December, then. What about Jacques?"

Once again, she counted on her fingers. "End of summer. There be a fat moon in the sky, for the light be comin' through the window as I labored."

"We can look up the moon's cycle on the almanac later, so we can pinpoint the date from last year."

"Why be it—" she corrected herself "—*does* it matter?"

"Good catch on changing the word. I hear you doing that more often now." He reached over and tugged on the end of her braid. "You wait and see what happens on birthdays."

Her brow furrowed. "Then why be you askin' now?"

"You learn these kinds of things when you're courtin', Antonia. I never had a chance to court you. And, there's precious little time to do so now with the little shavers around and all the work to be done." *And our trials of grief.* "Courtship is a time to dream about your future. Do you have dreams?"

Her eyes shadowed. "Just for my children to have an education."

"Henri is certainly on his way. He's losing his French accent, and I rarely hear yours anymore."

"I didn't have one before. Only came from living with Jean-Claude. He preferred to speak French and taught me." She tilted her head in askance. "What 'bout you?"

"I want a dairy farm."

She looked sideways at him. "You have that."

"A big one." As always when Erik talked about his goals, enthusiasm took him over. "Not just to produce milk and butter, but to make cheeses. Sell them in the mercantile, but also ship to other towns to sell. Get out from under the yoke of the Cobbs." He remembered the death of Annabelle Lee and her calf, and he inwardly winced. *Heavy losses.*

"Do you know how to make cheese?" she asked, gazing at him with earnest concentration.

"Yes, my family in Indiana produced several kinds we were known for."

"Why don't we make 'em cheeses?"

"I've been working to get other things in place. Figured I might be ready to start after Camilla was born."

"We should start." Her tone sounded firm.

We. He liked the sound of that. Daisy used to be more enthusiastic about the cheese making, but with her pregnancy, she'd been too exhausted to contemplate new endeavors. Couldn't even manage all the work she'd normally done, much less take on a new business.

Erik smiled at Antonia. "See, *this* is what courtship is—sharing dreams and making plans."

She gazed at his lips. "We already be married."

"You still deserve a courtship."

She watched him, an uncertain look, almost a question, in her golden eyes. *If we hadn't needed to get married, would you still have chosen me?*

Erik knew the answer was *no.* For Antonia wasn't at all the kind of woman he preferred—too tall, too independent, not a blonde with blue eyes.... *But... maybe my tastes were formed by my dainty Daisy, the epitome of femininity.* He pondered that idea. *If I'd never known Daisy, would I still have been drawn to petite blondes? Or would other types of women match well with me, too?*

Realization glimmered.... Perhaps *no* was the wrong answer, for as Erik adjusted to Antonia's hard-working nature, how she took on tasks usually done by menfolk, and to her kindness and strength, he found her attractive. He gazed over the windrows, seeing all the work they'd accomplished together. *Antonia does suit me in unexpected ways.*

On impulse, he set a fingertip to the pulse beating in her throat, and then brushed up and across her jawline, to let his touch linger under her chin. Slowly, he tipped her face toward his, giving her time to pull away.

His gaze lingered on Antonia's mouth. Her lips were fuller and darker than Daisy's. He'd given her quick kisses before, but hadn't lingered to explore, to become acquainted with the taste and feel of her. This time, when he lowered his mouth to hers, Erik allowed himself to experience every sensation.

Her lips trembled, then yielded, warm and soft.

He hesitated, pulling away a few inches to see her eyes.

Instead of the pain or disinterest he'd expected to see, her eyes looked wide and dreamy. He kissed her again, allowing his lips to explore hers and coaxing her mouth to open for him. When her tongue touched his, tentative yet welcoming, heat spread through him. His other hand cupped her face.

Henri stirred, shifted, in the process kicking Erik's leg and reminding him of their circumstances and the work still to be done. He drew back from Antonia and took a steadying breath.

She looked down, a flush suffusing her face, adding a becoming dusky tint to her cheeks.

From this angle, he could see her long eyelashes, her vulnerability, and wanted to gently press his lips to her eyelids. *Maybe when we've become more intimate.* "Have you ever kissed anyone but Jean-Claude?" he asked.

She shook her head.

He took her hand and played with her fingers. "Same for me. Only Daisy." He brought her palm to his mouth and nibbled kisses in the center, watching her flush deepen.

She moved as if to pull her hand away, and then she stilled, gazing over the prairie. "Be calm...peaceful here."

"A farmer can never have enough peaceful days," he said ruefully. "Unless his crops are in need of rain." He paused, reluctant to move. "Guess we'd better get back to work. We have to turn the windrows again so the hay will dry enough to take home with us tonight."

Still keeping her face averted, the color in her cheeks high, Antonia nodded and shifted to rise.

Before she could get to her feet, Erik placed their joined hands on her thigh. "You don't mind me kissing you?"

She shook her head, gave him a quick look, and then her gaze skittered away. "Different it be...but good, eh?" Her lips quirked into a smile, and she finally met his eyes. She touched her fingers to his lips. "'Spect we'll soon be used to each other, then just be *good*. Be no more *different*." She lowered her hand. "Makes me be feelin' sad and alive at the same time."

"I think you've just summed us up. Sad and yet alive. Different and good. I suspect about now, we couldn't ask for more."

"Guess you be right."

But Erik found he did wish for more. He rose to his feet, extended a hand, and helped Antonia up. Instead of releasing her, he shifted her to face him and circled her waist with his arm. He didn't have to bend far to reach her lips for another exploring kiss, languid and deep.

She placed a hand on his shoulder and slid her palm around the back of his neck to pull him closer.

Erik's arm tightened around her waist. He wanted to lay her back down on the blanket, to explore her body. Reluctantly, he lifted his head. "I'd forgotten how good kissing feels. I mean…the specialness of first kisses. I feel so alive right now, like I could scythe the whole prairie."

She chuckled.

The rare sound tickled inside his ribs. "Someday, maybe even soon, eh, I hope we both will be *only* alive and good."

❋ ❋ ❋

One by one, they moved the sleeping children into the back of the wagon to keep them safe and donned their head coverings to shade their faces. They walked over to turn the windrows, so the afternoon sun could reach the hay on the bottom. By unspoken agreement, each took the one opposite and farthest apart from the other.

Even though Antonia didn't watch Erik, or at least not much, she had a heightened awareness of his presence. When she wasn't sneaking glances at him, she heard scratching sounds from his rake and knew his location. His straw hat hid his face from her, and she wondered if he was thinking of those kisses just as she was.

Remembering the touch of his lips…her body tingling… made the turning of the windrows easier. As she separated and lifted the hay with her rake, she couldn't keep her thoughts from whirling around. She relived the kisses with Erik, the sensations in her body—ones she'd never thought to feel again, made more intense by newness and unfamiliarity.

She and Jean-Claude had always engaged in satisfying marital relations, although not so much after Jacques's birth. She'd assumed intimacy wasn't as important to either of them as before and figured when the baby was older, they might once again find their old patterns. Now she wondered if that would have happened.

But Erik's kiss stirred her in ways she'd never experienced. Antonia spent some time pondering why that might be and finally concluded that at age fifteen, as crazy as she'd been for Jean-Claude, she'd been young and virginal—her only kiss the one her husband had given her when he proposed. She'd been shy about her body and inexperienced in the ways of both marriage and intimate coupling.

Now, after years of marriage, living with a man in the close confines of small cabins and tents, birthing and nursing two children, Antonia was older, comfortable with nudity, and her body was riper for pleasure. She'd grown wise in the ways of men. A shiver tingled down her spine at the thought of intimacy with Erik.

She snuck another peek at him.

Erik straightened and stretched. When he caught her looking at him, he grinned. "You doing all right over there?"

Her cheeks heated. Grateful he was too far away to see the heightened color in her face, she flipped him a reassuring wave.

Yes, I be wanting more with him.

But at the same time, Antonia wasn't quite ready to step over the intimacy threshold into a real marriage, for when doing so, she'd be leaving Jean-Claude behind. At the thought, guilt and sadness haunted her.

Erik be not pressuring me. The realization made her relax. She'd come to trust this new husband of hers. She thought about the men she'd known—mostly soldiers and Indians, a few other hunters who were friends with Jean-Claude—and couldn't imagine one of them she'd want to be married to. She'd been lucky in the husband she'd ended up with.

A breeze blew tendrils of hair across her face, and she brushed them back. *Maybe our marriage be not just luck. Maybe we be brought together for a purpose.* Antonia imagined Jean-Claude as a puppeteer in heaven pulling the strings that attached him to his family, like a marionette performance she'd once seen. *Or maybe God himself had taken pity on their plight and arranged matters.* In her gut, the awareness felt right. A different kind of tingle—one of awe—slid over her skin, giving her goose bumps.

Antonia reached the end of her windrow at the same time Erik finished his.

He grinned again.

The man be full of grins since that kiss.

"Looks like yesterday's batch of hay is coming home with us tonight." He tilted his head in the direction of the rows of hay they'd raked from this morning's cutting. "Now to turn those."

The sun was dropping low when they finally rolled the dried windrows into large piles for the night.

They took the children out of the back, setting Camilla on the blanket, while Jacques and Henri were finally released to play a safe distance away. They took down the canvas top and then removed the ribs.

She changed the baby while Erik hitched up the team and drove the wagon to the two nearest haystacks, setting the brake. He only had one pitchfork, so he used it on the first pile, impaling the hay and tossing the forkful over the side of the wagon.

After nursing Camilla and setting down to play with her fingers, Antonia checked on the boys, playing hunting games nearby. With the children taken care of, she went to help Erik. She stooped and gathered huge armfuls of hay from her mound and threw them into the wagon, relishing the sight of the rising level. Several times, with Erik's help, she scrambled inside the wagon bed and stomped on the hay, enjoying the springy feel under her feet.

From time to time, her gaze would meet Erik's, and she saw a new awareness of her in his eyes—as a woman, not just the person who'd stepped in to take care of his baby and his home. And, she supposed, he could read something similar on her face. She saw him differently now—the solid way he stood, strong legs slightly apart, rooted into the earth, the play of muscles on his back and arms when he lifted the hay and threw a pitchfork full over the side.

Erik be like a mountain. Jean-Claude be a stream. Neither be better. Just different.

When they finished the first two piles, Erik moved the wagon down the rows. The load of hay grew higher, even with Antonia, and Henri—who left Jacques playing with Camilla's spoon—and came to join her, stomping to flatten the heap. Finally, the wagon bed could hold no more, and they threw the canvas covering over the hill of hay and anchored the sides to the wagon.

When Erik finished, he stopped to gaze at the boys.

Henri stood in front of Jacques, holding his hands. He'd let go of the little boy and back away.

With a wide grin, Jacques toddled toward his older brother until he caught him. Then the two would start all over again—release, step back, toddle. Eventually, Jacques's legs gave out, and he plopped on his bottom. "Haari!" Obviously pleased with his accomplishment.

Erik turned to her. "Tonight, when I do the milking, I want Henri to come with me. Time to start teaching him. He's a responsible boy."

The note of pride in his voice made her heart swell. She placed her hand on his arm. "Thank you."

"No need for thanks, Antonia. That's what a father does."

Camilla let out a hungry squawk.

Antonia moved toward her. When she stooped to pick up the baby, her muscles protested. She held in a groan. *Later tonight, I'm getting out the liniment bottle.* If she hadn't been so tired the previous evening, she would have thought to apply an herbal salve she'd learned to make from the Indians. When applied the liniment eased aches and pains.

But then again, it might not have been tiredness at all, but the bittersweet memories of rubbing the salve into Jean-Claude's muscles, or he into hers, and how the massages often led to marital relations. She hadn't been ready to touch Erik in such a familiar way, even if they'd kept to simple shoulder and neck rubs.

Be I ready now?

She wasn't sure.

CHAPTER TWENTY

Carrying a pail of grain and a large milk jar, Pa led Henri toward the trees in the pasture where the cows had already gathered waiting to be milked. "These ladies are docile enough." He shook his head. "When I was a boy, we sure had some ornery ones. Kick you. Kick over the pail. We had to tie their hind legs together."

Henri also carried an empty pail. In his haste to match Pa's wide strides, he banged the pail against his leg.

A few cows stamped and stared at him, so he held the pail away from his body lest he make noise again.

Pa motioned for Henri to come closer, gesturing toward the first brown cow. "This is Grandma Belle. She's a gentle old lady, matriarch of my herd."

Henri didn't want to ask what *matriarch* meant.

"Approach her slowly," Pa said softly. "Speak in a low voice and pat her side so she knows you're there. You don't want to scare her, so keep your movements slow. Then you can rub her head and nose like you would a horse."

"Hiya." Henri borrowed a greeting Daniel used each morning when he saw his friends at school. But instead of sounding friendly like the older boy, the word came out more like a mouse squeak. He tried again. "Hiya, Grandma Belle." He looked at Pa to see if he'd done it right.

Pa winked and jerked his thumb toward the cow, urging Henri ahead of him.

Reluctantly, his stomach cramping, he sidled toward Grandma Belle's head. Up close, the animal appeared much bigger than she did out in the pasture.

Pa set down the pail and lowered a hand to Henri's shoulder. "You made friends with my horses, Henri, and you're real good with the mules. You'll be just fine with these ladies."

Somewhat reassured, Henri moved to pet Grandma Belle.

The cow turned big brown eyes toward him.

Henri decided she didn't seem so scary after all. He stroked her nose, thinking that she smelled sort of like a horse, although with some mud and manure added in, and her hide felt rougher.

They moved into the barn through the back and filled a long shallow bin with small piles of grain, topping each mound with plenty of hay. After they opened the barn doors, in stepped cow after cow, right up to the bin. There was some head butting over the food, so Pa nudged each animal along until the five were evenly lined up and tied each animal to a post.

Pa pointed to a low stool. "This is where I sit to milk." He took a seat. "Place the bucket like so." He set the pail under the cow's udder and motioned for Henri to come closer. "Sit on the ground next to me so you can see everything."

Henri dropped into a cross-legged position. With a sinking feeling, he stared at four long teats drooping from Grandma Belle's distended udder. From this angle, the cow seemed even bigger.

"We wash off the udder." Pa dipped a rag in the warm soapy water in a pail he'd brought on an early trip to the barn and wiped off the cow. "Now watch." Pa took hold of two teats. "See my hand, like this?" He demonstrated with the teat nearest Henri. "Squeeze downward. With your smaller hand, you'll probably have to slide down like this. Keep your grip on the top, so milk doesn't flow back into the udder. Got that?" He glanced at Henri for confirmation.

Not at all sure he did, Henri nodded back.

"Good. Now, you're not to pull or tug, hear? She won't like that." Pa glanced at him. "The first squirt from each teat goes onto the ground, not into the pail. To clean her out, so to speak."

"Yes, Pa."

"Repeat with your other hand, going back and forth between the teats. Continue until that part of the udder looks deflated." Deftly, Pa milked Grandma Belle, talking as he worked. "You'll need to keep an eye on her back, for if she arches, she's about to drop cow pies. You don't want to foul the milk, so grab the bucket and move out of the way." Pa glanced at Henri. "Ready to try?"

What if I can't do it? But not wanting to disappoint Pa, he nodded.

Pa scooted back on the stool. "Sit in front of me and reach for the udder."

Henri took a seat. Held between Pa's strong legs, he leaned over and took a hold of the two nearest teats. They felt warm in his hands. His first squeeze didn't produce anything.

"Slide your hands."

He squeezed and slipped his hands down the teats. Some milk squirted out and splashed into the pail.

"There you go." Pa spoke with an encouraging tone. "Keep doing it. Not both hands together, though. First one hand, then the other. Find a rhythm."

The cow mooed, startling Henri, and he let go.

Pa patted his leg. "She's just talking to you. Get on back to milking now."

Henri bent to the task, feeling satisfaction every time he saw the white stream and heard the *splash-splot* sound as the milk hit the sides of the pail. After a while, his hands grew tired. He slowed, but kept going. The milk dried to a dribble.

Pa patted Henri's leg. "Let me take over and finish up the ole gal. We're not going to strip all the milk from her. When we're finished, we'll let the calves out, and they will do that."

Henri didn't want to stop, but he couldn't make his hands move anymore.

"You can help with the next one." Pa eased Henri out of the way. "Shake out your hands. That will uncramp them."

Henri stood. He spread his arms and flapped his hands, watching Pa's every move. This time, he better understood what Pa was doing.

Delilah lurked a few feet away, tail straight up and ears pricked. When he turned to her, she mewed and walked over to them, sniffing and rubbing against Pa's legs.

The cat had birthed five kittens, and after a few days, she'd allowed Henri near them. He loved to spend time with the little bundles of fluff in the morning and after school.

To his astonishment, the cat walked right under the cow.

"Meow." She sat on her haunches, front paws in the air.

Pa grinned at Henri. "Someone wants her supper."

The cat eyed Grandma Belle's udder.

Pa aimed a teat at Delilah and squirted milk at her mouth.

Delilah lapped at the milk as fast as she could. Some splattered on her face, but she didn't stop to lick the milk off.

Henri laughed. "Delilah has a white mustache."

Eyebrows raised, Pa sent him a glance filled with humor and pride.

Henri had never seen that look on Pa's face, and something warm and good and achy swelled in his chest. "Think you could do that with Jacques, Pa?"

"Sure thing. Just have to get him to smile. That grin of his is plenty bigger than Delilah's."

Henri laughed again, thinking of Jacques's *grenouille* grin and the surprised look he'd have on his face when Pa shot that milk at him. "Can we do it tomorrow?"

Pa winked. "We'll introduce Jacques to Grandma Belle. Might as well bring your *maman* along so she can see what a good milker you are."

❋ ❋ ❋

After Erik bore Henri off to help with the horses and get his first milking lesson, Antonia cleaned and fed two cranky babies. Once they'd gotten dry bottoms and food in their stomachs, Jacques and Camilla settled down. Because the evening was still warm, she washed up on the porch using the washcloth and Daisy's fragrant soap to clean herself all the way down to her waist.

Later, while she was cooking dinner, frying up the rabbits she'd taken from the springhouse, Henri rushed in, jabbering about learning to milk. He ran down the list of what he'd done, obviously repeating the instructions Erik had given him. Encouraged by her nods, he moved back and forth with her as she carried dishes to the table.

Here he be! The sight of her son's bright face made her heart soar. Up until now, she'd only caught glimpses of the happy boy he'd been before Jean-Claude's death. However, after those cheerful moments, Henri always retreated into his sadness.

His voice trailed off.

She leaned down and kissed his cheek. "Proud of you, I be. Now out to the porch and wash up."

Antonia set the table, including the serving pieces that Erik wanted but she thought unnecessary. *More dishes to be washing up after dinner.*

Henri skipped back inside, heading toward Jacques.

She watched with amusement, seeing a now-clean boy tell his little brother all about milking a cow, complete with hand motions. She laughed at his glee when he recounted Pa squirting the milk at the cat and promised Jacques a treat tomorrow.

Jacques's enthusiastic "Baa, Harri!" apparently served to encourage him.

Henri took the small boy's hands and tried to show him how to move his fingers as if clutching a cow's teat.

Through the open door, Antonia heard Erik's heavy footsteps on the porch, followed by the sound of splashing water. She pushed the frying pan to the cooler part of the stovetop. Picking up the liniment bottle from the table, she stepped through the door.

Bare to the waist, Erik bent over the washbasin.

Suddenly, she wondered if the liniment was such a good idea after all. Without his shirt, Antonia could see the breadth of Erik's shoulders and how his muscled back sloped to a narrow waist. The position showed his tight, well-formed buttocks and massive legs.

She inhaled a sharp breath, and with a sudden feeling of shyness, almost turned and fled inside. But a stronger current swept her across the porch, her moccasins silent on the wooden floor.

Straightening, he picked up the second bar, the one smelling of bay leaves, and rubbed the washcloth over the side of the soap. He tried to reach the center of his back and winced.

His arms must be sore. "Here, let me help." She set the bottle on the porch rail.

He paused, glanced over his shoulder at her, and his lazy smile widened into a slow grin. "Can't say I'll turn down your offer."

Antonia took the washcloth from him and placed it just under his neck. She slowly ran the cloth down his spine and across the bottom of his back, then moved her hand in small circles.

He shivered.

In almost sensual motions, Antonia stroked the cloth until she'd covered his whole back. She dunked the washcloth into the basin and rinsed it out. Picking up the ewer, she poured some clean warm water over the cloth and wiped the soap off his back. She switched the wet cloth for a towel and patted his skin dry.

"Thank you," he said, his voice thick.

"Once you be done, my liniment be helpful with soreness." She held up the brown bottle. "Later, I could rub some on you."

He cocked an eyebrow. "And you, wife? I'm sure you could use some liniment as well." The suggestive tone of his voice gave another meaning to the words.

Warmth swirled in Antonia's stomach, and she stepped back. "I have supper on the stove."

His blue eyes held a knowing look. "We'll do this liniment of yours after the children are in bed."

❄ ❄ ❄

Antonia shut the bedroom door behind her and hesitated a moment, listening to hear if the boys protested. She loved having the luxury of a separate room where the children could fall asleep, giving her and Erik a little time to themselves.

Instead of sitting and reading like she'd expected, Erik stood with a closed book in his hand. He'd turned down the lantern on the table. The yellow light had dulled to a dull orange glow, casting the rest of the room into dark shadows. He slid the book into the gap between two others on the bookshelf. "How shall we do this?"

Something about the tension in his body told Antonia he was as nervous about the idea of their massaging each other as she was. "With Jean-Claude and I, we, ah, just laid down. But..." Her voice trailed away, for she wasn't sure how to tell him that position had often led to other kinds of touches, ones she wasn't sure about.

Seeming to understand, Erik gestured toward the table. "I'll just straddle a chair." His fingers worked at the top button of his shirt.

Heat rose in her cheeks, and Antonia turned away, chastising herself for her reaction. *I haven't blushed so much since I be a girl.* She reached for the brown bottle on the table and uncorked the top, smelling the yarrow and other herbs she had no English words for.

Behind her, she heard a rustle as Erik removed his shirt. He laid the folded shirt on the table and turned the chair around, straddling the seat and crossing his arms over the back.

Antonia poured a puddle of liniment into her palm and stepped behind him, rubbing her hands together to coat her fingers and palms and warm the oil.

The lamplight played over the ridges of his bare back. Erik had the well-muscled body of a hard-working man.

The sight made her heart thump harder. She lowered her hands to his shoulders, first slicking the oil over his skin, and then skimming her fingers over the muscles, assessing where he felt tight.

"Hmmm."

"You be having rocks here under your skin," she teased.

"Feels like it."

She kneaded the muscles of his shoulders, paying particular attention to the tight areas.

Sometimes he made a sound, a grunt or groan, which told her when she'd hit a hurting place or one that felt good. She spent time on his shoulders and neck, then moved to probe with her fingertips between his shoulder blades.

Rubbing liniment over Erik felt more intimate than washing him had, for there was no cloth between her fingers and his skin. Placing her hands directly on his body felt like a whole new kind of exploration. She took her time rubbing, kneading, stroking, and imagining her fingers soothing all his aches and pains. She reached his lower back. "Stand and brace yourself against the table."

With a swing of his leg, Erik turned in the chair and rose. "I've never felt anything like this."

She stared at him in astonishment, careful not to let her mouth gape.

"Well, not so…" Erik waved his hand to indicate his upper body. "Daisy would rub on a sore spot if I asked her. But not the whole back like you just did. And she never volunteered to do so."

"I ain't be done."

He turned and lowered his hands to the edge of the table, bending so she could reach his lower back.

As she worked on him, Antonia mulled over what he'd just revealed. For the first time, Daisy didn't seem like such a perfect wife. She couldn't imagine a couple not using massages to relieve stiffness and pain and lead to a deeper physical and emotional connection.

With her thumbs and knuckles, she dug into his lower back, which must be aching from the bending and twisting he'd done the last few days. Hers certainly was.

Erik growled.

She laughed. "I'll be making the same noises when you do this to me."

"I'm massaging you?" He rotated to see her face. "I wasn't sure you'd be comfortable with that."

"Ain't sayin' it'll be comfortable. Fact that it be our first time doin' this." She smiled at him. "You should be knowin' by now...we've had uncomfortable firsts and will be a havin' many more."

Erik grimaced. "That we will." He raised his eyebrows and gave her a cocky leer. "I'm looking forward to *some* of those firsts."

"Oh, you." Antonia playfully swatted his arm. She circled her finger in the air. "Turn around and sit back down. Let me do your front."

He twisted his head from side to side and rolled his shoulders. "Much better."

"There be more to come." Her flirtatious tone surprised her. Rubbing Erik's front felt more intimate. As she kneaded his shoulders, Antonia was acutely aware of how close her breasts were to his face, of the heat pooling in her body, the rich scent of the herbs on his skin.

She didn't make eye contact as she worked. Instead, she kept her gaze lowered and concentrated on his right shoulder. But when she snuck a peek at his face, she saw his eyes were closed, which made her feel less tense. When she finished both shoulders and arms, she asked him to stand.

With that lazy smile she was coming to love, he obeyed. In the lamplight, the hair on his chest gleamed golden, the muscles were shadowed. She wanted to skim her fingertips over his hard flesh, and then trail kisses over the same path. *Not this time.*

Antonia rubbed her palm over his chest, pausing over his heart, feeling the beat—hard, fast, and so very alive. The rhythm echoed in the pulse thrumming through her body. If she concentrated, she could almost feel as if they flowed together, his blood to hers. She could have stood there, palm to chest for a long time.

Although reluctant to finish the massage, Antonia knew the evening was growing late for a busy farmer and his wife. They needed to be up with the dawn, especially with another day of haying planned. She moved her hand to knead the muscles between his arm and chest, eliciting a groan.

When her hands started to ache, Antonia patted his shoulder in a sign she'd finished.

Erik squeezed her into a hug, burying his face in the crook of her neck for a kiss. His body pressed against hers.

The touch of his lips on her skin tickled, and she squirmed.

Erik kissed her cheek. "Your turn, wife," he growled and released her. He reached for the liniment bottle.

With her back toward him, Antonia untied the strings of her tunic and rolled it down to her waist. The air was cool on her skin. She hitched up the bottom of her tunic to straddle the chair, leaning forward over the seat back. Intensely aware of her naked upper body, of the weight of her breasts hanging loose, she lowered her head to her arms, waiting in anticipation, listening to the sound of Erik rubbing his hands together.

His palms came down on her back, instead of her shoulders as she'd assumed.

The unexpected touch gave her a ticklish shock, and Antonia gasped and flinched.

Immediately, Erik pulled back his hands.

"No, no, I be fine. That be a good jump."

"If you're sure..." He splayed his hands over her back, hesitated, as if waiting to be sure she was ready before he moved, seeking her sore areas. "You're tense."

"I know."

His palms and fingers settled on her, soothing and sure. His hands were bigger than Jean-Claude's, his touch different, more exploratory but no less deft.

The sensations of Erik's rough hands on her body felt exquisite. Warmth from his palms tingled into her muscles. *I needed this.* Not just the massage for her stiffness, but a man's caring focus on her body. Like chilled butter set in the sunlight, she gradually melted into a deep sense of relaxation.

After he'd massaged her neck and shoulders, Erik moved to the middle of her shoulder blades.

An area that she hadn't known was sore until his fingers probed the muscles. She gasped at the sharp pain, and tears pricked her eyes. *Where did that emotion come from?*

"Too hard?"

"No. Just a hurting place." Her voice sounded wobbly.

"I expect you've been carrying far too many burdens lately."

'Spect so. Antonia blinked back tears, grateful for his understanding.

"Would you like me to stop?"

She shook her head.

"I'll go back to your shoulders for a while. When I return here, I'll start softer then increase the pressure." His fingers probed the area where her neck and shoulder met. He lifted her braid and pressed his thumb around the base of her neck.

The feeling of needing to cry ebbed. Antonia began to relax and enjoy the sensations he awoke in her.

The more Erik worked on her body, the more the tightness in her aching muscles eased. Pleasure simmered under her skin.

Antonia felt his mouth on her shoulder as he dropped a kiss on the exposed skin. She shivered, and a pleased hum escaped her.

"Like that, do you?"

Too much.

She didn't turn to face him, although she longed to do so.

"I want to love you tonight, Antonia," he said softly, his mouth near her ear. "And I think you want that, too." He paused, obviously waiting for her answer.

The silence stretched. She could only nod.

"But I'm not sure we're really ready or how we'd feel in the morning. I couldn't bear to feel guilty, as if we'd done something wrong, even if we know that's not so."

"I know. You be right." Antonia pulled up her tunic and fastened the ties. When she finished, she swiveled on the chair to face him.

He extended a hand to assist her to her feet and gathered her into his arms for a kiss.

His lips and tongue, the taste and feel of him, were familiar now, yet just as new and exciting as earlier today.

Erik's kiss was demanding, yet also patient, arousing her, as well as promising fulfillment in the future. He lifted his head and touched her heart with his forefinger. "We've been planting seeds, you and I, between us." He moved his finger from her chest to his and back again. "And with you to my daughter and me to your sons. The seeds have sprouted and are growing just fine. We need to see they are watered and the weeds kept away so they bear fruit. The harvest will come in due time when the fields are ripe and ready."

Touched beyond words, Antonia reached up on tiptoe to kiss his cheek. "You be a good man, Erik Muth, and I thank you for your patience."

"I have enough patience for *tonight*."

Left unspoken was a question, hovering in the air between them. *How long should we be patient?*

CHAPTER TWENTY-ONE

Two days later, Antonia and Erik stood at the window watching the drizzle mist the early Sabbath morning. Behind them, Henri still lay in bed, although he was awake. He'd been so hard to rouse that she'd taken pity on him and let him lie for a bit. She'd already changed and fed Jacques and had given him two spoons to play with.

Antonia held Camilla in her arms, gently rocking the baby. "Yesterday's cuttin' be lost," she lamented, thinking of all the work they'd done to make more hay. She glanced at Erik, wondering if he was upset.

His hair was still damp from driving the cows into the barn to be milked. "We had an unusually long sunny spell. I didn't expect even two days' worth, so we're ahead."

She raised a skeptical eyebrow.

"My outlook has changed, Antonia. Last year at this time, I'd have bemoaned the ruined hay." He shrugged. "Now I know what real loss is. So I'm seeing things differently. I'm focusing on being grateful to have hay for the livestock, and I have even more than I'd originally thought I could manage because you helped."

She pursed her lips, struck by the truth of his words.

Jacques banged on the floor with his spoons.

Antonia glanced at her youngest son.

With a wide smile, Jacques tapped again, apparently delighted at using the floor for a drum.

"I tell you, wife." Erik's voice changed from serious to playful. "I have a powerful hankering for fried chicken. Would you mind cooking up one for Sunday dinner tonight?"

"No, I be not mindin'." The agreement slipped out before Antonia realized she did, indeed, mind. She'd grown fond of the chickens and didn't want to serve any of them up for a meal.

"And, would you mind...." His voice trailed off.

"Mind what?" she prompted.

"Well, Daisy always made my favorite kind of fried-chicken, even better than Ma's—not that I ever admitted that to my mother on pain of being disowned."

Disowned?

"The recipe is in her box, there." He waved toward the shelf that held the tin box with the red flowers on the lid. "Daisy was particular about keeping everything written down. Her ma's and grandma's recipes are in there, too."

Antonia's stomach chilled. *Now be the time to tell him I cain't read.* Since they'd arrived at such accord, she didn't want to do anything to damage their growing intimacy. She'd seen how Erik prized book learning. *He'll be ashamed of me.*

"Would you try using her recipe? I promise I won't compare."

"And how could you not?" Antonia said tartly.

His expression fell. "You're right. I shouldn't have asked," he said in a deadened voice. "You just fry the chicken your own way." Erik turned back to the window. The drizzle has stopped. "I think we can go to church after all." He reached for his coat. "I'll go hitch up the horses and ready the wagon."

Antonia regretted her sharp response. But she didn't know how to explain. "Breakfast be waitin' for you. I'll fry some ham and eggs, quick like."

He frowned. "If we're going to town, then we probably don't have time. Can you make something for us to eat on the way?"

"Of course."

"Then, I'll get the milk and butter from the springhouse," he said, his tone back to normal. "And if you've eggs to spare for the mercantile, we'll take them, too. The Cobbs only open up the store for an hour after the service, but they'll still let me drop off everything beforehand."

"I have plenty of eggs."

"The more to sell then." He left the house.

Antonia made a scooting motion to Henri, who'd lain and watched them from his bed of furs. "School clothes, son. Be gittin' on with you now."

Henri's mouth pulled down. He was slow to slide out from the covering.

She shifted Camilla to one arm and walked over to ruffle his hair. "Natalia probably be there. You haven't seen her for three days."

The mention of meeting up with the older girl he idolized banished the sullen expression from Henri's face. Once on his feet, he hurried to the bedroom to change his clothes.

Antonia shook her head at her son, grateful he'd taken such a liking to the girl who was helping teach him. *Far better for him to be wanting to go to church and school than for me to be a pushin' him out the door.*

Now, who will be pushin' me out the door?

Camilla wiggled.

"You want to be gittin' down, do you?" Antonia dropped a kiss on her daughter's head, her lips brushing the fluffy hair, softer than the finest corn silk. "Sweet babe," she crooned.

Camilla gurgled a noise of pleasure and waved a hand, promptly smacking Antonia's chin.

She grabbed the baby's hand. "You be dangerous, little one." She kissed Camilla's fingers and laid the baby on her back next to Jacques, propping her up a bit with some folds of the fur.

The baby waved her spoon and kicked both feet, seeming just as delighted in her makeshift toy as Jacques was with his.

Antonia boiled eggs and sliced ham, wishing she had bread for they'd used up all of her last baking. Slowly, she walked to the bedroom, feeling no desire to change out of her comfortable clothes, go to town, and attend an unfamiliar church service with people she didn't know.

I can't avoid Sweetwater Springs for the rest of my life. But oh, how she wanted to. *I'm doing this for Henri and Jacques.* She glanced at Jacques and Camilla. *For my family, so we be part of this community.* The thought gave her strength. She would do *anything* for her children—indeed, had already done so.

You be knowin' some good people. Antonia thought of the Nortons, the Camerons, and the Carters, and realized she'd like to see them again. *Maybe goin' to church be not so bad.*

She stripped off her Indian garb and opened a bureau drawer, shoving aside the corset to reach her chemise, then had a sudden unpleasant thought. *I've regained the weight I'd lost. I might have to wear the corset to fit into the dress!*

Antonia let out a French curse she'd learned from Jean-Claude. Realizing what she'd said, she clapped a hand over her mouth. Feeling guilty, she lowered her hand and peeked out the door to see if her sons had heard her.

The boys sat across from each other, playing a game with Jacques's spoons.

Camilla lay next to them, her head turned to watch her brothers.

Good, they didn't hear me. Antonia quickly donned her undergarments, slid the dress over her head, and buttoned it. With relief, she realized the waist fit her perfectly. She glared at the corset and slammed the drawer shut. *I be spared the ordeal of wearing that contraption,* she thought, using some of the big words she'd learned from Erik. She made a mental note to try to speak properly while in town.

I'll have to be watchin' every word that comes out of my mouth. Antonia caught herself. *I'll have to watch every word,* she amended.

Erik strode into the house. "The wagon's in front," he called a moment before he appeared in the doorway of the bedroom. "I've packed up the food. There's straw in the wagon, and I've folded your bearskin and laid it across the seat." He stopped talking and gazed at her. "I like how that dress makes your eyes shine like gold."

Antonia could feel heat creeping into her cheeks. Jean-Claude had been fond of giving her extravagant compliments, most of which she'd laugh at and dismiss. But something about Erik's quiet words and the admiration in his eyes made her heart flutter.

With his forefinger, he tapped the side of his chin. "You've left your braid down."

Embarrassment made her good feelings flee, and Antonia wished she could follow suit. *How can I tell him that I've never worn my hair any way but loose or plaited, or maybe in two braids like the Indian women?*

She reached over to finger her braid and decided to admit her ignorance. "I don't know another way."

Erik rocked back on his heels as if stumped. Then he shrugged. "I can probably help. I saw Daisy do it often enough." He walked toward the bureau.

She moved closer. A white glass chicken sitting on a nest was positioned on top of the drawers near Daisy's comb and brush, which Antonia now used.

He lifted the hen. "Daisy kept her hairpins in here."

To her surprise, the hen separated from the nest, which turned out to be hollow. Antonia tried to hide her astonishment from Erik about not knowing such a thing and moved closer. Inside the nest, she saw a scattering of bent wires shaped like long narrow horseshoes.

"A hairpin." He picked one up. "My sister Kirsten once described it as 'a piece of wire used for the express purpose of stabbing a woman in the head and tormenting her with too-tight hairstyles.' She complained that wearing her hair up gave her headaches, and when no company was around, she refused to do so, no matter how much our mother scolded."

Antonia thought she might like Erik's sister. She wondered if Kirsten wore corsets at home but figured she couldn't ask him such a question.

In the mirror positioned above the chest of drawers, Erik's gaze met hers. He reached over to finger her braid. "Your hair's a lot thicker than Daisy's. You'll probably need plenty of these." He laid the hairpin back in the nest. "Tell me if I poke your scalp." He made a twirling gesture with his finger.

She turned her back to him.

He twisted the plait up and over the top, looping the braid around and around. "I like how your hair shines auburn in certain lights." His fingers brushed the nape of her neck.

An unexpected shiver trickled down her spine.

"There," he said, satisfaction in his tone. "Hold this for me, and don't let go until I say."

Antonia reached up and grasped the mound piled just above her neck.

One by one, Erik took a hairpin and eased the ends into her hair.

One went too deep, poking the back of her head, and she winced.

"Sorry." He pulled out the hairpin and tried again. "How's that?"

"Fine," she said, not sure that wearing her hair up like this was *fine* at all.

"Done."

She lowered her hand.

Erik stepped back and examined his work. "Not bad. The bun's a little lopsided, but not enough that I think anyone will notice. Well, maybe the people right behind our pew will."

Antonia thought a bun was bread. But in remembering back to her childhood, she realized both had a similar shape. She turned her head from side to side. The unaccustomed weight of her hair pulled but didn't hurt.

Erik strode over to a stack of three round containers covered with flowered wallpaper, next to the bureau.

Antonia had never looked inside them.

"Now for Daisy's Sunday bonnet." He lifted the lid of the first one and brought out a blue-gray cloth bonnet with velvet ribbons and flowers of the same color. Holding it up, he glanced from her dress to the hat. "Um." He shook his head, set the hat on the bed, moved the first box aside, and took off the lid of the second one. "Her summer hat."

This one was straw with shiny pink ribbons and pink and white blossoms on the top, like nothing Antonia had ever seen blooming. She imagined Daisy looked pretty wearing it. *But I'll look like a gawky walking flower garden.*

"I don't know, Antonia," Erik said in a skeptical tone, waving with his free hand, from her skirt to the hat he held. "Daisy set great store by her hats matching her dresses—or at least not clashing. I remember her nattering at...uh, *telling* me that much. But what do I know about female fashions?"

This whole business of hats be silly. Antonia thought back to their wedding. Although she hadn't really paid much attention at the time, Mrs. Cameron and Mrs. Carter had, indeed, worn hats that seemed a similar color to their dresses. Only Mrs. Norton, in her worn blue dress and faded black bonnet, hadn't matched. That thought gave her hope. *Maybe it doesn't matter after all. Or, at least, not to all women.* She pointed at the last box. "What's in that?"

"An old one that Daisy refused to wear any longer."

He slid the box out from under and pulled off the lid. Inside was another cloth hat. This one had faded to a sage green, and the ends of the ribbons were frayed. With a comical expression of dismay, he glanced between the hats. "Looks like it's a choice between blue or pink that don't seem like you at all, or this old thing."

In spite of the tension in her stomach, Antonia couldn't help but smile at the face he made. She reached out to touch the green hat. "If we trim the end of the ribbons, this be not so bad."

"All these choices are bad," he muttered.

"We be both havin' the worst kind of bad, so what does a hat matter?"

Erik shot her an expression of admiration. "You're right, wife." He laid the bonnet on the bed, walked over to a shelf, and lifted the lid of the sewing basket. He rummaged around inside before pulling out a tiny pair of scissors. Picking up the end of each ribbon, he carefully cut off the frayed edge. "There." He extended the hat toward her.

Antonia took a step, reaching for it. Her toes caught on her hem, pitching her forward.

As Erik moved to steady her, she did a quick step for balance, causing him to tread on her toes.

He caught himself, shifting his foot away from hers. "Did I hurt you?" He looked down to check.

"No."

"You're wearing moccasins, Antonia." Erik frowned.

Her stomach clenched.

"I didn't realize. I'm so used to seeing you in them. And on the day we bought your dress, I was too stricken to notice you weren't wearing shoes. You could have been wearing shoes made out of gold, and I still wouldn't have seen them."

Antonia realized he wasn't criticizing *her* but *himself,* and her stomach calmed. "I ain't needin' no gold shoes." She tried to lighten his mood. "Likely they'd be hurtful to walk in."

His frown remained.

She touched his arm. "I've managed without."

His expression hardened. "After church today, we'll buy you a hat and shoes. I don't want people to think I can't take care of my wife."

Why does be matterin'? But she didn't say so, for it obviously mattered to Erik. *He's plumb picky about it.*

The uncharacteristic frown lingered. His brow furrowed. "Now that I think of it, you need a shawl and coat. You can't keep wearing that ratty raccoon skin of yours."

"Why not? It be warm."

"For around here the coat is perfect. But for town…" As Erik said the words, a pained expression crossed his face.

"We can use the money I got from the furs to buy 'em," she offered, guessing what the problem might be.

"Absolutely not. I want you to keep that money," he said in a firm tone. "The milk, butter, and eggs I've been delivering have paid off your dress and undergarments. We've started building up credit at the store that we can use for these purchases."

"Oh. Credit be good."

He let out a sigh and rubbed his hand over his head, mussing his hair. "Antonia, after what we've been through…if something happens to me, I want to know you have money put by.

Not that you won't have the farm and all, as well as everything I've saved, which at this point isn't much." He pointed in the direction of the barn. "I put everything into that."

A movement in the doorway caught her eye. Antonia glanced over to see Henri watching them.

Her son tilted his head as if studying her, and his eyes looked troubled. "You don't look like *Maman*."

"I don't 'spose I do." She walked over to drop a kiss on his head. "But I still be your *maman*, and that be never changin'."

Erik handed her the bonnet. "Let's pack up the children and get in the wagon. I'll hurry and swap out what I'm wearing for my good clothes. We don't want to be late for church."

Antonia turned toward the mirror and set the hat on her head, tying the ribbons under her chin. A stranger stared back at her—not a trapper's wife in squaw clothes—but one who looked like any of the other women she'd seen in town. *Be this really me?*

The woman in the mirror no longer was Jean-Claude Valleau's Antonia. She was Erik Muth's Antonia. As much as she wanted to adapt and become like other white women, she grew sad at the thought of losing more of her connection to Jean-Claude.

❋ ❋ ❋

The pewter sky had cleared to shades of blue, ranging from eggshell to turquoise to slate, filtered through elongated layers of white and gray clouds. The sight was beautiful enough to make a man stop and stare if he wanted to look like a fool in the middle of Main Street, with all the Sunday traffic—families walking, riders on horses and mules, wagons, buggies, and a few coaches—converging on the church.

Erik had already delivered his dairy goods to the mercantile, and now for the first time, he walked with his new family through Sweetwater Springs to attend Sunday service. He carried Jacques, who seemed thrilled with his new surroundings and cast charming frog grins at anyone they passed.

Antonia walked next to him, holding Camilla and looking around with wide-eyed interest. She glanced at him and smiled. "Different today, eh?" she commented.

"Much better."

Henri shadowed his mother's other side, an uncertain expression on his face.

The closer Erik came to the building, the more apprehension built inside his chest. Memories overwhelmed him. He and Daisy hadn't made church service often, usually due to the weather or the press of farmwork. So when they did, the day became more than an opportunity to worship. The Sabbath turned into a social outing where they met friends, shopped for necessities and the occasional treat, and caught up on the latest news of the town and the greater world beyond the borders of Sweetwater Springs.

Somehow, living isolated on the farm, Erik had managed to make peace with Daisy's absence. That wasn't to say he didn't still have times of grief and acutely missing her. And he didn't think the guilt would ever leave him. But more and more, his new family—especially his wife—filled his thoughts. His growing relationship with Antonia provided healing, comfort, and even joy, not to mention sensual pleasures—both those they'd already explored and the future ones he'd fantasized about.

Surely, people will be kind and understanding of our hasty marriage, not judgmental. He didn't mind so much for himself, but for Antonia. He was established here, known by most. But she was a stranger and still coping with grief, and—he glanced at Henri—the boy as well, for all he'd seemed better.

Only one cutting remark causes harm. And if they hurt, he would, too.

No hint of nervousness showed on Antonia's face or in her upright carriage. Her expression remained calm. She'd left the raccoon skin coat in the wagon and now wore Daisy's blue shawl, which was too small and the color didn't become her.

When Erik studied his new wife, shame washed over him. He'd vowed to cherish this woman even if, in a haze of grief, he'd said the words to a stranger he'd met a few hours earlier, scarcely knowing what came out of his mouth. *But I haven't done a very good job.*

Perhaps because Antonia seemed to want so little for herself, he'd been blind to her wardrobe needs. Daisy would have set up a screech to get what she wanted—especially regarding clothing—and he'd assumed Antonia would do the same.

Will others see what I do when I look at her? The strength in her features, the gilded eyes, a smile that warms me when it appears? Or will they see the moccasins on her feet? A faded bonnet and a too-small shawl that's the wrong color for her dress—items they recognize as having belonged to Daisy?

Mrs. Carter's words, uttered in the store on the day of Daisy's death, came back to him. *A lady can wear rags, but as long as she holds up her head and carries herself proudly, people will see her, not her clothing.* She'd meant to chide Mrs. Cobb and Mrs. Murphy and bolster Antonia's confidence, but she should have directed them straight at him.

Maybe I'm taking on too much of Daisy's thinking. Plenty of women in this town only had one or two dresses that had to last for years. The same with their hats, shawls, coats, and shoes. Until now, Erik hadn't realized how he'd come to view the social world through Daisy's eyes, as well as his own.

Daisy had always approached church with an air of smugness that increased when she wore a new outfit, especially a fashionable one sent from her parents. She was secure in her appearance as a pretty, popular woman, with—she'd once told him—a husband who was both handsome and as strong as an ox. She'd basked in her popularity, smiling and waving at everyone and calling greetings to her particular friends. They'd stop a dozen times to have short conversations before they even reached the building.

Today, though, as the street grew crowded, few people did more than nod in their direction. Others slid their gazes away and quickened their steps. A few gave him strained smiles but didn't stop to talk. Here and there, someone openly stared at them.

Erik couldn't really blame them. He never knew what to say to someone who'd suffered the death of a loved one. Better not say anything at all, than something that might cause more pain instead of bringing comfort.

But he also noticed men stopping to talk to one another. From the serious expressions on their faces, he wondered what was going on. Maybe the storm damaged their places— homes, barns, livestock—although such discussions wouldn't exclude the womenfolk.... Erik shrugged. *I'm probably not the only one who shields my wife from unpleasant discussions.*

Antonia's face brightened. "There be Pamela and John. Oh, I hope to meet their children."

"I know them." Henri skipped ahead a few feet and waved. "Hiya, Lizzy!"

Erik exchanged an astonished look with Antonia and felt himself relax. The boy's despondency had weighed on him.

Lizzy Carter, holding her mother's hand, wore a blue dress with lace at the cuffs and sleeves, a frock that looked like it cost more than the price of a cow. She gave Henri a shy smile and curled her hand in a tiny wave, and then tugged her mother in their direction.

Pamela Carter, stylish in a brown-and-cranberry plaid dress with balloon sleeves—a new style Daisy had coveted until her parents satisfied her craving by sending her a gown of the fashionable design—glanced their way and smiled. She bent to say something to Lizzy, and the two came over to them.

"My dear Antonia." Pamela released her daughter and placed a hand on Antonia's arm. "I'm *so* pleased to see you are looking well." She glanced up at Erik. "And you, too." She leaned over Camilla. "Let me see this dear one."

Antonia held out the baby so Pamela could view her. "Oh, she's grown so! Such lovely eyes." She placed a hand over her heart. "The sight of her makes me teary."

Sadness welled in Erik. *Don't get me started.* He wanted to get through this day without becoming emotional.

Antonia shifted Camilla to one arm and took Pamela's other hand. "She be makin' me be teary sometimes, too."

Pamela patted her chest as if pushing down her rising emotion. "Enough sentiment." She lowered her hand. "Come meet my dear friends, Nick and Elizabeth Sanders." She gestured to a couple talking to John. The woman held a baby.

As with the Carters, Erik didn't know the Sanders except for an exchange of greetings. Even Daisy had been intimidated by the wealthy Boston belle who'd come to visit the Carters and ended up married to a local cowboy. The couple joined the Carters and the Thompsons as leaders of the town, although that group also included Banker Caleb Livingston, Reverend Norton, Dr. Cameron, the Cobbs—as unpleasant as they were—Ant Gordon the newspaper owner and his wife the schoolteacher, and now the new female sheriff, K.C. Granger.

Blonde, blue-eyed Elizabeth Sanders's beautiful countenance was one a man could stare at. *If said man wasn't married, of course.* She was plumper since the birth of her daughter but wore the serene glow of a contented wife and mother. The babe-in-arms, about five months older than Camilla, was bundled in a pink blanket. The mother glanced down at her child with a loving gaze.

I wonder if Daisy would have looked so after Camilla's birth? Somehow, he couldn't see her taking the same delight in her daughter as Elizabeth Sanders did in hers. The thought made him feel disloyal, even more so because he suspected Antonia enjoyed being a mother far more than Daisy would have.

Jacques wiggled to get down.

Erik clamped his arms around him. Once on the ground, the boy would be filthy quicker than a dog could roll over.

"Pa," Jacques demanded. "Paa!"

On second thought, perhaps it was better to let the boy get out his fidgets before the service, for containing a baa, haa, paaing Jacques would be well-nigh impossible. Erik set the boy on his feet and held his hand, taking small steps while he walked and hoping the toddler would stay upright and out of the dirt.

Jacques seemed content enough, at least for now, toddling along at Erik's side.

They reached the other couple.

John greeted them, his gaze lingering on Antonia's face. He gave a slight nod and a satisfied smile. "Antonia, may I say you are looking better than when last I saw you?"

"I could hardly not be," she said in a teasing tone.

John's lips turned up. "Yes, definitely better." He laid a hand on the shoulder of the man next to him, who wasn't much older than Erik. "May I introduce my godson, Nick Sanders, and his lovely wife, Elizabeth, who happens to be Pamela's best friend."

Antonia was taller than both women, closer to Nick Sanders's height, and not without her own appeal.

Elizabeth sent them a glance of compassion. "Pamela and John shared with us your tragic circumstances. I'm sorry Nick and I weren't in town at the time to support you through your ordeal."

Her genuine graciousness surprised him—*not* what he would have suspected from a former East Coast socialite. "We were well supported." He nodded at John. "A debt I can never repay."

"Nonsense," John said. "As I told you before, in this town, we help each other out."

Pamela laughed. "Why, the first day after I arrived here from Boston, newly married to John, the entire town turned out to welcome me."

Making a comical face, John leaned over as if to confide in Antonia. "And all of them came straight away to clean out and freshen up the hovel my house had become. Thank goodness they did, else Pamela might have turned around and high-tailed back to Boston."

The men laughed.

"Never." Pamela wrapped her hand around her husband's arm. "Luckily, they all brought food, else I'd have been sunk, for John's larder contained only beans and beef."

Elizabeth bent closer to Antonia. The breeze wafted a hint of her perfume. "How is the baby doing?"

"Everyone's wanting to be seeing...*to see* our Camilla. Perhaps I should just hold her up in front of me like a sign," Antonia joked.

"She's beautiful. Very like Daisy. Oh!" Elizabeth glanced at Antonia in obvious consternation. "You don't mind me saying that do you?"

"Why not?" Antonia asked with her characteristic straightforwardness. "Be...*it's* the truth."

Erik's chest swelled with pride. His wife was trying so hard to speak well.

"Seems like only yesterday Carol was that small," Elizabeth said with a wistful tone. "They grow so fast." She kissed her daughter's head. "I waited so long to have her, and I'm trying to enjoy every minute."

Humor glinted in Nick's blue-green eyes. "Perhaps not *every* minute."

They all joined in his laughter—a mutual sharing on the more *challenging* aspects of parenthood.

To Erik, the two baby girls looked similar—blue eyes, wispy blonde hair, and unformed faces—although Camilla was far tinier. "They could be sisters. Perhaps when they're older, they'll become the best of friends."

"Or bitter rivals, each the queen of a circle of admirers," Nick joked.

"We'll be fighting off the boys with a shotgun," Erik quipped. Not that he could imagine his little mite as a woman grown.

"No doubt about that," Nick agreed. "The thought of Carol as a young lady, looking as beautiful as her mama, is enough to keep me up at nights."

Erik could share in that vision. *Least I won't have to warn off fortune hunters like Nick will.* "Thank goodness, we have plenty of time before then."

Elizabeth handed her daughter to Nick. "Your turn for baby duty." She turned to Antonia. "I need to start the processional." With a smile of farewell, she hurried off.

Antonia stared after her with a puzzled look.

"Elizabeth plays the piano," Erik explained. "Music for the service."

The bell in the tower on the white clapboard church began to ring, the rich tones summoning the congregation to worship. As if being herded, everyone moved toward the door.

Only Sheriff Granger remained still. Even on a Sunday, the officer of the law was dressed like a man in a gray three-piece suit.

The idea of a woman wearing men's clothing had shocked Erik when he'd first heard the story. But after two months of exposure to Antonia, he thought differently. Now he approved of the sheriff's apparel. She couldn't effectively do her job wearing a dress.

Sheriff Granger watched them with cool gray eyes, nodding as they passed.

Erik dipped his head in return.

The sheriff returned to surveying the crowd.

He wondered why she looked so alert. He couldn't recall her being so stern before. Then again, he and Daisy had only attended a couple of church services between Christmas, when the sheriff was hired, and Daisy's death. Maybe he'd missed the sheriff's serious attitude.

Reverend and Mrs. Norton stood opposite each other at the foot of the church stairs welcoming their flock.

Mrs. Norton patted Erik's arm. "I'm so glad to see you, dear Mr. Muth. You and your family have been in my thoughts and prayers."

"Your prayers have helped."

"Good." She patted him again before stooping to say hello to Jacques and Henri.

Reverend Norton greeted Antonia by taking her hand between both of his own and saying something in a voice too low to hear.

Antonia smiled and nodded.

The minister touched Camilla's head, as if blessing her, before turning to the next person in line.

Erik swung Jacques into his arms, mounted the stairs after his wife and oldest son, and entered the church. Once inside, he removed his hat and guided Antonia to a pew near the back, in case one of them had to make a quick escape with a fussy baby. They took a seat amid other families with babies, and the single cowboys, who tended to group themselves by the ranch they worked at, packing the pews fuller than a pod stuffed with peas.

They claimed their spot. At the same moment, Elizabeth, sitting at the piano in the front corner of the room, began to play a piece that must be her favorite, for she often opened the service with the same music. As always, the first notes of the piano worked their magic on the congregation, for they settled down.

Erik had to set his hat on the floor underneath him, for there was no other spot for it, and Jacques took up his whole lap.

Antonia stared at Elizabeth, an enraptured expression on her face.

Erik suspected she'd never heard anything like the complicated music. *Well, most people in small Western towns probably hadn't.* Bach, Mrs. Norton had once told Erik when he'd asked.

During the service, Erik did his best to guide Antonia with gentle nudges, stand and pray; sit and listen to the reading; stand and sing; sit and listen to the sermon, so she'd be no more than a little behind the rest of them.

Jacques enjoyed the singing, pounding Erik's thigh with the palm of his hand, almost in rhythm to the hymns, adding an occasional, "baa, baa, baa!" Luckily, the other voices drowned him out.

Erik noticed Antonia wasn't singing, and he wondered if she didn't know the hymns or had forgotten them. *Maybe I can ask to borrow a hymnal, and she can learn some at home.*

Jacques fell asleep during the first few minutes of the sermon, much to Erik's relief.

Aside from some gurgles, Camilla was content to look around or hold Antonia's fingers.

After the conclusion of the service, the family filed out. Henri found a friend and darted away.

The members of the congregation must have gotten used to seeing Erik and Antonia together, for they received more greetings than before church, with the women nearest them wanting to coo over Camilla.

Unlike Sundays in the past, when Erik had drifted off to speak with the men, and Daisy had surrounded herself with her female friends, today he stuck to Antonia's side. Erik and Antonia hadn't taken many steps away from the building before the doctor's redheaded wife, Alice, snagged Antonia. She, too, held a baby in her arms.

Normally, he would have stayed to politely view the new arrival, but with a jerk of his head, John Carter, in serious discussion with fellow ranchers Wyatt Thompson and Nick Sanders, summoned Erik to join them.

Although he didn't want to leave Antonia, Erik couldn't turn down the invitation to speak with the three leading ranchers in the area. He shifted the sleeping Jacques to a more comfortable position for carrying and walked over to them.

John made an inclusive gesture, making space for Erik in the circle. "Sorry to pull you away from your bride, but we wanted to speak to you without our wives present. No need to worry them."

Wyatt Thompson, who owned the second largest ranch in Sweetwater Springs, exchanged a sardonic glance with Nick. "Our wives won't be pleased when they find we've been keeping things from them. We probably need to be more worried about the ladies going on a warpath than the Indians."

"Indians?" Erik said sharply, remembering the conversation from the day he'd married Antonia. With the press of other concerns, the loss of some livestock around the area had slipped his mind. Truth be told, some of his memories of that day still remained hazy.

John swung off his Stetson, scrubbed his high forehead, and frowned. "The thefts that started a few months ago have continued. As long as no one spotted any Indians again, there wasn't anyone to focus the blame on. We wanted to know if there've been any problems at your place."

"Not with disappearing livestock," Erik said wryly.

The grimaces that crossed the men's faces acknowledged the fact that Erik had suffered far greater losses.

Sheriff Granger, along with Ant Gordon and Caleb Livingston, the banker, joined them, nodding greetings.

Erik was a big man, used to towering over most others. Wyatt Thompson was about his size, and John and the banker were almost as tall. But Ant Gordon topped Erik by at least four inches. His size and dark angular features gave him the appearance of a villain in a penny dreadful novel. But in spite of his looks, he'd managed to snare the affections of the petite town schoolteacher. The man had been a foreign news correspondent before settling in Sweetwater Springs, and on several occasions, he and Erik had spoken of history and world events.

The sheriff was tall for a woman—topping Nick Sanders's height—with a solid build covered by the men's three-piece suit she wore. With her husky voice and brown hair tucked up under her hat, she could easily pass for a man.

Erik figured she hadn't dealt with more than drunken cowboys since accepting the job. But before that, she'd captured a murderer on the outskirts of Sweetwater Springs. Story was, she'd trailed him for weeks all the way from Wyoming.

"Sheriff Granger, what are your thoughts on the matter?" Erik asked, making sure to sound curious rather than critical. He didn't want to get her back up. Wouldn't do to offend the law.

"When something's reported, I go investigate."

"You, ah…go alone?" he asked.

"I deputized the blacksmith. When Red Charlie can spare the time, he comes with me. He still has connections with the reservation."

A smart choice for a deputy.

"Some losses I can put down to natural causes. But the others…" She shrugged. "They cover their tracks well."

The hard glint in her eyes told Erik she meant business. "They?"

Ant Gordon shifted to get their attention. "Hank Anderson, a small farmer out on the prairie past my house, rode to tell me that he shot and injured a rustler on his place. Seemed pretty sure he was an Indian." The newspaperman had a low, gravelly voice in keeping with his dark appearance. "In the morning, Hank followed the trail of blood—three sets of moccasin prints, one with a limp, and three sets of hoof prints—until he hit a stream, and the sign disappeared."

"Rode up or downstream, no telling," Sheriff Granger commented. "I'll head on out there and see for myself. Hopefully, I'll find where they left the water and pick up their trail."

"I haven't heard back from the Bureau of Indian Affairs. I think another letter is in order." John Carter snugged on his hat. "Now with one wounded, maybe they'll stop," he said. "But..." He shot a glance at Erik. "As your wife said, the Indians are starving." He sighed. "Can't blame them. I'd beg, borrow, or steal if my family was starving to death."

Erik thought of the boys, of his fragile daughter. *So would I.*

The looks on the other men's faces told him they had similar feelings. Only Caleb Livingston seemed to dissent, shaking his head and frowning.

"Stealing's against the law of God and of our country," Sheriff Granger said with a sharp slash of her hand.

"I agree," the banker interjected. "*Borrowing* is a better place to start."

Nick frowned at him. "You're in the business of lending money. Of course, you'd agree."

Caleb Livingston shot Nick a dark look.

Erik had heard the two had hard feelings between them due to Nick making off with the fair Elizabeth right under the banker's nose.

Wyatt Thompson pinned the sheriff with a stern look. "And neither of you is a parent." Their gray gazes held and clashed.

Erik had the sense that Wyatt didn't much approve of their new officer of the law, and he wondered why.

Wyatt broke the standoff to glance around the circle. "As fathers, we are given families to love and protect." He flicked the sheriff a critical look. "You might feel different if you ever have a baby, a child depending on you, whose very life is in your hands."

Erik remembered his desperation with newborn Camilla, knowing he had only hours to save her. *Yes. Becoming a father has changed me to my very core.*

Wyatt's gray eyes, burning with intensity, met Erik's, as if reaching across the few feet separating them. "I, too, lost a wife in childbirth. When I held my baby daughter for the first time, a fierce protective love seized me and has *never* let up, although my Christine is strong and healthy. The image of her mother."

The man's words punched Erik in the chest, for he'd felt the same driving love for Camilla.

The sheriff made a cut-off gesture. "Sentiments or not, we have a potential war brewing." Although she appeared perfectly composed, her voice held a chill. "If it's Indians, and they keep stealing, or if God forbid, someone from Sweetwater Springs is wounded or killed…" She shook her head. "Hotheads will rile things up. Those caught up in a mob become crazed and lose their ability to think rationally. We'll have a self-appointed vigilante posse sweeping onto the Indian reservation. They're just as likely to gun down the entire encampment, including innocent women and children."

John made a sound of protest.

The sheriff rode roughshod over any attempt to speak. "Later those idiots might suffer remorse, or believe their actions didn't matter because they only killed *savages.*" Sheriff Granger's tone made it clear what she thought about that. "Even if only a few are wounded or killed, the Indians might retaliate." She didn't have to say more.

John looked troubled. "Pray, God, it doesn't come to that."

"We won't let it," Nick said fiercely.

Wyatt's dark eyebrows drew together. "We'll speak with our men. Any cowboy of mine who joins that kind of mob will be out of a job, regardless if he's prosecuted by the law."

Ant crossed his arms in front of him. "I'll run an article in the newspaper urging calm. We can't keep the Anderson attack quiet for long. The town's already buzzing about the thefts, although we're trying not to worry the womenfolk."

Erik remembered the groups of men he'd seen talking before church. "That's a mistake," he said bluntly. "I'd as soon have my wife and her rifle at my side as any man. She's a crack shot." The truth of the words surprised him. "I think the women need to know. Prepare them. Warn them to be watchful. This probably isn't the time to wander off alone or with small children, picking flowers and such."

The sheriff eyed Erik with approval. "I agree." Her lips twitched. "Most of the women around here seem sensible enough. For those few ladies who don't take the news well—" she jabbed a thumb toward her chest "—send any hysterical female over to the jail, and I'll set her straight."

In spite of the gravity of the situation, that image made the men smile.

Well, I'll be. Our lady sheriff has a sense of humor.

She gazed at Erik, a thoughtful look on her face. "When this is over and I have time, I think I'll hold classes for women who want to learn to shoot, assuming their husbands or fathers can't or won't teach them."

"Nonsense," the banker exclaimed. "Too unladylike."

The others ignored him, something the handsome, wealthy man wasn't used to, and it showed in the flash of his brown eyes.

Ant's eyebrow peaked, matching his crooked smile. "Some things are best left to other instructors, not husbands," he drawled. "I'll sign Harriet up on the spot."

Caleb Livingston gave him an astonished look. "You're that sure she'd want to learn, are you?"

"I know she would," Ant said, all levity vanishing from his face. "My brother-in-law almost killed her."

Shaking his head, Caleb raised a placating hand. "I'd forgotten."

"I wish we could say the same," Ant said coolly.

"It's a good notion for the women to know how to defend themselves." Nick rocked forward on his heels. "I've already taught Elizabeth, and Pamela learned from John. But a female shootin' class might be good for them regardless." He touched a hand to his side, as if he had a gun strapped there. He didn't, of course. No one went armed to church.

Almost no one. Erik eyed the sheriff for weapons.

Sure enough, she had a bulge at her side, hidden by her jacket, as well she should.

He'd bet Nick had a rifle in that fancy carriage of his, just like Erik carried one in a special box built under the seat of his wagon.

The sheriff's expression sobered. She gestured at the ranchers. "As far as I can tell, livestock in your direction aren't disappearing."

The three exchanged glances, but it was Nick who spoke for them. "No losses that can't be put down to animals—tracks and all that. We have our cowboys riding around our spreads. And our men are on guard. Granted our ranges are wide, but except for the cattle, our livestock are near the ranch houses."

Sheriff Granger straightened her arm, hand pointing like a sword to the front of her. She pivoted in a half circle, indicating a target area. "There you have it, gentlemen." She lowered her arm. "That's a lot of territory for one sheriff to cover. In fact, the task would be hard for a posse of sheriffs.

The citizens living within the affected area need to take extra precautions. See that you put that in your article, Ant." She tipped her hat to them. "And I'm going to ride out to the Anderson place."

Wyatt raised a hand to stop her. "Take my oldest son, Hunter, with you," he said, referring to the Blackfoot boy he'd adopted. "He's good at tracking and shooting. If it's Indians causing harm, he'll be able to speak with them. Keep things peaceable. He'll surely convey understanding to the culprits, for I caught him in the same situation—stealing one of Mrs. Toffels's fresh-baked pies. Samantha up and adopted him right out from under me."

"I'll take Hunter along. Send him on over." Sheriff Granger nodded in farewell. "Good day, gentlemen." She sauntered off in the direction of the jail.

In silence, the men watched her go.

Erik rubbed Jacques's back. "I almost pity the culprits when she catches up with them."

"It's only what they deserve," Caleb Livingston muttered. "And if word gets out beyond our town—" his voice sharpened "—such an event will be bad for our businesses."

Your business. If we have Indian problems, no one will come stay at that fancy hotel you're building. But Erik didn't voice his thoughts aloud, even though he suspected the other men had similar ones about the banker.

He glanced over at Antonia, still talking to Alice Cameron. They'd been joined by Mrs. Gordon and Natalia, no doubt discussing Henri's schooling. "I'd best be getting back to my wife. If you have need of me, if there's anything I must know, leave word at the mercantile, for I'm there most mornings."

Even as he said the words, Erik realized including the Cobbs in their plans was a bad idea. Their hatred of the Indians was a well-known fact. "Never mind that." He glanced at Sheriff Granger. "I'll stop by the jail and see how you're progressing."

The tall man nodded. "Sounds good."

As Erik moved away, he thought back on the area the sheriff had marked out. His place lay just on the eastern boundary.

With one of them wounded, the Indians might become more desperate.

I've been negligent, too lost in grief, struggling to help Antonia and the boys adjust, learning to become a new father and a husband to a stranger, getting the crops in the ground....

That changes now!

CHAPTER TWENTY-TWO

Before walking over to rejoin his wife, Erik paused to take stock of the weather. Overhead, pale clouds veiled the sun. *Hopefully, it won't start to rain again.* But just in case, they needed to get going.

Still, Erik hesitated. He didn't want Antonia to know anything was wrong and spoil her enjoyment of their visit to town.

I'll tell her on the way home.

He felt Jacques stir and rubbed the child's back.

The boy lifted his head, glanced at Erik, and laid his head down for a few seconds, only to look at him again, his eyes still sleepy. "Pa," he mumbled.

"Yes, I'm your pa."

Jacques looked around. "Ma?"

"*Maman*'s over there." Erik pointed to her.

Antonia must have seen he was alone, for with a smile and a few words, she left Alice Cameron and came over to join him.

Lina Barrett, a plump Italian woman, practically pounced on them, corkscrew tendrils of black hair bouncing around her face as she moved. "Oh, I want to see that baby." She spotted Jacques and smiled. "And meet this one, too." She spoke with an appealing Italian accent.

Jonah Barrett, Lina's husband, followed her. He, too, held a toddler in his arms, a girl about a year older than Jacques, with her mother's curly hair and his bottle green eyes. "Mrs. Muth doesn't know you from Adam, my dear Lina. So she might not want to share her children with you." He winked at Antonia. "Mrs. Muth can't possibly know she's standing in front of the most maternal woman in Sweetwater Springs."

Lina flicked a wrist at her husband.

Erik smiled at their banter. "My dear, meet Lina and Jonah Barrett." He gestured to the Barrett daughter. "Although I don't know this one's name."

"Maria," Lina said, going on tiptoe to kiss her child's cheek. "My only daughter." She smiled at them.

Erik gestured to Antonia. "My wife, Antonia, baby Camilla, and this one—" he hefted Jacques so the boy could display his froggy grin "—is Jacques."

"Mrs. Muth, I'm delighted to meet you, although what you have gone through, *Madonna Mia!*" Shaking her head, she threw up her hands and shuddered.

"Please call me Antonia."

"And you must call me Lina. We will be friends." Her definitive nod set her curls bouncing again.

"I'd plumb like that," Antonia said.

"You'll hear the gossip soon enough, so I'll just go ahead and tell you." Lina waved her hand in a circle indicating the congregation milling around them. "I was a mail-order bride." She waited, as if expecting a shocked reaction.

Antonia's brows drew together. "What be...what's a mail-order bride?"

Jonah barked a laugh, and his green eyes twinkled. "She's got you there, dear. That's the first time you've had *that* reaction." He turned to Antonia. "I sent a letter to Mail-Order Brides of the West Agency in response to their ad about brides willing to travel west to marry strangers, sight unseen. I ordered up my Lina."

Erik stared at the man, a fellow farmer whom he didn't know well. But he'd heard tales of the morose man Jonah had been, of the drunken sot he'd had for a father, and of his first marriage to a squaw—all just before Erik's arrival in Sweetwater Springs. But he'd also heard of the change that had come over Jonah when he married Lina. The man had astonished the whole town by becoming a loving husband and father and a solid citizen of Sweetwater Springs.

Lina finagled Camilla away from his wife, rocking her and cooing Italian words that sounded like musical compliments.

Jacques squirmed to get down.

Erik gave in, setting him on his feet.

"Ma!" The boy toddled to his mother, falling against her legs, and then turned to look at Erik with a wide-mouth grin. "Pa!"

Jonah cocked an eyebrow. "Things seem to be settling in for you two."

"As well as can be expected."

"Good." Jonah hesitated and moved so his back was partially to the women who were engrossed in talking about babies. "My marriage to Lina was somewhat like yours," he said in a serious tone. "I was mourning a wife who'd recently died in childbirth, along with our second baby. I needed a mother for Adam and selected a bride I didn't know."

Another man with a similar story to my own.

He had known, of course, that women died in childbirth, but that fact had seemed so distant, not even a possibility he'd considered. To his shame, Erik remembered how he'd scoffed when Daisy had expressed fears that to him had seemed so unlikely.

Forgive me, Daisy.

Erik brought his attention back to Jonah.

"Our...*transition* wasn't easy," the farmer said. "We were very different from each other. The guilt I felt from Koko's death almost crushed me. I thought I didn't dare open my heart to Lina. But my wise wife convinced me otherwise."

Erik hadn't heard this story before, and he realized the man was confiding in him.

"Best thing I could have done," Jonah added.

"The guilt passes?"

Jonah nodded, his eyes grave. "Mostly." He took off his hat and ran a hand through his shoulder-length blond hair. "Hard to be grieving one wife and yet developing love for another." He put his hat back on. "Confusing as all get-out."

Erik let out a slow breath, relieved to be understood. "Yes."

"You can treasure the memory of one and love the reality of the other."

"I'm not there yet. Don't know if I'll ever be." He glanced over to make sure Antonia couldn't hear him. "I care for her, that I do. But to love again..." He shook his head.

"Give yourself time."

While Erik appreciated Jonah's sentiments, he wasn't sure the passage of time would be enough.

❋ ❋ ❋

When they left the store, Antonia glanced past Camilla in her arms at her shiny leather boots and turned them in the direction of the church where the Sanders and the Carters still lingered in conversation. With her new brown hat, coffee-colored netting fitted over the brim and crown, and an amber-colored shawl, she looked like the other church-goin' women.

She'd bundled Daisy's shawl around Camilla and tucked her moccasins, wrapped in brown paper, under her arm.

Although Antonia had balked at spending money on things she didn't think she needed and purposely chose simple styles, she'd just discovered the lift a new hat gave her spirits and was eager to see the ladies' reactions to her finery.

Not that she'd felt low. Everyone was so welcoming. Mrs. Cobb's vinegar glare at Antonia's corset-less waistline hadn't soured her day. *In the face of everyone's kindness, what does one woman's disapproval matter?*

Erik, carrying Jacques, stopped her with a touch on her arm. "You trying to parade your new finery through town?" he teased. "The wagon's at the livery, remember?"

Her cheeks heated, and she looked up at her husband's grin.

"So let's head on over there. But there's one more thing we have to do before leaving town."

"Camilla be needin' to feed soon," she warned, then caught herself. "I mean, Camilla will soon need feeding." She glanced at Jacques and back at Henri, both gnawing on oatmeal cookies. "Those cookies you bought will tide the boys over 'til we git to the food I brought."

"This won't take long." Erik placed his hand in the center of her back, steering her in the direction of the livery.

Even through the shawl, she felt his touch. Shivers radiated across her skin.

"Most of the churchgoers have already left. See—" he pointed "—only a few horses are in the paddock. Most of those belong to Mack Taylor," he said, referring to the livery owner.

Antonia had briefly met the man before church when they parked the wagon near the stable. Mack and Pepe, his stable hand, had taken charge of the horses.

Erik pointed. "Mack or Pepe have already hitched our team to the wagon. The Sanders' and Carters' teams are ready, too."

As they approached, Mack Taylor waved, his rheumy green eyes beaming. "Hey, you two. Have you heard the news? We were like fleas jumping around on a dog this morning, so we didn't have time to tell ya. Think everyone and his brother decided to attend church."

"Not sure," Erik responded. "Which news are you talking about? We have a lot going on in Sweetwater Springs nowadays."

Mack cackled. "That we do. But *this* news is about my boy, here." He waved toward Pepe. "Go on. Tell him."

Although Pepe dropped his gaze, when he looked up, a wide grin broke over his round face. He glanced at Camilla. "My Lucia, she...she's...."

"Come on, boy," Mack cackled, rubbing his hands together. "Spit it out. We've been telling people all day. I'd have thought you got it all down pat by now."

Antonia decided to put the stable hand out of his misery. "A babe?" she guessed.

"Yep." Mack grinned showing tobacco-stained teeth.

Erik buffeted Pepe's shoulder. "Congratulations!"

"I'm gunna be a grandpappy." Mack tottered out several jig steps.

Her husband's eyebrows raised in apparent surprise. "Well, then, congratulations to you as well, Grandpa Mack."

The man slapped his knee. "I like the sound of that, I do."

Antonia looked back and forth between Mack and Pepe. No two men could look more different—elderly Mack, with his reedy body and voice, white-haired, and a tobacco-stained beard. Pepe—dark-skinned, stocky, low-voiced, and apparently shy. But she could see the obvious bond between the two.

"I'm going to be a *papá*," Pepe said, awe in his tone.

His words echoed a bittersweet memory of Jean-Claude saying something very similar when he heard she was with child. Antonia remembered how he'd swung her around, and how she'd laughed, her heart full. With a nostalgic smile, she glanced at Erik, reckoning he might have had a similar reaction to Daisy's pregnancy.

Antonia didn't know how long Pepe had been married, but she could see he hadn't lost the wonder. "May your wife have a healthy time carryin' the babe and a safe birthin' for ma and child."

Her words, meant to be a blessing, had the opposite effect. Discomfiture settled in the air, everyone obviously remembering Daisy's death.

Pepe shot Erik a worried look.

Mack's eyes lost their gleam. He rubbed his beard and glanced at Erik's wagon. "You're all hitched and ready to go."

Erik held up a hand in a *wait* gesture and gave Pepe a reassuring smile.

Antonia figured only she could see the hint of sadness underneath.

"I'm sure all will be well with Lucia," Erik said. "Don't waste time worrying about what will be, for the future's in God's hands. Focus on the loving *now*—the excitement and anticipation of your babe."

The man ducked his head in a gesture of obvious respect. "Will do, Señor Muth."

Erik looked toward the livery. "Are the puppies ready to leave their ma?"

"They are, at that. Little rascals." His expression relieved, Mack grabbed for the change of topic.

"Puppies?" Henri said with an imploring look.

Mack jerked a thumb in the direction of the open stable door. "I put them in the first stall, but with all the people in and out of here playing with the critters, who knows where they ended up."

Puppies! Antonia thought in excitement, remembering a litter of fat mongrels she'd loved as a girl. All one summer, she'd played with them, until the soldier who'd owned them found new homes for each one, breaking her young heart.

Mack motioned toward the stable. "You all go on in and see."

Erik led the way inside, Henri almost skipping beside him in excitement. The building was empty of horses, but the smell of straw and manure lingered.

When they opened the stall gate, the puppies surged out, tumbling around their feet. They frolicked the wide aisle under the watchful eyes of their dam, a large hound with beautiful gray and black fur.

"Maman!" said Henri, obviously throwing his heart right into the midst of the bunch.

"Look at the size of their paws," Erik marveled. "They've gotten a lot bigger since last I saw them."

A quick glance at his eager expression made Antonia think he'd set aside his sorrow, and she relaxed. The pups had at least three-months' growth, she figured by their leggy look.

"They'll grow monster-size." Erik shot her an amused glance. "Sure are appealing little creatures, aren't they?"

"They be," she agreed, instantly captivated by a fuzzy gray and black whelp. Only holding Camilla stopped her from picking one up. *I wish we could take one home. Having a pup around the place is just what the boys need.*

Erik jiggled Jacques, pointing to the puppies. "Dog. Can you say *dog?*"

The little boy gazed at the puppies, entranced.

"Oh, oh!" Henri jumped up and down in excitement. "Can I play with 'em?" He glanced at Erik for permission, his eyes pleading.

Nodding, Erik chuckled. "Go ahead, son."

Henri squatted and held out his hands to the dogs.

Seeing the invitation, three of the puppies raced toward him. A fourth followed more slowly, and the other had no interest in Henri, being preoccupied with chasing his tail.

"Look out," Antonia warned her son, enjoying the puppies' playful antics. "Here be comin' the herd."

The three jumped on the boy, scrambling into his lap. In their efforts to reach his face, they toppled him backward onto the floor.

He lay there, giggling.

Triumphant, the puppies scrambled over his chest, licking his face and shaking their stubby tails so hard, their hind ends wiggled. One chewed on Henri's nose.

Her son shrieked with glee.

Erik bellowed out a belly laugh, the likes of which she'd never heard from him before. Seeing his enjoyment lightened her heart.

"Daaag." Jacques squirmed to get down.

"Yes, dog." Erik crouched to lower Jacques to the ground. With one hand, he kept the child back from attacking the dogs while he scooped up the tail-chaser and held him in front of the boy.

The puppy was already so big, his legs spilled over Erik's arms.

"Daaag!" Jacques grabbed for a paw.

Erik lifted the dog out of the way. "Gentle, boy. Be gentle."

Jacques knew what *gentle* meant. They certainly used the word with him enough when he played near Camilla.

The puppy found Jacques's nose even more interesting than his tail, and he swiped the boy's face with a pink tongue.

Jacques screamed in merriment.

The infectious sound of her children's pleasure swirled gaiety through Antonia. Something seemed to break loose deep inside her, bubbling up until she couldn't hold back any longer. Laughter burst out of her, joyous and freeing.

Erik glanced over. The smile of delight on his face crinkled the skin around his eyes. His chuckle was obviously as much from amusement at her as from enjoying the boys.

Her chest expanded, released from months of tightness. *This feels wonderful!* Antonia laughed so hard that tears came to her eyes. She wiped them away, thinking how much she'd rather cry from happiness than sorrow.

I never dreamed I'd be this happy again.

Guilt followed that thought, making her clamp down on her good feelings.

She paused, reconsidering.

My Jean-Claude, a man full of laughter and stories, would not chide me. He, of all people, would not have me shrouded in black, grim, and sorrowing.

"Life is for the living," her late husband had said more than once. "Laugh while you can."

She'd always thought he referred to those who'd died, but perhaps Jean-Claude was preparing her for his own leaving. Antonia felt a light touch on the back of her shoulder, but when she turned she saw nothing that could account for the feeling.

Perhaps Jean-Claude stood at her side—an invisible specter—relishing the sight of their boys playing with puppies and encouraging her to laugh...to love. The idea eased her guilt.

Mack marched in, his rheumy green eyes gleaming. "You all leavin' me out of the fun?"

"We are, indeed," Erik drawled. "And we're readying to head out and leave you with one less of the little monsters."

Mack winked at Antonia. "'Bout time. The critters are eating me out of house and home. The Thompsons took their puppy home earlier. Two less mouths to feed."

They untangled the boys from the dogs, Jacques protesting all the while.

Erik crouched to Henri's eye level. "Would you like to take a puppy home?"

The boy's eyes grew big. "*Oui!* Yes!"

"You've been such a big help to your *maman* and me, and you've studied hard in school. I think you're old enough to take care of a dog, eh?"

Antonia watched her son's excitement, and happy tears again pricked her eyes. *If Henri had a tail, he'd be waggin' it as hard as the pups.*

Henri pointed to the puppy who'd beaten her two littermates in the race to him.

Erik nodded. "I think that little gal will make a good watchdog and companion. What say you, son?"

"Oh, yes, Pa!" Henri gathered the pup into his arms, barely able to hold her. He buried his face in the fur, setting the bond.

Everyone laughed.

They allowed Henri to carry his puppy to the wagon.

Jacques toddled after his brother, the excitement of chasing Henri and the *daag* enough to keep him on his feet without any help.

They retrieved their bucket from where they'd left the food to chill in the livery's springhouse, bade good-bye to Mack and Pepe, and climbed on board the wagon, the boys in the back with the dog.

Once they drove out of town, Antonia settled Camilla at her breast. "It be feelin'...*It feels* good to laugh." She glanced at Erik, saw a troubled look in his eyes, and understood all too well what he was feeling.

"Very good. Until the guilt hits."

"For me, too. Then I told myself Jean-Claude would want me to be happy. He be...*was* a man who laughed often, and because he did, we did as well."

"Daisy and I didn't laugh much together." Erik's mouth turned up in a wry smile. "You might have noticed I'm the serious sort."

Antonia shrugged. "You have cause to be serious."

"We talked about the future a lot, Daisy and I." His smile died away. "The future that never came for us." He hesitated, gazing into the distance. "'Cept for that time at haying, you and I don't really do that. Perhaps that's just as well. Daisy and I concentrated too hard on what *will* be instead of taking the time to enjoy what is *now.*"

"*We've* learned our lesson then," Antonia said. Despite the seriousness of the conversation, she tried hard to speak properly. "Now we just need to remember it."

His nod told her he agreed.

Laughter from the boys made her turn to watch them.

Although she handed out food, the first part of the drive passed with everyone's attention on the puppy. So far, the boys were too excited to eat, and she'd let them be, figuring they'd settle down in a bit.

As she nursed Camilla, Antonia kept twisting to watch the children, then facing forward and gaily describing to Erik what the boys were doing. She wasn't sure who was enjoying the puppy more—Henri and Jacques, or she and Erik.

Finally, the boys wore out the puppy, and she fell asleep. No amount of attention from either child woke up the dog.

"Leave her be, you two," Antonia told them. "She needs a nap. She'll wake when we get home and be ready to play again." She had to give Henri a stern glance before he subsided. "You and Jacques eat now."

"I'll help him," Henri said.

"Good." Antonia turned forward, and they lapsed into silence, finishing the cold pheasant, washed down with milk in jars.

While she ate, Antonia thought through her encounters with everyone that day, feeling proud in how she'd managed to use proper speech during the whole time in town. *Or as proper as I know.*

The highlight of her day was talking with Mrs. Gordon and Natalia. She'd been nervous to meet them, in awe of their book learning. But both lauded *Henry*, as they called him, to the skies—saying the boy was intelligent; showed an excellent grasp of concepts, whatever that meant; was a hard worker; well-mannered; and so considerate of others. In the glow from their praise, Antonia had forgotten her discomfort about her poor speech and lack of education.

She exhaled a happy breath. In her prior life, she couldn't have even dreamed of such a wonderful day. As always, remembering Jean-Claude cost her heart a pang. But the feeling wasn't as strong as before. She wished he could have heard what Henri's teachers said about their son. But maybe he wouldn't have valued their opinions as much as she did.

But Erik will. She nudged her husband with her elbow.

When he looked her way, Antonia told him about the conversation with Mrs. Gordon and Natalia, enjoying the way his eyes lit up and his nods of agreement.

"Doesn't surprise me a bit," he said when she'd finished. "A bright boy, our Henri, *Henry.*"

She slipped her hand around his arm and squeezed, feeling the strength of his muscles. "Hearin' such from you makes me feel just as good as from 'em."

He slanted her his lazy grin. "Then I'm in excellent company." His expression became thoughtful. "We should think of college for him."

College? She gave him a questioning glance.

"More schooling after he finishes learning all Mrs. Gordon can teach him."

"There's more?"

"Much more. If he wants to be a doctor or minister or lawyer, he'll need a lot of education."

The glory of such possibilities blazed through her mind, and Antonia wanted that for Henri with an intensity that almost ached.

"From the time I was a boy, I wanted to be a farmer like my pa," Erik said in a reminiscing tone. "Had no mind to go off to college, although I think I'd have enjoyed my studies. No more land was available near my folks in Indiana, at least not any that I could get ahold of without paying top dollar. So I came out west to make my own way. Maybe Henri will want to be a farmer, maybe something else. I'd like him to have the choice."

The sun burst through the clouds, brightening the vast dusky sky and sending golden rays of light into the heavens. After living so long in the tree-shaded mountains, Antonia never tired of watching the wide-open prairie sky.

No matter what she was doing, or how she was feeling, Antonia liked to stop and look up, feeling as if the beauty of the sky uplifted and sustained her, offering a promise of hope...of healing. *I've journeyed far. Not just the trip from the mountains to Sweetwater Springs to the farm, but from the agony of Jean-Claude's death to remembering him with warmth.*

Erik cleared his throat. "Did you see me talking to John Carter and Nick Sanders and a few others?"

"I saw."

"The sheriff was there, too."

Her interest quickened. She'd only noticed a group of men, no female in the bunch. "John said the sheriff be a woman."

"Yep. Sheriff Granger was the one in the gray three-piece suit. 'Bout the same height as Nick Sanders."

She pictured the group. Even knowing about the sheriff, Antonia still couldn't believe she was a woman. "Why ain't she wearin' a dress?"

"Now don't go getting any ideas, wife. She's not wearing one for the same reason you didn't when we cut hay."

"Be that allowed?"

He tossed her a smile. "It's not against the law. Probably isn't even against the law to walk stark naked down Main Street."

She laughed. "That be a sight."

"Sheriff Granger came to us dressed as a man." He slid into his storytelling voice.

Erik's way wasn't as dramatic as Jean-Claude's—no exaggeration, speaking with his hands, comical faces, or different voices. But she'd learned to appreciate how he stuck to the facts yet still held her interest.

"She already was a sheriff in Wyoming. Some low-down varmint murdered a bunch of people in her town, and she trailed him all the way to the outskirts of Sweetwater Springs before catching up with him. Saved a little girl in the process," he said, pride in his voice. "Showing up in town with the desperado wounded and handcuffed was enough to get her the offer of a job, practically on the spot."

"What happened to the bad man?"

"Doc Cameron fixed him up so he could stand trial. The sheriff hauled him back to Wyoming where they strung him up right quick."

The very idea of such a woman awed her. "I want to meet her."

"I'll introduce you," Erik promised. "Anyway, wife, you're distracting me from what I wanted to tell you," he said in a teasing tone.

She rolled her eyes.

"The man in the group with us—the one who towered over me—is Ant Gordon. He owns the newspaper." His voice sobered. "Well, his neighbor brought word…"

As he relayed the story, Antonia's stomach turned tighter, and her peaceful feelings fled. She thought of the suffering the Blackfoot tribe must be enduring and felt helpless. Her arms tightened about the baby. "Do you think it be the Indians stealin'?"

"I don't know. Probably."

The urge to help the tribe was so strong her body trembled from the pull. Even though she hadn't seen the Indians in two years, Antonia remembered those she'd come to know, especially the children, so quick to make Henri one of their own. She wondered if she could take her money, buy food, and haul it out to the reservation—a journey of several days' travel. But even as she mulled over all the tasks—borrowing the wagon, taking Camilla with her, leaving the boys, wondering if Henrietta would watch Jacques—Antonia realized how complicated the plan was. *At least by myself.* She cast a speculative look at her husband. *But with Erik?*

"We have to do somethin'."

"What?"

Speaking quickly, she outlined her plan.

He let out a frustrated breath. "Let's just suppose I go along with your idea, which I'm not saying I will."

His resistance made her feel rock-stubborn. Her muscles tensed.

"We fill the wagon with bags of beans, flour, cornmeal, and other supplies. We drive it out to the reservation. Then what?"

"We give the Indians the food."

"And then?"

"They eat it."

"What happens after that?"

Antonia looked at him, baffled. "Why be you askin' these questions?" She thought the answer obvious. "They not be thievin' then. No more problems with them and us."

"But for how long, Antonia? How long can your supplies feed a whole tribe? A week? Two? What happens when the food is eaten up? We're back to square one."

She scrunched her forehead. *Square one?*

"A game reference—checkers or chess." Erik shook his head in frustration. "I mean, we're back to where we started. Your plan is only a short-term solution. You'd be throwing the money away."

"I be savin' people," Antonia said fiercely.

"I'm not saying you're wrong about that. But you must see the problem is bigger than a wagon of food."

Frustrated, she didn't want to admit he was right. *I be right, too.*

"Besides, we need that money set aside for the future. God forbid, what if the crops fail, or the cows die, or the barn catches on fire?"

"But what if *nothing* be goin' wrong?"

Erik gave her a sharp look. "This is a *farm*, Antonia. Inevitably, *something* will go wrong." He waited a beat. "Besides,

I saw how your eyes lit up at the thought of Henri going to college. That will take money. Far more than what you have stashed away. We'll have to save for years in order to make that opportunity happen. And that's just for one child. What about Jacques or Camilla? There're colleges for women. And any children we might have together."

Antonia looked down, torn between what he was saying and the emotion whirling around in her body. *Not helping feels wrong. But using funds my family might need also feels wrong.*

She wished she knew what to do.

CHAPTER TWENTY-THREE

Erik pulled the wagon into the yard and stopped in front of the barn. He set the brake, tying off the reins. "As much as I enjoy going to town, I like coming home even more." He winked, then jumped off the seat and came around to take Camilla from Antonia before helping her step down.

Her skirt tangled in her legs, and she tugged the material to free herself.

"I'm looking forward to that chicken dinner later," he said with a smile, handing the baby back to her.

Antonia's stomach clenched. She'd forgotten his earlier request.

"Daisy told me that Penny was the next hen she'd planned to use for dinner. Apparently, her egg production has slowed down."

She inhaled sharply. *Not Penny!*

Erik didn't notice Antonia's reaction. He went to the back of the wagon, leaned over the side, and lifted up the puppy. "Come on, *Schatz.*"

The dog woke up and licked his hand.

Erik gestured to the barn. "Henri, you bring your puppy and help me in the barn. *Maman*'s going to be busy cooking us up a feast."

The boy scrambled out. "What's a shots?" He reached for the puppy, gathering her to him and staggering a few steps with her weight.

"*Schatz,*" Erik corrected. "German for *sweetheart*. When I was a boy, we had a dog named *Schatzy*."

Henri kissed the dog's head. "I like that name. Can we call her *Schatzy*?"

"*Schatzy* is a good name for a dog," Erik agreed. The two walked into the barn.

Antonia gazed after them. Only recently had Henri begun going along with Erik without first glancing at her for permission or reassurance. She carried Camilla into the house and laid the baby in her cradle, then returned to the wagon for the sleeping Jacques and placed him on the bed.

Hoping the babies would nap for a long time, Antonia left the house and walked with a leaden heart toward the henhouse.

While they were at church, they'd left the chickens cooped inside for safety. When Antonia opened the door of the henhouse, the birds billowed out and swarmed around her, acting as if she was about to feed them for a second time.

Usually, she enjoyed the chickens' liveliness but not today. She looked at every one, seeing the coloring, the quirks that made each unique—even the black one.

With a sigh, Antonia turned her back on the flock and walked toward the porch. She paused, unable to resist a glance behind.

Penny tried to follow her, but several other more aggressive chickens boxed out the copper hen.

Antonia paused and bit her lip. *Don't be gittin' close,* she warned herself. *Penny be only a bird. Not like she be family.* But she couldn't scold away her feelings. With a determined whirl, she waded through the chickens to reach Penny. "Here, girl."

She picked up her favorite bird. "One last time, let's go sit awhile." *I need to nerve myself up.*

Antonia carried the hen to the porch and sat in the rocking chair. As she rocked and petted Penny, she wished the ritual they'd developed would comfort her now. But instead, she only felt dread.

The thought of eating this chicken had taken away the good feelings from her time in town. Antonia couldn't understand her own reluctance. Before coming to live on this farm, she never would have believed she could care for a *chicken.* Over the years, she'd killed hundreds of birds and all kinds of other animals—did so even yesterday.

But never one that brought me comfort...that I loved.

I've already lost so much.

Antonia tried to chide herself into a different attitude— after all, the death of a chicken to provide food for her family was nothing compared to the death of a husband.

But maybe I feel so strongly because of Jean-Claude's death. Maybe losing him softened me somehow.

I won't do it!

A wave of anger pushed Antonia out of her chair and off the porch and into the yard where she put Penny near the other chickens. She stormed into the house, took off her boots, hat, good dress, and undergarments, and donned her Indian tunic and moccasins.

After gathering everything she'd need for hunting, Antonia took her rifle from the rack over the front door and moved outside. She marched halfway across the yard before some common sense penetrated her intense emotion, and she attempted to rein herself in. *Descending on Erik like a lightning bolt during a thunderstorm probably not be wise.*

❀ ❀ ❀

In the barn, Erik bent over Shandy's front leg, cleaning out the gelding's hoof, packed with smelly muck. He was looking forward to finishing up the chores, so he could sit down to a special Sunday dinner.

Henri had put the pup in the wheelbarrow and was mucking out the mules' stalls.

His back to the aisle, he was focused on scraping out the caked-in dirt with a pick and didn't look up at the sound of Antonia's footsteps. "Cornell Knapp wasn't in church today," he said, keeping his gaze on the hoof. "Tomorrow, I'll ride out there to talk to him about using his bull."

Antonia barely registered his words, so focused was she on chickens, not cows. "I'll not be killin' Penny for dinner."

"You don't have to," Erik said absently, brushing away the loose dirt he'd dislodged. "I always killed the chickens for Daisy. I'll take care of it as soon as I'm done with Shandy." He lowered the hoof to the ground. "There, old fellow. One down, three to go."

"We ain't havin' Penny for Sunday dinner."

"Don't get all riled up, now," Erik said in a reasonable voice. "Just pick another chicken then." He swiped sweat from his forehead with his wrist. "'Bout time to raise up another batch of chicks so we have roosters for the pot. We can't afford to sacrifice a layer every time I have a hankering. But just this once. Let me know which chicken you want." Feeling as if he'd taken care of this chicken debate, he stepped to the horse's rump, and slid his hand down Shandy's hind leg.

The horse obliged by lifting the hoof.

"Don't be botherin' yourself."

The edge in Antonia's voice—one he'd never heard before—stopped him. Erik lowered Shandy's leg, straightened, and faced her. From this angle, he could see her through the open stall door.

Antonia stood with one hand on her hip, her color high, eyes sparking. She held her rifle with her other hand.

He recognized the signs of female wrath but wasn't sure what was wrong. "Why are you dressed like that?"

"We ain't eatin' any chickens."

"That doesn't answer my question," he said in exasperation and leaned an arm on the horse's back.

Her chin lifted. "I'm goin' hunting. I'll get us a different bird. Pheasant or such."

"What in tarnation is going on, woman? The Sabbath's not a day for hunting."

"The chickens be…"

"What?" he asked impatiently. "The chickens *are*…food?" He guessed at her answer and plowed on. "All the animals around here are food."

Henri popped out of a stall, the dog clutched to his chest. "Not my puppy," he said, brows drawn together in an anxious expression, eyes pleading. "Not Schatzy."

Oh, for crying out loud! Erik had forgotten the boy was still around. He barely kept himself from saying the words, instead reaching deep inside himself for patience. "No, Henri. Not your puppy or the horses or the mules or the milk cows. Just the pigs and chickens and bull calves are food."

"Henri, take the puppy and play with her on the porch, please," Antonia said, enunciating every word, apparently determined to get each one correct. "Your pa and I have some talking to do."

They both waited until the boy left the barn.

Erik turned to her. "Now, wife, what's got your dander up?"

Her eyes narrowed. "The chickens are special. I ain't kil-lin' and eatin' 'em."

Antonia was obviously too upset to remember to speak properly. He held up a placating hand. "I know Penny's special to you. Didn't I just say pick another one? How about that black one that's always pecking at us? Be glad to eat that critter."

Antonia set the rifle down on a straw bale and crossed her arms. "She be a good layer."

Why did women have to be so dang unreasonable? Heat started to burn in his chest. "You're the mighty hunter," he said sarcastically. "Yet, you can't kill a chicken?"

"I *can* kill 'em. I just ain't gonna."

"I just *won't*, not *ain't*. You don't say *ain't*."

Her expression grew mule stubborn, and her hands jammed to her hips. "*Won't*, then. I *won't*."

Erik threw up his hands. "Fine. Sabbath or not, go kill whatever dang bird you want. I'll pretend it's a chicken." He turned back to Shandy and once again reached for the horse's leg.

She lowered her arms. "Whatever bird I bring back won't taste like Daisy's chicken."

"Of course, it will," he said in a sharp tone. "Just follow the recipe."

Antonia took a deep breath. "I *cain't*," she blurted out.

"*Can't*, not *cain't*," he corrected. "It's not that hard, Antonia. Even I've done it a time or two when Daisy wasn't up to cooking."

"I *can't* read them."

"What do you mean you can't?"

"I don't know how to read, Erik. I've never had no book learning. Might as well be chicken scratches for all I know." Scarlet flushed her cheeks.

He caught a glimpse of shame in her eyes before she lowered her gaze. Stunned, he stared at her. He'd assumed Antonia hadn't much of an education but figured she had some. He thought back over some of their conversations, and anger built inside. *She's deliberately misled me.* In his book, that was as good as a lie.

❋ ❋ ❋

With bated breath, embarrassed plumb down to her moccasins, Antonia watched her husband try to absorb her revelation.

Erik shook his head, pain in his eyes. "Why didn't you just tell me? You've always seemed so forthright. I liked that about you. Now I find you've been keeping this secret from me."

He doesn't care about my lack of book learnin'? For the first time, doubt touched her, and Antonia suspected she might have made a grave mistake. "You want an educated wife. Daisy had schoolin'. You be readin' all the time."

"I wanted a *nurse* for Camilla," he said sharply. "Frankly, at the time, any breast filled with milk would do, and you had one, uh…two." His face flushed. "I needed someone who'd care for my daughter. Being a loving wife and mother is more important to me than being an educated one."

"You be wantin' both." She kept her gaze on him. *How did I go from bein' the angry one to wonderin' if I'm in the wrong?*

"Lack of education can be *changed*, Antonia. It's not like something set in stone about a person—as if I wanted a short wife and got you instead, so I chopped off your feet to make you what I want."

With a sinking feeling, she realized he was right. The secret she'd thought so shameful turned out to be small when she finally admitted the truth. But Antonia couldn't get a word in edgewise to tell him so because he barreled on without stopping. In the dim light his eyes were smoky blue and pinned on her face so she couldn't look away.

"To be honest, no, I haven't liked the way you speak. But with everything else going on, that didn't matter. I focused on *what* you said, not *how* you said it." The edge left Erik's tone, and he sounded tired. "I knew you were smart and would probably change your speech on your own."

He thinks I'm smart? She'd never thought that about herself.

"And your efforts have paid off. I've been proud of you. Until today, have I ever said a word of criticism about your language? Ever corrected your speech?"

She shook her head.

"Have I been unkind or done anything else to make you think you had to lie to me?"

"I didn't b—lie."

His jaw tightened. "Not in words, Antonia, but in deeds. A lie of omission."

She could guess at what a lie of omission meant.

He pinched the bridge of his nose before lowering his hand. "Would you judge me so harshly that you'd be afraid of my reaction?"

Antonia felt guilty, realizing she'd hurt him. Fact was, Erik seemed more upset with her for withholding the information than he did about her lack of education.

She spoke slowly so every word would come out right. "No. I didn't judge you at all. I judged myself. And I was afraid. I didn't want any—" Antonia groped for the word "—*setbacks* with our relationship."

His lips twisted in a wry grimace. "Well, we certainly have a setback now."

Silence hung between them, uncomfortable and filled with pain—for the first time, pain *between* them, not from their shared grief.

"Antonia, I can teach you to read," Erik said gently.

The words that would have brightened her heart if she'd heard them a few hours ago now only made her feel ashamed. Heart racing, she lowered her gaze to the ground.

"All you had to do was ask."

Something new winged through her. Someone cared enough to teach her. This man. *My own husband.* Antonia scuffed a few pieces of straw with her foot before forcing herself to meet his eyes. "I would like that, Erik."

"We'll start tomorrow night. We may not get much done until wintertime when we'll have plenty of time indoors."

"I'm sorry. I never meant to hurt you." The words seemed paltry, but she didn't know what else to add.

"There's no need for a chicken dinner tonight."

She nodded her understanding and picked up the rifle, preparing to leave.

"In the future, will you tell me when something is bothering you? Before the boiling over stage?"

Antonia paused. "I'm usually not much bothered."

"So I thought. But now I have to wonder. Anything else bothering you?"

Without hesitation, she shook her head.

Erik stared into her eyes for a few minutes, pinning her again—as if trying to ascertain if she was telling the truth.

Her stomach twisted, knowing she'd made him doubt her. Antonia broke eye contact first, turning to leave the barn, aware of the breach that had formed between them.

I must find a way to repair what I've done.

CHAPTER TWENTY-FOUR

The argument, brief as it was, made Erik draw back from Antonia, even though their behavior toward each other remained civil, and they still pulled together like a team. But their growing physical intimacy stuttered to a standstill.

In Montana, the growing season was never long enough to accomplish all a busy farmer needed to do. During the two weeks after their argument, as Erik went about his chores, he pondered why such a relatively mild disagreement had made such an impact on him.

Since he didn't have a ready answer, he tried to put the incident from his mind, only to have it pop up at the oddest times and tug at his thoughts. But with the summer flying by, and the two of them laboring from dawn to nightfall, he never had the time or energy to mend the rift.

Instead, Antonia and Erik focused on the crops, the livestock, and taking care of the children. She planted medicinal flowers around the porch that she'd uprooted on her hunting expeditions. Soon white Angelica and sweet clover, as well as yellow columbines and evening primrose, grew beside the steps.

They'd started experimenting with making cheese, and, one by one, big cheese wheels ripened on wooden shelves in the pantry, crowding out the other supplies. When he could,

Erik dug into the side of the hill next to the house to make a cheese cave.

The puppy and the children grew at a surprising rate. Jacques went from toddling a few steps to running, seemingly overnight. His vocabulary expanded to words beyond those ending in an *ah* sound, although he still uttered them with determination.

In the evenings, Henri studied so he could continue learning while school was out for the summer, and Antonia worked under Erik's guidance, proving all along she'd been learning with her son since he'd started school.

Her sharp intellect didn't surprise Erik, nor did her hard work, but her thirst for knowledge did. He wondered what her life could have been if she'd had a real education as a child. Would she have chosen a profession, as a teacher maybe? Or perhaps she would have gone into the other careers that had begun opening to women in the last few decades—a doctor like Elizabeth Blackwell or a journalist like Nellie Bly. *Our children will have those choices,* he promised himself, *to the best of my ability to provide them.*

Henrietta taught Antonia to can food, and his wife reciprocated by teaching her neighbor how to dry berries and other fruits and vegetables. The two of them took their children to gather the wild berries, chokecherries, and plums, often leading a mule to help haul babies, baskets, food, blankets, and a rifle. As the garden ripened, an increasing number of jars of fruit and vegetables lined the shelves in the pantry.

One day in the beginning of August, Erik surveyed the remaining *holz hausen*—the haystack-shaped woodpile—and knew he'd better take a trip to the forest if he wanted firewood to season before the autumn nights grew cold. Every year, twice during the summer, he and Rory O'Donnell drove together, spending several days chopping or sawing trees and splitting the logs, returning with a wagon laden with as much wood as the horses could pull, which he then made into several *holz hausen*. He'd already postponed the journey for too long.

This year, Erik had mixed feelings about being away from the farm. On one hand, he looked forward to the expedition, longing for quiet time in the forest, just he and Rory working in silence except for grunts and terse words spoken when necessary. But, as much as Erik knew he needed time away from the family, he didn't want to leave them, especially Antonia, without having another discussion to see if he could bridge the divide between them.

That night after the children slept, Erik took a seat at the table across from Antonia, instead of next to her as he usually did when teaching her. He placed his elbows on the table, fisting his hands together and lowering his chin on top of them. A freshly brewed cup of chamomile tea sat at his elbow, sending a fragrant herbal scent into the air.

For a moment, he stared at his wife. The lamplight burnished her hair and gilded her lambent eyes, playing over the curve of her cheek, fuller now than when she'd first arrived here. He memorized the picture of Antonia, planning to take the image with him when he left. *Too bad there's not a photographer in Sweetwater Springs.*

He regretted having no picture of Daisy, although her parents had a family photograph. *As soon as there's an opportunity, I'll have one made of our family.* "I want to talk to you instead of studying tonight."

Antonia gave him a wary look and sipped her tea.

"You might have noticed that the *holz hausen* is getting lower?"

She raised her eyebrows. "*Holz hausen?*"

"German for wood hut—our woodpile. Our last one is dwindling."

"I hadn't given it much thought. You're always so good about keeping the wood box full. I've never had to fetch any from the woodpile."

The compliment pleased him. "You might have noticed we don't have many trees around here, certainly none we can spare for firewood."

She chuckled. "And you don't use buffalo or cow chips."

He grimaced. "Thank goodness for that. Rory and I take two annual trips to the mountains to cut wood. I need to go in the next few days—day after tomorrow, probably, if he can make it. Then another in a few weeks. Building a *holz hausen* seasons the wood in about three months, instead of six or longer. Barring too many early snowstorms, we have about that much wood left before we're out. But this is Montana, and early snowstorms can happen. Best to be prepared."

"True."

"We'll be gone three days, getting back late. I'll take all the milk and butter with us and drop off everything at the mercantile, telling the Cobbs not to expect more while we're gone."

I'll stop by the bank on the way home and make my payment on the loan. The thought of having to do so soured his mood. That payment would take the rest of the savings in his bank account, and he'd be scraping the bottom of the barrel, at that. No funds would be left for the winter if a late-season drought or early storms caused his harvest to fail. *Might have to sell some heifers.* He forced the dire thoughts away.

"If not for the children and the livestock, I could go with you."

She can still surprise me. Erik grinned. "Bet you could chop quite a bit of wood, wife. We'd need to take two wagons if you were along."

Antonia returned his smile. "You'll be sore. You'll be needin' the liniment bottle," she said in a flirtatious tone.

She hadn't spoken like that since their argument, and he felt relieved that she'd inadvertently opened the door for the rest of what he wanted to talk about. "I'll be needing the liniment *and* even better, your hands on my sore muscles when I return." He paused. "Been a while, I know. I've missed our closeness. I just had a lot of thinking to do."

"Thinkin' *and* a feelin'." She looked up and held his gaze.

He nodded agreement. "Truth is, even with getting along well...our growing closeness and care for each other, we're still grieving. Maybe the wounds have scabbed over, but we still have them."

Antonia winced. "We're more sensitive, like bumpin' your arm on something when you already have a bruise."

She understands. "Yes. And we still don't know each other well. We were thrown into a marriage and have had to learn about each other. I think we've jogged along in harness well enough, but I guess we needed to have an argument to learn about each other—how we fight and how to make up—as well as the intimacy that comes afterward and helps mend the rift." He shook his head. "Listen to me speaking in all these analogies."

She looked at him in askance, reached for her teacup, and took a sip.

"An analogy demonstrates two similar things." He gestured back and forth between them. "Our relationship, working together, is like a team of horses pulling a wagon."

She laughed. "Then our marriage be the harness."

He smiled in praise. "That day, you caught me off guard when you became upset about killing the chickens—especially since I wasn't expecting it. You'd agreed to make fried chicken in the morning and seemed so comfortable while we were in town. And to be honest...ever since Daisy's death, I've been feeling guilt aplenty about everything I didn't do to make her happy. Or maybe all I did to make her unhappy. Having a second unhappy wife—I mean, I realize you are grieving and thus are already unhappy. But a wife *unhappy with me* seemed too much."

"I'm not an unhappy wife," Antonia said the words carefully, as she did when trying to speak properly.

He cocked his head, not sure what she meant.

"There's a difference between being sad about Jean-Claude and being happy with you. I be—am both." She scrunched her forehead. "But not so much since…"

"I needed to pull back from you for a time, do some thinking, lick my wounds, so to speak."

"Another analogy." Antonia's lips turned up in a rueful smile. "I've done a lot of thinking, too. I felt bad. Missed our growing closeness. Wondered if we'd ever have it again." She touched her chest. "Yet, in here, I believed we would."

He reached across the table for her hand. "I'm ready for closeness and intimacy again. Perhaps when I return." Erik realized he was making assumptions. "That is, if you are?"

She paused and touched her lips with her fingers, obviously thinking.

What if she says no? Erik's heart started to knock against his chest.

Antonia smiled. "I'd like that."

❋ ❋ ❋

Erik and Rory were two days late returning from the mountains, and worry shadowed Antonia's footsteps. After the third night passed without him driving up, she'd fretted while doing her chores, as well as the added ones of milking and seeing to the livestock. Every time she stepped outside or passed a window, Antonia paused to glance up the road.

The babies grew fractious, and Henri retreated to his previous silence. Even quiet, the boy was a big help to her, taking on as much as he could shoulder. She couldn't wait to share with Erik her pride in her son, for she knew he'd be pleased, too.

The puppy had grown too big for Henri to carry around. Schatzy proved to be a loving companion, entertaining the children as nothing else could do.

Then another day crawled past and a fifth. Antonia tried not to think of all the reasons Erik and Rory could be late. But the memories of finding Jean-Claude's body wrapped in the grizzly's great arms kept leaping into her mind, making fear churn in her stomach. *There are two of them,* she constantly reminded herself. *He isn't alone.* After thinking the words so often, she no longer had to pause to say them properly.

Sometimes as Antonia worked, she sent up a prayer, something she'd never really done in the past, taking comfort from the simple communication with God.

On the seventh day, the babies were sleeping, Henri off exploring the grassy plains with his dog, and Antonia was in the kitchen drying dishes. Normally, she'd be enjoying this time of peace, but concern for her husband gnawed at her innards.

At the sound of hoofbeats and wheels, her heart leaped with joy. *Erik's home!* Relief made her knees weak. She dropped the dishtowel, untied the apron protecting Daisy's altered dress, and hurried across the room. Flinging open the door, she halted, shocked to see a buggy instead of a wagon, and a tall man in a suit stepping down.

Disappointment seized her, and Antonia had to work hard to mask her feelings. *Why is he here?* Then all the fears she'd grappled with for days burst out. Thoughts of the worst flooded her mind, and she gasped, racing across the porch to meet him. "Tell me he's alive," she flung at him. "Please, may my husband be alive!"

The man stopped short and took off his hat. "Mrs. Muth," he nodded. "I'm afraid—"

"Nooo!" Antonia wailed. "Dear Lord, not another husband dead!" *Not Erik!* Her legs couldn't hold her, and she sank to the step. Sobs built in her chest, and she struggled to contain them, her body shaking.

"Uh." The man cleared his throat, took two steps, and crouched, grabbing her arms. "No. No, Mrs. Muth. You are under a misapprehension. I'm not here to give you bad news about your husband."

At first, the man's words didn't penetrate the pain whirling through her.

"Mrs. Muth!" He shook her arms.

In a daze, Antonia looked up at him.

He'd paled and his brown eyes held genuine concern, even though he'd spoken so sharply. "I'm Caleb Livingston, the banker. I tell you in truth; I'm not here to bring you bad news." Mr. Livingston checked himself. "At least, not that kind of bad news."

"Then Erik's not dead?"

"No, my dear lady." His tone sounded compassionate. "Or at least I have no knowledge of the state of his health. Come." He slipped a hand under her elbow. "Let me help you to a chair and bring you some water."

Embarrassed, Antonia allowed him to assist her to her feet. Finding her backbone, she drew herself up and straightened her shoulders. "My apologies, Mr. Livingston. You must think me the most weak-minded of females. It's just that... that...my husband and Mr. O'Donnell have traveled to the mountains to log for the winter's firewood. They are four days late getting home, and I've been fearing the worst." She bit her lip, forcing the words out. "The last time I had a husband who was late, the worst *had* occurred."

"I understand. Please—" the banker waved to the rocking chairs "—sit." He removed his hat.

Antonia managed not to betray how her knees trembled. She perched on the edge of the seat, holding the chair steady so it wouldn't rock. "Please forgive my reaction, Mr. Livingston." She laid a hand on her chest. "Now I feel quite foolish."

"Pay it no mind."

"You are kind." She gave him a direct look. The man was handsome enough to turn a woman's head. *If a woman didn't already love her husband.* The revelation about her feelings for Erik shocked her.

He gave her a half smile. "Kindness is *not* something I've ever been accused of before, Mrs. Muth. Bankers can't afford to be kind."

"*Everyone* can afford to be kind," she corrected.

"Perhaps you will not think so when you learn why I've traveled here."

Inside, Antonia still felt shaky, although her mind was beginning to clear. "Whatever the reason be, *does* not take away kindness. That is *not* how it works."

"No." His smile was wry. He gestured to the second rocker.

Mr. Livingston doesn't look like a man who sits in rocking chairs. Antonia nodded for him to sit.

He settled himself on the edge of the seat, having to find his balance, and set his hat on his legs. "How long did you say your husband has been gone?"

"Seven days. He meant to be away only three." She gripped the edge of her apron.

His jaw tightened. "In a discussion several Sundays ago, your husband indicated he intended to keep you appraised of the thievery situation in Sweetwater Springs over the last six or so months."

Antonia gave a hesitant nod, wondering if she would need to defend the Blackfoot again. "He did inform me."

"He also mentioned that you are a crack shot with a rifle. Seemed quite proud of the fact."

Mr. Livingston spoke as if he couldn't understand Erik's attitude, but pleasure bloomed in her.

"If Mr. Muth hasn't been in town in the last week, then he hasn't heard the news buzzing about the place concerning the Indian thievery. The word has gotten out, and gossip and panic are rife, with the Cobbs being the instigators of the anti-Indian sentiment."

Antonia clenched her hands.

"I can't say I blame them."

She bit her lip. *What does this mean for my Indian friends?*

"The town leaders held a meeting yesterday to discuss the situation. The sheriff isn't sure if the stealing incidences have escalated, or if more reports being made are because people now assume events of missing livestock are due to the redskins."

Oh, no!

"The sheriff's chasing her tail with having to check out each one. Unfortunately, many livestock disappearances appear to be from natural causes—wandering off, or animal predation, which is wasting her time and slowing the investigation. She also fears some unscrupulous people may be stealing from their neighbors and blaming things on the redskins, or perhaps are even butchering and eating their own livestock and then reporting them as having been stolen."

Antonia wanted to surge to her feet and pace across the porch. She forced herself to remain still, but her fingernails dug into her palms from the effort. "That is unfair to the Blackfoot."

"Recently, the majority of the reports seem to be heightened in this area. Shots were exchanged at the Hansen place." He waved in a northeastern direction. "Sheriff Granger spoke with your neighbors, the Knapps, on Sunday to warn them to stay alert. I'll stop by Mrs. O'Donnell's on the way home, so she knows to be on guard. The sheriff is sending out riders to cover the rest of the area."

"I thank you for your concern, Mr. Livingston. We will be watchful." She decided not to mention her connection with the Blackfoot and made a mental note to keep Henri close to the house.

"Good." He let out a breath. "Now for what really brings me out here…. Normally, I would speak to your husband, so as not to trouble you. However, since I've already troubled you…"

She gestured for him to continue.

"Mr. Muth took out a loan to build that." He lifted his chin, pointing in the direction of the barn. "He has quarterly payments due on the amount he owes, and if he's late, then there is an extra penalty. The money was due yesterday, Mrs. Muth. And thus, your husband is in arrears."

Arrears? "What is the meaning, sir?"

"Behind and owing a penalty," he explained.

Antonia had been so focused on the fact that Mr. Livingston might have brought her bad news about Erik's death that it hadn't occurred to her that because the man was a *banker*, he thus must be here about *money*. "Oh," was all she could say, while she gathered her scattered wits about her. "I didn't know." She wished the words unsaid as soon as they left her mouth.

"And why should you? Ladies have no need to be involved in business."

His tone was still kind, but the assumption made her hackles rise. "How much does he owe?" she asked.

He hesitated. "Perhaps I should save this discussion for when Mr. Muth returns."

Antonia thought of Jean-Claude's money. *Will it be enough?* "I will pay you, Mr. Livingston," she said in a firm tone. "But I need to know the amount."

With obvious reluctance, he named the sum and the penalty.

Antonia held in a gasp. Her chest tightened. *That will take almost everything I have.* "Has Mr. Muth ever been late before?"

"There have only been three quarterly payments so far. But he paid on the due date with each."

"In that case, sir..." She spoke every word clearly. "My husband would have paid on the due date this time, too. But since he's delayed in the wilderness and may be unable to travel...if I pay what's owed, will you forgive the penalty?"

He sat in silence, studying her.

"Just this once, please."

"Due to the circumstances you both have undergone. I will waive the penalty. Indeed, I owe it to you for frightening you so."

"Oh, thank you, sir," she said in relief.

His lips quirked. "Just don't bandy that fact about."

"We will be silent." Antonia rose. "I will get the money for you. Shall I bring you anything? Tea?" She gave thanks that they'd replenished the supply on their last trip to town. "Water?"

He stood and gestured toward the well. "Water will be fine. I'll get it myself. And if I could water the horses?"

"Of course. Let me bring you a cup."

Back straight, Antonia walked into the house and to the bedroom, her knees still shaky. She kept the money in a beaded pouch in the bureau.

The babies slept—Camilla in the cradle she was almost too big for, and Jacques sprawled on the bed. But even as she watched, he stirred.

She pulled out the money, counting the bills, her fingers shaky. With the money in her hand, she moved into the kitchen to grab a tin cup and then walked outside. "Here is your money, Mr. Livingston." She gave the funds to him, not by tone or posture conveying how loath she was to part with her savings, and her growing resentment with Erik for putting her in this position. "I apologize that you had to drive all the way out here to be paid what's owed you. That be...isn't right." She held out the cup.

The banker counted out the bills. Grasping her hand, he removed the cup. "I appreciate the chance to quench my thirst."

Did he think I'd be runnin' him off the place, offer no hospitality? She reconsidered. *Well, if the banker's visits always brought bad news to those already lacking funds, perhaps he had reason to believe such.* Antonia hesitated, then rushed out the words. "You be a good man, Mr. Livingston. You remember that, hear?"

In the house, Jacques cried out.

The banker tipped his hat to her. "Tend to your child, Mrs. Muth. I'll avail myself of your water and be on my way." He turned and walked down the steps and across the yard.

For some reason, Antonia thought the well-dressed man had a lonely set to his shoulders, for all he walked so upright. She turned to go to Jacques before the boy woke up his sister.

As she shut the door, Antonia felt like she was wrung out from all the emotions she'd just experienced—from terror, to love, to resentment, and now anger welled up inside her. She couldn't believe Erik had been so disappointed with how she'd withheld her lack of education, drawn back from her even, and yet he'd gone and done the same thing with keeping the loan a secret.

You wait 'til you git home, Erik Muth. You're goin' to git a piece of my mind for keepin' such important business from me!

CHAPTER TWENTY-FIVE

That night, Antonia had a hard time sleeping. The full moon beamed through the windows, making the room lighter than she was used to. Camilla was fussy, waking every few hours. After nursing the baby, she lay awake, her thoughts torn between worry about Erik, the reevaluation of her newfound love, and anger with him.

She wanted him home safe so she could fall into his arms in relief and then give him a scold that would make his hair stand on end.

Finally, she'd given up on sleep, getting out of bed, changing from her nightgown to her tunic and slipping her feet into her moccasins. Taking a blanket from Erik's bed, she moved across the floor and stepped outside.

Schatzy slept in a straw-filled box on the porch.

She woke the puppy, who wiggled with joy and licked Antonia's face. Wrapping the blanket around her, she settled on the rocking chair, with Schatzy who could barely fit on her lap. She watched the moon-washed setting and inhaled the scent from sweet clover blooming around the porch. Gradually, she allowed the rhythm of rocking and petting the dog to lull her into drowsiness. After about twenty minutes, chilled, Antonia crouched to put the dog back into the box.

The puppy whimpered, wanting more attention.

"Stay."

The dog had learned that word and curled into a ball.

Antonia gave Schatzy a final pat before going into the house. Yawning, she didn't bother to change again; instead she sank down on the bearskin next to Henri, kicked off her moccasins, and spread the blanket around her. Within minutes, she was asleep.

The bark of the dog startled her awake. *Erik!* Antonia sat up, her anger with her husband forgotten in the wave of relief washing over her. But something about Schatzy's bark—a deeper, more threatening sound accompanied by growls—told her something else had disturbed the animal. Dashing across the room, she grabbed the rifle from over the door.

"*Maman?*" Henri sounded scared.

"Get up *now*, Henri, and come here." Antonia handed him the rifle and took down the second one, grateful they kept them loaded. "Hold this for me." She peered through the window, careful not to expose her full face. Dawn had broken and replaced the milky moonlight with a sky tinged with pink.

As she half expected, Antonia could see shadowy figures creeping toward the henhouse. *They must be desperate, risking the dog waking us.*

"Stay here, right behind the door," she ordered her son. "But be ready to hand me the rifle if I say."

"*Oui, Maman.*"

Antonia opened the door and stepped onto the porch, her bare feet silent on the wood. She raised the rifle, aimed, and shot, plowing two bullets into the dirt, right in front of the men.

❋ ❋ ❋

Five days after they were due back, Erik pulled up the wagon in front of the O'Donnell homestead, setting the brake and tying off the reins. They'd taken advantage of the full moon, leaving hours before dawn and driving through Sweetwater Springs before most people had awoken.

He was so antsy to reach his farm, having missed Antonia and the children more than he'd thought possible. He was starving and filthy and couldn't wait for a meal and a bath. But first, Erik needed to drop off Rory, water the horses, and unload half the wagon.

"Home at last," Rory said with a tired sigh and a grin. The man sat next to Erik, a sapling on his lap, the roots wrapped in burlap—one of several pine saplings the two had brought as gifts for their wives. He propped the tree on the seat and jumped down from the wagon.

The door of the house flew open, and the twins and Charlie raced out, calling, "Da! Da!" They ran into his arms.

Rory laughed, hugging his children.

Envy stabbed Erik. He wanted that kind of welcome when he returned home but wasn't sure either Antonia or Henri was the type to run to greet him.

Henrietta followed behind her brood, a hand braced on her chest.

Rory extracted himself from the tangle of children and opened his arms to his wife.

"Thank the saints!" She ran into her husband's embrace and burst into tears.

Rory held his wife close, patting her back. "Now, now. I'm sorry to be a frettin' a you with our lateness."

The children all started talking at once.

Erik relaxed on the seat, giving the man a few minutes to enjoy his homecoming. Hearing the word *Indians* uttered by one of the twins made his ears prick. He leaped off the wagon, strode around the horses, and toward the family. "What's this about Indians?"

Henrietta pulled away from Rory and mopped her eyes with the bottom of her apron. "Such a time of worry, what with you two being late and wondering what might have happened—if you were injured or killed," she scolded. "I can only imagine what Antonia must be going through, given what occurred with Jean-Claude." She shot Erik a sharp glance. "And with the threat of the Indians, I didn't dare go check on her, nor send Charlie."

"Shandy cut himself on a spar." Erik gestured to the cloth wrapped around the gelding's foreleg. "We had to doctor the wound and to wait for him to heal." He brushed the air in an impatient gesture for her to hurry up with telling the story of the Indians. "We drove straight through town, not speaking with a soul."

Henrietta pushed back a lock of hair that blew across her face. "Mr. Livingston came by with news that the town is in an uproar about Indians stealing livestock. A few days ago, there was a shooting. I haven't gotten any more news."

Livingston! Erik held in a groan, realizing he'd missed the payment for the barn and would now also owe a late fee. Shame burned through him. The banker had driven out to collect. *The man must think I'm unreliable.*

Did he tell Antonia about the loan?

"Mr. Livingston said that there are thieving Indians in the area, that the sheriff is searching for them, and warned us to be on guard. Charlie's been keeping watch with the rifle, but it's a big job for a boy." She huffed out a long breath. "I declare, I haven't slept a wink."

Rory and Erik exchanged worried glances. His neighbor waved at the wagon. "Everyone, let's help getting the wood unloaded. Just dump the wood on the side. We'll stack it later.

Charlie, fetch some water for the horses. We won't take the time to unhitch them."

"Aye, Da." Charlie ran to the well.

"Henrietta." Rory pointed to the seat. "If you could take my bag. And I've brought you some pine trees. Let me grab them."

She clasped her hands in front of her. "Trees. How lovely of you."

Erik reached under the seat and removed the Winchester from the box he'd made to store it. He transferred the saplings to the floorboard and laid the rifle on the seat.

With everyone pitching in to help, the group made short work of unloading half the wood supply. No sooner had the O'Donnell family tossed the last piece aside than Erik drove the wagon in a wide circle, heading back down the track that led to the main road and home.

His stomach tight with fear, he was tempted to speed the horses. But he knew they were tired from pulling the heavy wagon such a long way.

Dozens of dreadful scenarios of Indian attacks flashed through his mind—his wife dead, his children left vulnerable or even kidnapped. *Surely, the Indians wouldn't kill the children?*

Except they had in the past. As we have killed their women and children. He thought of the Marias massacre when the army slew a friendly band of women, children, and elderly men. Although twenty-five years earlier, he was sure the Blackfoot hadn't forgotten the tragedy.

Almost sick with dread, Erik reined in his runaway thoughts, reminding himself the local Indians hadn't hurt anyone up to this point—or taken any children. *They can't even feed the ones they have.* With his mind finally under his control, he remembered his wife's capabilities.

But even able to think more rationally, he had a gut feeling that something was wrong.

Thank God, she's so self-sufficient! I can depend on her.

In that moment, Erik realized he loved Antonia. The emotion sideswiped him, filling him with astonishment and joy. He didn't know whether to laugh or yell and couldn't wait to tell her of his feelings. *Even if I can't be sure she loves me back, I want her to know. Please, God, may she be all right. May they all be!*

Finally, his house and barn came into sight, tiny in the distance, seeming to take forever to grow larger. Yet, he couldn't whip his team to greater speed, for sweat already lathered the horses' necks. *I can't ruin my horses because of my foolish fears.*

Three mounts he didn't know stood tied up near the water. They wore saddle pads instead of saddles, and feathers fluttered from one of the rope hackamores.

The sight of the horses made his heart kick against his ribs. Instead of driving any farther, he reined in the team, set the brake, and tied off the reins. With the rifle in one hand, he leaped down, running at an angle to the house. If the Indians watched from the kitchen window, they'd see him. But he had to take the chance.

Erik reached the side of the house and plastered himself against the wall where he couldn't be seen from the front. Wondering where Schatzy was, he scanned the yard, relieved not to see the body of the young dog.

His stomach so tight his breath was short, Erik slid around the corner to the front, pausing to remove his boots, for he couldn't possibly move across the porch without being heard. Cautiously, he ducked under the side of the porch railing and pressed his back to the wall.

The guttural sound of a man's voice, in a language Erik couldn't understand, came through the open door. The hair on his arms rose. Although he wanted to lean and glance in the window, he didn't want to be sighted.

Dropping to his knees, Erik crawled underneath the window, careful to keep the rifle from banging on the floor. On the other side, he rose to his feet, stepping to the edge of the doorway. The smell of frying ham drifted his way, and he wrinkled his nose, wondering if they were forcing Antonia to feed them.

His heart in his throat, Erik said a quick prayer, took a deep breath, and with one move leaped around and through the door, his rifle leveled.

CHAPTER TWENTY-SIX

Three Indian men sat at the table along with Henri. Two of them sprang up when Erik leaped inside.

He aimed the rifle at them, wondering if he could pull the trigger, killing them in front of his family. *If I have to!*

The braves were dressed in fur-trimmed buckskin with beaded designs on the front and sleeves. They had braided feathers into their hair and looked to be about eighteen. One long-faced Indian held Jacques on his lap. He paused in the act of feeding the boy a piece of toast.

"Pa!" Jacques yelled, bouncing on the man's knee. The boy grinned and stuffed the toast into his mouth, smearing his face with purple jam.

Schatzy let out a happy bark and ran to him, her tail wagging.

Even Camilla, lying on the bearskin, waved her hand at him.

The air smelled of pork grease, and his hungry stomach clutched.

Still holding the handle of the frying pan, Antonia whirled from the stove. Her eyes widened. "Erik, you're back!" She shook her head at him. "Put down that rifle," she said sharply. "Everything's all right." Her tone softened. "I know them."

Henri translated what she'd said to the Indians.

His arms suddenly weak, Erik lowered the rifle. Relief made his knees tremble.

The three braves didn't move, but their shoulders relaxed.

Questions flooded his mind. But the first one that tumbled from his mouth was directed at Henri. "Where did you learn to speak Blackfoot like that?"

Antonia moved the frying pan to the cooler surface of the stove. She wore an apron over her Indian garb. "We often spent weeks with the Blackfoot, and Henri learned to speak the language as well as any of the children. Two years have passed since we were there, and I thought he'd forgotten. But he's speakin' much better than me."

"I've been practicing with Hunter, Pa," Henri chimed in, his gold eyes alight. "He says I speak real good."

Erik's muddled brain took a few minutes to realize Henri referred to the Thompson boy. He tilted his head toward the braves. "But what are they doing here?" he asked his wife.

Antonia shot the Indians a guilty look. "They came by for a…uh…*visit*."

Erik figured he knew the kind of visit she was talking about.

"I'm feedin' 'em up, and then I thought we could talk about what's goin' on. Figure out what to do."

Ride for the sheriff is what we should do. But Erik didn't say so. He didn't know how much English the men understood. *Things are calm now, and I don't want to change that.*

The two men standing followed the conversation with their heads, until Antonia spoke Blackfoot words, and they sat again, looking uneasy.

His wife stepped away from the stove and walked toward him with a welcoming smile, her hands outstretched.

The lack of worry in her eyes or tension in her voice told him more than her reassuring words.

She placed her hand on his arm and rose on tiptoe to press a kiss to his lips. "I'm glad you're home. I've been right worried."

"Horse problems." He'd give her more details later.

"All that matters is you be home safe." Antonia lifted her chin toward the gun rack. "Put up the rifle." She patted his arm. "You must be starvin'. I know you didn't take enough food for all those days you were gone."

"You're not the only hunter in this family, wife." Relief had him injecting some levity into his tone but he held onto the weapon.

Antonia playfully wrinkled her nose at him before waving toward the table. "Let me introduce Samoset, Chogan, Ahanu." She gestured to each one. "Ahanu's the one whose leg was wounded a few weeks ago when that farmer shot him. He's healed, though."

The young men all gave him solemn nods.

Erik dipped his chin in acknowledgment.

Antonia pulled her eyebrows together in a frown of disapproval that she directed at the Indians. "These three were just boys when I saw them last. But now they're men enough to cause trouble."

Henri translated for her.

Samoset, the one holding Jacques, gave her a sheepish look, but the other two only stared coldly at Erik.

"Do they understand the problems they're causing?"

"I don't know." She shrugged. "I've been feedin' 'em. We've been exchangin' stories of the last two years. The government promised supplies to the tribe, Erik. But they never sent any," she said, pain in her tone. "So many deaths..." Her voice trailed off.

He suppressed an instinctive feeling of compassion. "I have to see to the horses," Erik said, torn between taking care of his team and protecting his family. He hefted the rifle. "You're sure about this?"

"They won't hurt us."

Erik took the Winchester with him as a precaution and walked out the door, thinking furiously. He stopped to pull on his boots before hurrying down the road to where he'd left the wagon. All through driving into the yard, unhitching the horses, and seeing to their needs, he sifted through possible ideas, mulling over various solutions to the three problems eating breakfast in his house. He didn't like any of the possibilities.

Turning the braves over to the sheriff, if he could even manage to do such a thing, would cause Antonia and Henri distress. But, although hard on him, upsetting his family wouldn't prevent Erik from doing what he felt was right. But turning in the Indians didn't feel right, either. Just letting them go would also be wrong, even if Antonia scolded the braves enough to put the fear of God—or at least the sheriff—into the men, in hopes they'd stop their thieving ways.

The Blackfoot are still starving, and I can't turn a blind eye to their needs.

Erik stopped to admire the Indians' horses, and a glimmer of an idea came to him. Once he walked inside the house, he hesitated on the threshold, realizing something had changed.

Tension hung in the air.

He cocked an eyebrow at Antonia in askance.

She was back at the stove, frying eggs and ham. "I told them how people are gittin' riled up, and the sheriff fears folks could get angry enough to attack the reservation, killin' innocent people. Now these three realize they've stirred up a hornet's nest and might bring disaster down on their tribe. They're scared down to their moccasins. Not that they'll show it. But they don't know what to do to make everything right."

"Give me a bit of time to think on it."

Jacques toddled over to him, reaching up his arms. "Pa."

Going with a gut feeling that he could trust his wife's judgment, Erik hung the Winchester on the rack above Antonia's two rifles. He crouched to hug the boy. "You've grown since I've been away."

Jacques patted Erik's face. Seemingly reassured, he pulled away and toddled to the bearskin, picking up a spoon near Camilla and plopping down on his behind.

Erik rose and walked over to pick up his daughter from the bearskin. He kissed Camilla's forehead, feeling the intensity of his love for her and knowing the Indian men must have the same feelings for their babies—and how such abiding love could drive a man to do anything to save his family.

Needing to feel his daughter safe in his arms, Erik carried Camilla with him to the table. He seated himself next to Henri and ruffled the boy's hair. "Glad to see you're taking such good care of things here, son. I'm proud of you."

To his surprise, the affectionate tone and gesture seemed to make the braves relax. Erik realized they must have wondered how he was treating Jean-Claude's family. Seeing their concern made him feel better disposed toward them. Not only were they *not* going to hurt his family, they'd been concerned that *he* was the hurtful one. That realization was enough to make him smile toward them.

Antonia set a plate of scrambled eggs and ham in front of him, followed by another piled with several pieces of toast spread with jam and butter.

Even with keeping Camilla entertained, Erik managed to ravenously devour his eggs and toast. One-handedly, he forked the food into his mouth.

Once Erik finished, he relaxed, rubbing Camilla's back. He looked across the table at the braves, speaking directly to them. "How stand you with horses? Do you have enough to trade for cattle and other livestock?" He glanced at Henri, nodding for the boy to translate.

After he did, the Indians looked at one another, talking among themselves and seeming to come to an agreement, for they fell silent and faced Erik. Samoset, who seemed to be the ringleader, nodded.

Erik outlined his plan for the Indians to trade their extra horses for cattle and other livestock, seeds, and plants. In addition, some of the white men working in shifts could travel to the reservation and teach them the best ways to farm.

He'd need the agreement and cooperation of the sheriff and town leaders, but Erik knew in his gut that enough of them would get behind this arrangement, even if haters like the Cobbs objected. The support and involvement of the leadership would be enough to make an informal treaty work.

The discussion and bargaining between the five of them, which sometimes turned heated, lasted all day. By the end of the discussion, the braves had agreed to ride to the reservation and speak with the tribe's chief and elders, returning to the farm in a week's time with the chief to negotiate with John Carter, Sheriff Granger, and other town leaders.

Erik remembered that Jonah Barrett had close ties with the Blackfoot through his first wife. *He should be involved as well.*

Since all three braves had extra mounts, they agreed those horses were to be sold, and the money divided among all those whose livestock they'd stolen.

Erik had a strong feeling that offering reparations would be enough to allay the townsfolk's need for justice. He planned to draw up a treaty stating what the five of them had worked out today, which could be amended at the joint meeting.

Afterward, he and Antonia stood together with Henri and Schatzy on the porch, watching the Indians ride away. The three took supplies with them—Antonia's dried fruits and vegetables, as well as portions of cheese and jerky she'd made.

The boy and the dog wandered back into the house.

Erik slipped his arm around Antonia's waist and pulled her against his side. "Well, wife, are you satisfied?"

She leaned her head on his shoulder. "If Jean-Claude were here—" her voice thickened "—he'd thank you for taking care of his friends. Their—" she hesitated, obviously searching for a word "—*plight* was a burden on his heart. Mine, too." She sighed. "We be...will have much hard work ahead of us to make this right. But I feel here—" Antonia raised her head, turned toward him, and placed her hand on her chest "—things will be better."

Erik dropped a kiss on her lips. "No one in this town is afraid of hard work. Most all are God-fearing. I'm pretty sure they'll help the Blackfoot." He tilted his head toward the house. "Come," he said in a suggestive tone. "Let's put the children to bed so we can have some time to ourselves."

✳ ✳ ✳

After the children were asleep, Erik and Antonia sat on the steps of the porch together, holding hands as they watched the fat moon rise into the swath of stars in the night sky. The breeze drifted the smell of grass their way and mingled with the scent of the flowers Antonia had planted.

Erik stirred and looked at her, seeing only the shadows of her face. But he knew her familiar features, her beautiful eyes, and that was enough. "Tomorrow, I'll ride to town and meet with Reverend Norton and Ant Gordon. They can take over from there—sending word to the others. I'll also pay Banker Livingston a visit and make the payment on the barn. I'll assure him I won't be late again." He tensed for her reaction.

"I gave Jean-Claude's money to Mr. Livingston, and he didn't charge me *arrears.*"

Shame balled in his stomach. "I'm so sorry. I should have told you, should have taken care of it before going for wood."

"At first, I was angry. But then, with what happened today, the loan didn't seem to matter anymore. You're home safe, and you solved the problem with the Blackfoot," she said with pride.

"We both did, and Henri, too."

"From now on, only honesty between us," Antonia whispered.

"I promise." Erik lifted their joined hands. "The day we married, I never expected us to end up here, like this." He pressed a kiss to her hand. "The best I hoped for was a businesslike relationship."

"We certainly have that." Laughter lilted in her voice. "When we wed, I was just grateful for a home for my boys and a daughter to love. Never expected more."

"I couldn't imagine ever loving a woman again as I did Daisy. But I was wrong." He stared in the direction of the graveyard. "A part of you will always love Jean-Claude, and a part of my heart still belongs to Daisy." He turned to her. "But all the rest is yours, my dearest Antonia. I realized as much today when I feared for your safety."

She smiled, tilting her face to his. "I knew I loved you when I fretted so over you being delayed."

"Perhaps…" Erik made a back-and-forth gesture between the two of them. "Our love is all the richer for having known

Daisy and Jean-Claude...married them...brought their children into the world."

"We be not takin' our feelings for granted."

"We know how fragile life is," he agreed, touching her cheek. "I want to love you fully, Antonia. Appreciate our time...God willing our *long* time together. Become husband and wife in truth."

"I've longed for such."

"Then why didn't you say so, wife?" he growled. "I've been ready to oblige you for ages."

She placed her hand over his heart. "Your body was ready. Sometimes, mine was also." She patted his chest. "But we needed both."

Erik rose and brought her up with him. Circling her waist, he pulled Antonia close, enjoying how her breasts pressed against his chest. He felt the power of his love for her—their mutual readiness to go forward in a natural continuation of their relationship.

Passion ignited flames that sizzled through his body, and he could barely form the words to commit to their joining. "Then, I say, wife, it's time to begin our marriage—our *real* marriage—for as long as we both shall live." He leaned down and touched his lips to hers.

Mystic Montana Sky
Book Six of the Montana Sky Series

Summer 2016

Influential banker Caleb Cabot Livingston has already lost out on several opportunities for love, due to his snobbish East Coast ways. Feisty Maggie Baxter is married to an abusive miner and is nine months pregnant with their first child. On their way to Sweetwater Springs, the Baxters' gypsy wagon collides with Caleb's buggy, killing Maggie's husband and sending her into early labor. Caleb is forced to deliver the baby girl, a harrowing and ultimately endearing experience. Little does Caleb know that the most difficult day of his life will lead to the special relationship he's been searching for—but only if he can change....

From the Author

Dear Readers,

I hope you enjoyed *Healing Montana Sky*, book five in the Montana Sky series and one of eighteen (currently) Montana Sky stories, including the *Mail-Order Brides of the West* novels.

If you are new to reading the series, you'll find many of the characters in *Healing Montana Sky* have their own stories: Pamela and John Carter in *Beneath Montana's Sky*; Nick and Elizabeth Sanders in *Wild Montana Sky*; Wyatt and Samantha Thompson in *Starry Montana Sky*; Harriet and Ant Gordon in *Stormy Montana Sky*; and Lina and Jonah Barrett in *Mail-Order Brides of the West: Lina.* The O'Donnells have a story in *Montana Sky Christmas*, and their trio of nieces find love in *A Valentine's Choice*, *Irish Blessing*, and *Easter Reunion* (the latter two available in spring 2016).

Still to come are Caleb Livingston's story in *Mystic Montana Sky* in the summer of 2016 and Sheriff K.C. Granger's story in *Montana Sky Justice.*

In many of my stories, healing from grief is a theme. Grief is a complex emotion, and some losses of loved ones always stay with us. Antonia and Erik's marriage of convenience after the deaths of their spouses was quite common in human history because both the man and woman were needed to deal with the laborious tasks of survival and raising a family.

In writing *Healing Montana Sky*, I had to strike a delicate balance between portraying the grief Antonia and Erik suffered from and also giving them a chance to fall in love again. In my "other" life, I'm a psychotherapist and corporate crisis and grief counselor, and the author of *The Essential Guide to Grief and Grieving*. I drew on my years of grief counseling to write this story.

Those who have lost spouses know that recovery takes several years. Often, the second year after the death is the hardest because the loss becomes more real. The second year is also when others think the bereaved spouse should be "moving on"—a painful message to receive. At least in our modern times, husbands and wives have resources, such as grief books and support groups, and the time to fully mourn their spouses before choosing if they want to move on to a new mate.

I hope you enjoy the Montana Sky series, and I look forward to bringing you many more stories in the future.

Debra Holland

Acknowledgments

In gratitude to:

My grandmother, Martha Muth Junger, whose stories of her childhood made me want to write.

Del Wardell, my second father. He and my mother have proven you can find love again after the deaths of beloved spouses.

My Montlake Romance editor, Maria Gomez.

My editors—Louella Nelson, Linda Carroll-Bradd, and Adela Brito—who always make my stories better.

To Delle Jacobs and John Mitchell, my cover artists.

My mother, Honey Holland, and Hedy and Larry Codner (my aunt and uncle) for being my beta readers.

I needed a lot of help in researching *Healing Montana Sky*.

Many thanks to:

Lisa Oates, MD, for help with Daisy's childbirth scene.

Heidi Howard, for her help in connecting me with Betty Yoder.

Betty Yoder, Amish owner of The Trading Post, in Salem, Kentucky, who recounted milking cows from her memories of her childhood in the 1930s. (Thank goodness, they have a community telephone.)

Lisa Steele of Fresh Eggs Daily (.com) for information on chickens, henhouses, and feeding, as well as story suggestions.

(Any livestock mistakes are my own.)

To all my friends at Pioneer Hearts, a Facebook group for the authors and readers of Historical Western Romance, for answering my questions, making suggestions when I asked for help, and their eagerness to read more Montana Sky stories. I'm truly blessed to "know" you!

About the Author

Photo © 2013 Randall Hill

Debra Holland is the *New York Times* and *USA Today* bestselling author of the *Montana Sky Series,* a collection of heartwarming historical Western romances. In 2013, Amazon selected *Starry Montana Sky* as one of their Top 50 Greatest Love Stories. Debra has received the Romance Writers of America's Golden Heart Award and has been a three-time finalist for the award as well. She is also the author of the Gods' Dream trilogy, a fantasy romance series, and *The Essential Guide to Grief and Grieving,* a nonfiction book. In addition, she is a contributing author to *The Naked Truth about Self-Publishing.* She resides in Southern California with her two dogs and two cats.

You can contact Debra at:
Website: drdebraholland.com
Facebook: facebook.com/pages/Debra-Holland/395355780562473
and facebook.com/debra.holland.731
Twitter: twitter.com/drdebraholland